Land Girls on the Loose

Hazel Stephenson

Copyright © Hazel Stephenson

All rights reserved. No part of this publication may be reproduced, stored in a retrieval system, or transmitted, in any form, or by any means, electronic, mechanical, photocopying, recording or otherwise, without the prior permission of the publisher and copyright holder, except for a reviewer who may quote brief passages in connection with a review for insertion in a newspaper, magazine, website, or broadcast.

British Library Cataloguing in Publication Data
A catalogue for this book is available from the British Library.

ISBN 978-0-9562863-1-4

Printed by Lintons Printers Ltd.
Unit 14B, Beechburn Industrial Estate,
Prospect Road, Crook. Co. Durham. DL15 8RA.

Acknowledgements

I would like to thank the following people:

My family for help and support.

Malcolm Proud for proof reading the book and correcting any spelling and punctuation errors.

Alyson Bailey for giving her time and expertise putting the cover blurb into order.

Everyone at Lintons Printers for their help and support.

Finally, an extra special mention for my husband Tony for travelling up and down the country with me on my engagements.

CHAPTER ONE

Ethel's eyes fluttered open as the weak sun shone through the thin curtains, trying to melt the frost off the insides of the window panes. There was no bird song as it was the backend of the year, and most bird songs cease at the end of July. Ethel looked over at her costume which was swaying on its hanger on the wardrobe door, and smiled. It was her wedding day. Gran stirred beside her, then rubbed her eyes and yawned. She looked at Ethel and asked, "Have we slept in our Ethel, as I've slept like a log, and I could do with me breakfast? Eh this is the last time we will share a bed our Ethel."

"Oh will you miss me Gran?"

"I will if you don't put me some more blankets on me bed; I'll bloody freeze to death."

Ethel put her hand over her mouth as she yawned; Gran looked at her and said,

"I knew you wouldn't sleep very well with those steel curlers in."

Just then the bedroom door opened and Linda came in carrying two cups of tea. Ethel was about to throw the bedding aside and swing her legs out of bed. When she saw the cups of tea she said, "Eh Linda, it's very kind of you bringing us tea to bed, but I was just getting up, however Gran can stop in bed and enjoy hers."

"Well just stay where you are," Linda retorted, "as everything is under control."

Gran took no persuading as she leaned over Ethel and grabbed her cup. "Eh I'm fair parched," she said, as she tasted a mouthful of scalding tea. "Drink yours our Ethel and enjoy it while you can, as tomorrow morning, you'll be getting up early again. Apart from today, your routine rarely varies."

"Mabel and Susan have gone to bring the cows into milk," Linda informed them, and Frank and Colin are feeding the pigs, geese and hens, they'll also be collecting the eggs. Me and Jennie have been busy downstairs, so after you have both drunk your tea, breakfast will be ready."

As Ethel was drinking her tea she confided in Gran, "Oh Gran, my stomach is churning, I'm getting nervous. I don't think I can face any breakfast."

"Don't be daft our Ethel, course you need your breakfast, I'm having mine. I can't manage on an empty stomach, and I don't intend trying."

"Gran," Ethel asked attentively, "I wonder what Wilf is having for his breakfast."

"Oh Ethel" Gran replied, "He will fettle himself something; he is a fool if he doesn't as he is only getting married. Now come on, drink your tea. I don't know why you are so nervous, as you've both been married before, and besides, didn't Linda say she would have our breakfasts ready, because I could do with mine".

"Gran I thought it was good of Margaret Emmerson to make my wedding cake," Ethel said gratefully.

"Yes it was Ethel," Gran agreed," but it might have helped to take her mind off other things, because tomorrow they are bringing Paul home, in an ambulance. By what Linda and Jennie said, David is not looking forward to it at all."

"Well it won't be very nice Gran, for Paul seeing the land girls doing the jobs he used to do before he went away to war. He was a fit, young lad then, and he is coming home tomorrow with half a leg missing."

"Well I think Margaret and David will have their work cut out looking after Paul," Gran said knowingly. "Margaret is a decent woman, but she tends to fuss. Remember when they went to the hospital to see Paul, he wouldn't speak to them at first. He only started speaking the night he realized they were coming home. Aye, I reckon their troubles are just beginning."

"Right Gran," said Ethel, "and on a happier note, I'm getting married today." Ethel drank the last drop of tea in her cup, and then she threw the blanket aside, swung her legs out of bed, and then padded across to open the curtains. As she drew the curtains back, she saw Susan and Mabel coming back across the field .They were the other two land girls who lived with her and Gran.They looked up at Ethel's window and waved. They would be delivering the milk today for Ethel and Wilf, and taking Frank and Colin with them to push the barrow. On a normal day Wilf pushed the barrow, while Ethel ladled the milk into whatever utensil the woman brought out to fill. Not this morning, as it was Ethel's wedding day.

"It was good of the Emmerson's to let Linda and Jennie have the day off so they could do all the jobs for me and Wilf."

"Aye, I like the Emmerson's, they are a nice couple our Ethel."Gran was speaking and nodding her head at the same time.

"Well I'm dressed now Gran. How are you managing?"

"I've got me stockings on our Ethel," she said, as she pulled her garters over her skinny knees to hold them up. Her pink, fleecy knicker legs came down to meet them.

"Do you want to put your new dress on now Gran, or is it too early for you?"

"Aye, it is. I might slop me breakfast, and eh, our Ethel, I'm fair famished."

As Ethel helped Gran downstairs, and through the sitting room, she looked at the sideboard with the pull out bed, and thought, "I will be in there tonight, with Wilf, and it will be legal, not like the other nights when I've sneaked in. Eh, I'm getting as bad as the land girls, but I'm lucky, as he is a good man."

Over breakfast Ethel asked Gran, if she would manage the short walk along to the church. Gran was looking thoughtful, as she was sitting chewing her breakfast.

"Of course I will manage our Ethel. You don't think I would miss your wedding, besides, it's only along the road, and Jennie and Linda will help me."

"Gran will be alright, Ethel. She will be supported between Linda and me," Jennie said with a reassuring smile.

"Our Ethel's done well, getting Wilf," Gran was saying to anyone that cared to listen, but everyone was busy. "Wilf is the salt of the earth and he works hard, idleness has never sat easy on Wilf's shoulders, not like her first one. I said what Jack was, the first time I met him, but he is dead and gone now, thank God!"

Just then, Frank and Colin came in from delivering the milk. They pulled out a chair each, sat down and waited of someone putting their breakfast on the table in front of them. Instead of Ethel seeing to them, Linda stood up, scraping her chair back as she did so. She grinned at Ethel as she said, "Auntie Ethel can't be doing your breakfasts this morning, as she is getting married to Uncle Wilf."

Ethel said, "After you boys have eaten your breakfasts, you'd better hurry and finish your jobs outside, then get yourselves washed and changed. I've put your clothes ready on your beds. You are both going to be dressed alike in grey knee socks, dark blue shirts, ties and grey flannel trousers that Uncle Wilf bought for you."

He had made sure that the boys had polished their black shoes till they shone. Mabel and Susan were already putting food out on to the table in the front room, ready for when the wedding party arrived home. The centre piece on Ethel's table was the cake that Margaret had made and iced. Linda and Jennie were going to make sure that the boys were tidy after they had washed the breakfast dishes, while Ethel helped gran into her new dress.

Ethel asked, "Would you like a pair of nylons to wear today Gran with your new dress? I have a spare pair that Linda gave me."

Gran looked shocked. "Surely you don't expect me to wear them! I will wear what I always do, me thick lisle ones. Anyway, folk won't be taking any notice of me. It's you they will be looking at."

Ethel was wearing a peach coloured costume, and on her head she had a pillar box hat with a veil attached. She also had matching shoes and handbag. As she looked in the brown, speckled mirror and put her hand tentatively to her hair, she thought, "Those steel curlers were worth the pain through the night". Then she thought that Linda had done a good job styling her hair into place this morning. As the house door opened again, Eva, Prudence and the four little girls, Shirley, Margaret, Rose and Violet walked in. Jennie just looked at them and gasped.

"Don't they look gorgeous? She said, what a good idea Eva, making all the dress's the same."

" No I didn't think of it Jennie," she laughed, "that was all the material that I could get hold of, but they do look nice in pink, and prudence knitted the white cardigan's." Ethel noticed they were wearing pink hair ribbons, white socks, and black shining shoes, with a strap over, Ethel bent down and encircled the four girls she loved them all, Margaret and Shirley were Ethel's granddaughters, while Rose and violet, were evacuees, that Eva had taken in, to stay with her and prudence was a school teacher, that had come with the evacuees, and was staying with Eva. Ethel looked at the girls and said "you all look lovely," and then she kissed each one of them,

"you look smart as well prudence," Ethel acknowledged, "that light green costume really suits you, I like your new hair style as well, as you suit that bob," There was a tap on the door and Ada came in smiling, Ethel walked over to her with arms out stretched.

"Oh it's good to see you Ada, I suppose Walter has gone along to see if Wilf is ready yet has he? Mind you look nice Ada I do like your dress."

"Well I knew I didn't have anything decent to wear Ethel, and as you know there isn't anything decent in the shops, and when you go into the shop, to see if there is anything half decent, they say we haven't got much, don't you know there is a war on, and I also let my daughter in law have most of my coupons for the bairns, because usually I can make do, but I found this bit material and I've run this up myself."

"Yes the shop windows soon began to reflect the restrictions, this utility seems to apply to most things, not that I go to the shops much" added Ethel.

"Well if everybody is ready I think we should be setting off along the road or we will be late for church," gran told them, "and if I sit here much longer I'll seize up." Along at Wilf's house Walter had knocked and walked in, then said,

"What's up with you Wilf? You do look flustered.

"I am Walter, I haven't worn me suit for about fifteen years, it's been hung in me cupboard, with mothballs in the pockets, and I never thought, I should of taken them out last week, and given this suit an airing, as it stinks of the bloody things, and I can't fasten the top button on me trousers, I didn't realize how much weight, I'd put on, lately with Ethel's cooking, but it doesn't look very good with me belly hanging over the top of me trousers, I wish the wedding was over Walter, then I can get back into me work trousers, there's plenty of room in them, as they are held up with me braces," he then picked up his white shirt, off the chair back, and attempted to fasten the collar to the shirt,

"I'm going to choke in this shirt Walter,"

"Well once the wedding is over, and we are back at Ethel's house," Walter tried to pacify him, you could take the shirt collar off, as Walter patiently tried to explain, Put your arm out, and I will fasten your cuffs for you Wilf, or we will be late for the church" As the two men stepped out of the door, Wilf felt it was the happiest day of his life, he had waited a long time for Ethel, but very shortly she would be his wife, and he had no qualms about living with gran, she was decent enough with him, she was straight, she told you what she thought, aye she didn't mince her words, there was also four land army girls living there, they were Linda Jennie Susan and Mabel, there was also frank and Colin, two evacuees, who desperately needed discipline, and care, when they arrived, but they have settled down and they are good lads now. Wilf turned and looked at Walter,

"By your very quiet Walter, have you something on your mind?"

"Aye I have Wilf, but I won't bother you now, with mine and Ada's problems, not on your wedding day." Along at Ethel's, everyone was ready, and heading to the door ,Gran had her black felt hat and coat on, Ethel turned and said to Gran,

"I thought you were just putting your thick cardigan on, as it's only a short walk."

"I know how far it is our Ethel, and I have got me thick cardigan on under me coat, I'm not sitting cold our Ethel, just because you're getting married." Linda and Jennie helped Gran out of the door, one at each side of her, holding on to one arm each, making sure she didn't fall, all the girls looked really nice, they had all made an effort, Linda was wearing a light blue dress with a jacket to match, Jennie had on a navy blue skirt and jacket, Mabel wore a flowered dress, and white cardigan, Susan wore a white skirt and green twinset, as they all walked out of the door, they met up with David and Margaret Emmerson, Margaret's eye's travelled over them all, then she said, "

"You all look very nice, and look at them little girls, don't they look gorgeous, and did you make them dress's Eva? As you trained to be a dress maker when you left school didn't you?" "Yes I did Margaret," Eva answered, "but I had to dress the girls in the same coloured dresses, as that was all the material I could get hold of and Prudence knitted the four white cardigans,"

"Well I think they all look lovely, smiled Margaret, in fact you all look very nice,"

"Aye we all scrub up well," answered gran. The small group walked along together, apart from Ethel and Ada, who walked along behind, the others, deep in conversation. Excitement was bubbling up in Ethel, she felt like a young girl again, and she did love Wilf. As Ethel walked in to the church, the organ struck up with the wedding march. Wilf was waiting, with a big smile on his face; as Ethel walked down the aisle on the arm of David Emmerson. The happy couple held hands as they took their vows, and within a short time it was over, and Ethel stepped outside as Mrs Robinson.

The weak sun was shining, but there was a nip in the air, so everyone was pleased to step in to the warmth of Ethel's house, quite a few people, who had stepped out of their doors, to wish the happy couple well, were invited back for refreshment's, there was plenty of food including meat, which in some places, meat was a commodity, that was becoming scarcer, and scarcer, but did not affect the country people that much, Linda and Jennie helped Gran off with her coat and into the chair while Susan took the fireguard away from in front of the fire, then put the poker through the bars on the grate, and it burst into flames, as it had been banked down while they had been out, A cold buffet had been laid out along with the cake and As Wilf and Ethel stood knife poised, ready to cut at the cake, that Margaret Emmerson, had kindly made for the happy couple, Gran said,

"By it looks a nice cake that our Ethel, I'm looking forward to tasting it," everyone stood chatting, and laughter rang out, as they all had a glass in one hand, and a plateful of whatever they had chosen off the loaded table, in the other, Everyone's troubles seemed to be forgotten this afternoon, apart from Ada who looked exhausted, as she sat so close to the fire that, she was burning her legs, something she must make a habit of, as her legs were all mottled and scorched. There was a knock on the door, and Tommy and Lizzie from the pub walked in, to join the happy crowd,

"Sorry we couldn't get away earlier," Tommy apologised, "but we have brought these to toast the bride and groom." As he handed over two bottles of whisky, Ethel beckoned them both over, to the well laden table, as she thanked them, for coming, also for bringing the whisky,

"Now come on Tommy, you as well Lizzie help yourselves," Ethel told them, as she pointed to the food on the table. Ethel felt as if she'd had a beautiful wedding day, and it was a grand afternoon. She looked round at everyone and thought, when she had agreed to take the four land girls in, and the two evacuees Frank and Colin, she would never have thought it was possible, for everyone of them to live in such close proximity, and get on so well. Ethel felt as if her happiness was complete. She looked over to where Wilf, was standing talking to Walter, David and Tommy, she thought, he had not seen her looking, but he looked at her and winked, and her stomach, turned a somersault, just then gran waved her over,

"I 'm so happy for you, our Ethel; I know Wilf will look after you, and that is what I have always wanted, to see you settled and happy, to a good man, but will you fill my plate up again? As that fresh air has really given me a good appetite, and I wouldn't say no, to a glass of whisky, just to keep the cold out you understand."   As the afternoon was turning tonight, people were starting to leave, a few of them had farms, so they had the milking to do, and people like Tommy and Lizzie, had to go and open the pub, the land girls, Linda Jennie Susan and Mabel, were going to do the jobs on the farm, for Ethel and Wilf tonight, and frank and Colin could feed the animals for them, Walter and Ada would have to walk, back to their cottage , which was a quarry cottage as Walter was a quarryman, Ethel had managed to waylay Ada ,out of earshot of Wilf and Walter, to find out what was bothering her, as it turned out, it is a problem, that Ada and Walter are having with one of their daughters, but Ada said, she would call later in the week, and tell Ethel all about it. As the last person went out of the door, Ethel flopped down in to the chair, and kicked off her shoes, while Wilf removed his tie, and opened his top button on his shirt. Linda said, "I will make us all a fresh cup of tea,"

"Aye and I will have a bit of cake with mine, if you don't mind cutting me a bit Linda please. "Asked Gran"

"Are you still hungry Gran"? Asked Ethel, "As you have eaten all afternoon,"

"Well I wouldn't ask for more cake if I wasn't hungry our Ethel, and it's a long time till I get me breakfast as I'm having an early night," gran retorted. The girls wouldn't hear tell of Wilf and Ethel milking on their wedding day, as Wilf and Ethel did offer. Frank and Colin went out to feed the hens, while Jennie and Linda milked the cows, and Mabel and Susan fed the pigs and the geese, then the girls went back into the house and got themselves ready to go out dancing, as tomorrow they would all be back at work, there would be no more, lying in for Ethel either, as tomorrow her and Wilf, would be up early, as usual, to milk the cows, and deliver the milk, Later as the girls went out dancing, and Frank and Colin were in bed, Gran said,

"Will you help me up to bed now our Ethel? Wilf turned to Gran and said, "There is no need to go to bed so early, I hope you are not doing it for us?" "

No I'm not Wilf, it's just I've had a busy day," later on when Ethel and Wilf were sitting in front of a blazing fire, Ethel asked,

"Are you happy Wilf?"

"Oh I am Ethel," Wilf replied with a twinkle in his eye, "I will be happier still," he said, grinning, "When I get you into that bed," as Ethel blushed,

Stepping out of the door the next morning, the slight chill in the wind hit Ethel, as she walked beside Wilf, to milk the cows, she would help him to deliver the milk, then Eva or Prudence, would bring the four little girls along to stay at Ethel's, as Eva was moving house today, it would be a busy day for Eva, Ethel's daughter, and Prudence, who had moved in with Eva, when she had arrived here to teach the evacuees, as Eva was moving into the house that Wilf had vacated, which was a bigger house then hers, also her late husband had worked for the railways and with him no longer there she had to move out as it was a tied house it went with the job, but she would have a lot more space in Wilf's old house, as there was four little girls, Eva's own two little girls and two evacuees and Prudence, Wilf had left her some furniture, so she could choose what she wanted, Linda and Jennie had gone to work, and after they had finished milking, and had taken the cows back to the field, they went in to Margaret's for a cup of tea, and a bacon sandwich, Margaret was rushing about, and getting more hassled, by the minuet, "

", I wonder what time the ambulance will arrive with our Paul." She asked, no one in particular, as she leaned over the bed, that had been brought downstairs, in readiness for Paul, and rubbed her hand over the counterpane, to make sure there wasn't a crease in it, "

"Come and sit down Margaret," David insisted, "and have something to eat, it could be tea time before our Paul arrives home, and he will not want you fussing," he warned her. As the girls were busy later in the morning, they saw the ambulance draw up, the driver opened the back door and let the steps down, Margaret was by his side leaning into the ambulance, saying ,"

"Oh I'm so pleased you're finally here Paul," she looked at the driver and asked if he would like some help to get Paul out, Paul scowled at his mother and said,

"He helped me in on his own, I'm sure he can manage to help me out", the ambulance driver turned to Margaret and said,

"It's alright missus, you go into the house and scold a pot of tea, and I will help him in," David saw the ambulance the same time as the girls, and he told them,

"I'm not going in there yet, there is enough fussing going on with Margaret, he doesn't want molly coddling," David had tried to warn Margaret, that Paul, wouldn't want to be fussed over, he wouldn't thank her, for fussing, he would feel a fool in front of these land girls, but she wouldn't listen," David could feel trouble brewing, but after a while knew he would have to go into the house or Margaret would come out looking for him. The girls saw the strained look on David's face as they walked in to the farmhouse for dinner. As they opened the door they heard raised voices, David and the girl's dinners were ready for them on the table and Margaret had persuaded Paul to sit with them. But he didn't look very happy, so Margaret tried to jolly him along,

"Should I cut your dinner up, for you Paul?" she asked him, they all jumped as Paul's fist, banged down on the table, making all the pots rattle,

"I can manage," he shouted, "I am not a bloody invalid altogether, there is nothing wrong with my hands," then he scowled across at Linda and Jennie, and said,

"I bet you two love this, do you feel as if you have come to a freak show, to watch me?" David had said nothing until now, he had been sitting with his elbows on the table, with his knife and fork poised, ready to eat his dinner, he glowered at Paul, then said,

"Now there is no need for that Paul, the girls has always come in, and had dinner with us, and nothing is going to change, so if you don't want your dinner, we want ours" then he looked straight at Paul, and added, "in peace."

"Then you know what you can do, with your bloody dinner." Paul shouted, Then he scraped his chair back, and tried, to lean over, for his crutches that Margaret his mother had propped against the wall, for him, she quickly got off her chair and rushed to help him, as she guided him to the settee he shook her hand off his arm,

CHAPTER TWO

It was a quiet little gathering that sat around the table as no one tried to make conversation, as the girls were wishing dinner was over and they were back outside working. Margaret was trying to hold her tears back as she looked at Paul's full plate he hadn't touched it. David felt like telling Paul not to be so childish, but then he thought he wouldn't like to be in the same position, having half a leg missing would take a lot of living with. After dinner was eaten the girls refused a cup of tea that always rounded off a meal, they were so relieved to be back outside as the atmosphere was tangible in the house. Once outside Linda breathed a sigh of relief and said.

"It's going to be bloody awful now Jennie having our meals with Margaret and David with Paul being there, looking for sympathy" and with a determined nod of her head said. "He bloody won't be getting any off me as there are a lot of people worse off than him."

"Oh look Linda" Jennie shouted over to her as she had started to walk away. "There is Judith heading down the lane with the big black pram"

"Aye" said Linda thoughtfully, "it's the same pram that our Jane used when I went home for a visit, and God knows how many kids she quashes into it now". Linda looked up and realized Jennie was trying to get her attention,

"Linda don't you think it's a bad time for Judith to come visiting with Paul in such a bad mood? Jennie asked worriedly. Linda thought about what Jennie had said and answered her.

"Well he is her brother, and she is probably concerned, Margaret and David are her Mam and Dad, but the way Paul is, will there ever be a good time for anyone to visit"?

Margaret scraped the chair back and stood up stiffly ready to clear the table when she caught sight of Judith coming down the lane with the children in the pram, she smiled at Paul as she said,

"Here's our Judith coming down the lane with the children in the pram, she will be pleased to know that you are home safe and sound, and you haven't seen the latest edition to the family yet, he's called Roy." Margaret was startled as Paul shouted,

"No I bloody haven't and I don't want too," as he shuffled around in his chair turning his back to her. Just then Judith manoeuvred the big black heavy pram into the kitchen, then leaned into it lifting Emma out, then putting her down to the floor on her feet, then as the little girl ran over to Margaret with her arms outstretched Judith smilingly walked over to Paul putting her arms around him, and saying

"It's good to see you looking so well Paul, I thought I would walk up the same day as you arrived home, or you might have thought I had forgotten about you," she said laughingly. Paul nastily pushed her away then turned his back. Margaret loved her son and felt sorry for the predicament he was in, but this was ridiculous, you could cut the atmosphere with a knife she could not allow this situation to carry on "Paul" his Mother, Margaret exclaimed,

"You are not being very sociable to your sister;" he then turned on his mother shouting

"Well I didn't ask her to come, and I don't want to see her or her brats."

Little Emma was standing holding on to Margaret's hand looking up at her with frightened eyes. Margaret cried,

"That is enough Paul, your sister has been very good while your Dad and me came through to see you, her and your brother-in-law Brian, moved in here, so that Jennie and Linda, could keep the farm going, everyone has been very good ,so stop being so nasty to everybody." Just then with all the shouting the baby started to cry, so Margaret rushed over to the pram to pick him up, while Judith rummaged in her bag for a clean nappy. As Margaret handed the baby over to Judith to get his nappy changed she looked down at Emma and said,

"Are you going to help Nan-na to make a cup of tea? And I think we might be able to find a cake." Emma reached for Margaret's hand, and skipped along beside her into the scullery.

Judith changed Roy's nappy, then went over and sat down beside Paul, with Roy in her arms,

"Right Paul," Judith said determinedly, "you might as well tell me what all of this is about as you are making everyone miserable, I walked two miles today pushing a heavy pram, and the welcome I got off you I might as well stopped at home."Paul retorted

"Well you are bloody lucky you have two legs to walk on and I didn't ask you to come in fact, I'd rather you'd stopped away." Judith relented and said,

"This attitude is not helping anyone Paul; we know it can't have been easy for you but you needn't take it out on us."

Margaret came through carrying a loaded tray Emma was walking close beside her eating a cake and looking cautiously across at Paul, as Margaret handed a piled up plate of sandwiches and cakes to Paul he took it hungrily, he wished he hadn't been so stubborn and eaten his dinner. Margaret knowing he would be hungry had filled his plate for which he was thankful. Margaret could see him out of the corner of her eye tucking in hungrily; she knew he'd had a long journey this morning, so God only knows what time he would have his last bite to eat. Little Emma was patting Margaret's hand and saying bed then she was pointing at it Margaret was watching Paul scowl at Emma, but she was only a bairn and didn't understand but Margaret knew it was upsetting Paul having his bed downstairs, she would try and get hold of a sideboard with a bed in it the same as Ethel's, but it was hard trying to get hold of things when there was a war on. Margaret walked to the door to call David but he was on his way in,

"I was just coming to look for you as I have scolded a Pot of tea," then Margaret looked past him and asked

"Where are the girls David? They have always enjoyed a cup of tea this time of day."

"Oh Margaret they are down the field hedging , I told them it was time for our afternoon drink of tea, usually they are ready for a drink, but between you and me ,I think it's the atmosphere, that our Paul is causing, that's why they refused." As the girls watched David's retreating back going up the field   Linda took the packet of cigarettes out of her pocket and gave one to Jennie, as they both sucked the smoke deep into their lungs Jennie remarked,

"A cup of tea would have been nice," Linda retorted,

"I would rather die of thirst, then go for a drink where that miserable buggers at," as she tossed her head in defiance. David was filled with a sense of impending doom as he made his way into the house, and wiping the sweat from his forehead with the back of his hand, he wished he'd stopped down the field with the girls when he saw Paul glowering at everyone. The fire burnt in the grate despite the heat of the day, it never went out as it heated the water and the oven, and David looked towards the oven, as there was an intoxicating smell of roasting meat, that made his mouth water. Margaret was throwing logs on to the fire simultaneously; David sat quietly while his cup of tea cooled on the table in front of him. Little Emma walked over to him lifting her arms wanting to be picked up, and when he had her in his arms she giggled,

"Well this is a nice surprise Emma are you going to give Granda a cuddle?" "Yes" she said laughingly, as she climbed on to his knee and wrapped her little arms around his neck. Paul looked around at them then carried on eating, because he was hungry, nobody seemed concerned about him; they were laughing and talking, how could they? When he had half his leg missing he was a bloody invalid. He looked up when he heard his mother's voice asking if he would like more tea or another cake he would have liked to refuse just to upset her, and then he would have ignored them, but he was still hungry and thirsty. Margaret got stiffly off the chair and went hurrying through to the scullery to do Pauls bidding. As she came back into the kitchen she pushed back damp hair and wiped the beads of perspiration from her forehead with the bottom of her pinny.

"Here you are Paul get that down you, and you will feel better on a full stomach." Margaret was trying to coax Paul in a conciliatory manner. I don't bloody want it now he shouted as he raised his arm and knocked it out of her hand .Little Emma started to cry David tried to soothe her by rocking her on his knee as he gave Paul a nasty look. He then made up his mind to go and fetch the land girls for a drink of tea he realized now why they had refused, bloody hell Paul had only been home a couple of hours, and he'd upset everybody.

"Come with Granda Emma," David told the little girl, as he pushed her gently off his knee, so her feet touched the floor, "we are going for a walk down the field, to fetch Linda and Jennie for a cup of tea." Then he turned and stared at Paul defying him to comment Paul sat angrily in the chair it wouldn't be long now until those bloody land girls came in their gobs going twenty to the dozen, he thought the one called Jennie might be a bit sympathetic, but her mate Linda was as hard as nails, The girls were talking about Paul as David approached them, As Linda had decided to walk up to the house and get a drink of water from the well. David was waving his arms beckoning for them to come, as little Emma ran down to them, Linda opened her arms and Emma ran into them giggling. The girls had a hand each of Emma's and they were swinging her as they walked, Linda was saying,

"If David hadn't of come and insisted "they pop in for a drink" it wouldn't have bothered me, as I had enough of him at dinner time, Jennie was looking uncertain,

"Don't you think we should show a bit of compassion towards Paul?" Linda swung round and faced Jennie,

"Have you gone soft in the head? She shouted, he isn't the only one who is suffering, have you thought about all those people who are killed and injured in their homes and shelters every night as the bombs are dropping, she shivered as she thought about the drone of the planes overhead, and the mournful wail of the sirens. She had witnessed all of that when she had gone home for a visit. As the girls arrived at the door David held it open to enable the girls to walk through, Margaret and Judith smiled as the girls walked in, and Judith laughed and said,

"Oh you have found my daughter as well;" Margaret bent over and picked the big teapot of the hearth ready to fill a cup each for the girls, David went over and sat in the armchair, then said to Margaret,

"Fill me another cup will you please lass as I'm fair parched." Judith went through into the scullery and came back with a piled plate of cakes, and offered them around. Paul thought they haven't even acknowledged me, they must think I'm a bloody piece of furniture; Jennie looked over at Paul and asked him if he was feeling better. Paul took his nasty temper out on Jennie as he shouted,

"How the hell can I be feeling any better now? Then I felt at dinner time you stupid bitch." Linda cast a venomous look in his direction, as she was unabashed with Paul, and said,

"I wouldn't bother even asking him Jennie, when he is being so childish, she then turned her back to him and bit into her cake." Paul started to shout, and point at the girls,

"I didn't think you two would have been made welcome round here, as land girls are known as wild and promiscuous, I would call the lot of you whores." David jumped out of the chair pointing his finger at Paul and saying in a slow threatening voice,

"If you ever say anything like that again Paul, you will be looking for somewhere to live, as I will not have people spoken too in my house like that you are a disgrace. I have said all I have to say for now as we have company but I won't forget he " threaten ." as he relapsed into an angry silence. It was so quiet in the house you could of heard a pin drop Linda later told Gran. Judith shuffled in the chair and spoke in to the uncomfortable silence. To Linda and Jennie,

"Mam was just saying she might try and get a sideboard with a bed in it, and then we won't have a bed taking room up all day."

Paul shouted, "Why don't you just lean me up against the bloody byre wall if I take so much bloody room up? " Linda looked at Margaret and then at Judith and asked,

"Has he always been like this? Because I couldn't put up with it," then she looked over at Paul and said,

"Never expect sympathy off me, as I don't give it, and I also have nothing to hide," she said with a touch of complacency. As the girls walked out of the door and headed back down the field Linda put her arm through Jennies to hurry her on a little, I have never known such a bad atmosphere,

"Aye it's alright for us Linda," Jennie was saying, "we don't have to live with it but poor Margaret's stuck with him and his nastiness."

"None of our concern Jennie," said Linda "Here takes hold of this shovel; we will start from opposite ends, and dig this bog out or the fields will be flooded when the rains come." The girls worked hard all the rest of the afternoon, the hedges hadn't been layered for a few years, and there was a lot of growth on them, usually David was meticulous about his hedges, but he'd had so much more important things to see too, before Linda and Jennie arrived, it had been another job he'd promised Margaret, he would do but had never found the time. Linda threw down her slasher, the tool that was used to cut the hedge, and shouted over to Jennie,

"Come on Jennie have a sit down and a fag and by the way it's your turn to get the fags out," as Jennie sat down Linda could see the perspiration running down Jennies back. Linda said,

"It's been hot today, but we have managed extremely well, but we are both good at hedging now she said triumphantly." Jennie looked at Linda, who had lain down on the grass, and had her eyes closed against the hot sun.

"Linda talk to me or you will be dropping off to sleep, we'll have to go and get the cows shortly, or we'll be milking cows tonight and wasting precious drinking time." Linda jumped up in a hurry when she thought they might be late for a few drinks at the pub before they went dancing,

"Come on then slow coach." Linda shouted as she ran over to pick up the long handled shovels, you can bring the slashers and the rakes and put them in the barrow, as the girls made their way up the fields in the hot afternoon sun, Linda said,

"You know Jennie, I never had a suntan before I came here, and look at me know," as she held her arms out in front of her then she stuck one leg out and said I'm pleased I cut the bottoms of these trousers",

Jennie laughed and said, "I hope we don't rue in winter." After the girls had put away the shovels and slashers, they made their way over to the well, and with cupped hands, they drank thirstily at the water. Linda looked towards the gable end of the farm house hoping Margaret, wouldn't see either of them, or she would have been out inviting them in for a drink, but as Linda and Jennie both agreed they did not want Pauls Company anymore today.

"Come on then Jennie, get a move on, sang Linda, "or we will miss precious drinking time", they both hurried up the field laughing so full of exhilaration as what tonight might bring. The girls trudged up three fields to collect the cows for milking, as the heat slowed them down, usually fly the dog ran away in front, then kept turning his head to see if the girls had caught up to him, but today with it being so hot he walked by their side. As they all set off back down the cows amber ling away in front, fly tiredly making sure they kept inline, Linda said to Jennie,

"After we finish the milking I'm going down to the river as its only four fields away," "whatever for?" asked a shocked Jennie, "I thought we were going out dancing tonight, but going to the pub first."

"We are" answered Linda, "but look at the state of us, we are saturated in sweat, and our feet are squelching in these boots." They started to milk the cows before David arrived to give them a hand, as he walked through the door, Jennie would of dashed forward to bring in another milk churn, but David's hand restrained her,

"I'll bring that churn in for you lass." he said as he wiped sweat from his brow.

Once the milking was done the girls unchained the cows, Linda saw them out of the door with a pat on their rumps, they would stay near the byre until the girls mucked out, then they would walk them back up the fields.

David said, "After you lasses have cleaned up here, you can get off home, I'll walk the cows back." The girls were shocked as he had never suggested that, before, as they turned questioning eyes to him he muttered, "I'm giving Margaret and our Paul a bit space," and he added," I'll enjoy the walk a bit peace and quiet".

"Right that's the day's work done then Jennie." Linda said happily, "come on Jennie I'am going in the river it will be refreshing "don't be spoilsports" she begged.

"I'm not" answered a thoughtful Jennie, "it's just a bit worrying,"

"What are you going on about now?" asked a bewildered Linda.

"I want to go in the river the same as you; I'm just a bit worried about going in there, in the nude what if anyone sees us?"

"Oh stop worrying Jennie you're going on like an old woman, nobody is going to see us." Linda was busy kicking off her saturated boots, as she looked over at Jennie, with hands on her hips and asked.

"Are you coming into the river with me or not? As she hurriedly threw off her shirt, bra, and knickers, Jennie could feel her cheeks turning red with embarrassment;

"I'm not like you Linda," "

"What do you mean by that?" Linda shouted at Jennie as she stood in front of Jennie without a stitch on."

I'm frightened anyone comes along. Do you think We should go into the water with our bra and knickers on?"

"Then what will we do?" shouted Linda "When we come out of the river, we will have to walk home, with wet knickers and bra on, but you please yourself because I'm going in now." Jennie finally made her mind up, and looked around cautiously, then hurriedly pulled her clothes off and ran into the river to join a giggling Linda. Once Jennie was in the water, she had to agree, that it had been a marvellous idea of Linda's, as they splashed, and threw water over each over, Linda was bobbing up and down on the water, then Jennie joined, in both totally unaware that they were being watched by the village idiot, and he was excitedly handling the girls' underwear, as he dribbled at the mouth it was only when the girls decided they had better be going that Jennie saw simple Simon as he was cruelly called in the village,

"Look Linda," Jennie shrieked, "what the bloody hell are we going to do?"

"I don't know, maybe if we stay in here he might get sick of sitting there, watching us and go away "

"No I don't think he will." Jennie said nervously, we can't stay here all night, and what will Ethel and all the rest of them think when we don't go home? Oh Linda I've just thought what if Roberts Mam, hears about us, in the river without a stitch on?

"Will you shut your mouth for a while until I think what to do Jennie? One thing is certain; I will not be stopping in this river all-night, because if I have too, I will walk over and grap my clothes off him, he shouldn't be holding our things to start with." Jennie was astounded.

"You can't do that Linda, you can't walk over to him with no clothes on" Linda was starting to lose patience with Jennie,

"Well either I walk over with nothing on, to get our clothes or you do." she told Jennie as she stared straight at her.

"Should we just wait a bit longer?" Jennie pleaded, "I'm sure he'll go shortly."

"Do you know what I think Jennie?" Linda was starting to shout. You must be daft if you think he is going to move from there when he knows we are in here with no clothes on,

"Oh I wish someone would come along and make him move," Jennie said wistfully. "Who would you like to come and see us?" Linda asked sarcastically, the bloody army? Then she made her mind up,

"I'm not waiting any longer, we are in this together, and we will both go and get our clothes together, come on she said, as she grabbed Jennies hand and they set off together out of the water, as they got nearer to Simple Simon, Jennie was blushing to her roots, while Linda strode on determinedly pulling Jennie with her, Simon watched them approaching and jumped to his feet shouting, "tits" as his hand was down the front of his trousers, and he slavered at the mouth with excitement, just as Linda and Jennie leaned over to grab their bra's and knickers off him, a voice shouted. "

"Stop leading my son astray you harlots' I don't know how you dare," she sneered at the girls "standing there with no clothes on have you any shame? Then she spun around with surprising agility for her size, and dragged the girl's bra and knickers, out of Simple Simon's hands, she then threw them down at their feet, and rubbed her hands together, as if they had something infectious.

"Come with me now," she barked at Simon, "and as for you two whores you might have damaged my Simon for life,"

Linda shouted, How the hell could we damage something that's not all there to start with, he's not fit to be out on his own."

"Come on Linda," Jennie said hurriedly, "let us get to hell away from here, and do you think that woman will keep it to herself or will she tell the entire village?"

"I don't know Jennie, but there is nothing we can do about it, but next time we fancy a dip, we'll have to keep some clothes on she laughed cheekily, come on Jennie have a laugh or you'll end up portentously like our friend Paul."

"Oh Linda I don't look as solemn as him do I?" Linda turned her head and looked at Jennie,"

"No I don't think anyone could look like him, now come on Jennie run or we really will be late, and missing valuable drinking time." The girls hurried up the lane, to go home to Ethel's, their hair was wet and dripping down their backs, their wet feet felt twice as bad as the boots were still wet with sweat, it was a relief to open the door but as they walked in six pairs of eyes looked curiously at them."

"Well what have you two been doing now?" asked gran, "as Wilf only brought half a tale back?"

"I told you all that I knew gran," Wilf said apologetically, "I was just walking back along the road, when I met David, he said he'd just taken the cows back up the field ,so no doubt you lasses would be home early. And then we heard, a noise so we turned around and there was simple Simon, hurrying along with his mother beside him, giving him a smack on the back of his head with every step he took, and fair shouting at him she was," Wilf was shaking his head and laughing, as he told what had gone on. "Then she started shouting at us, and saying she had found two girls down by the river with no clothes on leading Simon a stray."   Wilf realized then that all eyes were on him, so he asked, and looked at no one in particular, "

"Why everyone is looking at me I don't know."

"Oh Wilf," Ethel said, "Don't you see, the land girls that old Bertha was talking about, was our Linda and Jennie"

"What will I do, if Roberts Mam finds out?"Jennie asked piteously, "as I didn't particular want to go in the river with no clothes on."

"Well I definitely didn't drag you in." said Linda standing arms akimbo legs slightly apart as if she was looking for a fight.

"Well I suggest you girls go and get some dry clothes on, before you catch pneumonia" said Ethel as she was down on her knees, in front of the grate, rattling the poker between the bars, to send the ashes through to the ash pan, before adding more coal.

"And then you can tell us all about It." said gran sitting curiously on the end of the chair eagerly waiting for the next instalment. The girls felt a lot better after they had towelled their hair dry and were sitting around the table enjoying their mutton stew.

"I hope everyone isn't talking about us, when we go to the pub tonight Jennie said worriedly I don't know why people think we're fast."

Gran said, "Well you are certainly giving them plenty ammunition to fire at you."

"Well whether they do, or they don't I'm still going out" replied Linda looking unperturbed. "We have done nothing wrong, and besides we are good girls we were just unlucky that imbecile happened to come along."

"Of course you are." Wilf affirmed heartily.

"Years ago all the girls went into the river with no clothes on, mind you, they always had someone watching out for them, isn't that true Ethel?

Gran shrieked. "So you used to go in the river in the nude our Ethel."

"Well it's a long time since now gran." Ethel laughingly told her. Later on as the girls walked into the pub there was much hilarity, someone shouted,

"Here come the strippers." And some one said,

"Simon isn't as simple, as folk think; he stopped and got a right eyeful."

"Aye he was in the right place at the right time, but I bet he has a bad head, as his mother smacked it all the way along the road, laughed Eddie but I bet it was worth it, seeing these two well endowed lasses."

The weather was questionable as the night progressed, and thunder clouds were forming, Lizzie behind the bar had predicted that there was thunder on the way, as it was getting hot and stifling in the pub,

"There is no air in here." signed Lizzie as she fanned herself with her hand. The girls didn't seem to notice, as Mable and Susan the other two land girls who lived at Ethel's, had accompanied them along to the pub. The blokes, and the visiting GIs, who they had arranged to meet were all buying the girls drink, they never even heard the rumble of thunder, or saw the flashes of lightning, as the girls had started to sing run rabbit, and then straight on to the next one knees up mother Brown, with everyone joining in. Lizzie was standing quietly behind the bar, contemplating how jolly this pub was now with the land girls coming in full of fun and merriment, and a lot of the armed forces came as well. So as the thunder storm wreaked havoc outside and the lightning lit up the lanes and fields everyone carried on singing, until the door was opened so abruptly, and Burt, nearly fell in holding on to his porkpie hat which was dripping with rain.

"By God" he shouted to his friends, who were sitting at the top table enjoying a game of dominoes, "The weather is rough out there, its bloody fork lightning." As he made his way to the fire, Tommy was already filling Burt's pint, so before he walked over to the bar he took off his coat giving it a good shake as he did so.

"Hey up lad, steady on there, shaking your bloody coat we are getting wet sitting here," shouted Bill.

"Aye alright then," said Burt as he hung his coat over the back of a chair to drip, thus making a pool of water on Lizzie's clean stoned floor, while he stood in front of the roaring fire warming his backside as the steam rose off him. Mable gave Burt time to finish his pint then shouted him over to play the piano,

"Aye gan on, make the girls happy, play them a tune then they can have a bit dance."Dennis shouted over to Burt.

"Aye go on Burt I'll make it worth your while," Tommy told him as he carried Burt another pint over, as Burt put his hand in his trouser pocket to pay. Tommy shook his head and said, "No this is on the house, just go and give us all a tune on the piano." When Burt realised he could get some free beer he played until closing time,

Tommy didn't like shouting and telling everyone that it was closing time, when they were all enjoying themselves, but he was tired and wanted to get to bed, he laughingly told Lizzie,

"Those land girls will have thick heads in the morning, the amount of drink they have swallowed tonight." The girls had all got themselves a GI apart from Jennie, whose boyfriend Robert was a prisoner of war, and of whom Jennie was patiently waiting, for his return when the war is over, they intended getting married. It was still raining heavy when they all left Tommy's pub, Linda was giggling, that it was the second time today that she was soaked. Then she went on to drunkenly tell the GIs how she and Jennie were caught in the river naked. Jennie was wishing they were home as she was soaked, and embarrassed. She also knew she had drunk too much. When they arrived back home Jennie went straight inside, while Linda Susan and Mable stayed outside with the GIs. Jennie got into bed she felt sick, and dizzy, she tossed and turned hoping she wouldn't wake the rest of the house, but she needn't have worried as Ethel was awake in the sideboard bed downstairs, with Wilf snoring soundly beside her. Ethel raised her head from the pillow, and blinked the sleep from her eyes, as she punched the pillow into a more comfortable position, then pulled the pillow down to fit comfortably into her neck, then she sat up and cocked an ear, by them girls are still outside with them GIs but they will be getting more than they bargained for one of these days if they weren't careful she thought as sleep claimed her.

CHAPTER THREE

Just up the road from Ethel's, lived Grace Hughes's sister. Pat her husband Michael, and her widowed, mother-in-law Doris Green. Pat had just finished a full days baking, as she ran her flour, covered hands down the front of her pinny; and said I'll have a sit down awhile Mam, and drink this tea before it goes cold, before I start the tea. Pat and her Mother-in-law Doris sat in companionable silence, facing each other over a fire that was roaring up the chimney Pat sat back in the chair as she sipped the piping hot tea and signed.

"What is the matter lass, the older woman asked with concern, or can I guess?"

"Yes you know me too well, it's just the usual Mam; she looked around the room, to emphasize, I just wonder if we will be lucky enough to get some evacuees, as we have plenty of room, Doris Green felt for her son and daughter–in -law ,they had been married eight years now, and were still childless, Doris's son had suffered with a bad chest as a boy so he couldn't be conscripted, and when he had married Pat, he had got the caretakers job at the hall, the house in the grounds went with the job, it had three bedrooms and a room that they called a box room, Pat was often heard to laughingly say in the early days of their marriage

"We have too much space." And Michael would laughingly reply

"We will fill the house with children." But sadly it never happened; Pat came out of her reverie and said

"I'd better start the tea or Michael will be back before it's ready."

37

The older woman leaned over and held Pats hand knowingly,""I know you and Michael might never have kiddies of your own, but I'm sure very shortly you will have some evacuees, filling these empty bedrooms." Little did the older woman know that within the week her words would come true?

Hundreds of miles away from this quiet little village, in London, there were children cowering in the shelters.

One little family was, Maureen Winter with her three children, Mary who was aged eight, her sister Amy aged six, and their brother George who was four, Maureen always kept the shelter bag handy, so she just had to grab it on the way out, as the sirens started their woe full sound, the local paper said to pack a shelter bag, it advised people to put in rent books, insurance policies, identity cards, and birth certificates. She always kept the gas masks near the shelter bag, the children's masks were meant to look like Mickey Mouse, and they were red and blue, Maureen had just arrived home from work and after picking up the children moaning Minnie had started making the horrible wailing noise, she and the children started running towards the shelter, she didn't feel any safer sitting in this claustrophobic shelter, the local defence volunteers, liked to think they were looking after folks, Maureen didn't feel any safer with them helping ,as it was made up of the very old ,very young and the infirm, and in place of rifles which were in short supply, they practised with brush shafts.

"One old woman had asked, "How the bloody hell do they expect, to defend us with bloody brush shafts." Maureen was seriously thinking of evacuating her three children on Friday, as that was when another train load of kiddies were leaving the cities. It was getting too much having the children with her, she loved her children, and she was pleased her good for nothing husband had been conscripted, but she liked a bit enjoyment like some of the other girls at the munitions factory, and then there was Ritchie a G I she'd met a while ago when she'd managed to get a baby sitter for her children, she had been tied down to a bad marriage, and now she wanted some fun with Ritchie, and to ease her concisions, she was telling herself the kiddies would be safe, and she could go and see them now and again, she jumped as a bomb dropped very near, the German planes were over head, with their distinctive intermittent sound. The bomb had dropped so close to the shelter that she and everybody else got covered in dust as it swirled in the air. The bells of the emergency services were ringing frantically; George started to cry, Mary and her sister joined him as the planes roared overhead, then the explosions which were very close. The whistles of the descending bombs making her insides turn with fear George had his arms tight around her neck, she could see fear etched on the girls faces. If only she'd had a dependable husband who cared, but she had to make all the decisions, and one of them was not to go back to him when the war was over, Richie had asked her to go with him, but she couldn't leave her children. Another bomb had just dropped and the shelter was shaking, as minuets turned into hours, the bombardment carried on relentlessly. Some of the other children had started to cry, Maureen had a bad head, she could have cried with them, every bone in her body ached as well, and she had stood all day at her machine, then sitting in these shelters on a night made folk weary. Mary was asking for something to eat, so Maureen opened her shelter bag and offered them some paste sandwiches, that was all she could get hold of, then she put her hand down to the bottom of the bag, and pulled out a packet of *lucky strike* as she lit it and sucked in the smoke it made her feel more relaxed, she always had fags, Ritchie saw to that, the generosity of the Americans was greatly appreciated, people looked when you pulled out fags, Maureen could tell what they were thinking they will probably think I'm going to bed with a G I but I'm not bothered.

"I wish these noises would go away Mammy," cried Amy, as the ack ack guns started firing into the night sky, lit up by incendiary bombs being dropped, and the beams of the search lights, and the bombs still exploding in the distance.

"The bomb damage will be considerable," said the shelter attendant.

"Well I just hope we get out of here alive to see it," said one old woman.

She then turned her attention on Maureen, and said, "Your husband will be in the forces is he love?" then without waiting for an answer she went on to tell Maureen.

"I live on me own, so I only have myself to see too, my husband's been dead now for." then she pursed her lips as she was thinking, "Aye its nigh on fifteen years, been on me own ever since, he started bad with cold then it didn't take long until it turned to pneumonia, and then I lost him, she sighed. We had eight children, I see them all from time to time", then she looked longingly at Maureen's cigarette, Maureen saw her looking, and offered her one.

"Oh thank you." the old woman said, as she hurriedly took one out of Maureen's open packet, lucky strike eh,

"Oh and me names Ida, by the way "which street do you live in then?"

"Oh I live in James Street." Maureen answered comfortably; I was in two minds whether to come down here tonight as I hadn't been long in from work. I was thinking about just going under the stairs with theses three, as she looked at her three children.

"Oh I live about a ten minutes walk from here," insisted Ida, "I could go to another shelter that's a bit closer, but I like to see different faces, its gets a bit lonely living on your own. I have a little one bed roomed house its big enough for me." As Maureen took another cigarette out of her packet, Ida looked at her, so Maureen offered her another.

"Oh thank you I do enjoy a smoke." As Maureen leaned over and lit it, Ida took a good drag then blew out a mouthful of smoke and said,

"Well I'm pleased, I came to this shelter tonight, because it doesn't matter which one you go to, there's going to be explosions, and bombs going off but you meet different folk."Mary was cuddling Amy while Maureen was rocking George on her knee. Just as the all clear sounded, one of the firemen came into the shelter and hurriedly shouted,

"There's been four streets flattened, around here, they are Bells avenue, Parkinson Crescent, James Street, and Gregory Close." Maureen cried out

"No I live at James Street, what are we going to do? Where are we going to stay? I have nowhere to go." And then she started to cry, as bedlam broke out, as everyone was shouting about their homes being flattened, the children started to cry, those that were sleeping woke up with all the noise, the fireman was trying to appeal for calm, and make himself heard,

" if you all make your way to the church hall, the volunteers' are waiting there with cups of tea, and you can all stare there for the rest of tonight, as there are ferocious fires burning everywhere," Ida put a comforting arm around Maureen, and said ,

"Don't you fret love; you've shared your cigarettes with me tonight and we've got on well together, so you and those three bairns are coming home with me," Maureen was crying as she got ponderously to her feet, Ida seemed to take charge as Maureen was in shock,

"Come on you girls." Ida said as she took hold of Mary and Amy's hand, "You are all coming back to my house", then she turned and said "Come on Maureen you've got to make the best of it, I know you have lost your house, but how many will of lost their lives in this lot tonight?" As the little party made their way back to Ida's, the sky was red with all the fires burning, they were all coughing with the thick smoke, and the acrid smell, as they turned in to a yard Ida took the key out of her bag and opened the door, at the same time propelling her visitors inside,

"Come and sit down then I'll make a cup of tea," she explained as she rattled the poker between the bars to stir the fire back to life. The children started to cry and rub their eyes tiredly; Ida pointed to a door and said,

"That's my bedroom in there Maureen, take the bairns to bed they are worn out." Once the three children were tucked up in Ida's, comfortable double bed they slept while Maureen and Ida were contemplating what to do, while sitting next to Ida's fire with a welcome cup of tea in their hands. Ida was telling Maureen how lonely she was on her own, and they were welcome to stay as long as they wanted.

"I was going to have my bairns evacuated," Maureen said reluctantly,"

"I just don't want to part with them; do you think I'm being spiteful? Keeping them with me, and going through all this, she asked as she turned anguished eyes to Ida."

"I don't think you are being spiteful at all" Ida told her kindly. And you know you can all stay here as long as you want, but if they were my kiddies, I wouldn't want them living through all this horror, and I can't see it getting any better, God knows how long this war will go on for, and all the families split up," then the realisation that she was spreading gloom, and despondency, occurred to her, as Maureen burst into another flood of tears, and so Ida tried to redress the balance. As dawn broke, Maureen with the help of Ida, had decided to evacuate her three children, so leaving the children in the care of Ida Maureen set off to see the people in charge of the evacuation, the children, like Maureen only had the clothes that they stood in, at the church hall the misery was etched on everyone's faces, a lot of them had slept on the floor, the volunteers had done their best, but there was such a lot of homeless people, some of the children had got parted from their parents some parents were crying for their missing children. After two hours of been past to different people she had managed to get some clothes for herself, and George,

"I'm sorry," one of the workers told Maureen, "I can give you some knickers, socks and a coat each for your two daughters, but we don't have one dress in the place," as Maureen had wearily made her way back to Ida's the kiddies had been fed as Ida had kindly shared her rations with the children and Maureen had put their names down for the next evacuation, which was rescheduled for the next day, as Maureen broke the news to the children they cried, George didn't understand but he cried as he was frightened, and Maureen was cuddling the children and shedding a few tears with them, as Ida was also rubbing her eyes,

"Please don't send us away mammy," Mary begged her mother, what if we don't see you anymore? Who is going to look after us?

"You will be going to stay with some nice people who will love and look after you until this war is over. Then I will come for you and we will all be together again." Maureen said a quiet prayer to herself, "Please God let somebody love and take care of my children." Just then the wailing sound broke into Maureen's thoughts as moaning Minnie started up again. They thought the bombs were bad enough the doodle bugs were worse; they just dropped out of the sky,

Ida looked up at the sky, and said, "Come on Maureen we will go to the shelter at the end of the street, it will be packed but, it will be better than being out in this lot." The shelter attendant helped Ida Maureen and the three children inside as the planes were coming over. Margaret had her children in her arms as she listened to the drones of the planes over head, and the thunder of the ack ack guns firing back, no one could sleep while the bombardment was going on.

The old woman who was sitting near Maureen said. "It seems the city is taking another battering tonight, God knows when it will all end." The incendiary bombs were lighting up the sky with their red glow. The ARP was busy rescuing people from flattened houses, fires were erupting, and gas was a hazardous and a noxious smell. The raid continued throughout the night, as the all clear sounded the next morning, and people were stiffly getting up off the hard bench seats, as they made their way home, hoping that their homes were still standing. They found the air was filled with thick black smoke.

Ida looked at Maureen as she trudged miserably, up the street with her little family, then she patted her hand and said. "If it's any consolation, I think you are doing the right thing, having these bairns evacuated, as this is getting to be a nightly occurrence."

"I know they will be better out of harm's way, it's just letting my bairns go to strangers," cried Maureen as tears ran unchecked down her cheeks.

"Come on now," said the old woman, "I will help you," then as an afterthought she said, "Some of my grandchildren were evacuated," she omitted to tell Maureen that some had come home as well, as the people they were billeted with, had failed to look after them properly. As they neared Ida's door the van belonging to the WVS, services, came to a halt beside them, and one of the woman asked cheerily, "if they would like a cup of tea? Before they had time to reply, the woman told them the water and gas mane had been damaged, the woman also handed out tea and meagre sandwiches

Which Maureen later gave to Ida saying, "I couldn't face that sandwich I feel so upset at losing my children,"

Ida tried to jolly Maureen along saying, "It won't be for long and they will be safe, come on now let us go inside, and then we will all have a cuddle before we set off to the station."

CHAPTER FOUR

A few hours had passed and the little family were making their way to the station, for Maureen to put her bairns on a train with no idea where they were going, or when she would see them again. The station was full of human misery, and packed with wives and girlfriends saying good bye, to husband and lovers not knowing when they would meet again. Mothers were holding their children as if they wouldn't let them go; some of the grandparents had gone along to give moral support, the woman were openly crying, while the men had their handkerchiefs out blowing their noses, the children were clinging on to their mothers, Ida was thinking the sooner the train came the better, as this was a sea of misery. An official looking woman came around with a clipboard,

"Are these your children," she asked in a clipped tone I have you down here as having three is that right? Everyone thought that Cathy was hard faced woman, walking around with a clipboard checking on the families, but they didn't realize she had just put her own four children on a train two days before, and she was upset, and harassed,

"Right is there anyone else that I've missed she asked?" As a brassy blonde came hurrying in with a little girl about eight years old,

"Yes." the woman shouted, "you have missed me; my little girl is going as well."

"Really!" Cathy looked at the woman with raised eye brows, what is the little girl's name? The woman looked at Cathy as if she should know.

46

"Well its Beryl." She answered nastily,

"Well I'm sorry but your child's name is not down here on my list" Cathy told her as she scanned it,"

"Well I don't care someone will have to sort it out as I haven't got all day." Cathy tried again

Right Mrs what is your surname?"

"It's Ebdon and its miss actually."

"Well I'm sorry Miss Ebdon, your child will not be able to go, as there will be no billet sorted for her, you should have put her name down, all around them children were crying woman and wives were in their husbands arms not knowing when they would meet again if ever. Miss Ebdon suddenly grabbed hold of her boyfriends hand and said to him.

"Come on we are going." The boyfriend hesitated then asked,

"What are you going to do about her?" Beryl was standing on her own with tears running down her cheeks, just then the train came steaming into the station and disgorged its passengers. Miss Ebdon and her boyfriend hurried away leaving Cathy with a dilemma. mothers were giving their children last minute cuddles and instructions, and Beryl had no one to cuddle, so Cathy put her arms around Beryl's shoulders, and shepherded her on to the train, Maureen still had a tight hold of her three children, but Ida saw the guard standing holding the flag.

"Come on now Maureen, let the kiddies go to where they will be safe." Ida was saying as she untangled them from their mother's arms.

"I am going to miss you all." she cried as she bent and hugged them convulsively for the last time. At last everyone who was meant to be on the train, had finally climbed aboard. The carriage doors clashed shut, the whistle was blown, and they were off. Very soon the train passed out of sight, leaving only a cloud of steam, to show that it had been there, and left so many broken hearts.

Meanwhile hundreds of miles away in the peaceful countryside, Ethel was busy cooking dinner, when someone knocked on the door, she thought it was strange as everyone just walked in. On opening the door Ethel found Lillie and Lindsey, the two land girls who had just recently arrived,

"We were wondering if we could come in and wait for Linda." they asked Ethel."

"Of course you can," said Ethel as she opened the door wider and stood aside to let them through."

"I thought you two would have been at work this time of day, would you like a cup of tea? As I was just going to make one

Oh yes please they both chorused,"

"Have you two lasses been in bother then?" asked Gran and before they had time to answer Wilf walked in,

"Oh I'm just in time for a pot of tea," and then he turned to the girls and asked. "Are they all your possessions outside the gate?" Gran sat and nodded her head knowingly,

You two are leaving aren't you? That's why all your bag and baggage is out there. Lindsey looked despondently at Ethel and said,

"Yes it's true we are going home, but we have no money for the train fare," "well did old Lennie not square up with you? Or you have maybe left him in the lurch? And why are you going anyway?" Gran asked, as you have only been here a fortnight."

Lillie said,

"I will never ever come back into the country." "I won't either." Lindsey said determinedly. "It's eerie on a night, we have to walk away down the garden to the lav, and there are no buses, or picture houses, reality is far from the idyllic images that have been displayed on the posters, which we looked at before we came here." Ethel was standing looking thoughtful then she said,

"By the time the girls come home tonight, you'll not get a train back, as it will be too late." The girls looked horrified,

"What are we going to do?" Lillie asked Lindsey.

Ethel said, "You can have some tea with us, and then you'll have to go along and ask Lennie for the money he owes you."

"He won't pay us we have asked," said a tearful Lindsey,

"He'll have to," Wilf told them with some authority. "If he doesn't he won't be allowed anymore land girls, if you report him, for not giving you your wages". After tea the girls walked back to see Lennie, and after threatening to report him, he gave them their wages.

Lindsey told Lillie, "We have got our wages, but where are we going to sleep?" Gran had been wondering about that, so when they came back, she asked what they were going to do about a bed, for the night. "

"I don't know," answered Lillie I should have had more sense than to come in the first place, it's been an extraordinary and frightening time, reality is far from the idyllic images that were displayed on the posters, that we read before we came here, we thought life in the country would be easy."

"Aye then you got a shock." said gran knowingly. "There is a lot of hard work in the countryside, and the only available space in a bed here is mine, you can come in with me, gran offered as long as you don't snore and fart."

Linda said "Oh thank you, we will. Mam always said, better the devil you know." Gran's eyes narrowed, as she shouted.

"I hope you are not associating me, with the devil or you can sleep in that bloody field."

"Oh I didn't mean any harm Mrs Brown." Lindsey quickly tried to pacify her.

"Well if you are both stopping here and sharing my bed, you had better go up with me at nine o clock, as I'm ready for an early night."

"Oh we don't go to bed until after twelve." Lillie informed gran. "

"Well seeing as you will be sharing my bed." gran retorted, "you will go when I say. I am not having two giggling girls, waking me up after twelve o clock so let that be an end to it. "As nine o clock approached, gran started to shuffle forward in her chair. Ethel immediately jumped up to help her.

"It's alright our Ethel; these two lassies are going the same way as me." As gran looked keenly at both Lillie and Lindsey, and besides we've fed them, so it's only right they give me a bit help it will save you helping me upstairs our Ethel." As the three of them made their way upstairs Lillie thought,

"No one will believe me back home in the city that I went to bed at nine o clock with an old woman." but Lillie knew if she didn't do, as Mrs. Brown told her, she would definitely be sleeping in a hedge back, so she would put up with it tonight, and tomorrow she would be home.

Gran got into bed and pulled the blankets up and was soon snoring. Through the night the girls woke up cold and soon realized why. Gran was wrapped up in the blankets and what wasn't covering her skinny body was on the floor, Lillie whispered to Lindsey.

"I will go downstairs, and bring our coats up to cover us over, as we dare not pull them off her. I wish it was morning."

"So do I." shouted gran. "You are nothing but a couple of nuisances."

Morning came early for Lindsey and Lillie, as Lillie was woken with a poke in the back off gran's elbow.

"Come on get up you two." gran told them "

"What time is it?" the girls asked as they rubbed sleep from their eyes.

"It is five o clock and time you were up,." gran answered impatiently "you go to the stair top, and shout and tell our Ethel not to bother coming up here, to help me as she usually does," pointing her finger at Lillie, "as you girls can help me, I will sit on the edge of this bed," gran explained, "while you bring my dress and cardigan Lillie off that chair and you" gran pointed her finger at Lindsey, "can open that cupboard and get me clean drawers and stockings out," the girls were flabbergasted, Lillie thought this old woman was unbelievable. As gran Lillie and Lindsey made their way into the kitchen, the four land girls, Susan Mabel Linda and Jennie, were just finishing their breakfast, Wilf and the two boys Frank and Colin, were just finishing their mug of tea, and then they were going to milk the cows, and deliver the milk. The land girls quickly embraced Lillie and Lindsey, and said their goodbye's, as the door closed behind them.

Ethel smiling said, "I will cook you all some breakfast," the smell of bacon frying had hit the girl's nostrils when they had walked into the kitchen,

"Aye I'll have my usual," gran said, "I do like bacon and a couple of fresh eggs on a morning, you will just give these two an egg each wont you Ethel?"

Ethel was shocked, "Well no gran, I am going to give them bacon and egg the same as everyone,"

"Well you can't do that our Ethel; giving food away like that, they are strangers to us, we didn't know them before they came here, and once they go on that train we won't see them again, so I wouldn't be wasting good bacon on them."

"But gran, we have plenty, we have sides of ham, and bacon hanging from the ceiling in the scullery."

"Aye we might have now, but we won't have for much longer if you keep giving it away," gran retorted, and then she turned to the girls and said, "you can both have a fried egg each, as the hens are laying well, our Ethel can fry my bacon and eggs first, and after she has fried yours you can have a slice of bread each fried in the fat that the bacon has been cooked in and then you will get a taste of the bacon,"

"They are having bacon like the rest of us gran," Ethel seized on the opportunity to get a word in." like I said there is plenty of bacon hanging up and these two girls are not going from here hungry." Lillie put her hand over her mouth as she yawned; Ethel saw her and asked if she had slept well?

"No not really." Lillie replied, "why ever not?" asked a surprised Ethel, "Do you think it was the excitement of going home today to see your family?"

"No it wasn't, I was cold we both were, weren't we Lindsey/"

"Yes we were," answered Lindsey.

"Well I don't understand why," Ethel told the girls," gran has twice as many blankets on her bed as what the rest of us have, I would of thought, with all them blankets on and three in the bed you would of been sweating," said a bewildered Ethel.

"Gran had all the blankets, in fact they were actually on the floor at gran's side," Lillie said meekly. Gran looked over at the girls with narrowed eyes and shouted,

"you don't think I'm going to lie cold all night to suit you two, as you seem to have forgotten, that it is my bed, and my blankets, and after you have eaten those eggs, and bacon," she had to add, "you want to be getting ready to catch the train,"

"Oh there's plenty of time yet," said Lindsey off handily.

"Well just make sure you catch that train," warned gran, "as you needn't think you can come back here for another free meal, and I don't intend making a habit of sharing my bed either and after we have eaten our breakfast's you two girls can wash the pots for our Ethel, as you have no money for your bed and board so you might as well work it off."

"No it's alright." Ethel said," I'll soon do them."

"Well if our Ethel's going to see to the pots, you lasses can get a bucket each and fill them at the well it will save our Ethel having to carry water."

After they had collected the water from the well, they decided to say goodbye before gran had some more jobs for them to do ,so the girls picked up their possessions, and set off to walk the three miles to the station, as the girls sat and waited for a train to take them back to the city Lillie said,

"I will be pleased to see the back of this place, and that Mrs. Brown is unbelievable, fancy not going to let us have any bacon, but you know Linda told me last night, that the four of them, don't intend going back home to the city, after the war they like it in the country."

"Well they are welcome to it," Lindsey remarked, "I personally can't wait to get away; I'd rather dodge the bombs"

After an hour the train came steaming in to the station, an official looking woman with a clipboard got off first, then the children followed with the W V S ladies who had looked after them, while the children were disembarking,

Grace Hughes the local nurse and midwife was pedalling along to her sisters, Pat Green, to give her some news that would make her day. Pat and her husband Michael had been married Eight years and didn't have any children they would dearly have loved some but it didn't happen. Michael's widowed mother Doris, a kindly soul lived with them in a big house, in the grounds of the hall as Michael was the caretaker, Grace was puffing as she stood her bike up against the wall, and hurried inside the house, Pat saw her sister, and she came through rubbing her floured hands down her apron.

"Is there something wrong Grace?"

"No not at all Pat, I have brought you some news,"

"Well it must be important, the speed you've come up here."

"I have been sent to ask you if you can take three evacuees, they will be arriving very shortly I know it's, very short notice,"   Doris Pats mother-in-law, came through with a potato and knife in her hand,

"Did I hear you say, Grace, that we are getting some evacuees?"

"Yes that's right Doris, two little girls Mary is eight and her sister Amy is six and George their brother is four," Pat was smiling as she went out the door, to look for Michael to tell him the good news.

Two hours later, the WVS lady was standing at Pats door with four children, as   Pat opened the door she had a big smile on her face to see the children, but she was puzzled to see four, the WVS lady saw her looking and quickly said ,

It's alright we are not shoving an extra one, on to you, as this is an unexpected one, just then Doris came through,

"Come on children would you like some lemonade? I made earlier and a cake." Over a cup of tea, and out of the children's hearing, the woman told Pat all about the fourth little girl, how her mother had just left her at the station, and gone off with her boyfriend. Pat loved children, so she asked

"Where are you taking the little girl too?"

"Well that's just it," the woman confided in Pat,

"We have nowhere for her to go with such short

notice, we will have to walk her around the doors to see if we can get anyone to take her in. That's the fate of the kiddies that's not wanted I'm sorry to say. Her mother never even made arrangements for her to be evacuated, just left her at the station."

"Don't do that please." begged Pat, "I would hate to see her dragged around the houses, we have plenty of room, leave her here with us, another bairn isn't going to make much difference."

"Well are you sure?" would you not like to talk it over with your husband/"

"Talk what over with her husband /" Michael asked as he walked through the door and only heard part of the conversation. "

"We don't mind taking the little girl, as well as the three winter children, do we Michael?"

"No of course not Pat, you can't leave her with nowhere to go." It turned out to be an experience, with Beryl Ebdon, that left Pat wondering sometimes, if she had done right. And when she relayed her fear to Michal, his only comment was,

"You can train animals, so it can't be that hard, to train an unwanted child." Beryl was a disobedient child, from the moment she arrived, without a frock to her name the same as the other two little girls, after the official woman with the clip board had left Pat climbed on a chair and took the sitting room curtains down, then with the tape measure hanging around her neck measured the three little girls one by one, then proceeded, to cut up the curtains, then she had Michael drag out the treadle sewing machine,, out of the cupboard and by teatime the following day the little girls all had a new frock. Pat knew there would be some problem's as the bairns had been bombed out of their homes, and been evacuated to the remote countryside, a lot of the evacuees had never seen farm animals before, it was an extraordinary time for them and it must of been frightening being billeted with strangers. It wasn't as bad for Mary Amy and George, as those three were together, but Beryl was on her own, and Pat knew she had to win her trust, as she had never had any affection. It didn't take Pat long to run up three frocks for the little girls, come on try them on she beckoned, Mary and Amy, walked over to Pat, but Beryl hung back.

"I'm not wearing the same frock as them two." She told Pat.

"Well if you won't wear the frock I have made for you, I don't know what you will wear, as that is only fit for the bin." as she pointed to the frock that Beryl was wearing, which was too tight and short, and had definitely seen better days. Beryl stared at Pat uncomprehendingly as she sucked her thumb; Doris tried to jolly things along, as she told the children they could choose what they wanted for tea, the three winter children all chorused chips as Pat looked approvingly at Doris her mother in-law. Michael, Pat's husband was just making his way in and on hearing the children suggested taking them round to the hen house,

"Then Auntie Pat will fry you an egg with your chips," he told the children, the three winter children seemed eager to go but Beryl hung back uncertain.

"Do you not want to go and see the hens Beryl and fetch the eggs back for your tea?" Pat asked the little girl kindly, as she was still sat on her haunches on the floor, Beryl nearly had Pat sprawled across the floor as she rushed at her with her arms outstretched and tears running unchecked down her cheeks

"I don't want to go with him," she cried "he mightn't bring me back,"

"Well I'll come as well," Pat said as she tried to untangle herself from Beryl's arms, as they all walked across the field to the hen house Beryl clung on to Pat's hand

"Where is the hen house? Asked Mary as she was very inquisitive, "I can't see it," she said as she looked round her.

"It's just over there," Michael said as he pointed to the little wooden shed in the corner which was obliterated by the trees. As Michael opened the henhouse door there was a couple of hens sitting on the nest, and as the children walked in disturbing them they started to flap and squawk, Michael held the door open and the hens fluttered out, as Pat tried to comfort the children who had never seen hens before. As they all headed back to the house the winter children were running about whereas Beryl kept tight hold of Pat's hand,

"Can I stay with you forever?" Beryl asked. Pat did not want to upset the little girl as her mother could take her back anytime, but she did need to win her trust, and she doubted if Beryl would ever see her mother again. As pat and Michael walked back to the house with the children they all had an egg each in their hand for their tea, as they walked back into the kitchen, Doris was leaning over the fire putting a big pan of fat on to the hot coals to heat, she turned and smiled as the children walked over to her to see what see was doing, as they had never seen anyone cooking on a fire before, and she told them tea would soon be ready. Pat bustled about setting the table for tea; very soon Doris tipped the full dish of chipped potatoes into the pan of hot bubbling fat, then when they started to turn brown she put the frying pan on the side of the fire to heat ready to fry the eggs that the children had collected,

Down the road at Ethel's, Eva was standing at the table peeling cooking apples for Ethel, as Ethel had already made all the pastry and was busy lining two large pie dishes, with some of the pastry she'd just made, then she picked up the pieces of the clean chopped rabbit, and dropped them into the pie dishes then covered them with the pastry lid that she'd rolled out earlier, just then the door opened ,and Eva's four little girls came rushing in ahead of Wilf, Eva thought of them and treated them all as her own, as she had been looking after Violet and Rose Parker now for a year and a half, they were two little evacuees, their mother had been killed when a bomb had dropped on the pub where she was staying with her boyfriend,"

"If she had come and visited her two little girls like she'd promised," Gran was forever saying, "she would have still been alive". Eva had traced their father who was in the army, and he had been visiting his daughters ever since, and he seemed to take a shine to Eva, Wilf took off his cap and hung it on a nail behind the door, then sat down in the chair opposite Gran,

"Are we having a drink of tea Ethel?"Wilf asked then looked at Eva, she laughed at Wilf and said,

"I will scold a pot of tea Mam, as everyone will want a drink."

"Aye don't forget about me our Eva, and if you don't mind you can cut me a piece off that rice cake, as the rate things are going in here I can see tea being late tonight."

"It won't be late at all Gran", Ethel replied," It will be ready in time for everyone coming in."

"I have just been talking to Tommy from the pub,"

Wilf turned and told everyone they all stopped talking and turned their attention to him. "He was telling me, that Michael and Pat Green have taken four evacuees in; he was saying that three of the kiddies are brother and sisters, and seemed to be well looked after but the other girl, is a proper terror. Poor little lass it's a shame they were saying she had never know affection, her mother had just left her standing on the station platform and walked away with her boyfriend never giving that bairn a backward glance," Ethel shook her head and said ,

"Well Pat will likely get an allowance off the government for the four of them, and Mrs Winter will pay her contribution to her children, but I can't see Beryl's mother paying anything towards her keep, and there is a few evacuees going back to the cities if their families have stopped paying, as you can't afford to keep them on nothing she said with a sigh," as Ethel was speaking Colin had arrived at the door and when he heard Ethel saying about money for evacuees he had listened , and his heart plummeted like a stone dropped in a well. When he eventually sat down for his tea he just stirred it round his plate, his brother frank wasn't eating his either, as Colin had ran back across the field to relay what he had heard to his brother who was two years older than him. Ethel had a feeling something was wrong, so she leaned over the table and stroked Colin's hand asking what was troubling him." He started crying, tears running down his face he was crying so much Ethel looked at Frank for a explanation, after he explained what Colin had heard at the door Ethel got up from the table and cuddled Colin saying,

"Don't be silly we have never had any money for you two boys, and we know you have no one to go back too, that is why you will be staying with us." she said smiling.

"If you ask me, you deserved all you got listening at doors; folk that listen at doors never hear any good about themselves", said gran with a scowl, "and you're too soft with them our Ethel." Later in the evening his mind reassured , Colin cuddled Ethel then said good night, and made his way to bed, to lay awake for a while contemplating staying here with Auntie Ethel for ever as his eyes closed and sleep claimed him.

CHAPTER FIVE

Along at Pat and Michael's house the children had all eaten their tea hungrily,

"Will you bring the tin bath in for me Michael please?" Asked Pat, Beryl was horrified

"I'm not having a bath, and I'm not wearing that dress tomorrow neither," she shouted as Michael carried the bath in to the house and Pat started filling it with a pail, but first she had to ladle the hot water out of the boiler, that was joined to the side of the fire, Pat soon got the other three children bathed dried and into their night clothes,

"You are going to have a bath Beryl, whether you like it or not, as you are all going to sleep top to toe so get your clothes off now Beryl or I will undress you" it was a revelation to Pat and Doris, once Beryl was parted from her dress as she didn't have a stitch on

Where are your drawers at Beryl? Asked a puzzled Doris

Beryl shrugged her thin shoulders as she said "never had any" Amy and Mary didn't have a lot of clothes as they had been bombed out but they did have spare vest, knickers, liberty bodice and nightdress, whereas Beryl had nothing, as she had stayed with everyone on numerous occasions, when her mother had boyfriends staying and no one had seemed to notice or care how poorly she was dressed,

"You will have to borrow one of my night dresses tonight." Doris kindly told Beryl, "and I will run you one up for tomorrow night", as bedtime approached Pat said,

"Come on up the wooden hill it's been a long day," Pat began to climb the stairs with Beryl close on her heels, the children were soon sleeping soundly upstairs, in warm comfortable beds, and for Beryl it was the only time she hadn't gone to bed hungry.

Back downstairs Pat looked disparagingly at her mother-in-law Doris,

"Oh I do feel sorry for Beryl, Mam, poor little lass; I don't think anyone has ever cared for her." Doris looked up from her mending basket,

"Well she'll take no hurt here pat, and I don't think her mother will want her back in a hurry if at all." but the first disillusioning weeks were hard for all concerned, it had been a revelation to both Pat and Doris, as to what Beryl ate.

A long at Ethel's Prudence had just called in,

"Where have you been? Gran asked. "Posting another letter"

"Yes I correspond regular with my parents," answered Prudence," and I thought a walk would do me good to breathe some fresh air, did I hear someone say that Pat and Michael had got some evacuees, I just hope they are well behaved when they come to school, as I won't stand for any nonsense, I believe children should be seen and not heard." Prudence stood arms folded, feet apart commanding the attention of everyone in the room; gran leaned forward in the chair and said,

"If you are staying Prudence sit down and shut up, your voice is enough to put folk off their tea," As Prudence sat down Ethel past her a cup of tea and asked her if she would like something to eat,

"Yes please I wouldn't say no, Ethel thank you," as Ethel past a loaded plate over to Prudence, Gran said

"Right eat your tea prudence, let the meat stop your mouth, because I'm enjoying my tea, Prudence heaved a deep sigh,

Oh alright then gran she said resignedly it isn't easy trying to teach some of them evacuees you know,"

"Life isn't easy for anyone prudence, but it's no good making a song and dance over it and I think there is more to you than meets the eye as well." Prudence dropped her eyes and quietly ate her tea sometimes she felt as if gran could see straight through her. If gran only knew how right she was about prudence, and within a few months the truth would be out. Wilf started to laugh,

"I bet your day hasn't been anything like mine prudence, I was in the field sorting the pigs which ones to breed off and some to go to the butcher, when David comes over to the wall he had a handcart with him, I knew where he was going as the girls told me the other night that Margaret and David needed a sideboard bed for Paul, so I said they could have mine, as Ethel already has one, I offered it to Eva with her moving into my house but she had one as well, so Eva said,"

"I'll put your sideboard into the house I'm leaving someone will want it." I thought I'm not that busy I'll have a walk out with David and help him with the sideboard, as we walked we were talking about Linda and Jennie, I was telling David that when they first arrived here they had never seen a cow or a pig and they definitely didn't know the first thing about making a meal," Linda laughed at Jennie Mable and Susan and said,"

"That is true isn't it girls, but we are good cooks now, we've had a good teacher haven't we Ethel," As Linda put her arm round Ethel's shoulder. The first night you girls landed on the doorstep Ethel had made rabbit stew, I'll never forget the look on your faces, but as David said he couldn't have wished for better workers, anyway Wilf said, you couldn't' of guessed what happened next as we arrived at Eva's old house, David said, are you sure no one has moved in yet Wilf? As there is smoke coming out of the chimney, just then a woman opened the door with a headscarf on her head, which looked like a turban and a hessian pinny wrapped round her, she looked me and David up and down and asked what we wanted, well I explained about the sideboard, and Eva already having one but David needed it for his lad that had been invalided out of the war, well that woman just stood blocking the doorway, with her hands on her hips, she said well if you wanted it you should of got it out before I moved in ,so I told her we didn't know it had been let to anyone, well as you can see it has she said as she took a packet of fags out of her skirt pocket under the hessian apron, then struck a match and lit it, she was still staring at me and David as she took a huge drag off her fag ,and inhaled it deep into her lungs,"

I have rights you know me and my family have moved in, I could claim it." she said standing there with a fag in one hand the other hand on her hip, just then her daughter came to the door her jumper straining against her large breast, then she rubbed herself against me and David,"

Oh don't be so hard on them Mam," she said," with me being in business, as I'm always looking for customers," as she looked coyly at me and David, as the woman threw her fag end on to the step that Eva had whitened every week, the older woman seemed to make her mind up as she said

"I will sell you it " well I'd had enough of her so I said now look here missus it is my furniture so you can step aside as we are coming into get it, just then a weedy little man with the station uniform on came walking down the path, "

"What's the matter Mildred? The squeaky little voice asked the big woman; well she just leaned over and dragged him in by his tie, with one of her beefy arms,

"Get in there and don't ask questions that don't concern you," she shouted. The daughter stepped back outside and rubbed herself against me, Wilf sat and rubbed his chin as he said well I wasn't going to be got rid of that easy, can they come in Mam the girl called Lucy asked her mother you never know they might be customers some day, we walked in to the house and soon found out why she wanted to keep the sideboard, all they had was two shabby armchairs slovenly behaviour was evident. There was two dirty children sitting on the floor, they started crying when me and David walked in, just then the fat woman shouted see to your kids Lucy as the weedy little man gave us a nervous smile, and as me and David walked out carrying the sideboard Mildred came following behind and gave the door such a kick it shuddered on its hinges, David looked at me and said,"

"It's a funny do in there and no mistake, if I'd known what they were like I wouldn't have come,"

"Aye then you would of had to gone home and face Margaret, as she has her heart set on that sideboard I told him, but it was a real eye opener she'll cause some bother that one." Gran was busy making sure she had got the last bit of potatoes and mince off her plate then she looked up and said,

"Aye there will be a lot of lasses carrying their secrets under their aprons and our Ethel's one of them, "gran Ethel exclaimed "whatever did you make a comment like that for? "Well you haven't denied it, our Ethel;

"I was going to wait awhile before I announced it, as it is early days," said Ethel defiantly, as Eva turned as red as beetroot,

"Oh Mam I've just realized, I can't believe it. I will have a brother or sister younger then my children, oh how embarrassing I think I will go home,"

"See what you've done now gran, upsetting our Eva, I was going to tell everyone in my own time" Ethel felt harassed, perspiration ran down her back in this hot crowded kitchen,

"Stop making such a fuss our Ethel, it doesn't matter when you told Eva, she would have been shocked, at least now she has got time to get used to it,"

Wilf said, "I have a plan for the milk round as Ethel has plenty of work to do I am not going to have her walking round delivering milk, then he cupped his hands behind his head closed his eyes with legs stretched out, and then he seemed disinclined to say any more

.Mean while Three hundred miles away in London, Winnie Breaker was about to find something out, which would undermine all Prudence's principals' at the small village where she was billeted and teaching the evacuees, Winnie had left school a year ago at the age of fifteen, her and a friend Dorothy worked at the pickling factory, Winnie wanted more freedom then what her Mam and dad would allow, she was saying to her friend,

"You are very lucky Dorothy, having brothers and sisters around you, also having young parents, not like me having two old folk, and no one else to chat too, or share anything with",

"Well you have got an older sister," Dorothy replied, "much good she is." said Winnie irritably "or has ever been." She is sixteen years older than me, "

"Yes isn't that strange," Dorothy replied thoughtfully, "your sister is the same age as my Mam, I bet you were a mistake", laughed Dorothy, "come on cheer up Winnie," Dorothy pleaded, "I'm sure your Mam will give you back the stiletto heels, and the short skirt to wear this weekend."

"But what can I do about my makeup? Winnie pouted; "dad said he was going to throw it on the fire, as he didn't want me associating with those soldiers," "

"Well you do let them go a bit too far you know Winnie, I've been telling you about It." as Dorothy's Mam was forever warning her. And when Dorothy thought about it, she knew Winnie was getting herself a bad name, for being such a flirt, and she knew that Winnie went outside the dance halls with the G I's that is how she managed to have plenty makeup, and silk stockings, Dorothy was thinking about the conversation she had overheard two days ago when someone had remarked that Winnie would turnout like Prudence, but Dorothy hadn't understood as Prudence was a respectable school teacher, she was still trying to work it out as Winnie jabbed her in the ribs and asked her,

"Are you going to stand there all day gawping? The girls returned to work after their dinner break; it had been warm enough to eat their dinners outside, and they could also have a fag each before going back into work, the girls and woman who worked in the factory were known as rough diamonds, and Enid loved embarrassing the foreman, who was a very shy and quiet man, he was not eligible to join up as he had chest problems although he thought he would of been better off than being left with all these coarse woman. The poor bloke always changed colour when he came near Enid. As Dorothy and Winnie worked with a lot of woman of all ages they were no longer blushing girls, as Winnie made her way over to Enid she felt sorry for Rodger the foreman, as he had ended up in this pickling factory. Enid was laughingly asking him whose bed he'd been in last night and whose he would be in tonight.

Winnie laughingly said, "Leave him alone Enid he just goes home to his Mam don't you Rodger?"

Then she winked at Enid and said, "You should get a woman and try it Rodger, you never know you might like it." As the woman started to laugh, a middle aged woman who worked near Winnie and Dorothy shouted over,

"We all know you like it"

Winnie retorted, "Your only jealous because the fella's fancy me," Rita who was standing next to Enid shouted over,

"They only go with you Winnie. As they know you don't mind dropping your drawers." and then they all laughed.

Beryl who worked across from Winnie said, "I don't blame her for going out and enjoying herself, you're only young once."

Sandra joined in saying, "Well we all know what you get up too with your husband away."

Just then the girl next to her called Irene said, "I go out with the GI's. They are friendly they treat us well, and besides I like silk stockings, so I will carry on," then they all started to sing as their hands worked quickly. At five o clock the siren sounded and the woman all filed out grabbing their coats headscarves and handbags, they had been standing on the production line for ten hours, and as they walked out of the door they all lit their fags as they could enjoy a smoke as they walked home. Sandra walked out of work with the lasses, she would have to hurry home to see to her three children, and cook some tea under the eagle eye of her father, who thought that Sandra's mother had done enough, looking after Sandra's three children all day, without cooking tea for them. She hated living with her parents, it felt like being a young girl again, getting told what to do, but her husband was away fighting for his country, and she had been bombed out so she had no choice but to move in with them. They did not like her going to the dances but there was one at the camp this weekend and she had made up her mind she was definitely going. As Dorothy and Winnie walked home Dorothy offered to look after Winnie's makeup for her, if it would make life easier at home.

Winnie looked at her friend and said, "You are very lucky Dorothy, you and your sister's wear whatever you like, and your Mam wears makeup too she even shares it with you my Mam doesn't even own any, and does not agree with me wearing it. But I don't care." said Winnie with a defiant toss of her head.

CHAPTER SIX

The following night as the girls walked together from work, Dorothy asked "Would you like to come and stay at our house Winnie?"

"I don't know what to do," said Winnie with a shrug of her shoulders, Dad is so self-righteous,"

"Well you can come to our house anytime you want" offered Dorothy, "as Mam does not mind, she says. "More the merrier"

"Thank you Dorothy, I will and I'll bring my attaché case over for you to keep for me as it is full of makeup," Winnie often thought she was the odd one out in the family, as her Mam dad and her sister Pru as Winnie called her, although she preferred Prudence, they all had slightly hooded eyes, and they also had heavily dark features, whereas Winnie was blonde, she had asked Mam about it once she was old enough to notice

But Mam always said, "Ask no questions and then you won't get any lies." Winnie's blonde hair was bobbed; her Dad called her a tart, Winnie could picture him now sitting in his chair beside the fire, the bowl of his pipe between his thumb and finger, while he sucked on it, and then while he lectured Winnie he would use the stem of his pipe to point at her. Winnie came out of her reverie with a jolt as Dorothy poked her on the ribs,

"Oh Dot you gave me a shock." Winnie exclaimed.

"Well you were in a world of your own for a while Winn, and I don't think you've heard a word I've said."

"Do you dread going home Dot?" Winnie turned and asked her friend.

Dorothy stopped and looked at Winnie, "Well that's a daft question and no mistake, what has brought this on? I know you are not very happy at home, but surely it's not that bad, I know that your parent's are old, maybe they are just concerned about you, but you are welcome at our house anytime, as Mam says one extra doesn't make any difference with all our lot, and Dad says we are an impressionable age, Dorothy laughed."

"Well I don't care what my parent's think of me anymore," Winnie replied, with a defiant toss of the head, as they reached the bottom of the street where the two girls went their separate ways, Dorothy went along the street and down a long bank where her house was huddled together with a great many others, Dorothy stood on the street and put her hand through the letterbox and pulled out the string with the door key attached, then let herself in, as she turned to close the door she saw two of her sisters just coming down the street from work at the ammunition factory, she shouted,

"Hurry up you two, I'm not standing here holding this door open all night," she laughingly shouted at them, Winnie had also reached home, she opened the garden gate and walked down the narrow path between the small flowerbeds, her mother saw her making her way to the door and came and unlocked it, Winnie had tried asking her mother if they could have the key dangling on a string inside the letterbox, but she'd been unsuccessful , and when she had tried to persuade her and find out just what her mother had against it?"

Her mother had given a contemptuous sniff and said "Because it is common Winifred and I do not want to hear anymore about it'" Winnie still thought it would be better than her mother having to get up and let her in.

As Mrs Breaker opened the door to admit Winnie she said ,"Go and get a wash Winnie, and change your clothes, get rid of that repugnant smell of pickled onions' and vinegar I don't understand how you can work in such a place , and I dread to think what those woman are like who you are working with." Winnie hurried past her mother and ran upstairs, she knew she was lucky to have a bath on a night, as Dorothy's house didn't have a bathroom, they had to drag the tin bath inside, from where it hung on the wall outside, but there was humour and laughter at Dorothy's just then her mother's voice sounded upstairs,

"Don't use too much water dear, and do hurry up dear as Dad is waiting for his tea." Winnie knew what her mother would shout up to her, as she did the same every night, after Winnie had dried and dressed she walked into the living room where her parent where about to eat their meal, as she took her place at the table her Dad looked at her and said,

"If you had a decent job, you wouldn't need to bath before we eat every night and I wouldn't have to wait for my meal,"

"Well I do work, at the pickling factory Dad, I also work hard, and I like my job," Winnie retorted defensively, and I also like the girls I work with,"

"Yes dear but they do have a bad reputation." Her mother replied, as she passed her husband a full plate of dinner and then passed a good plateful to Winnie. "I think we will all sit and listen to the wireless tonight." Her Mother said to try and soothe the tension at the table. "After we have washed up after tea, what do you think Winnie?"

But she gave a surprised gasp as Winnie said, "I'm going out tonight; her Dad was busy shovelling food into his mouth so Winnie was spared the interrogation until he had eaten his tea. After tea as Winnie and her Mam were doing the dishes Winnie told her Mam she was going to Dorothy's later and could she have her attaché case back please?"

"No I will not give it back to you Winnie, your Dad and me don't like you wearing it, as it is only common people who wear make-up.

Winnie thought she sounded the same as usual which was sharp and authoritative, and she wasn't going to listen to her any longer, so she cried, "You can dry the crockery yourself.", as she threw the tea towel down and hurried into the hall grabbed her coat and handbag off the peg and then hurried out banging the door behind her. As she reached Dorothy's house, tears of frustration was running down her cheeks. Dorothy's mother was surprised to see Winnie standing on the step, with tears running down her face, as she opened the door to Winnie's loud and abrupt hammering.

"Whatever's wrong Winnie? Exclaimed Brenda, Dorothy's mother, "come on in and tell me all about it, surely it can't be that bad, as Brenda led Winnie into the kitchen Winnie realized someone must have had a bath, as the window had misted over with condensation, and a small pool of water was forming in the window bottom.

Brenda saw Winnie looking at the window so she said laughingly, "Oh it's only the steam off our Jimmy's bath, if you'd come earlier you would of caught him in it, and then she pulled out a chair from under the table and gestured to Winnie to sit down, as the grandfather clock chimed in the sitting room, Brenda picked up her woodbines and handed one to Winnie, after Brenda had lit hers and inhaled a lung full of smoke she said,

"Right Winnie tell me what is making you so upset,"

"Well its Mam and Dad, I'm sure they don't want me," she sniffed, "and they are so old fashioned, they won't allow me to wear makeup, there is never any laughter in our house, do you know that Mam has never smoked or worn makeup, I think they look on me as a nuisance," Brenda knew that Winnie was no shrinking violet but still felt sorry for her. They are proud of our Pru as she is a school teacher, but they look down on me, as I work in the pickling factory.

Brenda leaned over and patted Winnie on the knee and said, "There is some right nice respectable people work in that pickling factory," just then Dorothy came into the kitchen puffing on a woodbine, and asked Winnie if she felt better now she had talked to her Mam.

Brenda looked at her daughter and said, "I have told Winnie, if ever she needs help or somewhere to stay; she can stay here, as an extra one won't make a lot of difference, as the house would be full if we were not on different shifts."

Winnie started to get up off the chair , Oh I'm sorry Mrs Watson, you haven't been in long from work and I'm telling you all my problems, when you probably have jobs to do,"

Brenda waved her hand dismissively, "You sit still and have another cup of tea with our Dorothy while I go and take me curlers out. As she pointed to the scarf that was wrapped around her head, I go to work with me curlers in but they are hidden under me headscarf and then if I go to the pub on a night with some of the lasses I just have to comb me hair out. Oh and I just want you girls to be careful what you get up to with them soldiers." "We will Mam." Dorothy answered in a pained voice.

As Mrs Watson closed the door behind her, Dorothy said to Winnie "it looks like Mam is going out again tonight, Dad is on nightshift ,and it's not easy trying to get a seat in there." as she pointed to the sitting room door, "when they are all in". Meaning her brothers and sisters, so why don't we go out somewhere Winnie?"

"Come on then." Dorothy said breathlessly, as she reached for Winnie's hand, and pulled her up off the chair. "Come upstairs and borrow my clothes and makeup."

Winnie didn't need to think about it as she said, "Yes why not, as I don't fancy going home until I know they are in bed." One hour later saw the girls teetering down the street in their stilettos and silk stockings, with massacred eyes and bright red lips, Winnie started to giggle,

"I think we should find ourselves a soldier each,"

"Alright we'll look for a fella each," said Dorothy, as she knew that would cheer Winnie up, as she knew the situation at Winnie's home was worsening every day, as the girls turned the corner to cross the road near the dance hall, a jeep drew up full of GI's, as soon as the lads saw Winnie and Dorothy they started wolf-whistling at them.

One of them called out. "What are you two gorgeous girls doing tonight?"

Winnie replied," we are going dancing in there." as she pointed to the hall with the doors ajar. The GI's headed over to the girls.

The blonde GI put his arm around Winnie, and whispered. "Would you and your friend, like to come along to the pub with us? We will buy you both a drink," and when he saw the look of uncertainty on Winnie's face he added, "We will pay you into the dance as well."

The other G I grinned and said. "I bet you girls could use some makeup?"

Winnie turned and grabbed Dorothy's arm saying. "We are coming with you boys, aren't we Dot? As the Liquor or licca, as the G I's called it flowed, Winnie and Dorothy were beginning to feel lightheaded, and giggly.

Winnie leaned over and shook Dorothy's hand to get her attention, and then said laughingly, "If Mam and Dad could see us now they would say we are as bold as brass, but I'm not bothered anymore, as she started to hic-up, and cuddling up to Baz as that was what he had told her his name was. Dorothy saw Baz's hand travelling up Winnie's skirt, while his other hand was cupping her breast, and she was not stopping him, in fact she looked like she was enjoying it.

Dorothy caught the G I she was with, watching Winnie and Baz and she cringed, with embarrassment, as Winnie was looking unperturbed, so Dorothy said loudly. "Time we were going to the dance." As she got off her seat they all started to follow suit.

Baz kept his arm round Winnie as one of his friend who had been watching them in the pub grinned and said. "You've got an easy one there."

"Yes I've been lucky". Baz answered happily. As they all reached the dance hall door Dorothy walked in ahead of the G I's and paid her own admittance money, deliberately ignoring the rest of them, as Winnie and Baz went around behind the hall. Dorothy's night had been ruined, she couldn't go home and leave her friend behind, she got up and danced when asked but her heart wasn't in it. Eventually she saw Winnie coming through the door looking very dishevelled, but Dorothy's eyes widened in amazement as Baz took Winnie over to another G I and Winnie went back outside with another one,

Dorothy made her mind up she was going home and after the night she'd had with Winnie she could go to hell. Just as Dorothy headed for the door, the band struck up with one of her favourite tunes. Apple blossom time, but Dorothy was too upset to stay and listen, after such a disastrous night, and also the realisation that what people had said about Winnie was true. As Dorothy pulled the door open she collided with Winnie and the G I making their way back in.

Winnie realizing Dorothy was leaving without her. Looked appealingly at Dorothy and muttered, "Please don't go without me Dorothy and leave me on my own," Dorothy retorted, "Just like I've been on my own all night." The G I had sneaked quietly away.

"Please Dot." Winnie begged," look what I've got, I will share it with you."

Dorothy looked at the small bag of makeup and nylons that Winnie held out offering them to her, "No thank you Winnie, if I didn't have any makeup, I wouldn't touch that" she emphasized pointing her finger at the small bag of makeup, "knowing what you did, to own all that lot." Dorothy and Winnie had just stepped out of the door, when the sirens wailed their chilling warnings, it was eerie. Dorothy shouted,

"This is all I need, to finish off a bloody awful night", and stared at Winnie for being personally responsible for her miserable time, Winnie grabbed hold of Dorothy's hand,

"Come on Dot I can hear the planes coming over, we've got to find a shelter quick,"   she cried,

"Wailing Minnie, hasn't given us much time tonight, do you think we should run back to the dance hall?" Dorothy asked shaking with fright.

"No I feel safer in the shelters," replied Winnie "look at all them people hurry up the street there must be a shelter somewhere near,

"Yes I can see it now," Dorothy cried, "it's just so claustrophobic and I don't like it."

"Well its better than being killed," Winnie retorted, then mellowed and added, "it might not be for long." Once in the crowed shelter Winnie looked around her, as she heard the drones of the planes over head, the thunder of the ack ack guns firing back, as the incendiary bombs lit up the night sky, with their red glow, it was getting to be a nightly occurrence. Some people were trying to sleep; Winnie knew she would never close her eyes while the bombardment was going on, it seemed as though the whole city was taking another battering as she heard the sound of masonry crashing to the ground, along with the sirens from the emergency services, who were taking the injured to hospital, and the dead to the mortuaries, Just along the street from where all the people had been, the enemy aircraft dived through the searchlights, Barrage balloons were caught and ignited, they dropped to the ground screaming, as the German bombers' found their targets, the big guns thundered as they retaliated, the onslaught carried on all night, Winnie turned and looked at Dorothy who was as white as a sheet, her hands were resting on her knee but Winnie could see them shaking, she immediately, put her arm around Dorothy, and tried to reassure her, that they would be fine that these shelters were the safest places to be, Dorothy glared nastily and said,

"If you hadn't been giving it away at the dance hall, we could, have still been there, this is your entire fault Winnie and I will never forgive you," Winnie's heart was thudding as a bomb shook the shelter, one old woman dropped to her knees and started saying her prayers, while mothers rocked crying babies in their pram's as the old men sucked on their pipes, just then the door burst open and two sailors ran in causing Dorothy to jump as she was startled the same as everyone in the shelter, as nerves were jangling, one of the sailors looked at Dorothy and said,

"Sorry love didn't mean to startle you, but its bedlam out there, the whole city's ablaze." The other solider asked,

"Do you mind if we squash on this form beside you?" As he gave Winnie a meaningful look,

"No not at all answered Winnie." who was pleased that the sailors, seemed keen to keep the conversation going, as the tension was parable, it was to be along uncomfortable night, the sailors started to tell the girls all about themselves, Winnie saw Dorothy start to relax a little, and as morning approached and the all clear sounded the four of them felt like old friends, as the shelter door opened Sam one of the sailors said,

"I can't see us getting back to our ship today, as there are no trains running." Burt his friend said,

"Why don't we see these girls get home safe and sound?" So the four of them set off along the road, they hadn't gone far when there was a diversion, a gas main had been hit, and a row of houses had been demolished,

"We had better head back towards the dance hall, and go around the long way, as that is where we were at last night," stated Dorothy, as she scowled at Winnie, "and where I would have preferred to stay", Sam laughingly said,

"But if you'd of stayed there, you wouldn't have met us and look what you would have been missing" they all had sore throats off the gritty dust,and as they walked along the rescue workers were all digging, away at a collapsed building, debris and boulders were all over. The street had been cornered off. one of the men from the rescue team who had been listening intently, hoping to hear some cries or moaning, came over to them wiping swear from his brow,

"Sorry folks you can't get through this way," he shouted, as he raised his hand to indicate to them not to come any further, as he walked towards them he was saying,

"What is left of this building still isn't safe," "Aye" he said as he looked back to where he came from; "bad job that, all them young ones," he said, shaking his head, "dancing and having a goodnight out, and it got a direct hit and no survivors." Dorothy turned and gave Winnie, a sad smile and squeezed her hand in a friendly gesture. Winnie asked,

"Am I forgiven?" As she gave Dorothy a meaningful look, Burt looked enquiringly at the girls and asked Dorothy what Winnie was being forgiven for? "

"Surely you haven't fallen out, as. Life is too short,"

"Yes I realize that now," Dorothy said looking at Winnie, "now I have seen the remains of that dance hall." Later as the two girls walked into Dorothy's house linking arm's followed by the two sailors, no one could of guessed what an extraordinary night they'd had, as Dorothy's family were all at home each trying to get ready for work, the gas main was blown to smithereens the water pipes were fractured, Dorothy's mother informed them as they stepped into the house, No one could have a cup of tea or a wash, there was a covering of soot all over, The curtains were in tatters and blowing in the breeze through the broken glass, in the windows. The girls were shaking their heads in disbelief as Dorothy's mother told them, how the pickle factory had been bombed,

"It was so loud it shook these houses, we didn't think these houses would still be standing when we came out of the shelter this morning." She stated. Dorothy's Mam was unperturbed that the sailors had arrived back with her daughter and friend. As people shared whatever rations they had.

"Well you'd better introduce us all to your friends, Dorothy." Her mother told her as Mrs Watson rose off the chair and came over to shake hands, with Sam and Burt, who told her

"We hope we are not in the way Mrs Watson.?

"No not at all lads," she told them, as she gave them a reassuring smile," it's always crowded in here, you just have to make the best of it, as she looked meaningful at the empty teapot.

I will have to be going shortly," Winnie told them, "only could I have a word first with you Dot?

"Yes course you can Winnie," Dorothy answered her in a friendly tone, as she knew if it hadn't been for Winnie carrying on with the G I's last night they would both have been buried under the dance hall.

"I will walk you up the road Winnie," Dorothy conceded, "and then we can have a talk in private".

"Oh it must be something top secret," one of Dorothy's brothers Alan chuckled as he was heading for the door to go to work. Then Mrs Watson shouted after them,

"Before you girls, go for your private chat, you want to be going up the munitions factory, as they are taking people on, and from last night you don't have a job."

"Right oh Mrs Watson," Winnie replied, "I will go home and get changed, and then I will come back here for you Dot, is that all right?" As the friend's set off along the straight feet crunching on broken glass, as there was not a house in the street that had its windows in, Winnie immediately started to apologize, for last night and as Dorothy was in a better mood, she said,

"Look Winnie just forget all about it, lives too short," then looking very sheepishly said, "I could do with a lipstick and mascara." After the makeup had been shared, Winnie hurried home but dreaded facing her parents, After a cold walk Winnie arrived at her door to find it locked, as usual, but she didn't have to wait long in answer to her knock as he parents had seen her walking down the path, Mrs Breaker opened the door looking reproachfully at Winnie, and asked frostily,

"Where have you been all night? And what time do you call this, come into the sitting room," she commanded, "your father wants a word with you." Winnie had been hoping to sneak upstairs; her father was sitting in his usual place, beside the fire in his armchair, smoking his pipe, He looked up at Winnie under his bushy eyebrows that met in the middle, there was no laughter in those eyes, how there was in Dorothy's Dads,

"I prophesied you would be trouble Winnie from an early age," he said as he pointed the stem of his pipe at her, "also I forbade you to wear makeup, your mother never did, and also you had better find yourself a respectable job young lady, as you are getting lead astray at that pickle factory."

"I am going after a job today dad, as soon as I get changed."

"Oh" answered a shocked Mr Breaker, he couldn't believe the change in Winnie, so she had finally come to her senses, maybe last night's harsh words had done her good, and then before he had time to speak she said cheekily,

"The pickle factory got bombed last night, so I'm hoping to get a start at the munitions." Then before he had chance to speak she made for the door and ran upstairs, and then she kicked her bedroom door shut and threw herself on the bed, Winnie must of dozed off, as the sound of the bedroom door opening woke her, she rubbed her eyes sleepily and yawned, as her mother came into the room , she walked over and perched herself on the bottom of Winnies bed, she only managed to fit one cheek on as she was such a big woman, as she sat down the springs cried out alarmingly,

"Why have you come into my bedroom?" Winnie asked her mother suspiciously.

"Dad and I don't want you going to work in the munitions factory, as it will probably make you worse then you are now, and I have heard there is a lot of loose woman, working there and we don't want you mixing with the likes of them," Winnie jumped furiously off the bed saying.

"That's the trouble with you two; you don't know what I want, as you have never been interested in me, just because I'm not brainy like our Pru, you have always thought I'm not as good, so I will work where I want with my friends," Mrs Breaker thought she had better try again to get Winnie to knuckle down, and be less trouble to them, it hadn't been easy looking after Winnie , when there was such an age difference, Mrs Breaker eased her heavy body off the bed as the springs squealed with delight, Mrs Breaker called to Winnie as she disappeared into the bathroom,

"Just listen to me Winnie, surely there is an alternative to working in a factory, with rough woman," she said encouragingly. Winnie was thinking it might be good times to ask for her attach case, makeup and some of her clothes back, so she replied,

"Please could I have my things back Mam?"

"No you cannot," Mrs Breaker spat, as she stared at Winnies retreating back, as Winnie went back into the bathroom to get ready to go to the munitions factory with Dorothy for a job she despaired of her parents ever caring about her, she closed the bathroom door then stood with her back against it listening to her mother's slippered feet, descending the stairs, after a quick wash and clean clothes on she made her way downstairs, slipping her coat on as she walked, she picked her bag up to go out of the door as her mother called her. Winnie put her head round the sitting room door; her mother was sitting in the armchair opposite her father with the fireplace between them, Winnie thought they looked like bookends, her mother's hands were never idle, her knitting needles worked so fast Winnie often thought she was having a race with those needles, while the ball of wool bobbed about in her pocket of her crossover pinny, Winnie gave a gasp of dismay, as her dad was saying,

"If you go to work in a munitions factory, you can go and live elsewhere." Taking the pipe from his mouth and spitting into the fire which sizzled and crackled.

"But where am I supposed to work?" she shouted exasperatedly. Mrs Breaker looked at her husband and said,

"We can't do that, what would our Prudence say? Then as an afterthought she added, "And she still sends money",

"So she should and I don't care," bellowed her husband, she left us with all her troubles," he told her callously.

"Well I am going, I am truly sick of you two," she said as she squared her shoulders defiantly, and stared at her dad, with a resentful expression on her face then walked out banging the door so hard that it shuddered on its hinges, as an act of defiance, and then calmly lit a fag and threw the match down on the recently swept footpath, and walked back to Dorothy's house. As Winnie rounded the corner she met Dorothy's Dad heading the opposite way,

"Well hello young Winnie," he said happily, "I bet you are on your way to our house,"

"Yes I am. Mr Watson Is Dorothy still at home or has she gone without me? As I intended being here sooner,"

"No she hasn't gone without you Winnie," Mr Watson answered as he heaved his bate bag further on to his shoulder, "you hurry along now, I'm sure there will be a cup of tea left in the pot, we finally got the gas and water back on, by its arum do when you can't have a cup of tea, well I'd better be off as we have a ship sailing in tonight with a full hold to empty, so we will be working all through the night, ta- ra for now," he called to Winnie as he walked away. What a nice man Dorothy's Dad was, Winnie thought as he walked away, how she wished her Dad was like him, on arriving at Dorothy s house, Winnie tapped on the door and walked in ,as she had been told to do, make yourself at home Dorothy's Mam was always telling her, Winnie always felt more at home here then at her own Mam and Dad's, Dorothy was still doing her hair in front of the mirror, when Winnie walked in, she turned and said,

"Your late, I thought you had changed your mind"

"Winnie probably had some jobs to do for her Mam," Brenda, Dorothy's Mam, spoke up for Winnie, "the same as you and the rest of them have helped me today, eh that soot took some shifting," she told Winnie, "my hair was covered in it, after I'd been outside shaking mats and curtains, but I've managed to get me hair washed and curlers in ready for tonight," as her hand went instinctively to her scarf on her head that was covering her curlers, just to make sure they were still intact, then she picked up the teapot and poured Winnie a cup. "Here you are Winnie, you look as if you could do with it, after you have been down to the munitions, come back here for tea and a chat." Mrs Watson said invitingly, and patted Winnies hand reassuringly as she and Dorothy walked out through the door, and closed it behind them.

Winnie looked appealingly at Dorothy and cried "I wish I had parents like yours Dot."

"What has brought this on again Winnie? Have you had a row, at home? Because I told you to tell them about the munitions as soon as you went in, also that we were sitting in a shelter all night, as I'm sure they worry about you Winnie."

"They wouldn't worry about me." Winnie said sullenly," in fact they told me if I started working in the munitions, I have to find somewhere else to live." Dorothy stopped walking and looked wide eyed at Winnie as if she could not believe it,

"Surely they don't mean it Winnie?" Dorothy tried to console her; Dorothy had only been in Winnie's home a few times, and there seemed to be an atmosphere, although

Dorothy thought, Winnie might have her own bedroom, while my brothers and sisters are all squashed in together, but I would not want to swap my life with Winnies. As they arrived at the factory gates they had to hand over their matches, and Dorothy whispered,

"I hope we can still work together Winn."

"Well we'll soon find out," answered Winnie, the way my lucks going I'll probably not even get a job as she sighed miserably, As the gates opened to allow the girls to walk through, a voice shouted,

"Are you two coming through, or are you going to stand there all day looking gormless." Dorothy pushed Winnie forwards,

"Come on Winnie hurry up, or neither of us will get a job, and if you are not bothered, I am." The foreman stepped outside as the girls made their way along to his office,

"Oh so you are the slow coaches are you?" he asked, "I saw you dawdling along, do you want a job? Or not, as there is plenty more wanting work," he said, in his aggressive tone and his face as hard as granite, Yes we both want a job they chorused. Right look sharp then I haven't got all day, as they stepped into his Office he walked behind a desk and sat down while the girls stood in front of him,

"Now I don't have to tell you we make explosives, so no matches' will be brought in, or anything which will cause a spark, if you do it will be instant dismissal", Winnies mind was starting to wander, until she felt Dorothy give her a sly dig in the ribs, and the foreman was saying,

"I expect you to do overtime, and if you do, you will earn eighteen shillings a week on piecework, have you any questions?" he asked, as he raised his eyebrows enquiringly at the girls. Then when no answer was forthcoming as quick as he expected he told them,

"You can both start here at seven o clock in the morning, and I don't care if you are bombed out, or had no sleep, I like good timekeepers." We'll be here on time shouted Dorothy as she linked arms with Winnie and hurried home to tell her mother the good news.

When the girls arrived back at Dorothy's house, there had been no need to tell her mother, as Brenda could tell by her daughters face as she walked in with Winnie, Dorothy's three brothers and two sisters were also in the kitchen, waiting of the potatoes boiling in the pan on the fire so they would be able to have their tea, Mrs Watson also had a dish of mince and onions in the oven which was a rare treat, it amazed Winnie how everyone managed in such a small space, they hadn't been in long when Marion walked in carrying the baby in her arms, while three year old Robert left loose of his mothers skirts and ran over to Brenda, she picked him up and swung him around, while he squealed and giggled,

"You have just come in time for tea Marion," Brenda told her daughter.   Marion said,

"Oh are you sure there is enough to go round Mam?" fifteen year old Michael was sitting on the settee, spoke up and said cheekily,

"It will be alright our Marion; Mam will tell us to eat extra bread to get filled up." They all laughed, as they knew it to be true,

"I will go home for my tea Mrs Watson." Winnie offered,

"You are having tea with us Winnie," Brenda told her as she threw the butt of the cigarette on the fire, just missing the pan of potatoes, "I invited you earlier, to stay and have tea, there will be plenty of food as that big pan is full to the brim." Marion said,

"It is hard trying to make nourishing meals when everything has to be queued for."

"Well you have all-day to do it Marion not like me," Brenda retorted, "I work, and I still have to queue, where as there is only you and the two bairns, while Bens away in the army."

"Yes I know that Mam," Marion said in a wheedling voice, "but I don't feel very well again, I feel sickly." She said, as she cast her mother a sheepish glance, "you know Ben was on leave just over two month ago," but Marion never got chance to say anymore, as Brenda forestalled her, as Michael was sitting listening, and he couldn't keep his mouth shut, so Brenda was shaking her head to indicate not to say anymore, after tea fifteen year old Michael went out into the street to play, with his thirteen year old brother Alec, and twenty year old Ronnie was going to the pub, as he was going back to camp in the morning,

"Now you girls, it's time to sort some problems out, as we are all girls together," Brenda informed them, "Now our Marion it seems to me you could be carrying again, have you missed your monthlies?"

"Yes I have Mam, two in fact," she answered miserably," sometimes I wish my husband didn't come home." she said bitterly.

"Well he always leaves you a reminder that he's been, that's for sure." sighed Brenda, "but you should think yourself lucky, your husband is alive; as there is a lot of woman out there, who are left to bring the bairns up on their own, through no fault of theirs, now those girls that get themselves pregnant, and no wedding ring on their finger, are a different kettle of fish, if my girls were in that predicament, I would have no hesitation in kicking them out."

"You wouldn't do that Mam," Marion said, "you have always looked after me through my pregnancies."

"Yes but you were legally married, so just think what you girls are doing with them lads", she threatened or you will be looking for somewhere to live," Dorothy and Winnie stood up,

"Thank you for my tea Mrs Watson I had better be going, I don't know how my Mam and Dad will react, when I tell them I am starting work at the munitions factory tomorrow,"

"Well go home and see what they have to say about it," Brenda advised, "as it is no good speculating."

Winnies feet felt as heavy as lead as she made her way along the street, she was dreading going home, she knew her parents wouldn't listen to her, they never did, everything Winnie did was wrong, as she walked down the garden path the front door was opened by her mother as she reached it, and she knew by her mother's unsmiling face that all was not well,

"Where have you been till now Winnie?" her mother asked nastily, and scarcely looked at Winnie, and then she turned back into the sitting room, and sat back in the chair she had just vacated opposite her husband, who was sitting looking at his pocket watch, which was hanging on a chain, then he put the watch back into his waistcoat pocket, and looked up at Winnie, and asked,

"Have you thought about what your mother and I were saying to you this morning? we are not prepared to let you come and go as you please, as you are going to mend your ways he explained emphatically, so what have you got to say for yourself?." Winnie felt so despondent why her parents couldn't be more like Dorothy's she didn't know.

"I have got a job" she told her parents," as her insides turned with apprehension, "I start at the munitions factory at seven in the morning, with Dorothy"

"Well that girl is no better then she should be," her mother sharply replied. "If she was a decent girl she wouldn't want to be working there, whatever is her mother thinking about letting her go? I take it she has told her mother." Mrs Breaker insisted. "Yes," Winnie argued, "Mrs Watson suggested it, as two of Dorothy's sister's work there." Mrs Breaker clucked her tongue in annoyance, as she said;

"Mrs Watson has no right to involve you Winnie and you will not be going that sort of woman has no self-discipline, so let that be an end to it." Weariness was starting to overwhelm Winnie, as she yelled,

"I am going to work at the munitions, and you two cannot stop me." Her mother looked at her with cold accusing eyes, and said;

"After all we've done for you; well you can get your things and go," Winnie's heart plummeted as her mother made no attempt to hide her hostility towards her,

"If that's how you both feel I will go tomorrow," Winnie felt her brave act diminishing, her stomach was churning, she couldn't think straight, she never thought it would come to this, that they would actually through her out, as she brought her mind back to the present, her Dad was speaking.

"Did you not hear what I have just said to you Winnie? No I thought you hadn't." he said nastily, as Winnie shook her head. Mr Breaker cleared his throat,

"I said under the circumstances you had better go now."

"But where can I go?" Winnie cried, "I have nowhere."

"Go back to where you have been all day." he retorted. And then he picked up the newspaper and gave it a good shake, and settled back in the chair with the newspaper up in front of his face as he read. Winnie ran upstairs and dragged the old brown suitcase out from under the bed, and threw her things into it, as she snapped the case shut she looked around the room and thought I've never been happy here, and then the thought hit her, as I was never wanted, as she made her way downstairs tears were stinging her eyes, she poked her head round the sitting room door, and asked,

"Could I have my attaché case please?" Her mother was knitting, and her father was still reading his paper, both completely oblivious to Winnie, then her mother looked up and raised her eyebrows, saying,

"When you return the suitcase you may have your attaché case," Winnie opened the door and went outside there was nothing else to say, the gate creaked as she swung it open, and as she trudged on down the street, towards Dorothy's wondering what lay ahead of her, tears rolled down her face, and from deep inside great sobs poured out of her.

Prudence was sitting in Ethel's house, she had been to the post box to post a letter and some money to her parents, she yearned to see Winnie and often wished that she could bring Winnie up for a visit, but she kept reminding herself that everyone had to make sacrifices, as there was a war on, and she had no doubt that her parent would give Winnie all the love and discipline that a girl Winnies age needed. Prudence was oblivious to the fact that Winnie had been gone from her Parents house now for the past four months, as the same night as Winnie left, Mrs Breaker had penned a short letter to Prudence, which her husband had taken to the post office for her, the next day, but during the night a bomb had dropped in the street reducing the post office to rubble, and burying the letter. As Prudence sniffed appreciatively at the smell of Ethel's cooking circulating the room. Winnie and Dorothy were walking home from work, with their collars turned up against the cool wind; they were tired as they had already spent three nights in the shelter so far this week, but they had the dance to look forward to, tomorrow night and as both Sam and Burt were arriving tomorrow, the girls were getting excited, although they were getting concerned about their skin, they knew when they stated work at the munitions that they would eventually have the yellow skin, yellow canaries everyone called them, Winnies skin was covered in blotches, and her eyes watered, Dorothy was sneezing all the time, and she had strange blotches as well , their job was to pack the shell cases with T N T, powder, they had to fill them full and then smooth them off level, as the girls turned off into the street where they lived as Winnie had moved straight in with Dorothy's family, they saw old mother Riley, coming towards them with her daughter, Dorothy had lived in this street all of her life, and had never heard anyone call the woman Mrs Riley, she had always worn a cap and a pair of men's boots, that were too large for her, no one was quite sure how many children she had, as a lot of them had left home, as she got closer to Winnie and Dorothy she gave them a toothless grin.

"Now girls have you just finished work?" She asked them, then not waiting for an answer, said, "My daughter used to work there, same as you, at the munitions but it's a while back, but then she ended looking like you two, Doctor told her she was allergic to the explosives." Both Dorothy and Winnie looked at the young woman standing beside Mrs Riley, thinking that it was her; that Mrs Riley was talking about, Mrs Riley seeing them standing looking at her daughter, grinned and said

"Oh it's not this one, she has never worked, she's simple, and she would never be able to fill the shell cases as she is boss eyed," Dorothy looked at the cross eyed girl and felt sorry for her, as Mrs Riley was explaining, that if her daughter got a start they would have a long wait for the shells, as "I have to tell her everything twice, and then I end up doing it myself." Ta ra for now Mrs Riley Dorothy said,

"We must be going as our tea will be ready."

"Oh alright then girls," Mrs Riley replied, and then she gave her daughter a push to let her know they were going on their way again.

"There is no need to push me Mam." Mary, Mrs Riley's daughter told her, as they set off along the street after leaving Winnie and Dorothy. Mary was wearing a shapeless dress and down at heel shoes,

"I wish I had some nice clothes Mam," Mary remarked.

"Whatever do you want nice clothes for?" Mrs Riley was shocked, "you never go anywhere, and you ought to think yourself lucky that I feed you, so hurry yourself up, and when we get home you can make me a cup of tea,"

It was a full house at Dorothy's, as usual, as everyone was at home; Mr Watson was propped up in the chair beside the fire with cushions, he had hurt his back at work, lifting something heavy in the hold of the ship, although he maintained that he would try and go back tomorrow, as no work meant no money, Brenda was scandalized,

"You know you won't be able to manage Jim," but she knew it would be hard trying to manage without his wages, it didn't matter how ill people felt they still dragged themselves to work, Dorothy went over to her Father, and handed him the baccy she had managed to get for him, as he liked his pipe, as her mother elbowed her out of the way, while she lifted a heavy pan off the fire, then wiping the sweat off her forehead with the back of her hand, as someone knocked on the door.

"Will you answer the door?" Brenda shouted at Michael, who was standing near, "as I only have one pair of hands." It was apparent to Winnie that they were grossly overcrowded, but at the moment she didn't know what to do, about finding somewhere else to live, Michael had answered the door and invited Sam and Burt into the sitting room, Winnie was pleased to see them, they were standing turning their caps round in their hand's, wondering just what to do, as the room was full of people.

"Should we come back later?" Burt asked anxiously.

"No we are ready now," answered Winnie, as she picked up her handbag, as Mrs Watson shouted at their retreating back's,

"What about your teas?" As the door closed behind them, Sam put his arm around Dorothy, as Burt did the same to Winnie, as they approached the cafe down the street, the sailors steered Dorothy and Winnie through the door, and they sat down at the table nearest the fire, the tired looking waitress came over with her notepad and said,

"We only have sausage and chips left, but you can have a slice of bread each with it," Burt looked around the table and said,

"It doesn't look as though we have a choice." When the food arrived the black sausages tasted like sawdust, and the cold chips were covered in fat and the cold weak tea had no sugar or milk in it, as Burt and Sam paid the bill, between them, Winnie said loudly,

"We won't be coming here again."

The waitress heard her and replied, "Please yourselves, don't you know there is a war on?"

"As If we didn't know," Dorothy said jeeringly, "we are walking round like bloody yellow canaries' the four of them walked round most of the night enjoying each other's company, Burt said ,

"We are not sailing until next week, why don't you two girls come away with us?" For a couple of nights, Winnie accepted without hesitation, while Sam turned questioning eyes on Dorothy, she waved her hand dismissively,

"I will not go," she stated,

"Why not?" asked a bewildered Winnie, "we are all squashed in your Mam and Dads house, if we are all in on a night the last ones in have to sit on the floor, and you are turning your back on a weekend away from it. Dorothy glared at Winnie in astonishment,

"Well I didn't know you felt like that, having to squash in with my family; you were only two pleased to move in with us, when you had nowhere else to go." Sam said in an alarmed voice,

"Come on girls don't fall out, look there's a pub over there, we will go and have a drink, inside the pub the girls went and sat down, while the sailors went to the bar, to buy the drinks,

"I am sorry," said Winnie in a wheedling voice, "are we still friends Dorothy?"

"Yes you are my best friend, and if we do go away for the weekend what will we tell Mam and Dad? Dorothy asked worriedly, Winnie replied laughingly, with such a full house they might not miss us, As the sailors walked back to the girls Sam was carrying two pints of beer, while Burt had two glasses of port and lemon, Dorothy told Sam she had changed her mind, and she would go with him the following weekend, but Winnie and me will have to think about what we are going tell Mam.

"I am sure you girls will come up with something," Burt told them as he smiled encouragingly, " but whatever you're going to tell her, you must stick to it, you'll both have to sing from the same song sheet," Dorothy gave Sam a shy smile, as she nestled in his arms, and didn't resist when he cupped her breast, Later as Sam and Burt were walking Dorothy and Winnie home the eerie sound of the air raid siren screamed out its warning that the Luftwaffe bombers were approaching, and flying low with their unrelenting attacks, the moonlight was so bright, as the four young people walked down the street, bombers moon people had started to call it, as they hurried towards the nearest shelter, as the noise of the incoming planes were getting louder, they started to run and as they neared the shelter door the warden was shepherding people inside, and as the four young people were the last in the queue the warden followed them in closing the door behind him, as the bombs began to drop from the bright sky, everyone shuffled their backsides on the hard uncomfortable benches, trying to settle down for a long night, and trying to make the best of a desperate situation, some of the men started playing cards, while a few woman started knitting, while others checked their handbags, making sure they had birth certificates, marriage certificates, and life assurance policies, after bags had been checked and all papers were there, the snapping shut of the handbags could be heard, as the ferocious bombing went on unrelenting, everyone had settled down when the shelter door burst open, two old ladies who were sitting near the door started screaming that Hitler had come to the shelter, everyone held their breath their eyes wide with fright, when a big woman shuffled in wearing carpet slippers, on her huge feet, a long black coat flapped open to reveal a tight brown dress which hugged her rolls of fat, and her massive bosom sticking out in front, she scowled at everyone as if they were personally responsible for her predicament, and then she turned and barked at the wiry little man who was following close behind, clutching a large handbag. Everyone started to shuffle closer on the benches to make room for the pair, the woman walked over and then flopped down taking the space up of two people, and then started to push the men each side of her, to make room for the wiry little man, and then after checking her head to make sure her hairnet was still intact, she barked,

"Sit yourself down Herbert, your neither use nor ornament, leaving me in bed until the last minute, and then having to hurry to this place, I told you to clear the rubbish out from under the stairs, and then I could of sat in there, you never know what you might catch sitting in here so close to strangers." The two men sitting opposite shouted over,

"We didn't ask you to come into this shelter missus, if we are not good enough you can always go back out and dodge the bombs."

"Yes I agree with you," said another woman, "who does she think she is?" Everyone was murmuring in agreement, and staring at the large woman, she then snatched her bag off Herbert and started rummaging in it, while he glanced anxiously at his wife, and then he said to her in a nervous voice,

"I think I have put everything into the bag that you wanted Doris." The man sitting next to Doris was busy filling his pipe with tobacco; he struck a match to light it and got it stoked up Doris screamed at her husband and knocked the man's arm, as she shouted,

"you are bloody useless, you haven't brought my teeth off the chair, near the bed, the man who had been lighting his pipe got such a shock ,when she screamed, he dropped his lit pipe on his trousers and the hot ash dropped out, he jumped up off the bench and started to dance as his trousers caught alight, a woman sitting nearby drinking a cup of tea out of her flask tried to help ,by throwing the hot tea over his burning trousers ,as they had started to burn very close to his manhood, as he was rubbing his flat hand over his smouldering trousers, the shelter was in a uproar, Dorothy and Winnie didn't know where the most noise was coming from, as the harassed mothers had got the babies to sleep only to be wakened again, by all the carry on, the big woman started to shout to anyone who would listen ,

"I'm in a fine pickle now; he hasn't brought my teeth." The man who had dropped the hot ash out of the bowl of his pipe on his trousers, now stood and stared threatenly at Doris, then said in a loud nasty voice, as he stood in his wet and holed trousers,

"Shut your mouth you stupid cow, going on about your bloody teeth, they are dropping bombs not bloody fish and chips." Everyone started to laugh even Herbert, until she gave him a dig in the ribs and a look of contempt, as her cheeks flushed with indignation. The tension around Doris and Herbert was palpable. Herbert sat back crossing his arms, sighing wistfully, he knew patience was diminishing fast for his wife in this centre; it was the same wherever they went as she was so sanctimonious. Then he closed his eyes as sleep claimed him. The raid continued throughout the night, it seemed a long time to Dorothy since the sirens wailed their chilling warnings, she hated these claustrophobic conditions, Sam realizing how tense and frightened Dorothy was feeling tightened his arm around her. Dorothy was also wondering if she was doing the right thing, agreeing to go away for the weekend, but she knew Winnie would be disappointed if she didn't, as her hopes were pinned on it, she smiled as she thought about Winnie, you had to admire her for her optimism, Dorothy was brought back from her thoughts by the massive woman who was shouting at the woman sitting next to her, rocking a baby to sleep in her arms, but wasn't having much luck, Dorothy looked at the loudmouthed woman , in the tight brown dress, which hugged her rolls of fat, her legs were wide apart, her stomach hanging between them, while her massive bosom jutted out in front of her,

"I did not want to come here," she shouted, mutinously, waking her husband who spoke appeasingly to her, as she folded her arms over her ample chest, as the rest of the people had made it abundantly clear they did not want her there, it was with relief that the all clear sounded, they all got stiffly off the bench and Sam put a protective arm round Dorothy, and propelled her through the door to start another day.

CHAPTER SEVEN

Hundreds of miles away at Ethel's Wilf walked along the road with his surprise for Ethel, he had been very secretive, only Frank and Colin knew what Ethel's surprise was, as they had been helping Wilf to mend the roof on the old stable, and cleaned all the rubbish out, and the boys had put fresh straw down while Wilf went to collect the horse, the boys then positioned themselves on the wall, awaiting Wilf's return, as soon as the boys saw him walking the huge horse along the road they ran to him,

"Go and tell Auntie Ethel to come outside, and see her present," Wilf told the boys, "but don't tell her what it is,"

"We won't," the boys chorused, they ran excitedly into the house nearly knocking Prudence off her feet, as a few minutes earlier a perfunctory knock had heralded the entrance of Prudence, and she was still lingering on the doorstep.

"What's all the rush for?" shouted Gran, "is there a fire somewhere?"

"No" Colin said, as he jumped from one foot to the other, "Uncle Wilf said, Auntie Ethel has to go outside, and see her present,"

"Well why can't he bring it in?" asked Gran,

"Because he can't", answered Colin, just as Frank gave him a kick on his Shin to indicate he'd said enough,

"Come on then," said Ethel eagerly,

"Let us all go and see what Wilf has outside for me," Prudence and Eva helped gran out of her chair, while everyone else hurried outside, Ethel could not believe that Wilf had been and bought her a horse, it was a big brown shire horse, with huge hairy feet Ethel hurried over to stroke it,

"Oh I've always loved horses Wilf,"

"Yes I know that Ethel, but I have bought this horse for another reason as well,"

"Oh well what is the other reason Wilf?" Ethel wanted to know,

"It is going to pull the cart with the milk churns on, so I won't be pushing a hand cart again, I will be filling people's jugs with milk,"

"But that is my job Wilf," Ethel cried,

"not any longer it isn't Ethel, in your condition, you have plenty of work in the house," and then Wilf looked at Ethel tenderly and said, "you choose a name for her Ethel," as she stroked the horse's mane, "

"Sally," the girls chorused,

"Sally it is then," said Ethel laughingly, the four land girls were just coming along the road when they heard Colin say,

"What a daft name for a horse, isn't it Frank?" and Frank answered knowingly,

"Well what did you expect, with lasses choosing the horse's name, because all lasses are daft," Linda ruffled Frank's hair and said,

"In a few years time you won't be saying that, you will be chasing the girls," as everyone stroked the horse, Prudence stood back, and when Susan beckoned her over, Prudence said,

"I don't like horses, I got bitten once, with a horse that was delivering milk before I arrived here, and in fact I don't like any animal, I don't know why I bothered to come outside and see the thing ," Gran turned and looked straight at Prudence and said,

"I know while you came out with us, because you didn't know what Wilf had bought our Ethel," gran erupted furiously, but you are so damned nosey, and besides this horse mightn't like the look of you," Wilf thought he had better defuse the situation, but before he had time Prudence was nearly blown off her feet as she stepped behind the horse, being a townie she was totally unprepared for the horses bodily functions.

"Come on then" he beckoned to the children, "we will take Sally to her stable, and give her some hay he said laughingly,"

Later as Wilf came back in to the house he observed with a wry grin at Ethel, while she was beating the batter for the Yorkshire puddings with a fork, that although gran had put Prudence in her place earlier, she was still stopping for tea although a smile would crack her face, as Mable collected a handful of knives forks and spoons out of the drawer, to set the table, Wilf sat down in the chair with his stocking feet on the brass fender, and a cup of tea cradled in his hand, to wait of the woman putting his food on the table.

"I hope you don't mind us all coming for tea again tonight Mam, as I know it's not easy for you expecting the baby as well as looking after everyone, Ethel looked tenderly at Eva so pleased she had come back along the next day to make up with her, after she had flounced out, after gran had told her Ethel was having a baby,

"You don't mind about the baby do you Eva? Ethel asked her, I know it must have been a shock to you,"

"Of course, I'm alright now Mam, it was such a shock, thinking that I would have a brother or sister younger then my own children, but I've had time to think about it, and I don't mind she said smiling at Ethel."

"Well it doesn't matter, whether you like it or you don't our Eva", gran informed her, "that bairn will be born, so you will just have to accept it, I don't know why you kicked up a fuss in the first place, at least Wilf did the right thing and married her,"

"Gran" a sigh escaped Ethel's lips, as she swivelled round leaning elbows on the table and admonished her,

"You make it sound as though Wilf and I had to get married,"

"Well you could hardly do anything else, with you being in the family way, anyway I don't see what you are making such a fuss about our Ethel, you are married now, and Wilf could do with his tea and I could do with mine, Wilf leaned over and gave Ethel a playful smack on her backside,

"Come and give us a kiss Ethel," he said, beaming with pride, as Ethel turned as red as beetroot, and everybody laughed including gran.

Linda said, "By its good to get home and have a laugh, as its miserable at the Emmerson's"

"Is Margaret keeping any better Jennie? Ethel asked worriedly As Grace said she was going to call and see her when she gets time,"

She told you she would call when she got time our Ethel, well if she didn't gossip so much she would have plenty of time, I like Grace, Gran concluded, but by, she can gossip."

"It's a sad do and no mistake" said Ethel shaking her head knowingly, "Paul went away to fight, a strong healthy lad, and came back a cripple, and having to watch young lasses doing the work that he used to do can't be easy for him, and I do like Margaret, but she is a fuss pot she will have to learn to let Paul to do things himself, Wilf was looking forward to his tea, with the intoxicating smell of meat coming from the oven, as Ethel opened the oven door to stick a fork in the big piece of pork, the Yorkshire puddings had risen so much they were nearly touching the top of the oven, the carrots and cabbage was simmering on the fire alongside the huge pan of potatoes, which Linda was lifting off the fire in readiness to drain the water, Wilf knew he'd done well getting Ethel, he had loved her a long time and she was a good cook, and the land girls were leaning fast, they were a grand bunch of lasses.

The land girls tackled every job with gusto and the next morning as Linda and Jennie biked down the quiet lane to Emmerson's Farm it started to rain, Linda shouted to Jennie,

"Well Gran did forecast this, after it was so hot and clammy last night, she said it was likely to thunder," the rain came down with big heavy drops, Linda said,

"We will be drenched before we get the cows in for milking,"

"Well it could have been worse" Jennie reckoned, "this is summer so it's still warm; if it had been winter we would have been frozen,"

"Yes we have that to look forward too," joked Linda, "at least the cows are moving quicker than usual," they were pushing and shoving each other, to be the first through the byre door, as their full bags swung between their legs, then as the two girls and cows were happily in the byre out of the rain Margaret came bustling in with two towels in her hand,

"I thought you girls might need these," she wheezed,

"Oh thank you Margaret," the water is running down our backs off our hair," said Linda,

"We are soaked," said Jennie as she was chaining the cows up, just then Margaret started coughing again, and holding her ribs, Linda looked at her and said, "You shouldn't be out in this rain, and that cough is not getting any better,"

"Aye well I haven't got time to be laid up, as there is plenty of work to be done inside and out," and with a deep sigh said, "and there's our Paul to see to as well, I had better go and see if he needs anything now," she said, as David came splashing through the puddles,

"I have helped Paul to get up and dressed," David told his wife, and I helped him down the garden to the lav, he wouldn't 't put a coat on, so he is sitting in the house wearing a wet jumper," David waved his hand, as if he was dismissing Margaret, and told her, "You go and see to him lass, as I can't get any bloody sense out of him."

Margaret started to hurry across the yard, as she made for the warmth of the house her breath was coming in gasps, and her chest was very sore,

"Oh now Paul" she said as soon as she was able to get her breath back, are you sitting there waiting for your breakfast?

"Course I'm sitting here, did you think I would run away when you went outside, running after them bloody lasses, I can't stand them, and have you forgotten? I don't have two legs, so I can't run away," Margaret pulled out a chair that matched the table and flopped down heavily, sweat was standing on her brow, and her legs felt weak, she thought, "this won't do sitting here, David Jennie and Linda, will be in shortly for breakfast," she hadn't even lifted the hams down yet from the rafters, and she would have to slice it before setting the frying pan down on the red hot coals, David would have a busy day to day, as he was going to start and cut the fallen trees up with the crosscut saw, before Paul went away to war he was on one end of the saw and David on the other, but once Paul had gone, one of the men from down the lane had helped, but he was too old and infirm now, she sighed , she knew she could not manage to help David today, and the girls were still busy ditching, Margaret didn't even know how she was going to manage to cook meals , she looked up as the backdoor opened, and David, Jennie and Linda, walked in, she hadn't realized she had been sitting over an hour, Margaret started to get up with the palms of her hands flat on the table, to help ease herself off the chair, just then she started coughing again, she reached into her pinny pocket for a hankie, as her eyes were watering, Linda seeing what was happening took charge, she put her hands onto Margaret's shoulders, and eased her back onto the chair, Jennie had gone through to the scullery, and proceeded to slice the ham, to fry with the eggs,

Linda saw Margaret shivering, "I think you should go to bed Margaret," Linda advised her,

"Oh I couldn't I have never been one for lying in bed, she was appalled and then she looked around worriedly at Paul.

David looked over at his wife and said, "Do as Linda said and go to bed Margaret as you are ill." As Margaret stood up with the help of Linda another thought struck her and she turned and asked her husband." What are we going to do about the pigs carcasses? David said, "Theses lasses will manage, Ethel will have shown them how to go on." Linda put her arm round Margaret's waist and said, "Come on Margaret, the sooner we get you tucked up in bed the sooner we'll get the jobs done," it was a slow climb upstairs as Margaret was finding it hard to breathe, she was clinging tightly to the banister rail, although Linda was holding onto her, it was a relief to both Margaret and Linda to get inside the bedroom, Linda just had time to turn the blankets back as Margaret flopped down on the bed, Linda put her hand under Margaret's pillar and produced her nightdress, "come on Margaret, hands up let us get your clothes off and your nightdress on, then you will soon be tucked up in bed." Margaret turned pleading eyes to Linda as she said, "don't take me drawers off lass." as she fiercely held on to the elastic waist band, Margaret felt so tired as Linda lifted her legs and swung them into bed, then Linda tucked her arm under Margaret to haul her up the bed so her head was on the pillar, and her eyes closed straight away.

As Linda stepped back into the kitchen, Jennie was serving the breakfast, David came over to the table, and sat down picked up his knife and fork and started eating, Jennie was just going to pick Pauls plate up and carry it over to him, when Linda put out her hand and stopped her. "Where do you think you are taking that?" Linda demanded. Jennie looked shocked. "Well its Pauls breakfast, and I'm carrying it over to him." Jennie declared. Linda turned and looked at Paul as she told him. "If you want your breakfast come to the table like everybody else or do without." Then she pulled out a chair and started to eat her own, as Paul reached for his crutches scowling at Linda as he did so, then he made his own way to the table, where he sat and glared at Linda, while she totally ignored him, and speared a piece of fried ham with her fork and promptly dipped it into her egg, then she sat and enjoyed her breakfast as if Paul was not there. David was very quiet over breakfast; he was wondering what the hell he was going to do. There were meals to be made, Margaret was ill in bed, and she must be very ill to give in and go to bed he thought as the only time Margaret had stayed in bed was when she had the family and even then she got up too early and earned herself a telling off from Grace the midwife. Then there was Paul to see too as he couldn't get around very well, mind he could do more if he tried, David knew that Linda wouldn't molly coddle him, and maybe it was a good thing. As David cleaned his plate with his bread he said, "I do like a bit fat, it keeps the cold out." "Aye," Linda told him, "that's something that Grans always saying." David shoved his chair back a little then sat with his elbows on the table supporting his head with his hands; he looked at Linda and Jennie then asked them. "How are we going to sort this out girls? as I can't go and get our Judith, as the bairns are full of cold, Linda looked at Jennie and said, "I have been thinking about how we are going to manage, "Jennie could help you outside David, and I'll see to things in here, as I'm sure things will run smooth in here," as she narrowed her eyes at Paul, "as I can cook the meals and look after Margaret, If someone will give me a hand in cutting the pigs down we can all make a start."

"Where does Margaret keep the sharp gulley?" Linda asked as she vacated her chair and started to clear the table. As David stood up he said, "I don't like putting all this extra work on you lasses, more so Jennie, having to saw the wood with me but there is nobody else available." Just then Paul scraped his chair back and shouted, "that's right, rub it in, I can't do bugger all." Linda retorted, "You will never be able to do anything, if you don't try, but don't expect me to run about after you because I won't," then she looked at Jennie and said. "I won't let her either," "You are a hard faced bitch," Paul shouted at Linda. "I will have none of that talk in here Paul," David warned him," As he struggled to retain his patience, "things are bad enough without you fighting with everyone." Jennie got up and started clearing the rest of the things off the table, while Linda put the kettle on the fire to make Margaret a hot drink, and she would fill the stone water bottle as Margaret was complaining she was cold. As Linda made upstairs Jennie asked David, "If he would give her a hand carrying the pig carcasses into the scullery? Ready to cut up and cure on the stone table," As Jennie walked to the stone outhouse with David, he had a grin on his face as he remembered how soft hearted Margaret was with the pigs,

"Every year," he told Jennie, "when it came to our turn to have the pig slaughtered, Margaret cried, he laughed I told her she would never make a farmer crying over a pig." Jennie was interested now,

"Did she not like the thought of them being killed?"

David said, "Well it's like this, all country folk like to keep a pig, we always had a pig at home, mother fed and looked after it, so when Margaret and I got married I bought a piglet in the April, it was a few weeks old, and I kept it until the end of October and then I sent for Jim to come and kill it the same as everybody else did, they are about eighteen stone when they are killed you know lass, Margaret should of been outside helping me, but instead she was in the house crying over the pig, by the time the next pig was killed she was out helping me as I told her they are not pets they are food."

Jennie said, "Piglets are cute, and you do get attached to them, Ethel and Wilf, have a lot of pigs, we help feed them some nights."

"Yes they have Jennie, but they breed them" David said thoughtfully, as he opened the door of the outbuilding and there was the pig hanging from the rafters. Jennie rubbed her hand over the pig, and it was smooth as all the hair had been scraped off, she knew it was done as soon as it was killed, as she had seen Ethel and Wilf doing it.

"Can you hold on to it Jennie?" asked David as he stood with his arms outstretched, reaching up to cut it down, after a struggle they managed to lift it down and carry it round to the scullery, David asked Jennie, and Linda "if they would manage alright, as he told them you might as well get the pigs done together as I don't need a hand yet with the wood, until it stops raining, and when it does I will call for one of you." As David walked out of the door Linda turned to Jennie and said,

"at least we are not working outside getting soaked. Jennie saw Paul leaning forward out of his chair trying to watch the girls, so she nudged Linda, and asked Paul, "Why don't you come through here and join us? Rather than sitting through there on your own,

"Why" Paul sneered, so you can scorn me, as I can't do anything, while you two bits of lasses hump an eighteen stone pig about.

Linda retorted, "You could help, there is nothing wrong with your hands."

"Well I suppose I could help but I need to see me Dad first." Jennie offered to go and find David for him "would you like to see him now Paul?" Before he had chance to answer, Linda asked him what he wanted his Dad for.

Paul snapped, "What the hell has it got to do with you?" Linda stood legs slightly apart hand on hips, starring at Paul. "Well it has a lot to do with us actually, us girls have to cure two pigs, make a midday meal, see to your Mam, who if you haven't forgotten is upstairs in bed ill, and then we have to go out and help your Dad with the farm work, so whatever you need you could ask me or Jennie, rather than your Dad having to run back here for you."

"Oh yes clever clogs are you going to take me to the bloody lav?"

"Linda sharply replied, "No I am not, and no one is going for your Dad as she looked meaningfully at Jennie, you have your crutches and I will guide you down the two steps at the back door."

"Oh I suppose you two will stand there and have a good laugh when I fall down the steps and break me bloody neck." Linda ignored him as she opened the drawer and took out two sharp gulley's while Jennie went to bring the salt peter, Paul felt awful he was a grown man and he had to sit around all day while everyone worked and he knew there was more work than what these two lasses could cope with, when he looked over at the girls they were busy turning the huge pig over. He missed his mother and she had only been in bed a couple of hours, she would of run outside for him if he had asked her to go and bring his Dad, he needed a pee, he also realized that the girls would not run after him the way his mother had done, so he shuffled his backside to the edge of the chair and reached for his crutches, just then Jennie saw him struggling, and was going to help him when Linda realized what she was going to do and stopped her.

"Don't go helping him Jennie, or he will never manage, on his own and we have numerous jobs to do today." Pauls temper was rising as he listened to Linda; he would show that hard hearted bitch that he could manage, and a push with one hand on the chair arm and the other holding the crutch and he was out of the chair, he smiled to himself, he had managed, but his biggest hurdle was getting to the lav, down them damned steps, as he hopped into the scullery

Linda said, "You managed alright then."

"I must of done I'm bloody here," Paul shouted.

"No need to be so sarky", Linda told him, "I will help you down the steps," she said as she opened the back door, he was very nervous,

"How the hell are you going to manage me? I will probably fall then you will have to go for Dad to help me up."

Linda said, "The trouble with you Paul Emmerson you have no confidence and I haven't got all day to stand here, so come on Paul, just try and I will help you." Linda pleaded, as she had heard the nervous uncertainty in Paul's voice. Paul could feel his self shaking; he would appeal to Linda's better nature.

"Please go and get me Dad Linda, you said you had a lot of work to do, and we are both wasting time standing here." Paul did not have time to refuse as Linda took him by surprise; she put an arm around his back to move him forward and her other arm was loosely in front of him to stop him from falling forward, and had him down the steps in no time at all.

"Now you can manage the path to the lav, I will go back inside and watch through the window for you coming back." Paul was amazed at the strength that Linda had in her arms, but then he realized she was doing the same job as the men used to do, and there was plenty of strenuous work, to be done on a farm he thought sadly, he knew, as he used to do it. Neither Paul nor Linda knew that David was watching them, as he had been going to fetch Paul, as he thought he might need to visit the lav, but what he saw surprised and pleased him, he knew Linda would never fuss over him, and it was the best way of making Paul do something for himself, he stood and watched Paul come out of the lav and make his way slowly up the garden path, just then the backdoor opened and Linda stepped outside ,and put her arm round Paul, to help him back inside. David saw Paul hesitate but Linda had no intension of stopping until she had him safely up the steps and back into the house. David smiled to himself as he went back to work he felt sure that Linda would soon sort Paul out now there was a force to be reckoned with.

Paul looked at the girls and said, "if either of you girls wouldn't mind bringing me a chair I could help you as I know it's hard work pushing the salt peter down into the joints, and rolling all the pieces into the salt.

Jennie said "I will have to go and help your Dad now Paul, as it has stopped raining and we have a tree to cut up into logs." As Jennie put her willies on then lifted the latch and went out, Linda told Paul,

"We have already cut the two hams off, the pig," as she brought a chair and a sharp gulley for him, Linda was surprised how quick and thorough he was with the huge pig, Linda said, "I will do the messiest job and scrape the small intestines and then we can use them as sausage skins," by the time David and Jennie came in for dinner the table was set ready and Linda was busy serving it out, and the pig was cured. The potted meat had been made, and the internal fat had been boiled for cooking lard. Linda was sweating as she lifted the heavy stew pan off the fire as Jennie had taken the pan of potatoes outside to drain, after the girls had dished the dinners out, Linda said, "I'm going to take a small plate up for Margaret, with a cup of tea,

David looked up and asked, "Are you not going to have yours first lass?"

"No I had better go up and see to Margaret, I should have gone up earlier", Linda apologised, "only we have been busy haven't we Paul,"

"Well I haven't done a lot really." Paul exclaimed, but he was pleased to have been a help today,

"If you had not cut all that pig up I would not have had time to cook the dinner," Linda told him, as she set off upstairs with a tray for Margaret. As Linda walked into the bedroom she noticed Margaret's face was bright red, and she was lying so still, as Linda stepped nearer the bed she saw Margaret's face was wet with sweat, as Linda spoke to her Margaret opened her eyes then closed them again, she felt so ill she couldn't keep her eyes open. Linda pulled the blankets back off Margaret then put her arm around her to enable her to sit up and have a sip of her tea, and then she noticed that Margaret was wet with sweat, so she walked out of the bedroom and shouted of Jennie to come and help change Margaret's nightdress and bed sheets, and then they had managed to get her to have a few sips of tea but she refused anything to eat. As the girls walked back in to the kitchen to finish their dinner

David asked them, "If Margaret had eaten anything,"

"No," answered Jennie, "she has only had a sip of tea,"

David looked thoughtfully as he said, "you know us country folk don't bother much with Doctors, but I reckon a couple of days in bed might just do her good, get herself rested up a bit," then he turned to Linda, and said "I've been wondering about our teas, as you two girls go home after you do the milking, so I thought if you wouldn't mind if I helped Jennie to do the milking if you would fettle our teas lass?" as he looked pleadingly at Linda.

"Yes we will help you all we can," Jennie told David, "wont we Linda?" and so as the girls biked up the lane and headed back to Ethel's three hours later then they should of been, Jennie asked Linda if she was still going out tonight ,?"

"Well of course I am, why? Are you not, Jennie?"

"Well it's just with us being late home; I thought maybe you wanted to stay in."

You know me Jennie I like to enjoy myself and besides there is a whole lot more land girls coming so the more the merrier," Linda said laughingly, as she pedalled as fast as she could.

Back home at Ethel's, Gran was asking how Margaret was keeping, Ethel thought the girls had done well to get through all the work as well as looking after Margaret and Paul. Linda sat back with her hand covering her mouth as she yawned for the second time since they had arrived home. "You seem tired Linda." Ethel remarked,

"Yes but I'm just doing my bit for the war effort," Linda replied.

"No doubt that was what you were doing last night under my bedroom window." Gran retorted. "You girls seem to be doing more than your fair share with all these different soldiers, mark my words you'll live to regret it. But! I don't suppose you'll be the only ones."

CHAPTER EIGHT

The next morning Ethel had rose earlier, to black-lead the range with zebo polish, before everyone was out of bed, she was busy polishing the fire irons and fender with brasso when Wilf came back in from feeding sally, the horse some oats. Ethel sat back on her heels and smiled at practical, dependable Wilf his trousers were tucked into his wellingtons and wearing his flat cap, the kettle on the fire started to boil, as Wilf dropped into the chair to wait for his breakfast. Ethel had scolded the tea then as she was frying the bacon she heard a noise in Grans room.

"Look after this bacon Wilf." she told him as she hurried upstairs to see what was happening with Gran. As Ethel lifted the sneck and opened the door she saw gran sitting on the side of the bed trying to get her clothes on, and getting more vexed by the minuet as she struggled to get her legs in to the stockings.

"Whatever is the matter gran?" Ethel asked her, Gran turned and looked at Ethel,

"What are you asking me daft questions like that for our Ethel can't you see I'm getting up, and trying to get some clothes on."

"Yes I can see that gran, but why didn't you wait until I came to help you like I do every morning?" Gran was incensed; "it is no good coming for me our Ethel after all the bacon is eaten, had you forgotten that I was still in bed and hungry."

"No I had not Gran." Ethel's patience was diminishing. "Wilf and I got up early," Ethel told her as she helped her dress. I had the range to black-lead, and Wilf has been to see to the horse." Just then the land girls came out of their bedroom.

"We have not slept in have we Ethel?" asked Jennie.

"No" replied Ethel wearily, it's just Gran, she thought she might be missing her breakfast." Gran turned to Ethel with a questionable look on her face.

"I thought you told me our Ethel, you were polishing the range."

"Oh I was Gran Ethel was feeling harassed and the day hadn't started properly yet, why are you asking again."

Gran sniffed and said, "I can smell bacon."

"Yes that is because I heard you upstairs, and thinking something was wrong I left Wilf frying the bacon." Gran looked triumphantly at Ethel and said, "Just as well I got up, and then I won't miss my breakfast."

Ethel felt as if she had done a day's work already as she put the baking board and rolling pin on the table ready to bake the pastry, the fire was blazing as it heated the oven for Ethel's cakes, she already had the bun tins with the fairy cake mixture in the oven, as she paused to shove the hair out of her eyes, then proceeded to spoon the fruit cake mixture in to the large tin.

"Why don't you sit down and enjoy your cup of tea our Ethel?" asked gran, as her cup of tea was steaming gently in front of her. "I haven't time to sit yet gran." answered Ethel as she was standing at the table peeling cooking apples before making pastry for the pies. As the wooden clock on the mantelpiece began to chime   Grace the midwife tapped on Ethel's door and was making her way in.

"I thought I would call and see how you were getting on Ethel."

"Well I'm glad to see you Grace," remarked gran "I think you should have been calling more often but never mind you are here now. Our Ethel's as big as a house end, she must of been further on then she reckoned when she got married, or filling up with water." gran said as an afterthought. Just as Grace tried to get a word in Gran said, "There could be two in there as twins run in our family." Grace watched as Ethel rolled out the last of the pastry for pies and mixed the dumplings for tea to go in the mince. "You are always busy cooking Ethel." Grace admired Ethel she kept them all well fed, and Mrs Brown could try the patience of a saint, but at least you knew where you stood with her Grace presumed.

"Aye our Ethel has been busy this morning black leading the range, she does it frequently. Just examine our Ethel, while your here Grace."Gran told her. Ethel looked appalled, "Grace might not have time Gran," Ethel sharply replied.

Course she has Ethel, she can always make time for a cup of tea, I've never known her refuse yet."

"Well if you don't mind Grace." Ethel said resignedly, "As I am big for five month."

"Unless you're further on then you are telling us." Gran said suspiciously, and then she looked at Grace and said. "She did spend some nights in that pull out bed in the sideboard with Wilf before she was married. I was cold in bed on me own, but I have extra blankets on me bed now, and I don't get disturbed with our Ethel creeping into bed in the early hours," and as an afterthought said. "Well at least she's respectable now."

Ethel looked daggers at gran then said, "I'm just going to pop to the lav Grace."

"Oh that's fine," Grace remarked, "I'm not in a hurry Ethel." As Ethel went out of the door, Grace was just going to sit down, when gran said, "Just put the kettle on and make a fresh cup of tea Grace, you might as well make yourself useful while you're waiting for our Ethel." Ethel's expression was mutinous as she came back indoors to find Grace scolding a pot of tea under Grans guidance.

"Is that alright for you now Mrs Brown" Grace asked Gran? As she poured her another cup of tea, then she looked at Ethel "I'd made it too weak," she said dismally. "Gran said to add some more tea leaves I hope I haven't used too much of your tea ration," said a worried Grace.

"No of course you haven't, if I hadn't told you to put extra in the pot it would have been a cupful of hot water," grumbled Gran.

Grace looked at Ethel and said, "You have to try and make the rations spin out, it must be terrible living in the city and having to queue for everything."

"Well I like to taste the tea, if I wanted water I'd get a cupful out of that pail, and while you're standing doing nothing Grace pass me a few biscuits out of that cupboard." As Grace reached inside the cupboard Wilf walked in and seeing Grace handing Gran biscuits rubbed his hands together saying,

"I'm just in time for a pot of tea, oh and Grace is making it." As he took off his cap and hung it behind the door on a nail, then he ran his fingers through his receding hair. As Grace reached for another cup for Wilf, Ethel's face darkened, she gave a big impatient sigh.

"I'm sorry Grace that you've had to make a pot of tea, I'm sure gran could have waited," Ethel stated as she squirmed with embarrassment. Ethel couldn't believe it when she saw Prudence walking past the window heading for the door, Prudence often called in but Ethel was in a bad mood with Gran, and Wilf ,"Fancy asking the midwife to make a pot of tea," she thought.

Then the door opened and Prudence came walking in full of herself as usual, "I have just heard there is about thirty girls on their way here, and they are all land girls oh I can see a lot of trouble ahead."

Ethel said, "Are you still spreading doom and despondency Prudence?" but the sarcasm was lost on Prudence.

Gran gave a contemptuous snort; "there is nothing wrong with land girls." she thundered, "look at our four, they are all good hard working lasses, you don't want to meet trouble half way Prudence as you are not through yourself yet."

"But a lot of these girls will be coming from impoverished families they've survived practically on nothing; I don't suppose anyone's thought about the consequences." Said prudence looking thoughtful, Ethel's eyes rolled to the ceiling as she made for the door, indicating Grace to follow.

Ethel and Grace made their way upstairs out of the way of prying eyes, "I know I am big for five month Grace, I just hope there is only one." said Ethel worriedly.

After Grace had finished the examination she shook her head at Ethel saying "I'm not sure Ethel, as one could be lying behind the other, but I will call again in about a month then we might find out more." As they entered the kitchen Prudence turned and asked Grace

"Have you heard there are thirty land army girls coming?" And without waiting for an answer carried on saying," they will all need accommodation."

"Yes just the same as you needed somewhere to stay Prudence when you came here." Gran replied.

Later as they were having tea Prudence repeated what she had been told "There is always a feeling of camaraderie among us land girls." Jennie confessed. As it is a hard life out in all weathers, fighting the elements when wind rain and snow sweep across the open fields and of course when we first arrived here none of us knew anything about animals so we have helped each other." She said smiling at the rest of the girls.

Wilf quickly drank his tea and glanced over at the boys, "are you about ready then? He asked them. The boys got off the chairs and pushed them back under the table. Wilf reached for his cap and the three of them went out the door.

"Where are they going now Ethel?" Asked Prudence,

"I have no idea Prudence but no doubt there will be plenty of jobs to keep them busy until teatime." Ethel had no idea that Wilf and the boys were busy harnessing Sally the horse, as he was going to the next village to buy a wireless as a surprise for Ethel and he presumed gran would enjoy it as well. As Wilf backed sally between the shafts of the cart the boys jumped on, then Wilf climbed on and getting hold of the reigns he said gee up lass as sally's ears pricked up she was tossing her head with anticipation as she set off down the lane, the wind had picked up but it didn't deter Wilf as it started to rain, but Tommy coming along on his motor bike upset sally as it backfired sally was nervous never having seen a motorbike so she started to rear up as Wilf said "steady girl Whoa there." As sally stopped and tossed her heavy mane, Wilf had climbed down and was stroking her long nose and talking kindly to her. The boys had got to their feet to join Wilf but he indicated with his hand to stay where they were. "I am going to walk with her." he later told the boys when he had quietened sally down.

Ethel thought they had arrived back home when the door opened but it was Ada, she had recently started calling, with her tales of woe; she poked her head around the door and said "I hope I haven't called at a bad time?" As she walked over to the chair sat down.

Gran said, "Well bad time or not, it looks as though you are going to stay and make yourself comfortable."

Down the road Wilf was still walking leading the horse, and talking to her gently as she seemed to have got over her fright. But the rain was coming down heavier. As they reached the shop Wilf opened the door and a bell tinkled overhead. Mrs Peacock the owner of the shop asked if she could help as she saw Wilf looking round in bewilderment at all the goods on offer.

"I would like a wireless," he told her, "but I don't know anything about them," he said as he rubbed his chin thoughtfully, the boys were rushing about looking at everything in the shop, "well you have some nice looking wirelesses in here," Wilf told her, "but I am still not sure which one our Ethel would like."

"Well may I make a suggestion?" Mrs. Peacock asked.

"Yes that would be grand," Wilf exclaimed, "or we will be here all-night he laughed."

"What colour is your furniture at home?" she asked Wilf.

"Well the sideboard and the small table that this wireless will sit on is mahogany."

"There you are then." she excitedly told Wilf, "this wireless with its beautiful mahogany cabinet it will look lovely,

"Oh I will take that then," he said as he put his hand in his pocket for some money.

"Don't forget you will need an accumulator." Mrs Peacock pointed out to Wilf.

"I think I will buy two accumulators and then when one is down here getting charged we will always have a spare, how much will it cost to charge them up?" Wilf asked.

"It will cost sixpence," Mrs Peacock replied, "but it is entertainment for all the family." she smilingly told Wilf. The boys carried an accumulator each out of the shop while Wilf carried the wireless and placed them on the cart. The rain had turned into a downpour, so Wilf reached for his raincoat and wrapped the wireless in it, and then he wrapped the accumulators in a hessian bag, as the boys jumped on to the cart and wrapped a hessian bag each round their shoulders. Wilf led sally by the bridle for a while, and just as he was going to climb on to the cart Tommy rode past again and the motorbike backfired, which unsettled sally. Wilf decided he might as well walk but he would have a word with Tommy the next time he saw him. Wilf was wet and weary as he carried the wireless indoors the boys were just as wet as they carried an accumulator in each.

Ethel cried out, "you are soaked Wilf where is your rain coat?"

"It's here Ethel I wrapped the wireless in it to keep it dry." Ethel hurried through to the front room and brought the small mahogany table where she gave it pride of place tucked nicely into the corner as Wilf placed the wireless and accumulator on side by side.

"Right you two just put the spare accumulator there and we'll go back outside and see to the jobs, it's pointless staying in here and getting dried out to have to go out and get wet again, also I have sally to dry off and bed down."

Ada sat close by the fire with her legs slightly apart and her knicker legs just over her bony knees enjoying the heat, as her cup of tea cooled in front of her; she had a hard life and a long walk home from work every day so she looked forward to a daily cup of tea at Ethel's and a chat, as Ada hadn't heard from her daughter for a long time, and she was worried for the safety of her daughter and grandchildren, who lived in the city. The last thing Ada had heard was, her son-in-law had been killed in action. Ada didn't have much money but she had been sending a little every week to her daughter but there had been no correspondence for a long time from her so Ada had stopped sending money and thinking the worst wanted to go and try and find out what had happened to her family, as time went by Ada got more upset. She had enlisted the help of Susan one of the land girls who lived with Ethel. Susan had lived in the rectory three streets away from Ada's daughter before she had came to Ethel's Ada was a country woman who had never been further then six mile away from home, she would never have managed in a big city on her own.

Susan had no intension of ever going back home to the city she was pleased to leave behind, as her parents had never wanted her, but once Ada had found out that Susan knew her way around she never let it rest.

Gran said, "She's like a dog with a bone, but you have to feel sorry for her I wouldn't like to be in her position, and I don't know if Susan has made the right decision to go with Ada to help her find her daughter and grandchildren, as I think there will be a lot of heartache whatever happens."

Later in the day after the farm work was done and everyone had enjoyed the meal that Ethel had cooked. Wilf decided to get the wireless going, after a good while Gran was beginning to wonder if Wilf knew what he was doing, as his big calloused fingers fiddled with the knobs, all they could hear was a screeching, crackling noise, but after a while when he finally got it tuned in and heard the newsreader giving out the news Gran was elated, as she smilingly told Wilf by you are a clever lad, and I never thought that I would see one of them as she pointed to the wireless, as Wilf sat beaming from ear to ear, as he winked at Ethel.

Just then Susan and Mable came downstairs, as Linda and Jennie walked in.

"By you two are late," Mable said, is Margaret any better?"

"No she isn't." Linda answered with a deep sigh, "and David doesn't think she is bad enough for a doctor."

Gran said, "Country folk don't bother much with doctors, we can usually put ourselves right, give her a few days and she'll be as right as rain folk don't want a fuss, but a bottle of camphorated oil and a bit of vick for her chest might help her." Later as everyone who was in had gone to bed leaving Ethel sitting in the chair in front of the fire, and Wilf was in the other chair with his legs stretched out to the fire, and his hands cupped behind his head. The wireless was playing dance music which Ethel was thoroughly enjoying. The curtains were drawn across the windows, shutting out the cold wet and windy night. Wilf turned his head and looked at Ethel and murmured sleepily. "By this is grand, what a difference a wireless makes lass."

"Aye it does Wilf everybody got a bit enjoyment out of it tonight." Ethel agreed. "I think we had better bank this fire down for the night there is a bucket of small coal in the corner that Colin brought in earlier."

"Aye I will do it for you Ethel as soon as I've drank me coca, let's hope the weather improves a bit before morning or we will all get soaked."

As the whole house slept there was a ferocious downpour battering the windowpanes and making the doors creak, but they all slept on unaware of the stormy night. As morning approached and Ethel drew back the curtains after giving the fire a good poke and the flames came to life she got a shock when she looked out of the window. Branches had been snapped off the trees, and some of the outbuildings had parts of their roof missing. Wilf would have to mend them today if the weather calmed down a bit. By the time everyone else got up Ethel had a good fire burning in the grate, and the kettle boiling on the red hot coals. The girls drank the scolding sweet tea and talked to Wilf and the boys while Ethel fried the bacon, just as she was frying the last slice before cracking the eggs into the pan she heard Gran stirring upstairs, so Linda took over the cooking while Ethel went upstairs to help gran. As Ethel walked into the bedroom she said,

"I hadn't forgotten about you Gran, but I am trying to cook breakfast so everyone can start work."

"Well it's no good coming for me after all the bacon has been eaten." Gran sharply replied.

"It's alright Gran there is plenty for you."

"Well I am up now, so I might as well have it while it's hot, and I'll have an egg with it I like to start the day on a full stomach."

As the girls wheeled their bikes out through the gates Ethel wondered if they would be able to stop on them as the wind had risen again and there was still a heavy downpour. Wilf and Ethel kept all the hessian sacks so they had plenty on hand; Wilf had walked round the buildings to get some sacks for the girls to wrap around their shoulders to keep them dry. As Wilf and Ethel walked towards the byre they were pleased to see the entire roof was intact, as they opened the byre door they could feel the heat off the cows as they lay two to a stall, the cows turned and looked at them as much as to say, "surely it's not milking time yet? We are just lying resting. Then they lumbered to their feet like a room full of old woman. As Ethel sat between two cows in the stall milking she thought they must be trying to see who could swish their tails the most as Ethel kept getting a bat across the head. As Ethel finished milking the two cows Colin and Frank came in from eating their breakfast.

"Right Ethel theses lads will take over." Wilf walked over and told Ethel, who wasn't very pleased but she had to admit in her condition it was uncomfortable. "You go in the house lass, and have a chat to gran and another cup of tea." he told her tenderly. After Ethel had walked out of the byre Colin sat on the milking stool that Ethel had just vacated and soon had the milk splashing in to the pail between his knees, the boys were both deft hand at milking now, they were two different boys now to what they were when they came as evacuees to Ethel's. When Ethel had first taken them in they were filthy, cheeky and didn't know what a good meal looked like until they sat at Ethel's table, but with good meals, discipline and love they were two boys to be proud of. Ethel always referred to them as her boys as they would never be able to go back to their birthplace, as the mother had ran off with a boyfriend leaving the boys with a grandmother that didn't want them, and had told them as they boarded the train not to go back to her as she didn't want them.

Soon all the cows were milked and the frothy buckets of milk were emptied into the churns. Wilf walked around to the stable and put sally between the shafts and led her round, while the boys lifted the churns on to the cart. Wilf walked back round to bring the wheelbarrow in and two shovels, so they could clean all the cow muck up out of the channels. Wilf was sweating as he shovelled the steaming muck. But worse was to come as they walked through puddles of water delivering folk's milk. As Wilf lifted the ladle out of the churn to fill whatever utensil folk brought to their door to fill, the wind was whipping it out of the ladle, the rain was coming down like stair rods and hitting the churns, and hands, making them red raw, but it did no good complaining. When they finally arrived back home they lifted the empty churns off the cart and settled sally down with a dish of oats, then they all went into the house to get changed as they were soaked to the skin. Even with the hessian bags around their shoulders it hadn't protected them from this kind of weather. While Ethel prepared them all a sandwich and a sweet cup of tea Wilf went back outside to the outbuilding and came back in with two huge buckets of small potatoes to boil for the pigs, he knew it would take a few buckets to go around all the pigs that they had now but Colin and Frank were on school holidays so they could keep bringing them round for Ethel to boil and take the steaming mashed potatoes back and feed the pigs. As Wilf went to collect the potatoes, the boys went to the henhouse to collect the eggs and give the hens some corn. As the boys opened the henhouse door the hens had fluttered over each other to get out, but Frank thought they were not too sure now if they should have been in such a rush, to get out in this weather, as the rain was soaking their wings and feathers, some of them gave up on the weather and walked sedately back in where it was dry. The cockerels decided to stay out a little longer to show the hens that a bit of rain didn't matter to them, as they strutted about on their clawed feet trying not to sink into the mud. As Wilf finished his sandwich he sat in the chair with his stocking feet resting on the fender in front of the fire enjoying his second mug of sweet tea. As Ethel stoked the fire up for a day's baking, and Wilf would have to go back outside after his mug of tea to see what he could do with the building to stop the rain getting in.

As Susan and Mable arrived at John Rains farm they were drenched, Mr Rain as the girls had been told to call him was standing just inside the byre door. As the girls got off their bikes he stood and waited while they propped them up beside the byre wall then he stood aside to let the girls enter the byre.

He said, "Oh so you still came then, I didn't think you would."

Susan asked, and why is that?"

"Well because you two are lasses, and I thought you might have been a bit soft."

"Well you would have been in a right pickle if we had stayed at home wouldn't you Mr Rain? But we are soaked." Susan pointed out to him. Mr Rain stood and rubbed his chin and then he seemed to have an idea, as he splashed through the puddles into the farmhouse. The girls had just got the cows udders washed when he came hurrying in. Susan could hear his chest wheezing as he came over to them with a message. "Mrs Rain said to go across to the house now as she is sorting you some dry clothes out." All the time the girls had worked for the rains they had never been across the threshold since they had left to go and live with Ethel. Susan tapped on the door and raised her eyebrows at Mable, as much as to ask if she should open the door as Mable was shivering, so Susan lifted the sneck and eased the door open just enough to call Mrs Rain, she finally came and opened the door a little wider so the girls could slip through. There was a dirty hessian sack laid on the stone flagged kitchen floor. Mrs Rain shuffled over and pointed to the sack saying,

"There is some old clothes in there, they used to belong to Mr Rains dad, I was once going to use them in a prodded mat, but then I thought they might come in handy, I know they are little better then rags but they will do for you two," and then as an afterthought she said, "I will put your clothes on the pulley above the fire to dry."

On their way back across the yard Mable said, ".We look like two bloody clowns." As Mable and Susan walked back into the byre Mr Rain said

"I see the missus has fixed you up then, and it has taken you twenty minutes so you can both stay back tonight and work that twenty minutes up, we can't let the weather get in the way of work."

As Linda and Jennie pedalled along the road together in the rain, Linda asked Jennie if she would like to do the breakfast today for everyone.

"No thanks Linda I can't handle Paul like you do."

"That's because you are too sympathetic Jennie, and then he take advantage."

"Don't you think you are a bit too hard though some time Linda?"

"No not at all look what happened yesterday, he wanted one of us to go and fetch his Dad to help him to the toilet, and when we refused he managed alright once I had helped him down the steps."

"Yes I know Linda, but it must be frustrating for him."

"Yes I agree Jennie, but there are a lot of people worse off than him."

As the girls arrived at the farmyard David was just opening the back door. "Would you girls mind going for the cows together this morning?" He asked them. "While I see to Paul." As the girls splodge over the wet fields Linda said disparagingly,

"David looks worn out this morning, and he hasn't been shaved for a couple of days, I have never seen him with stubble before."

"Well Linda it can't be easy for him at the moment." Jennie reflected but Margaret might be a little better this morning," she said optimistically. Only after they had finished milking did the girls find out how ill Margaret really was. She was refusing food and only having a sip of water; perspiration was running down her face back and between her breasts, the bed was wet where she was lying. Linda was downstairs busy making breakfast as she went into the kitchen to set the table she looked over at Paul who was sitting in the chair while David rolled his mattress and bedding up into the sideboard.

"Good morning Paul." she called over to him, "it's not a bad day today now the rain has stopped, and I am hoping it keeps dry so I can peg the washing out."

Paul scowled at Linda, as he shouted, "What's so bloody good about today? Every day is the same for me; I'm just a bloody cripple, no good for nothing."

Linda thought "Oh that's the way the land lies this morning is it?" as she cracked the eggs in to the frying pan. Linda thought "he ought to think himself lucky there was a lot of lads in the city who had come back from the war with a lot more injuries then him, and they wouldn't be sitting down to bacon sausage black pudding and fresh fried eggs for breakfast." Linda carried the hot plates of food through as Jennie followed with the big brown teapot. David got out of the chair then walked over to the table pulled a chair out ready to sit down then he turned and asked Paul if he needed a hand to get out of the chair.

"No thanks," he said contemptuously, "she can bring it over," as he pointed a finger at Linda.

"I will not Paul," Linda retorted angrily at his audaciousness. "I am not your servant so get off your backside and come to the table like everybody else." David winced, he would have liked to carry it over to Paul but Linda was right it was time he tried to help himself, and when he thought about it he had just been telling Margaret not to mollycoddle him before she took bad. Paul was making his way over to the table with a thunderous look on his face. Linda watched him tucking into his breakfast there was nothing wrong with his appetite, as he leaned over for another slice of bread to mop his plate with and washed it down with a mug of sweet tea. Then he banged the empty mug down on the table and scraped his chair back as he reached for his crutches, he never spoke to anyone as he made his way to the chair that he had vacated less than twenty minutes ago, and sat down morosely for the rest of the morning.

Jennie went upstairs to check on Margaret and she came back down with a worried look on her face, "I think you should go for the Doctor." she told David.

"No nothing of the sort it's just a bit of flu," he informed her, "we country folk are never ill enough for a doctor, not with all this country air, usually ailments like colds and flu is better worked off. But I must admit Margaret has got it worse than usual but she'll be as right as ninepence in a few days." Jennie just looked at Linda and shrugged her shoulders it seemed to her there was a lot of stubborn men in this family. Well there was nothing else she could do, she might as well make a start with the farm work and there was plenty to do. Linda dragged the poss-tub out of the cupboard, and then went in again for the big heavy mangle, as she was sorting the colours to put into the poss-tub she looked up through the little window in the corner and saw some big black clouds she hoped it wouldn't rain until the washing dried, she was sweating as she pounded the clothes and wisps of damp hair kept falling into her eyes. Steam was running down the little window as Linda lifted the wet washing out of the tub and dragged it over to the mangle; it was hard work turning the handle so the big wooden rollers would squeeze the water out of the clothes. After she had put two loads of washing through the mangle she poked her head through the kitchen door to speak to Paul, but he was sitting with his eyes closed. Linda thought he had maybe closed his eyes when he heard her footsteps so he didn't have to speak to her because surely he couldn't be tired. Oh well she didn't have time to worry about him with his childish ways. Linda opened the backdoor then bent down to pick up the big wicker basket full of clothes when the wind blew the door shut with a bang, and Paul who had been asleep woke with a jump. He swivelled round in his chair shouting.

"Are you trying to give me a bloody heart attack?" But Linda didn't hear him as she was on her way to the clothes line, her big wraparound pinny that she had borrowed off Margaret was billowing in the wind. She thought to herself. "If this wind keeps up, these clothes won't take long to dry, as long as those big black clouds don't get here first." After she had struggled against the wind to get the washing on the line she would have loved to sit down for a while but the poss-tub had to be emptied and put away, then she would have to drag the huge heavy mangle back into the cupboard, and then it wouldn't be long before everyone wanted their dinners, but first she would go and check on Margaret.

Linda told Margaret that she had suggested to David that a Doctor should call. Margaret shook her head as she said. "No don't bother with a Doctor and don't go worrying yourself over me, I will be as right as ninepence in a few days." Linda went back downstairs she was pleased she had put the potatoes in the oven earlier as they would be about ready and the rabbit stew was simmering in the big pan with the lid bobbing up and down letting the steam escape.

Linda looked over at Paul and asked. "Is this moody look natural for you or did you get it with years of practice?"

"Oh you think you are so bloody funny, but what have I got left?"

Linda turned on him, "Well from where I'm standing you have a lot more than other folks, you have good grub, a comfortable warm bed and everybody running around after you."

"Well you don't." He retorted sullenly.

"No and I never will, its time you stopped feeling sorry for yourself and considered other folk for a change."Linda had just realized Paul had not asked her to help him down the steps she wondered if he had managed on his own, when she was pegging the washing out, and then she doubted it as he wouldn't be able to manage the steps on his own. Paul brought her out of her thoughts when he hollered.

"What are you starring at me for?"

"Oh I was just thinking you haven't been down to the lav this morning."

Paul exploded, "Have I no bloody privacy with you? Or are you hoping the wind will blow me off my feet. No I mean my one foot then I could be laid in the garden all day. Is that what you want? And don't worry I do know when I want to go to the lav." Linda never heard the rest of what he was saying; she looked up as the wind blew the rain at the window. She pulled the door open so hard that it swung back against the wall, and then banged shut, as she ran to retrieve the washing off the line, that had been nearly dry. It was a heavy downpour as Linda staggered into the kitchen under the heavy weight of the full wicker basket. Today was getting worse by the minuet for Linda, and it would be another eight hours before she was back at Ethel's. She knew it would have been easier outside doing the farm work with David, as that was what she was used too, as she had never done any house work until she came to Ethel's. But Jennie would have had to look after Paul and he would have had her run off her feet fetching and carrying for him, it needed someone strong minded to see to Paul. She knew David and Jennie were on their way in as she heard them scraping their willies on the boot scraper at the backdoor. The bottom field they had been working in was like a quagmire. They came in shaking their heads just like the dogs, and then they took their coats off and shook them. Linda saw a puddle starting to form on the floor and thought I have mopped that floor once already this morning. As they were sitting having their dinners Linda asked David if he would mind finishing off the stew at teatime, "I will peel a pan of potatoes, then mash them to go with the stew." she offered, "as I have a lot of jobs to do this afternoon." Paul looked across at her and sneered contemptuously.

"Oh is there too much work for Linda to manage?" He asked. The look he gave her was both mocking and challenging. David was eating his dinner, thoughtfully,

"Is your dinner alright?" Linda asked David hopefully. "Only you are very quiet and I know you are worried about Margaret." David seemed to have made a decision as he swallowed the last piece of food off his fork then looked round the table making sure he had everyone's attention while rubbing his chin, his brow furrowed in concentration.

"Yes this is something that I've been thinking about all morning." He replied with a sigh. "I know it will be a week or two before Margaret's back on her feet, there is a lot of work to be done on the farm." He looked at Linda and Jennie as he said. "There is even more work then we can manage, so if you girls can muddle through today just doing the jobs that need doing, such as looking after Paul and Margaret, until I get back and then we will milk and get the rest of the outside jobs done." Paul looked shocked his Dad would never leave the farm in the middle of the day when there was such a lot of work to be done.

"Where are you going Dad?" Paul was anxious to know. The loud ticking of the grandfather clock was the only sound that disturbed the air, as David answered, "I 'm going over to see your mothers sister, your auntie Gladys, she lives on her own since your uncle Lennie died, she has time on her hands so I'm sure she'll not mind helping out here." Then as an afterthought he said. "I will bring her back with me tonight." Paul gasped the colour draining from his face with shock.

"Surely you are not bringing that bloody old battleaxe here? We can do without her."

"She will be here tonight Paul and you had better keep a civil tongue in your head, and while we are talking about being short handed on the farm there is help coming next week." The girls turned questioning eyes to David as he held his hand up as Linda was going to ask what was happening.

"We are threshing in two weeks time and we will not be able to manage all the extra work on our own, so the authorities' have agreed we can have some p o w s, they will start work here next week."

Paul exploded his face mottled with fury he stared at David in astonishment. "You are not bringing them here, look what they did to Me." he shouted nastily lighting up a cigarette and blowing a cloud of smoke in David's direction. David stood up averting his eyes and scraped the chair back from the table. As Linda picked the teapot up off the hearth to offer David a cup he shook his head as a cup of tea usually rounded off a meal. Linda cleared the table as Paul sat in his chair sulking, then she took a cup of tea upstairs for Margaret. Linda was extremely concerned by Margaret's condition, as she slipped her arm under Margaret's shoulder to ease her up to have a sip of tea. Margaret's nightie was wet with sweat and she hardly had strength to sit up, while Linda changed her. As Linda made her way back downstairs she felt her concern mounting for Margaret the sooner Gladys arrived the better and then she could do the job she came to do.

"Do you think Margaret will be pleased to have her sister here with her while she is ill?" Jennie asked Linda.

"I should think so," said Linda thoughtfully. "I definitely will be, she will have a job on her hands looking after Paul. I know we are threshing next week and it is hard dirty work but it will be easy, compared to looking after Paul." Linda picked up the empty bucket and took it to the meal house which was a small stone building that stored dry food for the animals and poultry, then looking round she found the small shovel which had been left on the window sill as she reached into the meal bin she disturbed the mice, she turned and glared at Jennie. "I see you forgot to replace the bin lid this morning again Jennie, after you fed the hens."

"Oh I'm sorry Linda I was in such a rush to get all the jobs done; it's just with you seeing to the jobs in the house and looking after Margaret and Paul we are short handed out here." Linda started to wish she'd kept her mouth shut as it hadn't been easy for none of them apart from Paul who tried to make life hard for all of them, and that was why he was sitting in the house on his own now.

Linda put her arms round Jennie and said, "No it's not your fault Jennie, as you said we have been short handed, but David will be back shortly with Margaret's sister, so I will half fill this bucket with meal then we can go to the tap in the yard and stir in the water then the hens can have their crowdie."

"Yes we will Linda." Jennie laughingly said, "And I will put the lid on the meal tin." Later as the girls made their way across the fields, Linda looked thoughtful as she asked Jennie, "What time did she think David would be back with Margaret's sister?"

Jennie said, "Well it will depend whether they walk back, or manage to get a lift off Harold with his horse and cart." The girls parted at the five barred gate that led into the farm yard, Jennie went to feed the pigs while Linda went in doors to check on Margaret and make a drink of tea for everyone.

"I'm back she called out to Paul."

"I can see that." He replied nastily. "It's the use of my leg I have lost not my eye sight." Then Linda saw his mouth falling into his familiar sulk. As the kettle began to sing on the red hot coals Jennie came hurrying in to say, "She had seen a car coming up the road so hopefully David and his sister in law may have got a lift." She looked over at Paul but he was uncommunicative. "Look." pointed Linda. "The car is coming down here it's just crossing the bridge." Linda hurried over to the window to get a better look, just as David and his sister in law stepped out of the Doctor's car. As Jennie scolded the tea the three of them walked in.

Gladys went over to the girls and kissed them on the cheek saying. "I have heard all about you girls, David said he would never of managed without you, but I'm here now." As she turned and took a pinny out of her bag and proceeded to tie it round her waist, and then went over to Paul but he just turned his head and ignored her. David had taken the Doctor upstairs; Margaret was sleeping and running a high temperature, but woke when the Doctor put his cool hand on her brow, she tried to sit up but without Jennie or Linda's hand supporting her she flopped back down after she had been examined the Doctor spoke to David saying. "Just as well I came, your wife has pneumonia I can see she has been well looked after, but it will be a long time before she is well again, he rubbed his chin as he said "would it make it easier for you David if I admitted her to hospital?

"No I'm not having Margaret going to hospital, she has never been into hospital in all her life, and besides I have just brought Gladys up to stay and look after her, and I have got two good lasses for the farm work and our Judith comes and gives a hand when she can." David and the Doctor were still having a conversation as they walked down the stairs. As they stepped into the kitchen Gladys was waiting to find out what was ailing Margaret.

The Doctor spoke and included them all as he said. "Margaret will need a lot of looking after if she is to get over the pneumonia, she has been well looked after by these two girls but I should of been called in earlier, I am pleased to know that you are staying here to help as well Gladys." Then he turned to Paul and asked. "How are you doing now young man it s a while now since I saw you, are you managing to get a round alright with the crutches?" Paul scowled at him as he said, "What do you bloody think? I walk ten miles a day? You're just like the rest of them." Then he turned his head and ignored as he heard his father's intake of breath with embarrassment, as Gladys mind was trying to assimilate what she had been told, as pneumonia was a terrible illness and not everyone pulled through it David should of came for her straight away but it was no use crying over spilt milk she was here now and she would do her best for Margaret. The Doctor started to put his pork pie hat on his head as David handed him his two shilling and sixpence. Then the Doctor said. "Thank you David I will be back tomorrow." As he handed Margaret's tablets to Gladys, Linda opened the door for him, and as the Doctor made his way through the yard his driver old Harry got out of the car with the starting handle in his hand and strode purposely to the front of the car in an attempt to start it, sometimes it took a few turns to get it going he was lucky tonight after one turn the engine burst into life. The Doctor was already in the car gathering his thoughts.

Harry jumped in beside him and asked. "Where would you like to go to now Doctor?" When there was no reply, Harry repeated his question.

"I 'm sorry Harry what did you say?"

"I was just wondering Doctor where do you want to go next, only you have never said a word since we left Emmerson's farm."

"Oh yes you've just reminded me I have to call and see old Mrs Wilkinson."

"Right Doc." Harry replied,

The Doctor cleared his throat. "I know I can trust you Harry not to talk about the patients." and after a long drawn out breath said. You know I went to see Margaret Emmerson tonight at the Emmerson's farm, and they are sociable people, Paul was always a canny lad so is his brother and sister, but tonight when I went over to speak to Paul he was so derogatory, and I've been thinking about him since I walked out of their door.

"Why is that Doctor? Maybe he isn't well, and may be a bit downed cooped up in the house all day."

"No Harry I think all this nastiness off Paul stems from feeling useless and its time he got off his backside and tried to get on with his life."

"So what can anyone do for him?" asked Harry

"Well the hall is a convalescent home now as you know we visit it plenty, and I think it would do him good to have some physiotherapy, I know Paul can be very stubborn and at the moment has a bad attitude problem but if we can get him mobile I think he will be a changed man."

Harry shook his head. "I can't see Paul going there, and who is going to be tough enough to go with him? Because if Margaret was fit enough she isn't strong minded and Paul would have her in tears."

The Doctor laughed, "I am going to be at the Emmerson's farm every day until Margaret has pulled round, so I am going to talk to Paul, and I have someone in mind to accompany him."

"Who will that be then?" Harry enquired.

"It will be the strong minded one; I will tell her in the morning her names Linda." And with that sorted in his mind he sat back to enjoy the passing countryside.

Along at the pub Tommy wished his life was easy, all this trouble and it wasn't his fault, but once Lizzie got hold of something she was like a dog with a bone. Tommy thought it is only my sister's daughter coming to stay for a while, to hear Lizzie talk you would think it was the bloody devil. Tommy was just coming through from the cellar when Lizzie shouted "Have you filled the coal scuttles and rubbed all the tables down? I know I will have to manage on my own tonight."

"I don't know why you are making such a fuss Lizzie it's only our niece, my sister's lass that's coming to stay a while."

"Well you can please yourself Tommy Gibson, niece or no niece I say she will be trouble just like your sister, but you can look after her because I'm not." Tommy thought he would keep quiet and give Lizzie time to calm down a bit, she was a good woman but he had never won a row with her yet. He had tried talking to her the other night and she had vexed him so he had shouted at her then they had a big row, and he'd ended up sleeping in the spare room so in future he would try and keep the peace."

Lizzie was busy at the sink when Tommy walked into the kitchen. "I'm not happy about this at all Tommy; it will all end in tears."

"No it won't lass; I'll put my foot down with Elsie the minute she steps down from the train, I know it's a long time since we saw her, she was only a little lass and If our Polly has got herself another fella the bairn maybe feels left out."

Lizzie promptly turned round and faced Tommy saying. "She is not a little lass Tommy. She is fourteen, and if she causes any trouble at all she is out, and you with her if you let me down. Our three bairns are all up and married they have never been a hap'orth of bother so I don't see why we have to be lumbered with your sisters troubles."

Tommy was weary he hadn't realized how much bother there would be when that letter had arrived last week from his sister Polly, he hadn't seen her for years she had left the dale in a hurry more years ago then he cared to remember, breaking his mothers heart, she was a one for the men, and got herself a bad name. And then one day she arrived back as if she hadn't been away with two kiddies and no man. Aye when he thought about it Lizzie had been good then taking her and the bairns in, his sister never did a hands turn and didn't have a penny to her name. Lizzie was the one who looked after them while Polly lay in bed, and the night it blew up he had never seen Lizzie as mad, she had told Polly to find somewhere else to live and get her lazy self out of bed on a morning. Next morning when they got up Polly had gone leaving her children behind he had to hand it to Lizzie she hadn't kicked the kids out, she brought them up as her own and they look on Lizzie as their mother. "I have been thinking Lizzie. Elsie could maybe help you for awhile till she can find a job." Tommy wished he had kept his mouth shut as Lizzie said;

"I am not having her here under my feet all day, and if she's anything like her mother housework will be more as an afterthought rather than a habit."

"Well the bairn will need to do something Lizzie until she makes friends with the local and land girls."

Lizzie turned and stared at Tommy with her hand on her hips. "For God's sake Tommy, how many times do I have to tell you she is no bairn, and besides she has a job to go too?"

Tommy looked shocked. "What are you talking about Lizzie? The lass hasn't arrived yet so how can she of got a job."

Lizzie sharply replied. "She has just left school so she needs a job we cannot afford to keep her, so I have got her one. She starts at the hall or should I say the convalescent home for the sick and wounded servicemen on Monday morning."

"When did this come about Lizzie? You've kept this quiet, don't you think Elsie should have had time to settle in first, it's bound to affect her having to leave our Polly."

"Now look here Tommy, I am sick of hearing about Elsie, and your sister Polly, I think Polly has a cheek asking us to take another one in for her while she goes off with a different fella, if she thought anything about her daughter she would of taken her with them, but as it is Elsie is coming here, so as long as she behaves herself she has a home here with us and a job to go too on Monday, and you will be going to the station to pick her up on the motor bike shortly."

The big black train stood at the station blowing out steam waiting for its passengers. The station was packed everyone coming and going, among those people rushing for the train was Maureen Winter. It had been nine months since she had stood on this same platform saying good bye to her three children who had been evacuated, she had not seen them since and it broke her heart The only thing that had helped was the long letters she'd received from Pat the children's foster parent and her mother in law Doris, about the children. Maureen rubbed the back of her hand across her cheeks as the tears kept coming as her other hand held a small cardboard case, and the ubiquitous cardboard box containing her gasmask. Nine months ago she had put the three children on the train Mary, Amy and George, and said she would be with them in a few weeks, but she had gone back to work in the munitions factory for a short time to get some money. She had no home of her own so she had stayed with old Ida, which had suited them both as Ida was lonely on her own, Maureen missed the children desperately and how she hated her job but it cost her ten shilling and sixpence every week for the first child and eight shilling and sixpence for each additional child for the foster parents who the children were billeted with. Maureen only earned three pounds a week in the factory. She knew the government reimbursed parents with six shillings a week per child if parents couldn't afford it but Maureen had it to pay as her husband had army pay until he had abandoned her and left her destitute. But although she was working, she couldn't even go on the cheap day return

147

tickets the railway offered. Maureen's job was to weigh the cordite into linen bags and sew the gunpowder on the top, this was put into twenty five pounder shells, but it was her friends who had died today in the accident those who had been putting the detonators on the top. Maureen was still crying as she was running now for the train, it had affected her badly. The night before when the bombs were dropping and she was on the late shift she knew old Ida would be safe enough as she always went to the shelters. Maureen guessed it was for company as well as safety, only a stray bomb had landed on the shelter killing everyone. And on the same day Shirley hadn't tucked her hair into her turban properly and it had caught in the machine scalped her she had died before they got her out of the factory. Maureen rubbed her nose on her coat sleeve as she remembered Ida taking her and the children in when they were bombed out. She had been lucky today when so many of her friend had been killed and badly injured, so now she was going to her children, she had just got to the turnstile to buy a ticket when the train was ready to go, she paid for the ticket and ran as the guard had the flag raised.

Maureen cried out. "Please don't let it go without me." The station was packed with men and woman in air force blue intermingling with army khaki, sailor's wrens American soldiers and the girls in brown and green. The W L A. The man standing near the guard saw Maureen and tapped the guard on the shoulder and pointed to Maureen running as fast as her legs would carry her, he dropped the flag as soon as Maureen climbed aboard she was lucky to get a window seat, she was leaving the city behind but she would see the fields as the train sped by on her way to Teesdale. The whistle went and the train was off. Maureen had no idea what to expect as she had never been in the country before but she was on her way now, to see her beloved children and whatever life threw at her now she would always have her children with her.

Maureen woke up and looked around bleary eyed, she felt disorientated, her legs were stiff but there was no room to stretch them out, she had a kink in her neck as her head and body had been squashed against the train window. She regretted not having something to eat earlier today as the thick stale cloying smell of cigarettes and pipe smoke, along with an odour of stale unwashed bodies was making her feel nauseous. Maureen looked over at the girl sitting opposite she was as thin as a pikestaff and her belongings were stuffed in an empty sand bag, and later as the night was getting darker she was almost indistinguishable in her black clothes. Maureen smiled at the girl sitting in her miss matched clothes her woollen skirt showing under the black coat which was too big for her needed darning, she resembled some of the girl, Maureen had seen, that lived in the filthy warrens of slums where disease flourished and starvation was part of everyday life, and where the cold penetrated their thin clothes and bare feet. Maureen felt sorry for the girl as a tear rolled down her cheek, so she leaned over and patted the girl's knee, just as the train pulled into another station making room for the girl to sit next to her. The girl named Elsie gave Maureen along scrutinising look before moving across the carriage to sit next to her.

CHAPTER NINE

"Hello I'm Maureen are you going far?" Maureen tried to make friends with the girl.

After a long silence the girl Elsie, said. "I'm being sent to live with my Uncle and aunt." as she rubbed her nose on her sleeve.

Maureen smiled at the girls as she asked her, "Where do they live?"

"In the Dales that's all I was told I have not even met them." Elsie answered sourly. Maureen was beginning to find the silence between them oppressive and Elsie's expression more sombre then joyful. Maureen lit a cigarette and wondered how much longer it would take to get there. Just then the whistle blew and more service men and woman boarded the train so Elsie was squashed up close to Maureen.

The American soldier who had caused this quash said. "I'm sorry honey are you all right, would you like some candy?"

"Oh yes please, I haven't had anything to eat today." The solider handed some candy and chocolate to Elsie, and smiled kindly at Maureen as if they were together. Maureen was hungry herself but she wasn't going to have the solider thinking that the girl had anything to do with her as she did look unkempt.

"We have just met on this train she said as she pointed to Elsie haven't we love." Elsie nodded her head to agree as her mouth was full of chocolate.

The solider introduced himself. "I'm Dale pleased to meet you; we are on our way to camp."

Maureen said "I'm on my way to see my three children I haven't seen them for nine months, I hope they haven't forgotten me."

Dale tried to reassure her. "Oh they will be watching for you, as they will be excited I know I would be if I could see my Mam, but when that will be I don't know." he sighed.

Maureen rubbed a tear from her eyes as she told him. "They don't know I'm coming." Then went on to tell him how she had lost poor old Ida, and some of her friends being killed at work. The solider listened sympathetically as he shared his cigarettes with her. Maureen had forgotten about Elsie as she hadn't been inclined to talk, but as the girl wiped her mouth on the back of her hand she nudged Maureen and said,

"I'm frightened, I have never been in the country before and I know I won't like the animals, I have always lived in the flat above the cafe where my Mam worked, but she has gone off with her boyfriend Ralph, she said she couldn't take me. I have to live with my Aunt and Uncle." Then she cried. "What will I do if they don't want me either?"

Maureen's heart went out to the young girl as she put her arms around the thin shoulders. "Now come on stop crying I will look after you, will there be anyone there to meet you off this train?"

Elsie hic upped and rubbed her nose on her dirty sleeve. "My Uncle is supposed to be meeting me on his motorbike."

"I will wait with you then until your Uncle arrives." Maureen thought she must be mad offering to help when she didn't know where she was heading and it would be dark soon. She was wishing she hadn't come, but she was desperate to see her children. Elsie was feeling tired, her eyes felt heavy she couldn't keep them open, it wasn't long till the rhythm of the train lulled her to sleep. Maureen thought Elsie was just sitting quiet until she felt her head loll on to her shoulder, and then she realized Elsie was sound asleep. The solider said I get off at the next station as he stretched up to the luggage rack to retrieve his kitbag, as the train slowed down he leaned over and kissed Maureen on the cheek and whispered. "Hope everything goes alright for you." Then he was gone lost among the steam and smoke off the train as the stoker threw more coal on to the blazing fire next to the boiler, to keep the steam up. After an hour had passed Maureen was feeling uncomfortable she tried to shuffle as her left side had stiffened up with Elsie's weight against her, but as she moved Elsie's eyes opened.

The girl looked horrified, "I'm so sorry." she said as she moved as far as the small space would allow.

"That's alright." Maureen said smiling down at Elsie; "I should think we will soon be getting off, and I'll be pleased to stretch my legs, only it is awfully dark out there, I should have waited till tomorrow and come in the daylight."

"I am pleased you didn't as I would have been on my own, as I only have you." Elsie told her truthfully.

"It will be alright once your Uncle comes and picks you up." Maureen tried to jolly her along. As the train chugged into the station Maureen's stomach churned she didn't know what lay ahead it was dark and just starting to thunder as the heavy night became unbearable, she had also taken this girl into her care. As Maureen opened the train door and stepped down on to the platform the warm rain splashed her face, she turned around to make sure Elsie was following; she took the small hand torch out of her bag as she said. "I think we will follow this path it will probably lead to the road, this torch doesn't give off much light but I suppose it's better than nothing. Just then a crack of lightning suddenly illuminated the road ahead a great clap of thunder followed almost at once. Maureen instinctively got hold of Elsie and hurried her over to the gable end of a house to shelter. "Did your mother write and inform your Uncle when you would be arriving?" Maureen asked Elsie. I don't know answered Elsie as it started to pour down.

Up at the pub Tommy was trying to kick the bike into life. Two men who had been visiting the toilets stopped to watch Tommy.

"I don't think it's going to start tonight Tommy I would leave if I was you." One of them remarked Tommy was getting impatient with it, tonight of all nights, it had let him down, and he should have been at the station. Lizzie was busy in the bar people were holding their glasses up and trying to get her attention.

Linda was waiting at the bar she had been stood for a while and saw Lizzie getting more and more frustrated, so she lifted the hinged flap and went behind the bar saying to Lizzie. "I'll help you tonight, seen as you are on your own Tommy mightn't belong." She speculated hopefully.

Lizzie nodded and smiled at Linda and as she walked behind her to reach for a bottle she whispered. "You land girls are good girls." Meanwhile outside Tommy was wet and weary, he tried once more to kick the bike over and then he would have to walk the three miles to meet his niece, only he would have to walk the three miles back. Then he thought what if she isn't there he was over an hour late now, one last kick and the bike roared into life. Tommy jumped on the bike hoping she hadn't wandered off if he had to look for her it would be like looking for a needle in a haystack as he had never seen her before and it was dark.

Maureen looked round the side of the gable end and sadly said. "I can't stand here any longer Elsie; I am going to walk into the village."

"Please don't leave me." Elsie cried.

"Come with me then as we can't stand here all-night." They picked up their possessions and set off towards the village. Tommy was looking for his niece on the top road, he had had ridden up and down and couldn't find her, and he couldn't go home without her, he was sick of today. Lizzie wasn't sociable towards him because of his niece; the bike had refused to start until it was nearly too late and now he was soaked and God knows where the girl had gone. He made his mind up he would go down to the village and ask if anyone had seen a young girl he couldn't even give anyone a description of her.

Maureen and Elsie were walking wearily into the village holding on tightly to the torch which was illuminating a path through the darkness, when they heard the motorbike; they turned round as the bike passed them. Tommy was looking for one girl, on her own, not mother and daughter as he thought they were. Tommy rode round and as he came upon the couple again he noticed their bags and thought they might have seen his niece, he pulled up beside them and switched the engine off so they could hear him.

"Sorry to bother you," Tommy shouted. "I am looking for my niece; I was supposed to pick her up over an hour since only the bike wouldn't start." Before he had chance to finish what he was saying Elsie cried. "Are you Uncle Tommy?"

"Yes I am." Tommy said smiling, but hoping this wasn't his sister Polly or there would be all hell let loose with Lizzie if he took her back to the pub.

Maureen stepped forward saying. "We met on the train and I have stayed with her, I couldn't leave her on her own until you came but now you are here. She leaned over and kissed Elsie on the cheek saying "take care, and good luck, I hope everything works out." As she picked up her case to walk away Tommy said, "I haven't thanked you yet for taking care of Elsie, and where are you heading too? "

Maureen turned and said. "I'm on my way to see my three children, who are evacuees living with a family called Greens, Pat and Michael; I don't suppose you know of them? Oh I wish I'd come up here in the daylight."

Tommy smiled at her. "I do know the family very well, they live near me lovely people they are, your children have been well cared for. Come on, who is getting on behind me?" he would reciprocate her for what she had done for Elsie. Neither Maureen nor Elsie had been on a motorbike before but Maureen could see the girl didn't want to ride on the pillion so she said. "You get into the sidecar Elsie, and I'll get on behind your Uncle." Tommy didn't go fast but Maureen was still terrified, as she thought it was perilous in the dark as the lights on the bike were no better than a candle, and she was going up a lonely road on a motorbike with a man she'd never met before, but she kept telling herself it could of been worse she could of spent the night walking round, and round. And now she would see her children.

Tommy turned down a dark lane the branches were leaning over the lane from one side to the other as if they were joining hands, as she got off the bike an owl hooted in the distance. It disturbed Maureen she had never been in the country before and didn't think she was going to like it, her confidence had faded and she was visualizing stuck in some field all night.

The lights were on in the house that Tommy had pointed out to her, as she stepped off the bike. Just then the door opened and light spilt out and a man stood in the doorway with his shirt sleeves rolled up to his elbows. Michael Green lifted his hand and acknowledged Tommy, while he looked at Maureen and asked. "Can I help you?"

"I have come to see my children." She cried, "Mary, Amy and George."

"Oh you must be Mrs Winter, Come in." Michael ushered her into the house. Pat his wife looked up and they exchanged significant looks and then she poured the scolding water out of the kettle, as she made their nightly cup of cocoa, while Doris his mother was sitting engrossed in her knitting, she finished the row she was busy doing then laid the knitting aside while she turned and spoke to Maureen, as Pat handed her a welcome cup of cocoa.

"Well it is nice to meet you Mrs Winter." Doris said to Maureen. "Have you been travelling all day, or did you finish work early?"

"I have finished working in the munitions for good; she felt overwhelmed with misery and tears where not far away. My friend's hair was hanging out of her turban and it got caught in the machine and scalped her, she died before they got her to the hospital." She said with a sob.

"I expect you're eager to see your children." Pat said smiling at Maureen. "Come on they are sound asleep but it will be a wonderful surprise for them in the morning."

"Oh dear." Maureen cried out with her hand to her mouth. "I didn't realize it was so late, and I haven't found anywhere to stay yet, I'm sorry you must think me such a fool turning up here late at night and nowhere to stay." Michael had been sitting quietly listening to his wife and mother, talking to Maureen.

Then he spoke saying. "Course you have somewhere to stay lass, we have plenty of room here."

"Yes we have." Pat told her. "And you're very welcome I daresay you could do with a bit of company as well."

"Thank you." said Maureen with feeling, as tears of gratitude rolled down her face.

Pat lifted the sneck on the bedroom door and both woman tip-toed quietly across the bedroom floor. Maureen saw George first, sleeping soundly in his single bed. She leaned over and gently brushed his cheek with her lips as a tear slid down her face. As she straightened up Pat put a comforting arm around Maureen's shoulder as she led her over to the double bed, where Mary and Amy lay cuddled up together under the thick patchwork quilt. Maureen stood looking down at her sleeping daughters with their fair hair spread across the pillows. She would have loved to wrap her arms around them and tell them she was here and she loved them. But instead she went back out of the bedroom as quietly as she had come in, her face wet with tears. Anguish and frustration had made her more tearful.

Back downstairs in the kitchen Doris had made them all another hot drink and a thick ham sandwich and a thick wedge of cake for Maureen, as she guessed that Maureen probably hadn't had a bite all day. They all sat talking until late, as Maureen's feet sank deep in to the bright peg mat that covered the stone floor and told them all about Ida, and then looking after Elsie. "I just hope they look after her at the pub, mind you her Uncle seemed a decent type."

"She will be well looked after as long as she doesn't cause any bother." Doris remarked. "Lizzie and Tommy brought three kids of their own up, and then Polly came to stay with her two little girls and not a man in sight, you know what I mean." she shook her head as she tooted. "Unmarried and bold as brass, she left all the work to Lizzy and when Lizzie pulled her up about it she packed her clothes and went leaving the two little girls with Lizzie and Tommy to bring up. The two girls are grown up now and two nice girls they have turned out, they look on Tommy and Lizzie as parents. Then out of the blue they get a letter saying Polly is going off with another fancy man, and she is sending her third daughter up here." As Doris had been talking Maureen had eaten the food they had made for her she hadn't realized how hungry she was.

Michael stood up saying. "It's getting late, I suggest we go to bed you three can talk in the morning."

Pat handed the paraffin lamp to Maureen and said. "There will be plenty of room for you in the double bed with your daughters." Maureen was very tired but didn't think she would sleep a wink, but as soon as she slipped in beside her girls her eyes closed.

"Mammy" Maureen heard the cry, and opened her eyes as three little faces were looking down at her, all talking at once, she opened her arms as they all fell into them Maureen could hardly speak for the lump in her throat. Just then the bedroom door was banged opened and Beryl stood scowling in the doorway. Then she ran downstairs into Pats open arms.

Down the village at the pub, Lizzie was leaning over the fire, frying bacon for breakfast. Elsie had fallen asleep straight away last night she had been dreading, meeting her Auntie Lizzie, who she had never heard of till last week and she was unsure of her welcome although Uncle

Tommy seemed kind enough. The feather bed had been comfortable with plenty of blankets something Elsie wasn't used too. And now as she crept into the warm kitchen she didn't know what to say to her Aunt.

Lizzie turned and looked over her shoulder as she heard her niece approaching. "Are you hungry Elsie? As we always have bacon and eggs for breakfast, you can butter the bread while I finish frying our breakfasts."

Tommy walked through the door yawning and asked. "Did you sleep well Elsie?"

"Yes I did." She answered shyly.

Just then Lizzie pushed a plate full of eggs and bacon in front of her saying. Come on eat up, you need some meat on those bones, and after we have eaten our breakfasts we will have to go and get you some decent clothes I have a few coupons and I'm sure Rita at the shop will be alright if I haven't got enough, you have brought your ration book haven't you Elsie?"

"Yes it's in my bag." She stood up to get it.

"Sit down Elsie." Lizzie demanded, Eat your breakfast there's plenty of time, as long as we get you some decent clothes before Monday."

"Why Monday Auntie, Am I going somewhere?"

Lizzie carried on eating her breakfast as she said, you have left school now haven't you Elsie? So I asked for you a job up at the hall which has been requisitioned and is now a convalescence home for servicemen."

Elsie's face was a picture of woe, and she felt deflated. "I thought I was going to stay with you and Uncle Tommy." She didn't relish the thought of been moved to some more folk she didn't know.

Lizzie smiled at her. "Of course you're staying here with us, but you have to have a job and the hall is just up the road so you will be able to walk up every day, so eat your breakfast up and then we will go and get you some new clothes." Tommy had eaten his breakfast and now moved over to sit in the armchair beside the fire to enjoy his mug of sweet tea before he started work in the cellar. As he sat down he looked over at Lizzie and Elsie still finishing their breakfasts and said as he looked thoughtfully.

"Do you remember Lizzie, when I took those clothes coupons to buy some new clothes for Ethel's wedding? And I never bought anything; well I've just thought I've still got the coupons upstairs so you might as well use them today."

"Right we will Tommy and if you hurry up and drink your tea you can give me and Elsie a ride to the shops."

Along at Pat and Michael Greens house things were hectic. Everyone was sitting down to breakfast; Doris could see they were both worrying, about the lodge just down the road, it had stood empty now for a while, and then last night Pat and Michael had been told to get everything sorted as they were caretakers for the hall, and lodge, as there was a whole lot of land girls on their way. Doris didn't know where they would start, as there were so many things to do. Mary and Amy where smiling at Maureen while little George had never left his mother's side, Beryl had a scowl on her face as she had refused to sit at the table and eat her breakfast, and then she had knocked Marys drink of tea over her so Marys dress was to change, then she had ran back over to the settee and refused to come back to the table and eat her breakfast. Michael had enough of her antics over the time she had been with them so he walked over and picked her up and unceremoniously placed her back on the chair, and with the threat of spending her day in bed she started to eat her breakfast.

Maureen said. "I'm going to have to make some arrangements, but seen as I don't know my way round here, or know anyone I was wondering if you could help me please?"

Pat had been dreading this happening she knew the children's mother could call anytime and take their children back but she loved these children as if they were her own.

"What do you want to do?" Pat enquired hoping her voice sounded normal as possible. Maureen said. "I don't know anything about country life, but I have made my mind up I'm not leaving my children again although." she added. "You have been like a mother to them." Pat thought about it and then said. "I will help you all I can, well we all will, if you can wait for a few days, as we have been told we have to have the grange up and running within a couple of days as there is a whole lot of land girls coming. "Oh I don't mind helping to clean out the lodge I would feel as if I am paying you back for letting me stay." "Oh I couldn't let you start cleaning that place out you've only just come here." Doris was sitting listening.

And then she said, "I know it has nothing to do with me, and as you know Pat I never interfere, but I would take Maureen up on her offer as there is a lot of things to do and you haven't much time."

Maureen stood up shoving her chair back and with the palms of her hands flat on the table pushed herself up, saying. "Right that is settled then, where do I start?"

An hour later saw the little party making their way down the road armed with buckets sweeping brushes floor cloths and Pat carrying her jars of black-lead. She looked at Maureen as she nodded towards old Jim sitting on the seat with his dog beside him. "This is Jim sitting on this seat just down here," she told Maureen. "He is a good talker I think he gets to know what people are doing before they know themselves." She laughed. "And he likes to see what's going on but he has an opinion on everything."

They had reached the seat Jim looked up and asked. "Who's this then?" He asked Pat as he pointed to Maureen. "I've never seen her round here before, and where are you all going? With your arms full of cleaning tackle" Pat remarked. "We haven't time to stand and talk this morning Jim, but we are going to clean the lodge, as there are a lot of land girls on their way here and that is where they are going to stay."

"Oh I don't think its right." he said as he took the pipe out of his mouth. "These bits of lasses putting the bull to the cows, no I don't see that being right." He said as he shook his head. "You can't put lass to do a man's job I don't think it's right, mind you," he said as he pointed the stem of the pipe at Pat. "I do think them lasses that live with Ethel are a hardy bunch, outside working in all weathers, not like them bloody P O Ws. Have you heard about them?" And then not waiting for an answer he said. Those prisoners are having better working conditions then the land girls, oh Aye they won't work out in wet weather, and they work a shorter day, and they get a lift to the farms in a wagon or sometime a coach, and Linda that works at Emmerson's farm she puts Paul in his place, a real good worker her and her friend Jennie I think her name is." Pat said, "I'm sorry Jim, but we must go otherwise the lodge won't be ready for the girls."

"Oh just a minute could you tell me before you go." Jim shouted, as they started to walk away. "Who is going to be in charge then? A warden probably as somebody, will have look after them?" Pat stopped and looked at Jim.

"Do you know Jim I bet nobody has thought about it, I definitely hadn't oh dear that's another problem I'd never thought about." As the two woman made their way through the garden gate,

Pat said. "I am sorry you have to clean on your first day here."

"I don't mind." Maureen replied. "You have looked after my children for nine month."

"I will be sorry to see them go though." Pat miserably told Maureen. "Oh but I have to get a job first and somewhere to live, so we might be with you for a while yet, but first thing on Monday I will look for a job." As Pat was putting the key into the door she turned and laughed at Maureen. "I have found you a job." Maureen didn't understand. "What do you mean Pat?" "Well you can be the new warden looking after the girls and live here, that way you have a job, and a home, the children are just down the road from me and I will be on hand if ever you need me." Maureen was astounded. "But who will give me the job I don't know anything about cooking for thirty girls oh dear I don't think I can do it."

Pat turned the key and the old door creaked open, it was freezing inside the house as there had been no fires lit for two years. They walked straight through the long passages to the huge kitchen where they put all the brushes and cloths, Mary, Amy and George ran upstairs to see what it was like, as Beryl had stayed with Doris. Pat stood with her hands on her hips surveying the dirty kitchen and big cooking range surrounded by mouse droppings. Maureen picked up the brush and headed upstairs to see the mess she would have to clean, While Pat made a start on the range before she could light it. An hour later Pat sat back on her heels and surveyed her handiwork, she had just finished cleaning and black leading the kitchen range, with the black lead that came in blocks like soap, Pat had kept it in a jam jar then poured water over it then working at it to produce a paste which she had brushed on to the range then she had polished it till it met with her satisfaction.

Just then Maureen came through to the kitchen looking hot, and flustered, some of her blonde curls had escaped from her turban as she had brushed out all the bedrooms, she smiled when she saw the range shinning and a good fire starting to burn. Pat said. "I think we deserve a cup of tea,"

Just then they heard the door open and Doris came in smiling holding a big brown teapot, in one hand and two cups in the other. "Run up home she told the children and fetch the bag of food I've put up." "I have put both sugar and milk in to the teapot; I thought you wouldn't mind I thought it would be easier to carry if it was all in the same pot."

"Oh thank you." Both women chorused. "Aye I thought you would both be ready for a drink, I've done my share of cleaning it dries your throat, more so with all this muck and dust."

The children came running in carrying the bag as Michael followed carrying three wooden chairs. "I thought you might like to sit and drink your tea." he told them. "And you can stay here as well." He told Beryl. "I will be busy this afternoon." Then he turned to Pat saying. Oh that smoke is not going out of the chimney I should think after all this time it will be full of birds nest we are lucky the fire is not burning well he turned to Maureen as he said it never does when the chimney is damp. He ran his hand through his hair as he said they will need some furniture for this place, I'll have to have a look in the attics where all the spare furniture is kept, and I wonder if Walter is busy tomorrow. I will ask him to help me bring it down." "I have found a home and a job for Maureen." Pat told her bewildered Husband and mother- in –law. "How have you done that?" I don't understand you have been here all morning." Doris Said. "Well they are going to need a warden to look after this place, and the land girls will need meals, Maureen needs a job and she would like a place of her own and she will be just down the road from us." Michael and his mother looked knowingly at each other and smiled they both knew what was behind the job; it was so Pat could still see the children.

The door opened again and it was Sarah, who lived across the yard in Badger cottage, which belonged to the lodge, her husband had worked all his life for the estate so when he retired he could stay in the house rent free.

"It Is true that this place is opening up again? I have just come down the road and met old Jim; he said we are getting about thirty land girls. Just think about that. Thirty land girls on the loose." "Oh." She chuckled. "There will be a lot of woman keeping an eye on their wayward husbands."Pat looked locked in thought as she said "I suppose some of them will play away," then she laughed as she said, "Will you be keeping an eye on Charlie? Sarah laughed as she said. "He'll not play away lass, it takes him all his time to play at home and then she started to cough your chimney needs cleaning I bet there is a jackdaws nest in it." "Yes I'm going to clean it once the range has cooled down." They were all laughing and never heard the woman knocking loudly she had come in her car to sort the accommodation out for the land girls.

Mary heard the knock so opened the door and invited her in. The woman were shocked to see this stuck up woman standing in the kitchen and looking at them as if they were something she'd stood in. Pat was the first to stop laughing so she asked. "Can I help you love?"

"I have come to look over the accommodation for my land girls who will be arriving in the morning." Pat repeated "In the morning.". "They can't come tomorrow we are nowhere near ready." As she held her arm out to emphasize because all the work that needed doing.

I am Mrs Dixon; and I need to talk with whoever is going to be the warden here and I want this contract signing.

Maureen stepped forward saying. that is me, I'm going to look after the girls .Mrs Dixon looked Maureen up and down then with a sniff said I will be back next week to go through the paper work with you when there might be somewhere to sit without being disturbed and you will need their ration books as soon as they arrive and I hope you're going to get some fires going before the girls arrive." "Could you not of come a week or two earlier to warn us?" Pat asked "I have all my calls worked out, it is not my fault if you woman cannot clean the place in time or have someone to clean the chimneys." Pat felt the desire for pacification go out of the window. "Right Mrs Whatever your name is if you don't mind going we can get on and we will have it ready for the girls." and then she shepherded the stuck up little woman to the door. Pat stood still after shutting the door on the stuck up little woman, her mind trying to assimilate what she had been told.

Doris knowing her daughter in law better then what Pat thought shouted. "Don't stand there wondering how you are going to manage, we are all here to help you." The four women, and Michael and Charlie worked till ten o clock that night, cleaning, carrying furniture, bedding, and doing whatever needed doing. So it was agreed between them, that Maureen and her children would move in tomorrow morning, and Sarah who had time on her hands and would welcome extra money would work there helping with the cooking and cleaning. Pat stood smiling it was working out, but as she said. "We could do with a young girl to run messages and help to clean, also to help with all the washing up." "I know just the girl." Sarah told her. "I met her with her aunt this morning, she was going to start work at the hall but someone had called and said the lass that were leaving had changed her mind. I will send Charlie down tonight to say there is a job for her here, he will be pleased to do that errand he will be able to have a pint she laughed."

Maureen got a shock on Monday morning when the young girl turned up, and said "I'm so pleased to be working for you Maureen." "And I'm pleased to have you Elsie" She answered." Maureen knew the voice without turning round.

Waterloo station was packed with all nationalities', in every coloured uniform. The noise and giggling was coming from the green and brown. The land girls were on the move.

The train came steaming into the station. The doors were opened and some clashed shut just as quick as everyone clamoured in hoping for a seat. The land girls pushed and shoved with the best of them, carrying all their worldly possessions in borrowed and battered cases. Ruth jumped in and had her makeup out and putting extra lipstick on before the rest of them had found a seat; her hair was swept back in elaborate curls. "Does anyone want to borrow this lippy?" She asked, as she held it out to anyone that needed it. Betty was digging in her bag shoving her elbows in to Jean's ribs. Jean asked. "What the hell are you doing Betty? I'm going to be black and blue before this bloody train sets off." "I'm looking for me fags." Betty Answered. A good looking yank leaned over and offered his lucky strike around, as they all took one so he had to take another packet out of his bag; he smiled at Jean and asked."Where are you going?" "We are going to Teedale." She laughed, as she inhaled a lungful of smoke.

A few days had passed since Dr Hardy had first examined Margaret, and the medicine he had given her had at least eradicated her pain sufficiently to be able to rest properly while her breathing slowly improved. She was a long way from being well, but she was getting properly looked after. Dr Hardy was calling everyday and every time he called he took notice of Paul, who used to be such a lovely lad, but he looked so sad now, probably due to Margaret's incapacitation. Dr Hardy made his mind up if he was to help Paul he had best do it while Margaret couldn't interfere so after seeing to Margaret he walked over and sat down beside Paul. Dr Hardy cleared his throat as he looked at Paul saying. "I have something in mind for you young man, I would like to see you walking again unaided, and so I am going to see the physiotherapist up at the hall you will have to go up there and they will get your legs moving properly and then in time we can have you fitted for an artificial leg he looked at Pauls leg as he was explaining, well you don't need a full leg it is only the little bit above the ankle and a foot. "Its bloody plenty isn't it?" Paul shouted he was so angry his jugular vein looked as if it would burst. "I know it's not easy for you Paul that is why I am going to get you an appointment." "Well you needn't bloody bother because I'm not going." Dr Hardy stood up picking his pork pie hat off the table, and saying I will be back tomorrow again to check on your wife David, and I'll be having another talk with you young man as he pointed across at Paul. As Dr Hardy was making his way across the yard to his car he saw Linda and Jennie heading towards him, so he waited. As the girls got nearer he took off his hat and acknowledged them. "Could you help me Linda? He asked her. Yes if I can Linda answered hesitantly, but what is it? The Doctor explained what he had in mind for Paul. Linda was puzzled, "but what has it to do with me." She asked. "Well I think if you talk to him he might be agreeable." Linda said, "Oh no." as she backed away. "Paul and I don't see eye to eye now so he wouldn't listen to me." "Would you please give it a go Linda; I think if anyone can make him understand it will be you." As Linda and Jennie walked into the kitchen Paul bellowed. "I saw you talking to the bloody Doctor about me; well it's got nothing to do with you." "Yes I know that." Linda said smiling at Paul I told him you were so selfish you would rather sit here being waited on hand and foot, although there was enough work here to keep an army going I also told him you had ostracised yourself from former friends, I think you rather like sitting here being miserable."

"You bitch do you think I like being crippled?" Linda stared at Paul saying, "You must do or you would do something about it." Linda drank her cup of tea off in one go and refused a piece of cake, as she wanted to get back outside. Jennie did the same although she could have enjoyed a cake but she had a feeling Linda needed her. Gladys didn't know what to make of it. "The time you two have been here it was a waste of time calling, and it's a wonder the tea didn't scold your throats." As the back door closed behind the girls Linda said thanks for coming with me Jennie I couldn't stay in there any longer, I know Paul and me rub each other up the wrong way but I'm trying to help him I would go with him for the exercises to his legs but I think I have gone too far and the gulf widening between us is in danger of becoming unbridgeable.

The rest of the afternoon Paul was left in the kitchen on his own as Gladys was seeing to Margaret who was still very ill and everyone else was busy outside. Paul was sitting fuming about Linda how dare she say he wanted to stay like a cripple he wanted to be normal again. She had no idea what he had gone through in the army no one had he had kept it to himself. The bitch telling the Doctor he enjoyed being like this. Well she could think all she liked as his mind was made up he would show her, bloody miss know all just wait till Doctor Hardy came back in the morning.

The next morning Dr Hardy called early to see Margaret the rest of the house were having a late breakfast, as two cows had calved along with all the rest of the farm work they hadn't had time to stop. As the doctor came downstairs he popped in the kitchen as Gladys always had a drink of tea ready for him. "I will quickly drink this he smiled, and then I'll be on my way, also I'm pleased to say Margaret's temperature is staying normal, but I will still be calling everyday for a while as pneumonia is a nasty thing"

"Can I have a word before you go?" Paul asked as everyone went quiet. "Yes course you can." answered the Doctor. "Do you want to talk to me in private?" "No I don't. I want to tell you while Linda is here, seeing as she knows I like sitting here all day being a cripple and doing bugger all I will have the physiotherapy as soon as you can sort it for me." The atmosphere was strained until Linda jumped up putting her arms around Paul's neck saying. "That's the best thing I've heard in a long time, and don't worry you don't have to go on your own as I will be with you." Paul knew he should have been thanking Linda for instigating him, for if she hadn't of goaded him he would have sat here forever, but he didn't feel like thanking her. Paul looked up as he realized everyone was looking at him, he said as he looked at Linda, "I don't want you to come with me, but I don't suppose you'll take any notice, you will likely still tag along" as he sighed in resignation. Linda was sitting drinking her tea letting his brusqueness wash over her as it was second nature to Linda, as she thought Paul had acquired a hard exterior and showed little emotion, but it was just veneer that hid his vulnerability, she knew Paul better than he knew himself.

CHAPTER TEN

The next morning started early for everyone, Maureen woke and wondered where she was until she heard voices, and saw her three children looking down on her telling her that everyone was up. "Oh dear have I slept in?" she asked the children as she hurriedly threw the bedclothes aside and put her feet on to the bedside mat making sure not to touch the cold oilcloth.

"Go downstairs." she told her children. "Until I get dressed I won't be long." and then as the children left the room she yawned and realised although she was tired last night she had slept badly. Today the land girls were arriving how she was going to cook and look after thirty young women she had no idea. As she walked into the kitchen everyone was sitting eating breakfast apart from Michael who appeared hair tousled and braces round his hips.

"Come on have some breakfast." Pat told her as she patted the seat beside her.

"I don't think I can face any." Maureen told her as she sat down. "But a cup of tea would be welcome."

"You need some food inside you." Doris told her smilingly. "A good breakfast sets you up for the day." As Michael sat down at the table Pat got up and passed both Michael, and Maureen a plateful of egg and bacon that had been keeping warm for them. Maureen picked up her knife and fork as she knew it would be rude to leave such a good breakfast especially in wartime, and these kind people had welcomed her and her children into their home.

Pat looked keenly at Maureen as she said. "I expect you're a little nervous this morning, as I know you're not looking forward to the new job but you will be fine, you have us just up the lane and Sarah is helping with the cooking and you already know the young girl Elsie is she called? Who travelled up with you?" Maureen nodded and smiled as she cut a piece of bacon and dipped it into her fresh egg, and then looked over at her three well fed children and made her mind up she would enjoy her breakfast and then go and open up the lodge her and her children's new home and wait for the land girls.

Down at Emmerson's farm the morning had been particularly arduous for Paul, and consequently he was not in the best of moods. He was nervous; he didn't want to be like this all his life, he had tried twice this morning to have a shave, and just when he thought it was safe to put the razor blade to his throat to take off his whiskers Linda came dashing in from outside nearly knocking him over, as she took off her coat with a flourish nearly knocking the razor out of his hand, as he clung on to the table with his other hand, he turned and bellowed at her.

"You weren't happy knocking me over, you had to try and make me cut me bloody throat. Can't you see I'm trying to get a shave?"

Linda swung round glaring at him. "Don't you know, I'm rushing around trying to get all the work done so I can go with you?"

Paul shouted. "I didn't ask you too, in fact, I would rather you stayed here but no doubt if they start twisting my leg about you'll enjoy seeing me in agony." Gladys came bustling through to the kitchen to see what was going on.

"What is the matter now Paul?" She asked him. "You should be happy." And then before he had chance to shout at her she walked away, to meet the doctor coming downstairs from seeing Margaret.

Linda walked through at the same time as the Doctor told her. "You will be going up to the hall this morning with Paul, or should I say the convalescent home." "Oh yes" she said emphatically. "I have been rushing about all morning so I could take him."

Paul heard her as he was coming through the door on his crutches. "You don't have to go with Me." he scowled. "I can go on my own."

"Well I don't know how you're going to get there this morning, as it is still raining hard and you can't hurry on those crutches." Linda pointed out. Doctor Hardy said. "That's not a problem; I have to call there so I will drop you both off." The weather was atrocious torrential rain pouring relentlessly down from a cloudy sky. It was a slow walk to the Doctors car as Linda didn't like to run and leave Paul so her hair was soaked. His driver got out and turned the starting handle on the car.

As they made their way up to the hall they saw a bus standing on the grounds. The Doctor looked and said. "I wonder what that is doing here. It can't have brought anymore patients or I would have been told about it." The driver stopped the car right outside the main door with the canopy over so it saved them getting any wetter than what they were. As the main door opened to allow them in, Linda saw it was extremely noisy and heaving with people and then she realised. The land girls had arrived. They had been forced to come here as there had been no food delivered to the lodge. Maureen, Pat and Sarah had been smoked out when they had lit the big range, as there had been a huge Jackdaws nest on the top of the chimney so the smoke had come back into the room, so while Michael cleaned the chimney the land girls had been sent up to the hall and were staying there for dinner.

The hygienic smell of carbolic reached Linda's nose as she made her way along the corridors with Paul hopping along on his crutches by her side, "right." she said complacently "When your name is called, I will come in with you."

"There is no reason why you should come in with me Linda; I can manage on my own there was no need for you to come here with me." Just then one of the land girls walked towards them smiling seductively at Paul.

"Do you know where the toilets are in here?" she asked, looking directly at Paul and completely ignoring Linda. Before Paul had time to speak,

Linda said. "You will have to go and look for them the same as I will if I need to go."

"I was only asking." Ruth retorted. "And I wasn't asking you, I was asking him." as she looked at Paul and smiled. "I'm Ruth by the way." she said to Paul as she held out her hand Paul shook hands as Ruth started to walk away saying. "See you around I hope".

Linda was fuming as she turned and looked at Paul. "Who the hell does she think she is coming over to you as if she has known you for years?"

"Well she seems alright I suppose." said Paul. "As far as Land girls go."

"And what is that supposed to mean? And, after I've come here to help you."

Paul looked stunned. "How do you mean? You have come to help me, I didn't want you."

Linda said. "Well if that's all the thanks I get, you can come on your own next time." Not another word was spoken between them, as the big clock on the wall ticked away another hour. Linda left her seat and hurried to the toilet, she had come here with Paul she was determined she was going in with him to see who ever could help him. Just as she was walking down the corridor a nurse approached her and asked "if she would like a cup of tea?" "Yes please." answered Linda. "And could I have one for my friend?" Paul looked up as Linda held the cup out to him. "Thanks." he muttered as he accepted the hot tea and drank it gratefully.

"What did you just say?" Linda laughingly asked him. "That is the first decent word you have ever said to me."

"Well I've had a long time to sit and think, and Mam and Dad seem to think a bit about you." He never said no more as the nurse called him in; Linda jumped up and passed him his crutches. "I suppose your coming in then." Paul said but Linda noticed it wasn't said nastily.

Maureen knew it would be a huge task feeding all the girls. Sarah looked over at Maureen and could see the worry etched on her face, and felt sorry for her as she seemed nice lass. Sarah was just going to go over to her when Michael, having finished cleaning the chimney lit the big black range, and then sat back on his heels looking at the woman and saying.

"I have cleaned the main chimney so you woman can go and light all the fires." He rubbed his hands together as he said. "It will take a week or two to warm this place up and draw the damp out of the thick walls". Sarah put a protective arm around Maureen as she said. "Come on, let's get these fires going, I know you have no experience but make sure you get their ration books as soon as they set foot through those doors, and you have run your own home and raised three children and I'll be here so we will manage, besides we have a generator for lights so we won't be dependent on paraffin lamps."

Maureen felt very much disorganised as wardrobes, dressing tables bedding, and huge cooking utensils were carried in, she thought just as well it is such a huge kitchen as they had to use a trestle table and benches for the seating arrangement at meal times with so many girls arriving together. Maureen had never seen so much cutlery, plates or cups. She was just wondering what she would cook in them when a loud knock at the door startled the woman, and as Maureen was closets' to the door she opened it and realised the food had finally arrived. As the delivery men were leaving after filling the kitchen with sacks of potatoes, flour, and all the ingredients Maureen Sarah and Elsie would need to feed thirty hard working girls, Pat was just closing the door when she heard the noise of thirty girls laughing, and talking, and the sound of heavy shoes, announced the arrival of the land girls. Maureen after much deliberation jumped up smiling and announced. "Everything is finally ready."

Sarah couldn't believe her eyes, as the girls trooped in. laughing and talking, their eye brows were plucked, their lashes stiff with mascara, and lips blood red, all the girls were wearing their land girl's uniform, but four girls were wearing very short skirts and thin jumpers with their nipples showing through. Sarah was astounded and appalled she thought. "These lasses will take some watching, it won't be long before they have a tumble in the hay, and most likely end up with more in their bellies then food. As the local men and wayward husbands would welcome them with open arms, but their mothers wives and sisters would be less enthusiastic". Maureen led them all in to the recreation room and insisted they form an orderly queue, or as Maureen would of called it the girls sitting room. It had warmed through in this room, although the windows were running with condensation as the heat was drawing the dampness out of the walls. Maureen clapped her hands to demand peace and quiet.

"I am Mrs Winter your warden I think we should all introduce ourselves, there is some house rules which we all have to live by, but I will not go into it all tonight but you will all have a rota I will arrange it all tomorrow, as I expect you would like to go and choose your rooms and partners," and then she beckoned for Sarah Elsie and Pat to come and stand beside her and introduced them to the girls saying. "I expect you show them respect as well as me, as they will be making your lives comfortable and helping to make your food. Right girls one at a time call your names out and then go upstairs and make yourselves at home while I make us all a cup of cocoa."

"Do we have to?" Jean asked as she stuck her head arrogantly in the air.

"Yes you do if you want to stay here." Maureen told her irritably with a new found confidence that she feared she'd lost earlier. Sarah and Pat gave a knowing smile Maureen was the right woman for the job.

Next morning at half past four, Maureen slid her feet out of bed on to the cold oilcloth that covered the wooden floors; she shivered as she reached for her clothes off the chair that she'd stood beside the bed, the night before. She smiled as she looked over at the other two beds in this huge room. Baby George was tucked up in a single bed, as the two girls were in a double bed together. As Maureen made her way downstairs she knew she'd made the right decision to come here, she had her children with her, a roof over their heads and a job, hopefully she could manage as she was on her own now, she hadn't told anyone but before her husband was killed he had left her for another woman.

The knocking on the door brought her out of her reverie as she turned the key and drew back the bolt Sarah came hurrying in from her cottage across the yard followed by Elsie from the pub. From then it was chaotic as the porridge that was steeped last night was heated up and stirred until it was thick and creamy, and while Elsie sliced bread and toasted it on the toasting fork over the fire, Maureen brewed huge teapots of tea between going to the stair bottom and calling the girls a second time. The girls finally came stumbling bleary eyed to the table and proceeded to eat what was put in front of them, as Maureen Sarah and Elsie hurriedly tried to cut bread and make sandwiches for the girls dinners which they wrapped in greaseproof paper as the wagon was sounding its horn outside to try and hurry the girls, Maureen rapidly handed out the sandwiches.

Lennie hated this job on a morning. "Why woman took so long to get ready he didn't know but he smiled to himself as he thought he would get his own back, they kept him waiting. Well he would give them a merry ride." Just then the door opened and the girls came pushing and shoving towards him through the darkness. Then they climbed into the back of the wagon where they seated themselves on the bench seats that ran along the sides. Lennie set off and roared round the next corner as the girls screamed, as they slid off the bench. And then, further along the road he stopped quickly where as the girls all tumbled forward banging their heads on the partition that separated them from the driver. Valerie shouted. "We are not bloody putting up with this, we will tell the farmer about him when we arrive that's if we manage to get there."

Maureen closed the door behind the last girl and let out a deep slow sigh, and then walked in to the kitchen where Sarah was stirring the last of the porridge and Elsie making a fresh pot of tea. "Come and sit down lass." Sarah told Maureen. "And then we'll have a welcome cup of tea."

Ruth was sitting in the back of the wagon with the rest of the girls, trying to put her mascara on without poking herself in the eye. "I wish he would slow this wagon down a bit or I'm never going to get my make-up on." as she took the lipstick out of her bag and proceeded to cover her lips blood red. "I think it's ridiculous expecting us girls to get up at such an unearthly hour well I am not going to put up with it." she said as she reached intoher bag for nail varnish.

Valerie who was sitting next to her stared and shouted. "I don't believe you Ruth, you can't paint your nails now, they won't be dry before we get there, and then what will you do?"

Ruth tossed her head arrogantly. "Well I won't be doing anything until my nails dry and besides once that nice looking farmer sets eyes on me he'll give me the best job."

Old Walter stepped out of his house as the wagon arrived bringing him some help. "What have we got here?" he shouted with pipe in his mouth and thumbs tucked behind his braces as he stretched his neck to look into the wagon. "I have been told I can have six girls" he said as he swung back on his heels. And then he pointed to Ruth, Valerie Betty Jean Brenda and Ivy. The girls climbed down from the wagon. Walter didn't waste any time telling the girls. "You will be potato picking in that field over there." as he pointed to a gate. "Go through that gate," he told them. "There are some buckets for you" and then he turned and asked. "Have you done it before? Then he went on to explain. "I have put sticks in the ground all round the field so each picker keeps their own section, that man there," he said as he pointed with the stem of his pipe to the man on the tractor. "is a contractor and I have him to pay, so I want you girls working not playing about, so go and get yourselves a bucket each and make a start, as standing about talking is costing me money"

"Where do we collect the gloves from?" Ruth wanted to know. Walter gave a nasty laugh as he said. "I've never heard anything like it." Wanting gloves he said to himself as he walked away.

Potato picking was a strenuous job. The man on the tractor was drawing behind him the potato scratter, it lifted the potatoes and the tines on the spinner revolved to spin potatoes out of the ground he timed it so as the girls got to the end of the row he arrived to dig out some more. Ruth wasn't very happy she kept looking at her manicured nails covered in wet soil, her nose kept running, she kept rubbing it with the back of her hand, as she straightened up to take another full bucket of potatoes to the edge of the field to tip into the pile of sacks waiting to be filled. She put her hand on the bottom of her back, her muscles had tightened with all the bending, she reached inside her overalls pocket and pulled out a packet of lucky strike and box of swanvestas, as she drew the smoke deep into her lungs her moment of enjoyment was short lived, as Walter came hurrying over to her his face as red as beetroot demanding. "What do you think you are doing? Standing about smoking in my time," Ruth sneered at him as she put the cigarette to her lips. Walter leaned over and snatched it from her mouth, then threw it to the ground and stood on it. "Let that be a lesson to you." he warned. "I will not stand for idle woman on my land, now get back to work."

Ruth was shocked she wasn't going to let him speak to her like that. "I don't have to stay here and take orders like that from you." she warned him. "Well you either pick the potatoes and do as I tell you or bugger off back to where you came from." As Walter walked away Jerry stopped the tractor calling to everyone that, "it was dinner time". As the girls walked over to collect their sandwiches that Maureen, Sarah and Elsie, had prepared for them earlier, Jean asked if she should go and knock on Walters's door to see if his wife would make them a hot drink. "Well you can go if you want Jean." replied Brenda. "I will go with her to carry the cups." said Ivy.

The girls were hoping Walter's wife would answer the door as he would likely refuse Jean knocked at the door and a huge woman with a big round face and little piggy eyes answered the door and hollered. "What do you lot want now?" "Please could we have a hot drink?" Enquired Jean. "There's a tap in the yard." She growled and closed the door with a bang. As the girls stood together eating their food Jerry did feel sorry for them but as he told them.

"Walter is not an easy man to work for; he doesn't bother me as I'm a contractor, I just dig the potatoes out and then go on to the next farm." The girls were thirsty as they made their way across the yard to the pump and washed their hands and then used them as cups to enable them to get a drink. It was a tired miserable little group that Lennie picked up later for the return journey; Ruth said. "I'm not going back to Walters tomorrow," as she looked at her nails despairingly. "You will have to." Jean told her. "As he picked us I think we will have to stay until all his potatoes are harvested." "I don't have to do anything I don't want to do Ruth replied bitterly as she opened her compact up and looked in the little mirror at her face. "Look at my face." She cried. "I have no makeup on, my mind is made up I shall not be going back there tomorrow". Mary who was sitting in the back of the wagon feeling every bit as tired said. "We are all tired; you know, we have been threshing all day." Ruth didn't wait to hear any more because as the wagon drew to a halt to drop the girls off Ruth scrambled to the back of the lorry in order to be first off so she could run upstairs and be first in the bath, but as she opened the door of the billet Maureen was standing arms crossed.

"Where do you think you're going with dirty boots on? You can go round the side and leave them in the porch they will dry in there and drop the dirt rather than in here." Ruth stamped off to do Maureen's bidding, thinking if she was quick she could still claim the bathroom before the others, but she hadn't bargained on meeting Elsie who stopped her from going upstairs. "Mrs Winter is going to speak to you all first" Elsie informed her.

Ruth's temper rose as she started to shout at Elsie. "Who the hell do you think you are?" Maureen was just walking back in to the house and ready to defend Elsie when she turned on Ruth, shouting.

"Don't you come in here shouting at me, as I won't put up with you, I'm only doing what Mrs Winter told me too and it's about time you did the same?" As she clattered the pans as she tried to control her temper. Later on in the night as Sarah was sitting having a cup of cocoa with Maureen, everyone had been fed, and bathed or had a good wash down. Elsie had gone home back to the pub. Maureen's children were in bed, the land girls were in their recreation room, or as Maureen liked to call it their sitting room, some of the girls were writing letters home, some were singing and shouting as others were trying to have a conversation. Sarah laughing told Maureen. "The worm has turned;" Maureen looked at Sarah for an explanation. "You know who I'm talking about Maureen." Sarah said.

"Little Elsie she gave as well as she got tonight with Ruth." "Oh yes." answered Maureen. "The transformation from the timid girl, to the one that will put the likes of Ruth into her place, it was worth seeing."

"Well I'm going home now to my cottage across the yard, and my old man Maureen." said Sarah yawning. "It's been a long day." "It has Sarah." answered Maureen as she followed her to the door to lock it. "And it was a good idea of yours, Sarah, to make the sandwiches tonight save us rushing about tomorrow morning." Sarah laughed as she said. "I know someone who won't be going tomorrow she will be eating hers here." Yes I think your right Sarah I don't think Ruth will take kindly to having a boss.

Ruth was the only one upstairs, her hair wrapped in pipe cleaners and ponds vanishing cream on her face, she wished she'd never come here. Her family had told her she would never manage and she thought if she went home now her family would say, we told you so. Her face burnt when she thought as how her brother and his friends had laughed at her in the uniform before she left. Well she decided she was not going home and she was not going back to picking potatoes for that horrible Walter neither. They would have to find her another job, and tomorrow was another day, as she pulled the blankets up around her neck and was soon sound asleep.

Next morning Maureen and Sarah were very surprised to see Ruth up and ready for another days work. Sarah turned and looked at Ruth as she put another slice of bread on the toasting fork and held it in front of the fire. "I didn't think we would have seen you up early this morning and going to work I thought you said yesterday that you were not going anymore," Sarah reminded her. Ruth reached over and grabbed two slices of toast that Sarah had laid on the plate ready to butter, as she placed them on the table Maureen buttered them for her as she had just finished buttering the bread.

As Ruth bit into her toast with butter running down her chin she said brusquely. "If I don't go back there, I might have to go home and I don't fancy that, nor do I fancy picking those potatoes, roll on tonight." Sarah was just straightening up after leaning over the fire toasting all the bread and asked Ruth. "Why what is so special about tonight?" Ruth smiled condescendingly and said. "I will be going to the pub and you never know Sarah, I might find myself a fella." Sarah sniffed audibly as she made her way to the table and said, "Well you might and then again you might not, and my name is Mrs Foster to you girls so make sure you use it. Just then there was a loud noise outside and Lennie was sounding his horn impatiently. Then he saw the porch light shining through the door hurrying towards the wagon, he was watching to see if the other lass was coming, Ruth he thought was her name, and as he stared in to the early morning light he saw her hurrying towards him with the rest of them, he smiled to himself that lass wouldn't last the week he would put money on it. Rosey was last into the wagon as she climbed over the tailboard Lennie was setting off and Rosey nearly fell backwards if the other girls hadn't grabbed her she would have fallen back on to the road which amused Lennie as he skidded round the corners so the land girls slid up and down the bench seats with their sandwiches and bottle of tea in their bags.

Walter was waiting as the wagon made its way through the farm gate and he started giving the girls their orders before they were all out of the wagon. Then he stood rocking on his heels with a mocking smile on his face facing the girls. "Well I have decided to give you girls a different job today, something I think you will all enjoy."

he spoke in stentorian tones. " "Well I'm pleased to hear that." said Ruth as she dug her elbow into Valerie's ribs to get her attention. "I want you girls to spread muck, there is a big heap over yonder go and find yourselves a barrow there's plenty about and a fork each, fill the barrows with the forks it might be heavy going as it has been there a long time, but it will do you girls good to do a bit work," he sneered, "then take the barrows across those fields," he pointed with the stem of his pipe, "and spread it." The girls walked towards the byres and got a shock the pile of dung looked like a mountain,

Ruth said, "He cannot expect us to shift this lot with barrows." "I do and you will, you are supposed to be helping on the land." The girls hadn't realised he was following them. Just then four men came towards them and the girls stood and stared.

"No need to stand and stare at them." Walter barked. "They are German prisoners of war and I'm told they are good workers, so you girls make a start and fill those barrows." The girls filled the barrows with the muck which was heavy stuff and the smell that emanated from it penetrated into their nostrils, it was also a long walk to the field so the girls took it in turns to push the heavy barrows. All morning they spread the dung with the forks as their backs ached and hands became sore and blistered by the pitchforks back muscles ached and still they carried on. Until dinner time. As they sat down in a corner of the field they saw the prisoners of war were already tucking into their sandwiches. "I wonder how long they have been sitting there," said Ruth, "because if they are having long dinner breaks so are we." The girls were aching so much they could hardly sit down, but they were all ready for a drink of cold tea out of their bottles, it didn't take the girls long to eat their sandwiches and were soon reaching for their cigarettes.

"This is no better than yesterday." Ruth complained on an exhalation of cigarette smoke. "I'm going over there to see them men," said Valerie, "and find out how long they are going to be here."

"Do you think it's a good idea? I won't be speaking to them." said Betty stoutly.

"Well I'm going over there," said Valerie. "You won't like it if they take our jobs what would we do?" As Valerie made her way over to the men they looked away until Valerie was face to face with them.

"How long are you lot here for?" Valerie asked, "As we work here and don't want you lot taking our jobs." One of the men who gave his name as Hess said, "We come here and do as we told," then he pointed to the other three and introduced them as, "marcell, Adalwolf, and Riek." Then he sat down as if he didn't want to say anymore.

Ruth looked up as Valerie walked back to them," "Did they tell you anything?" she asked. "They only told me their names and they come here as they are told too that is all Valerie said as she arched her back to ease the stiffness, as the rest of the girls started to stub out their cigarettes' ready to spread some more dung.

When Lennie came to pick them up at night he found six weary girls waiting for him it took them all their time to climb over the tailgate of the wagon, but Lennie didn't spare them any as he bounced through the potholes. When Sarah saw the state of the girl's hands she said, "Oh dear I should have told you to spit on them it hardens them up" "Is there some kind of cream or something we could use Mrs Foster? Rosey asked her hopefully. "No I'm afraid their isn't lass." Sarah shook her head. "But just keep spitting on them and that will do it." The girls found out within a few days that Sarah had been right after all, and the hot meal was very much appreciated that night as the girls knew it was a hard task feeding them all.

Ethel had been busy all day although she knew her time wasn't far away, she had a drawer lined out ready in the big linen press, it was a huge cupboard that took up most of one wall it had two doors that opened at the top two small drawers underneath and then three long drawers in the bottom. She had done the washing this morning as it was Monday, people always did their washing on a Monday even if they didn't feel well. As ailments like colds, flu sprains and rheumatism, were largely ignored and worked off. She smiled to herself as she thought she would have a job to work this complaint off.

The morning had started like any other morning, Ethel had risen at five o clock and gone through to the kitchen and stirred the fire into life with the heavy brass poker, and then went to the foot of the stairs where she shouted and told everyone it was time to get up. As she walked back into the kitchen the kettle had started to boil, as the lid bobbed up and down on the boiling kettle. Wilf picked up the cloth which they used to lift hot kettles and pans off the fire as Ethel spooned tea into the teapot out of the caddy. This was Wilf's favourite time of day he liked his first cup of tea of the morning and he had risen early all his life so that was no hardship. The boys Frank and Colin came rushing through their hair all tousled and sat down at the table, followed by Linda Jennie Susan and Mabel. On hearing Gran getting out of bed Linda turned and went back upstairs to help Gran. As Ethel leaned over the fire frying egg and bacon for everyone her back ached but she kept quiet as she didn't want Wilf making a fuss. Ethel jumped as Gran shouted.

"What are you standing daydreaming about our Ethel? Because while you're in a different world to us that bacons burning and I don't want burnt offerings for my breakfast," Ethel quickly turned the bacon over it wasn't burnt it was just well browned. "Are you feeling alright Ethel?" Wilf was concerned. "Yes I'm fine Wilf," answered Ethel as she straightened up and rubbed her back. Linda came over and gently pushed Ethel down on to a chair while she took over the cooking. Jennie started to butter the bread, while Susan offered to stay at home and help Ethel. "No I'll be fine," said Ethel. "You girls get ready for work, and then Wilf and the boys can get the cows milked, and I will wash up while they deliver the milk." Linda and the girls were not convinced that Ethel was alright so as they went out of the door Linda said. "If you need anything Ethel send one of the boys for me." As they all went out together

Gran said. "I know you're not well our Ethel and I can count those babies are due,"

"I think you mean baby gran, as Grace can only feel one when she examines me and she is the midwife, and I don't think she takes kindly to you telling her she is wrong."

"I know that our Ethel but she is wrong look at the size of you but if Grace thinks she's right you must have an elephant in there." Just then the door opened and Eva walked in.

"What are you doing here at this time of a morning Eva?" Ethel asked. Eva was busy removing her coat as she said.

"Prudence offered to get the girls ready for school as soon as she heard Linda's bike coming down the lane."Ethel was surprised. "But I never asked Linda to come for you." "I know you didn't but just as well she did, as you don't look well so I'm here to help you."

189

Gran said. "it would be a good help to me Eva if you make another cup of tea as I'm fair parched, and I'm pleased you've come otherwise if our Ethel is ill today I might not have got any dinner, so now your here you might as well get started because you know what Prudence is like she won't want to look after those bairns longer then she has too, and if you have to go home sooner than we thought you might not of got all the jobs done, not that I take any looking after as I'm easy going." For the rest of the day Gran made sure Eva didn't have time to stop and chat telling her it was for her own good she might as well get as much work done as possible it would save her coming back tomorrow or if Ethel had given birth then she would have to come along to cook some meals. "As I can't be going without my dinner at my age." she said. Just then Wilf came hurrying in his face as red as beetroot.

"Whatever is the matter Wilf?" Ethel asked concerned at the state Wilf was in. "Oh I've rushed about this morning Ethel I have been worrying about you."

"Well its time you slowed down a bit Wilf, you are no spring chicken, and there is nothing ailing our Ethel she is only in the family way, she isn't ill."

"I'm pleased your here Eva to help Ethel with the washing, Wilf said smiling. Eva picked up the kettle and went to fill it from the pail that stood near the door. "I bet you would love a pot of tea wouldn't you Wilf?" Grans head shot up. "Well if you're making one I might as well have another." Later in the day while Eva possed the clothes Ethel sat at the table peeling potatoes for dinner, then once that was done she scraped her chair back and with her hands flat on the table she pushed herself up on to her feet.

"Where are you going now Ethel?" Gran was watching Ethel like a hawk.

"I am going to get the lamps they need seeing too Gran I can't sit here idle even Wilf has offered to help with the washing." I don't mind helping Ethel besides I'm only going to be turning the handle. Ethel returned bringing the lamps and candle holders with her, as Wilf Gran and Eva turned questionable eyes on Ethel she said. "I'm just going to trim the wicks, wash the glasses and fill these ready with paraffin, and then I will polish the brass candle stick holders with brasso then that will be another job done."

"You are looking very flushed our Ethel."

"I'll be fine Gran." Ethel said with a wan smile.

"Are you feeling any better Mam or would you like me to run along and get Grace?" "No I'll be fine love." Ethel looked tenderly at her daughter, if this baby was as good as Eva then she would have two good ones. Eva pushed a strand of damp hair out of her eyes as Ethel offered to help with the mangling. "You look tired our Eva." Ethel told her. Wilf looked over. "I will help, what do you want me to do Eva?" "Well I'll feed the sheets in and turn the handle and you can catch them on the other side."

"No I'm not letting a woman do the heaviest job." joked Wilf I will turn the handle until the water is out of all the sheets and clothes." "Oh thank you Wilf as my arm was beginning to ache, by the way how is Susan's arm keeping?"

Gran said. "Its festered I told her what would happen you can get some nasty scratches while you're hedging."

"Aye and in later years racked with rheumatism and arthritis isn't that right Gran?" asked Ethel. "It is Ethel, but I've always had you to look after me, some folk won't have been as lucky."

Towards tea time Ethel was feeling tired and weary bedtime could not come soon enough tonight. She had been busy putting all the little white matinee jackets and nappies vests and all the other paraphernalia that a baby needed into the rest of the press drawers , Ethel smiled when she realized all the knitwear she had made or been given she would have far too much stuff for the baby, but Gran had gone on, and on about there being two so Ethel had made enough stuff for two but Ethel knew by the way she felt that she would know for sure in the morning if she managed to go that long.

CHAPTER ELEVEN

Linda heard movement downstairs; she was just about to return luxuriously to sleep when she heard Ethel crying out in pain, in a moment Linda was out of bed. All sleepiness gone, She dressed quickly so as not to disturb the others. As she was passing Gran's bedroom door the groaning of the bed springs indicated Gran was awake and trying to get out of bed. Linda tapped lightly on Grans door and opened it just wide enough to get her head round and ask if she could help?

"Yes please Linda, our Ethel's in pain and I'm going to sit with her." The chronic arthritis that gnawed at her joints twisting her fingers and toes into gnarled lumps was very painful and excruciating so, in her deformed feet. Gran walked painfully downstairs holding the stair rail with one hand and Linda with the other. As Gran entered the sitting room where Ethel and Wilf slept in the sideboard bed Ethel was sitting on the bed while Wilf stood wondering what to do first. Gran walked over to Ethel and spoke soothingly saying "it's alright now our Ethel, I'm here to sit with you and I'll sit until it's all over and done with".

Gran soon took over sending Linda along for Grace and Wilf into the kitchen, to stoke the fire into life, and the big iron kettle on to boil for a cup of tea and Grace would need hot water.

Grace rubbed the sleep from her eyes as she heard someone banging franticly on her front door; she threw the blankets aside and hurried to the window as she pulled the curtain back to peer out she saw Linda looking up at her and waving her arms. Grace quietly dropped the curtain back into place and hurried downstairs as fast as her buniond feet would allow. As Grace opened the door a little to allow Linda to squeeze through, a blast of night air hit Grace who was shivering in her nightie.

"Could you come along to Ethel's quick Grace please? Gran has sent me Ethel has started bad." Linda felt as If her lungs were on fire as she had ran along to get Grace, thinking it would be quicker than going to the outbuilding to fetch her bike as she busied herself with the practicalities.

Grace whispered so not to wake her husband. "I will get dressed and come along and don't worry." She told Linda as she patted her shoulder reassuringly. Linda's head was in a whirl wondering what job to do first as she made her way home. Her chest was still sore after having run all the way to honeypot cottage for Grace but she needn't have bothered as Gran had everything under control and everyone busy, while she sat and stroked Ethel's hand and refused to go and sit in her chair in the kitchen. "I am staying here with our Ethel, and that's final." She told everyone. After Linda had left to go for Grace, Wilf had put the kettle on to boil and then Gran told him. "Go and make sure the boys, Colin and Frank, go straight out of the front door when they come downstairs, and walk around to the back door instead of walking through the sitting room as they normally do." As she told Wilf, "It's no good two young lads seeing our Ethel in this state." It was Linda who ushered Frank and Colin out of the front door they went out under protest the air so frosty it took their breath away. Linda hadn't been home long when Grace arrived, and asked. "Has anyone had been for my sister Pat yet?" "No not yet." Gran replied. "There is no need to get Pat out of bed too early; Wilf can tell her when he and the boys deliver the milk."

While Grace examined Ethel, Wilf went to milk the cows with Frank and Colin. One by one the other three land girls, Susan, Mabel and Jennie made their way downstairs to help in any way they could. Ethel was lying on the bed writhing in pain while Gran gently rubbed the sweat off her forehead, with a damp cloth and said to Grace. "Go through to the kitchen, and if the girls have eaten their breakfasts send one of them to tell our Eva, what is happening as she will want to be here. After all it will be her brother or sister that is coming into the world."

Mabel had reached Eva's door, and wondered how to knock and wake Eva without waking the whole house. But on reflection thought, there is no way I can knock quietly, so she gave a good loud knock on the door.

Presently she heard footsteps on the stairs, and creaking as Eva opened the door a little and peered round wondering who it could be at this time of day, to be followed by Prudence, who was known for not missing anything, and forever inquisitive. As Eva saw who it was she panicked saying. "Mam has started bad hasn't she Mabel? I must come at once." and then she turned towards Prudence saying. "Will you see to the children for me? As I must go and see Mam."

"I could come along with you Eva," Prudence offered. "And Linda can stay here and get the children ready for school." "No." Eva said tersely. "There will be enough people along there, without you Prudence, just stay here and see to the children please." Then she remembered Mabel was still standing there so she said. "Thank you Mabel, you go on ahead and say I won't be long." And with that she ran upstairs to get dressed before running down the steep bank to see her mother.

Ethel rolled on the bed in agony till dinnertime; Grace had remarked to Gran as she yawed, that "maybe she needn't have got out of bed as early as it was now dinner time and the baby hadn't put in an appearance yet." "Yes that's as Maybe." Gran said. "But I like to be on the safe side, if I'd waited and you had gone out our Ethel might have given birth without you. Well as it is you were here in good time." "Yes I suppose so." Grace said with a sigh. Ethel cried out as a gush of water escaped between her legs, and she started to push as Grace said to Gran. "Would you like to go into the kitchen until it's over, and then I'll give you a shout?" "No I do not I have sat here all morning, and I'll stop till the babies born, so as I'm sitting at the head end you had better see to the bottom end as that is why your here."

Half an hour later as Wilf walked wearily in for a meal that would of been cooked for him, but which he couldn't face, he heard the cry of a tiny baby his face lit up with joy, as Eva bustled through excitedly to tell him he had two boys, gran had been right all along, and Ethel's face had been wreathed in smiles as Grace had put the two tiny bundles into Ethel's outstretched arms.

Wilf walked into see Ethel and his twin son's looking very proud, and happy that everything had been alright. "Well have you two thought of a name yet for these two?" Asked a relieved Gran, "Oh we have a name for both of them haven't we Wilf? Ethel asked smilingly. Wilf cleared his throat and explained. "We have talked about names haven't we Ethel, and we both like William and Robert."

"Then that's what they will be called Wilf," Agreed Ethel. "Well I know what folk are like round these parts," said Gran, "and I bet they end up called Bob and Bill." "Well we won't be bothered will we Ethel? As long as they are healthy." smiled Wilf.

Prudence was busy teaching her classroom of children, they all seemed fractious today. The head teacher had given Prudence the small children to teach today, and she didn't like having to teach small children, she could manage the older ones but these five year old children cried, wet themselves and some had even gone to sleep. Prudence sighed she had a lot on her mind. She knew she ought to go home to her parents and visit them and Winnie, she had arrived here two years ago just before the evacuees, so that her and the rest of the teaching staff could get things in order, she had been lucky moving in with Eva. When she thought about it she was lucky to get here at all, as her father had told her she had responsibilities' at home, looking after her daughter, Winnie, Oh dear Prudence thought if anyone found out she had a daughter she wouldn't dare show her face again here but she was safe in the knowledge that she would never be found out, her parents had even gone as far as telling Winnie that Prudence was her sister. It brought Prudence out of her reverie as the bell rang, and she had made up her mind to write and let her mother know she was coming to visit.

Back home in London Winnie and her friend Dot were wondering what to do, they had been going out with Burt and Sam for a while, they had even managed to get away for a weekend now and again with them, without Dots mother realizing Dot had been very nervous at first with Sam but once she had got over the initial shock as to what would happen in bed with him she looked forward to being in his arms and in his bed she knew she was getting more wild and promiscuous like Winnie but she was in love, and she knew her nearness had affected him alarmingly when they had been forced to spend the night together in the shelter. The following night had been worth waiting for. As soon as they had reached the cheap hotel room he had been filled with desire, fumbling to unbutton her blouse before the door was closed, as she had moved over to him suggestively. And then helped him remove her clothes, and soon his hands were travelling over her body, and then she felt his weight upon her, the warmth of his body between her thighs, and she responded rapidly, as she arched her back and moaned with pleasure, it only took a few seconds to reach his climax, as he smothered her with kisses, before reaching over for his cigarettes and matches. Dot lay smiling beside him thinking she was truly his now in spite of unmentioned pregnancy fears, as she couldn't face the disgrace of illegitimacy, she was thankful for her monthlies the following week. But as time went on Dorothy was following suit with Winnie and taking risks with whichever G I they met at the dances, as she liked the idea of makeup and nylons as much as Winnie. Brenda noticed a change in Dorothy, also the amount of things she seemed to be accumulating, but when asked she looked so innocent. Brenda was wishing she had not offered Winnie a home, but she sighed when she thought about it, Winnie wasn't such a bad girl but she seemed to be leading Dorothy a stray lately by the bits of conversations she had heard.

The girls were walking back from work when Winnie said. "I wish we hadn't gone out with those two GIs again last week, just our luck for Sam, and Burt turning up when we least expected them."

"I thought you weren't bothered about seeing Burt again?" Dorothy challenged Winnie.

"Well I am now." Winnie cried "I think I'm expecting." Dorothy stopped and stared at Winnie and asked. "But is it Burt's baby?"

"I don't know I have been with the yanks the same as you and I thought all I would have to show for it would be nylons and makeup." she answered as she gave a wan smile. "But now I am in a mess, please don't say anything to your Mam Dorothy or she will kick me out and I have nowhere to go."

Dorothy was inquisitive. "How do you know you're expecting Winnie?" I have missed my monthlies and that is why I hurry out of your house to the lav on a morning as I don't feel very well."

Winnie looked suspiciously at Dorothy and asked. "Why are you asking me all these questions? I thought you would have been telling me how stupid I was to get into this mess." And then Winnie stared at Dorothy as the truth dawned on her." I know why." Winnie laughed. "You are in the same mess yourself." Dorothy looked at Winnie with tears in her eyes and said. "Oh Winnie I think I am what are we going to do I cannot tell anyone if Mam and Dad find out they will go mad, I think they would kick us both out, but I am still hoping I'm just late probably with worrying about it."

Just then Winnie pointed across the street, "look Dorothy," she said excitedly, there is my Mam and Dad over there quick come around here before they see us." Before Dorothy had time to think Winnie had pulled her out of sight of her parents. "Why are we hiding Winnie?" Dorothy was surprised. "You haven't spoken to them for months." Winnie peered round the corner making sure her parents were out of sight before she turned to Dorothy saying. "Do you not remember when I left home, or should I say they told me to go they wouldn't let me have the rest of my things, my attaché case for instance, so now I know they are both out I'm going to collect my things, so come on Dorothy hurry up." Dorothy was horrified. "We cannot go in there Winnie we will both get into bother if they get the police as we will be breaking in." Winnie laughed at Dorothy. "You are daft at times Dorothy, we will not be breaking in, I know where they leave the backdoor key." "I don't want to go Winnie I'm frightened they come back and catch us." "Some friend you are." Winnie stormed at Dorothy. "Oh please come with me Dorothy." Winnie begged. It won't take long I promise. "Oh alright Winnie but be as quick as you can as I don't want to be in that house when they get back." Then another thought crossed Dorothy's mind. "What if your mother has thrown your things out Winnie?"

But Winnie had a determined look on her face as she said. "Well we will soon find out wont we Dorothy?" As the two girls made their way back up the road Winnie was quite happy saying to Dorothy. "That was a bit of luck wasn't it Dorothy." When she didn't answer Winnie dug her in the ribs with her elbow and said. "Cheer up we won't be in there long or if you are that bothered I will go on my own."

"No I will come with you Winnie, besides this will be the first time I have been in your house, I will be able to have a look at your bedroom you were lucky you know having a bedroom all to yourself." "Come on down here." Winnie shouted as Dorothy was going to carry on walking along the road. "We will go down this path and in through the back door." Winnie explained to Dorothy. Mam always leaves the key under the mat, as they got to the door Winnie hurriedly lifted the mat and pulled out the key, then smiled up at Dorothy. Winnie inserted the heavy key into the lock and turned it then the door opened on to a tidy kitchen. Dorothy couldn't believe how big the kitchen was compared with her mothers, and as she was standing gazing about her Winnie got hold of her arm and said. "Come on Dorothy we haven't got all-night." Winnie ran upstairs with

Dorothy hot on her heels. At the top of the stairs Winnie through open her bedroom door and Dorothy stood wide eyed.

"This is a beautiful room Winnie; I have never seen a room as nice." Dorothy said as she walked over and stroked the pink bedcover and looked around at the matching curtains, and the big dolls sitting on the dressing table. "I can't believe you would give all this up to come and quash in our house with all us lot, it's amazing." "Well you didn't know what it was like living with them Dorothy I would much rather live with you. Will you take the rest of my clothes out of the wardrobe for me Dot Please? While I try and find my attaché case and all the stuff Mam has hidden."

Winnie laughed as she said. "I bet Mam and Dad will be livid when they realize I've been in and got my things." Moments later as Dorothy was folding clothes for Winnie, she asked her. "What are you doing down there Winnie looking under the bed?"

"I think they have thrown some of my things out Dot." She told her friend tearfully. Then Winnie jumped to her feet as an idea came to her. "I am going to have a look in Mam's bedroom; she might have kept them in there."

"Do you think that is wise?" said Dot who was alarmed at the thought of looking in someone else's bedroom. "What if they come back and catch us Winnie I'm getting worried so will you please hurry up?" As they walked into her Parents room Winnie pointed to a huge bag on the floor and said. "Mam takes that bag to the shelter with her, although they have their own shelter in the yard." Dorothy was surprised. "Oh why didn't they use the public shelter as it is only over the road?" "Oh Dad said he would rather die than share a shelter, he said you never know what you might catch being with so many people." Dorothy watched horrified as Winnie tipped the full bag on to the floor.

"What are you doing now Winnie?" exclaimed Dorothy. "Surely you didn't need to empty that bag on to the floor as you can see there is no attaché case there."

"I will need my birth certificate as well as my personal things as I will never come back here." Dorothy jumped when Winnie opened her birth certificate and cried out. "I knew I wasn't wanted." and started to cry big tears running down her cheeks and she was shaking her hand holding the certificate was trembling. Dorothy rushed round the bed and put a comforting arm around her "What is the matter Winnie? What have you found that is so terrible." Winnie held out the paper with a trembling hand. "Look at this Dot." she cried. "I am not theirs." Then she gathered hand full of papers and tossed them all around the room Dorothy tried to control Winnie but Winnie was past caring, she screeched at Dorothy. "Do you know who my bloody mother is? Only our Prue and I thought she was my sister." Then she sank to her knees and cried. Dorothy was beginning to wish she hadn't come. After a while when Winnies sobs had subsided Dorothy suggested it was time to leave. "You have got all your things now Winnie I think we should be going before they get back." Dorothy didn't want any more bother tonight besides she had her own problems. As the girls headed towards the stair top the front door opened and Winnie pulled Dorothy back into the bedroom. Dorothy's stomach was churning she wasn't sure what to do now and if Winnies Mam or Gran as it turned out happened to come upstairs, she shivered it didn't bide thinking about. After the girls heard the sitting room door close they crept quietly downstairs and out of the back door where Dorothy took a deep breath and let out a sigh of relief. Dorothy's house was a good walk from Winnie's parents, or grandparents after what she had found tonight. As they entered Dorothy's her mother was surprised when they carried all the bags in. "Your teas are in the oven keeping warm." Brenda told them. "They might be a bit dried up now, where have you both been?" she asked, as she removed her steel curlers in front of the spotted mirror. Brenda felt sorry for Winnie after being told what they had found out, but she couldn't say she was surprised as she had thought for a long time now that there was a big age difference with Winnie and Prudence, but who would of thought it, straitlaced Prudence but she thought it often happened that the older girls had the babies and pretended they were older sisters, but what could you do she wouldn't like to be in that position.

The next morning Dorothy experienced a feeling of nausea followed by vomiting it was only then she thought back and realised she'd missed the last two periods.

Brenda sipped her tea and mulled over the situation, she was disillusioned with the situation, but she thought at least they hadn't concocted a lie. Dorothy felt ill, the days were growing hotter everything thing seemed dusty and heavy with all the bombing, even though there was no clouds at all the air was oppressive, because of the lack of breeze coming through the propped open door. Brenda felt the seriousness of the situation was beyond their comprehension. Brenda stared at the two girls as she shouted

"I have always warned you." she said as she stared at her daughter Dorothy, all those lads were after were a good lay, Brenda was uncompromising, in her moral views she was staring in desperation trying to control threatening tears but she couldn't manage she laid her head on her arms that were resting on the table and cried. While Dorothy flushed at her mother's blatant description, her brother who was home on leave sneered at both girls.

"We are not tarts you know." said Winnie. He laughed derisively, and replied. "Course you are." He knew this was an extra worry for his mother to bear, as he had often thought that Winnie was of doubtful reputation, and as he put his arm around his mothers shaking shoulder while she sobbed at her daughter's downfall, he couldn't help thinking his sister wouldn't be in this mess if they hadn't taken pity on Winnie. Brenda lifted her face towards Dorothy as she asked wide eyed with terror, "What am I going to do Mam?" Then seeing the fear mirrored in her daughters eyes she took pity on her, as she looked over towards Winnie and smiled wanly as she realised Winnie had no one at all to turn too. Brenda seemed to make a quick decision. "There is nothing we can do today till your father gets home." she shook her head as she said. "I dread to think what he will do, but you two had better get off to work as you are going to need all the money you can get, Will Sam and Burt stand by you?" Brenda asked as an afterthought." While the girls faces suffused with colour.

Dorothy's brother shouted, "Oh I know now, they are not the fathers are they?"And you don't know the fathers as you have both slept with any one for nylons and makeup. Well I'm getting out of here." he shouted as he grabbed his jacket off the back of the chair As he stared nastily at both girls, then he had banged the door so hard on it shuddered on its hinges Brenda had been in the process of getting off her chair, and on hearing this flopped back down with a thud. "Go on get to work out of my sight." she cried, "as I don't know which way to turn" her voice was uncharacteristically unkind. As the girls walked to work they were filled with trepidation. Dorothy was still sniffing,

. "Will you stop that?" Winnie glared at Dorothy. "Those lasses in there are going to want to know what is wrong." "But we can't just ignore these pregnancies cried Dorothy I wish I'd never listened to you."

"Now look here Dorothy I did not force you so don't go blaming me, you can come with me if you want too." Dorothy slowed down and asked. "But where are you going Winnie."

Winnie gave a harsh laugh. "Well I'm going to see my Mother, Prudence of course; she has kept me well out of her life up till now, so I will go to her and make up for lost time won't that be a wonderful surprise." Just then Winnie slipped her arm through Dorothy's and hurried her along saying. "Come on Dorothy or we will be late and we need all the money we can get because very soon we will be on the train to Teesdale." And as the girls popped unobtrusively through the factory door no one could have guessed the drama they'd just left behind.

The girls hung their coats up on their pegs in the cloakroom, among the entire gossiping woman, who were busy fastening overalls and tying turbans around their heads. Dorothy felt herself heave as she walked towards her bench, the acrid odour of explosives thick in the air. Helen who was standing beside her who was on her way to the crane asked her if everything was alright as she looked a bit peaky. At the sound of Helens voice Dorothy jumped then said.

"Oh I'm fine thanks Helen I was just deep in thought." Helen didn't believe her but just whispered. "If you ever need someone to talk to I'm here." Dorothy knew she would have to do something she'd heard the talk among the woman in this munitions factory, which were no better than they should be, it is very easy for people to be wise with hindsight. Helen was still looking at her as she climbed the rope up to the cab of the crane she controlled one of many, which moved shells back and forth across the factory floor. Dorothy looked over at Winnie who was singing along with the woman as if she didn't have a care in the world. When the whistle blew reminding the woman it was bate - time Dorothy was one of the first out of the door, but not looking forward to the solitary paste sandwich, which was wrapped in greaseproof paper. As she sat on the low stone wall Winnie walked over to her and hissed "you're going to have to cheer up some of them lot," as she motioned with her head, "are wondering what's wrong with you."

The air left Dot's body in a long sigh, as she said. "I don't want to upset Dad, as he is so kind and gentle and he trusted me and now I've let him down"

"Well he will have to be told." said a heartless Winnie, "and besides you won't have to tell him as your Mam will do that as soon as he gets home from work."

"You don't understand do you Winnie? I don't want him to think badly of Me." said Dorothy as fresh tears threatened. Just then the whistle sounded indicating everyone should hurry back to their benches to pack more shell cases. As the final whistle sounded and everyone was reaching for coats and hand bags Dorothy was dragging her feet as she dreaded going home and facing her dad.

"Get a move on Dot." Winnie shouted in her ear as she walked behind her. "Or we'll be here all night." "I'm in no hurry to go home." Dorothy told Winnie once they were outside and lit their cigarettes, "You don't seem bothered Winnie."

"Why should I bother about what folk think about me, because no one is bothered whether I live or die?"

Dorothy wrapped her arm around Winnie when she saw tears running down her friends face. "This is partly to do with finding out that Prudence is your mother isn't it Winnie?" Dorothy felt sorry for Winnie. "How do you think I feel Dorothy how would you feel if no one wanted or cared about you?" they made their way home to Dorothy's in silence each wrapped up in their own thoughts. As they walked through the door Dorothy had a crumpled soaked hankie in her hand fresh tears cascaded silently down her face she was dreading facing her Dad, who was sitting at the table eating his tea as the girls walked in. He took out his watch glanced at it returned it to his waistcoat pocket. And then he turned on Dorothy and Winnie saying.

"Well this is a right mess you've both got into and no mistake,I never thought I would live this day to see one of my children disgrace themselves how you have done Dorothy, your mother has come up with an idea to save your blushes and the child being called names. We suggest you go to your auntie Thelma's until the baby arrives and then you can come home and hand it over to Marion your married sister, to bring up as her own, and after you handed the bairn over you would always be its auntie no one would ever know."

"No I'm not giving my baby away Dad I don't care what people think about me but it's my baby and I'm keeping it." Dorothy's Dads neck turned a dull red the colour creeping upwards into his cheeks. Dorothy's Mother Brenda stepped forward trying to defuse the situation saying.

"I warned her to wait until her wedding night for intimacy, but I suppose these things happen, more so in wartime."

Mr Watson raised disbelieving eyebrows, saying to Winnie. "And what are your Mam and Dad going to say about this caper as you have brought disgrace on them too."

"I don't have a Mam and Dad to tell Mr Watson, as I've just discovered that Pru, who I was always led to believe was my sister, is my unmarried mother" Winnie said with a sob in her throat and eyes luminous with tears, impulsively her lids blinked rapidly.

"Oh well that explains it like mother like daughter and our Dorothy has been led astray." answered Dorothy's dad. Winnie was not going to let Dorothy's dad put her down like that although she lodged with them she'd had to cope with Dot's brothers scathing glances this morning she also felt it was unfair criticism of her. The arrival of Dot's two younger brothers cut short any further arguments'. Brenda said we have no right to be dictatorial with you Winnie but we are concerned for you."

There is no need Mrs Watson, because tomorrow is Friday the last day of work this week so on Saturday I will be on my way to surprise Prue, and if you want to come with me and keep your baby Dot you'd better get packing. While Brenda broke into uncontrollable sobs,

Mr Watson stood up and finished his tea in one gulp, "I'm not having a palaver like this every night." He shouted, as he reached for his cap and jacket then made for the door then closed it behind him with a bang.

Brenda looked appealingly at her daughter and Winnie and said. "I wouldn't normally mention something like this but there are certain woman that could maybe help you both as you are so young and you've been very venerable."

"No Mrs Watson." Winnie sharply replied. "I'm going to Teedale with or without Dorothy," as she turned questionable eyes at Dot.

It was a long sleepless night for both girls, as Winnie realised she would have to go back and face her gran parents wrath as she needed Prudence's address and it was the only way to get it as they corresponded regular with Prue, the last time she had been back there she had crept into the house with Dorothy to collect her attaché bag and make-up and if Gran hadn't left her shelter bag open Winnie would not of found her birth certificate and realised she was illegitimate, she had been so upset she had scattered the contents of the bag all over the room, thinking she would never be in this house again, and now she would have to go back for Prue's address. Lying beside her in the narrow bed Dorothy was not asleep neither although her eyelids were closed the tears rolled down her face from closed lids, she wished she could turn the clock back, she didn't want to leave her family and friends, her mother had told her, "she should of thought about that." But she was not going to give her baby away although it would be to her sister she couldn't bear the thought. Winnie turned towards her and the bed springs creaked, "are you asleep Dot?" she whispered. Dorothy gave a big shuddering sigh, I cannot sleep it will be our last day at work tomorrow and we cannot breathe a word to anyone as Mam said they would be suspicious us both going away so quick and I dare not mention it as if anyone finds out why we went it will come back on my younger sisters. Thinking about her sisters made her cry all the harder as she wondered when or if she would ever see her family again. After an uneasy sleep Dot woke to her younger sister shaking her shoulder reminding her it was time to get up, Winnie lying close beside her rubbed her eyes and yawned. Come on then Dot last day to day we'll have to make the best of it, as the girls walked into the kitchen there was an unbearable silence, Mr Watson hurriedly drunk his tea and reached for his jacket as if he couldn't bide being in the same room. Dorothy stared at her mother Brenda, out of swollen pink rimmed eyes as she and Winnie reached for their coats, as her brother stared at them, she choked back a rush of tears the animosity her brother bore towards her now made her wary of antagonizing him so the sooner she was on her way the better.

The girls walked down the road neither of them wanting to go into work today Winnie said we will have to try and not draw attention to ourselves today or we will be bombarded with questions and I have enough on my mind having to go and face Mam, tomorrow she turned and asked Dot, "you will go with me wont you Dot? Because it's as much for your good as it is for mine because if we don't get our Prue's address I don't know what we will do." Yes I will Winnie I realise we can't stop at my house now after the atmosphere this morning the sooner we go the better. As they walked towards the factory gates the early morning mist shrouded the rooftops and the girls both felt sad as this time next week they could be anywhere and it didn't seem as if anyone was concerned. The woman who worked in the factory were rough diamonds always talking and laughing Dorothy joined in the laughter not knowing what she was laughing at but did not want to bring attention to herself when the final bell sounded the girls hurried out, and instead of heading back to Dorothy's house they were on their way to see Mrs Breaker to hopefully get Prudence's address it was Mr. Breaker who opened the door to Winnies tentative knock, and squinted at her asking what she wanted and after she had explained he said.

"I thought you had called to apologise after going through Mrs Breakers shelter bag and I presume you know your origin now after you scattered all those private papers."

"Yes and I'm sorry could I come in as there is something I have come to ask you?"

No you cannot we are eating our evening meal so you will have to call again tomorrow when it is more convenient for us then he closed the door.

Winnie was upset. "Look how they treat me dot," as she gulped audibly. "Well tomorrow we will have to comply with him and then I don't want to see them again."

Dorothy grabbed hold of Winnies arm and said with a look of horror "We won't be able to go tomorrow as we will have to come back here for the address, well I'm not going home for tea, come on Winnie we will go to the cafe and then we will sit in the park as I know they don't want me at home now, tomorrow can't come soon enough." The girls had an uneasy night wondering what they would do if they were refused Prue's address. They rose early their bags were packed ready, Brenda offered them breakfast saying. "It could be a while before they got another meal." But the girls couldn't face it Dorothy s heart was hammering in her chest. Brenda was resigned to the fact the girls were going and thought it best all round as she had younger daughters and didn't want anything like this washing on to them. As the girls picked up their bags Brenda encircled them in her arms and told them to take care, and write to let her know where they were at, and as the girls closed the door for the last time she rubbed the tears from her eyes with the corner of her apron.

It was a long walk to Mrs Breakers carrying all of their possessions as Winnie knocked on the door it was opened straight away Winnie thought nothing has changed they would likely be watching out of the window. Mrs Breaker was a formidable woman with a heart of Ice. "What do you want?" She barked at Winnie.

"Please could I have our Prue's address?" not wanting neighbours to know what had gone on Mrs Breaker stood aside and said "you had both come in for a minute, and besides I want a word. What did you sneak in here for? When I was out, scattering my personal papers all over, And I want the truth." she hollered. "Or no address." Mrs Breaker dropped her heavy body into the chair as the springs creaked in protest, and sat with her hands in her lap looking at the two girls standing nervously in front of her. "Well." she said nastily "The sooner you tell me the sooner you can both be on your way." As Winnie told her about the sorry mess they were both in she saw her grandfather sitting in the chair he raised an eyebrow at his wife it was steeped in meaning, and his wife didn't offer platitudes, nor did she feel compelled to help, instead she slowly made her way over to the sideboard drawer and passed a piece of paper over with the address on, that they had so badly wanted. "Here is the address, now please close the gate as you leave I don't like the gate swinging on its hinges it looks so common." Winnie and Dorothy stared at her completely nonplussed and walked out of their lives for good.

CHAPTER TWELVE

The station was hot and stuffy; Dorothy's heart was thudding like a sledgehammer as she followed Winnie to the platform she had all her possessions in a carpet bag, she wished she could of stayed with her family but she couldn't let her sister bring her child up her mother told her, "she would live to regret going with Winnie." but Dorothy felt as if she had no choice. Winnie turned to look for Dorothy "Come on Dorothy hurry up or we'll never get a seat, look at all those land girls queuing to get on the train." After a while of shuffling in the queue, they climbed the steps on to the train and were pushed into seats as people were hurriedly getting aboard as the whistle sounded, and very soon they were chugging out of the station, as tears ran slowly down Dorothy's face as she wondered when she would ever see her family again.

One of the land girls leaned over and Patted Dorothy's knee when she saw how distressed she was saying. "Come on love we are all in this together, it is the first time for most of these girls, I have worked on one farm before I didn't stop there long, I had to catch a bus on my own right out in to the country after the bus dropped me off I had a three mile walk down a narrow lane and it was teeming down no one came to meet me and by the time I arrived there I was soaked, on reaching the farm yard the farmer saw me and shouted, "take your things inside and then you can go down the field and start hedging." Some of the land girls had been listening, and Rosey said, "Well I would of turned round and gone back home, I wouldn't put up with it." Mary another of the land girls said. "My sister is a land girl and the first farm she was sent too didn't feed her very well so she moved on to another and s still there, If they had needed anyone else my sister said she would of asked for me to go there." Another girl opened her packet of craven A and handed them round everyone smoked and soon everyone was laughing and talking. By now the destination Dorothy and Winnie were heading for was only an hour away, and Dorothy's nerves were as taut as piano wire. The rest of the girls were laughing and talking with Winnie joining in as if she hadn't a care in the world while Dorothy looked out of the dirty window and wondered if Winnie's sister would send them straight back to where they had come from, she didn't have long to wonder as the train chugged into the station and there was pandemonium as everyone reached for cases handbags and pushed their arms into coat sleeves, Dorothy picked up her carpet bag and proceeded to follow Winnie once onto the platform they couldn't believe how quiet the country station was in contrast to the busy station they had left behind. Lennie was waiting with his wagon to pick up the land girls as the land girls were queuing to climb into the wagon Winnie and Dorothy kept on walking, then as Lennie caught up to them he stopped and shouted.

"What the hell are you two walking for when I have been sent to fetch you?" Winnie shouted back. "We are not land girls."

The land girls in the back of the wagon shouted. "It doesn't matter; come on girls climb in there is plenty of room, if we all shove up." As everyone moved another little bit along the seat to fit another two in, as Dorothy and Winnie climbed up unceremoniously and dropped into the back of the wagon. Lennie whistled as he bounced the wagon along the road, he wasn't bothered about his passengers in the back of the wagon, just as the girls attempted to light a cigarette the wagon jerked over a pothole in the rough road and everyone rose an inch or two before settling on the bench again, and the land girls swearing like troopers.

"Come on then tell me why you two are travelling up here and not in the land army?" Rosey asked Dorothy and Winnie. And before they had time to answer Rosey asked. "Are you running away for some reason?" Jackie dug her friend in the ribs saying. "Leave them alone Rosey it's none of our business."

Just then Lennie shouted. "Where abouts do you two lasses want dropping off at? Seeing as you're not going to the same place as the rest of them,"

Winnie said. "I don't know as I've never been here before."

"Well I know everyone round these parts so if you tell me a name I might be able to help." Winnie said. "The woman we are going to visit is called Miss Breaker but I don't know which house she lives in." Lennie whistled as he said with a grin. "Well I didn't know that miserable bitch had any friends, but I do know she lives with Eva, Ethel's daughter."

"Will you drop us off there then please?" Winnie asked. Lennie said. "They are at Ethel's having their dinners today so I will drop you here, at Ethel's door." As they climbed out of the wagon with all the goodbyes of the girls ringing in their ears, they cautiously made their way to the door, just as Ethel's Sunday roast had just began to sizzle in the oven.

"Whoever' is this knocking on the door our Ethel? Surely there is no one else coming for dinner or there will not be enough to go round and I'm not sharing mine." Prudence who was the nearest to the door jumped up saying, "I'll get it." Then she opened the door and came face to face with Winnie.

"Oh my God what has happened? What are you doing here Winnie and who is your friend," Prudence asked her voice full of enmity. As the colour left her face. Prudence had been living in trepidation knowing that someday, something like this would happen.

"Prudence." Gran called to her to bring her out of her reverie. "If you know these lasses bring them in and close the door the draught is blazing this fire away."

"Well you had better come in then girls." Prudence told them frostily as she stood aside to allow them into the kitchen.

"Who are these lasses then Prudence are you not going to introduce us?" Gran wanted to know.

"This is my sister and you must be her friend are you?" Prudence glared at them; "it is a long way to come just for the day, as I doubt you will be able to get a train back tonight."

"We are not going back tonight or ever." Winnie told her triumphly. Prudence's shock was evident as she said. "Mam and Dad will be worried about you Winnie."

"They don't even know where I'm living, as I have been living with Dorothy and her family, haven't I Dorothy? As she turned towards her friend,

Ethel was busy and sick of walking round them so she said. "Sit down you girls and I'll make you a cup of tea." just then Linda, Jennie Susan and Mabel walked in and heard Ethel mention tea Susan said. "You go and have a sit down Ethel you shouldn't be doing all this work as the twins are only a fortnight old."

"Yes I've told her that." Eva said, That is why, I'm coming along each day to give her a helping hand." Eva was looking thoughtful as she said,

"If you are going to have your sister staying with you Prudence, have you got somewhere else to live? As my house is not big enough for all of us, and so unexpected, or did you know they were coming?"

"No I did not Eva, and our Winnie is just being silly thinking she can come here to me, and besides Mother and father will be worried about her."

"No they will not." Winnie retorted. "They kicked me out along time since,"

"Well you will have to go back and make your peace or go back to Dorothy's house, as I cannot be doing with you here after all you are the parents responsibility not mine."

Dorothy drew in her breath and let out a long shuddering sigh, and then started to cry, "Just tell them why we are here Winnie, tell them we are both pregnant and we have nowhere to go."

Prudence started to admonition them her authority ringing in their ears, as she sniffed her disbelief but she could feel her hands shaking as she held on tightly to the chair back and wondering what Winnie was going to say next, and also wondering how much she knew. Prudence thought she had things under control when,

Winnie said. "Don't try and be the high and mighty with me Mother," as the air left prudence's body in a long sigh, "I found my birth certificate so I thought; as you were my mother I would come to you for help." Winnie was unrepentant as she said nastily "You made a precipitous exit from my life and I was left with them, I was never allowed to bring friends home or have a normal upbringing like other lasses, now I know why". Prudence had ensconced herself in the fireside chair as her legs felt like jelly and she didn't know which way to turn.

Ethel reached in to the oven and took out two huge trays of Yorkshire puddings, Eva dished out the vegetables as Wilf carved the meat, the land girls drained the big black pan full of potatoes and set two extra places for dinner. Gran said, "I think we should all eat our dinners and then work out what is best for these girls as I've always believed it's better to sort out a problem on a full stomach." Prudence cried. "I don't think I could eat a bite after all this bad news." Gran added her two penn'orth to the proceedings chiming in with. "Don't be so melodramatic prudence, you were just as bad yourself seemingly it's like the kettle calling the pot black. Ethel felt sorry for the girls but she knew there was nothing she could do to influence things one way or another but she would help if she could. Chairs were scraped on the floor as people tripped over each other to get to the big table the two boys Frank and Colin, sat beside the four little girls of Eva's to eat their dinners and Gran had hers on her knee so the four land girls Wilf Ethel Prudence Eva Winnie, and Dorothy all sat at the table Dorothy said, "It is just like being at home as I come from a large family," and then tears came into her eyes as she realised she might never see her family again. Ethel saw the tears and clicked her tongue and shook her head. Saying, "Don't upset yourself Dorothy we will work something out." Dorothy was full after the huge dinner she was very surprised when Susan got up and took three huge dishes of creamy rise pudding out of the oven while Linda went into the scullery for the cream if her Mam could have seen all this food, then as a tear slipped down her cheek she thought she had better put her family to the back of her mind for the present. Dorothy raised enquiring eyebrows at Winnie but she was tucking in with gusto her equilibrium had reasserted itself while Dorothy was very frightened but had a feeling Ethel would help her if she could. Wilf moved to the chair at the side of the fireplace with the morning paper tucked under his arm as soon as he had eaten his dinner, he felt this afternoon would be all girl talk so as soon as he had half an hour with his paper he would go back outside with Frank and Colin. Just then the fortnight old twins woke up and there was plenty willing arms ready to hold them. As Wilf smiled tenderly at Ethel,

Gran scraped her dish clean and licked her lips saying. "I've been thinking while I've been eating my dinner, I know our Eva hasn't got a lot of room but you can t see two lasses with nowhere to go so if Eva could make room for Winnie we could take Dorothy in, if that is alright with you our Ethel." "Yes it is Gran; I was just going to suggest it, only we don't have a spare bed." Linda said, "she can share our double bed cant she Jennie?" Prudence bristled with indignation, saying. "I thought I was sorting these girls out seeing as they came to me for help, although I do condone their promiscuous behaviour." Gran replied, "I don't think, you are able to condone anyone Prudence, seeing as you are unmarried and your daughter has turned up I think you will have enough bother with her, and besides it is our Eva's house." Winnie said, "Well I'm pleased that's sorted out I'm finally going to live with my mother." Linda had been upstairs for her curling tongs and after putting them through the fire grate to heat she turned to Dorothy and put an arm round her shoulders saying, Don't worry, it will be fine but you'll be needing a job until its born, that might be a problem."

"Well it needn't be." Ethel spoke up, "Pat has been coming and giving me a hand when our Eva's been busy, so if you would like to work here for a few weeks Dorothy that might suit us both." Dorothy attempted a smile but her throat was tight with unshed tears of relief, the anguish she had felt at leaving her family had subsided into a dull ache. Mabel and Susan finished washing the crockery and while Susan put the things away Mabel took the bowl of water outside to empty.

219

"I might as well go out at the same time." Winnie said as she walked towards the door, "As I need to go to the lav and I don't suppose you have one indoors." "No we don't." Gran shouted at her.

"Oh we had a bathroom when I lived with Mam, oh I mean Gran." She said her voice ominous as she looked at Prudence.

Gran looked at Prudence and said, "I think your past has come back to haunt you, she'll dance with the devil that one, but don't you put up with any mischief off her Eva, as its your house just make sure she does as she's told."

"Don't worry Gran I'll see to it that she does as I tell her." Prudence said worriedly. "I would just like to ask you all something." "Well don't look so worried Prudence." Ethel tried to cheer her up, "Whatever it is you know you can ask us."

"Well it's just I don't want people knowing that Winnie is my daughter, you know what people say about unmarried mothers, and me being a teacher I would never have respectability, so I thought I would tell everyone she is my sister, that is if you folks would say nothing." Ethel was the first to speak, "We will not tell a soul Prudence, you can depend on us, and it is your business."

"I heard that." Winnie said nastily, "All these years you've passed me off as your sister and you're still trying to do it, well I know different so I'll tell people the truth."

Eva said. "We are going along home now Mam." then she turned towards Winnie saying in a heavy voice. "You will be living under my roof, and doing as you are told, or you will be on the train back to where you came from, do you understand? I will not put up with your cheek." Winnie dropped her head as colour flooded her cheeks, and the land girls exchanged meaningful glances as they knew Eva was very much like gran. Dorothy had been feeling very frightened when she realised her and Winnie were going to be living apart, but now everyone was being friendly towards her the panic was subsiding, and commonsense reasserting itself she knew she would be alright here with Ethel and Gran.

Up at the lodge Pat held her hand to her aching back, she felt tired and worn out she had been down at Ethel's everyday helping to cook meals while Ethel had been laid up after giving birth to the twins, and now she hadn't been back home long as she'd been helping Maureen cut the sandwiches for the land girls bate for tomorrow. She sighed breaking the thread to the pillowcase with her teeth and then reaching into the basket for another garment she still had plenty left to do as she glanced at the basket of mending. Doris, Pats mother-in-law, helped Pat a lot, but now she put away her knitting needles and rubbed her tired eyes and was thankful that it was time for bed. Sarah usually buttered the bread and prepared the porridge for breakfast, but her son was home on leave for three days, and Maureen thought it was only right that she spent time with him. The girls had been shocked to see such a big nice looking fella, who had gathered the heavy logs up in the yard and carried them into the woodshed for them as if there was no weight in them at all, The girls thought he was sweet on Maureen They had heard all about him and his three brothers and found it hard to believe he could use a needle as good as any woman. Rosey remembered the night Sarah came across and saw what a mess the girls were making trying to mend their clothes the basket was full and no one seemed able to sew. Sarah had come over every night to learn the girls. Margaret, Rosey's friend had no idea at all and very little patience, and one night she had thrown the socks she was darning on to the floor and started to cry , saying, "It's no good I cannot sew." Sarah said, "I will have you all good with a needle before I'm finished with you, I have four sons all over six feet tall and I learnt them to cook and sew the same as I learnt my two daughters so you girls won't put me off. She had been right all the girls could mend their clothes now.

Ethel's kitchen was a busy and homely place, smelling of cooking, and wax polish Dorothy felt relived as Ethel had looked consolingly at her saying. "Cheer up you are staying with me now. I will look after you." Gran was nodding her head agreeing with Ethel saying. "You would do well to go around with the land girls Dorothy as that Winnies life will never flow in calm waters." Upstairs the land girls were getting ready to go out, Linda was standing in front of the mirror that was attached to the wardrobe door turning one way and then the other. "Hurry up Linda," Jennie told her, "you have stood in front of that mirror since we came up here to get ready."

"Aye well I want to look my best answered Linda we have competition now or have you forgotten about those land girls that arrived at the lodge." "We will be alright." Susan said "as all those yanks descended on the village yesterday." "Yes well I want to make sure." said Linda as she put more rouge on her face.

"I wonder if I should go downstairs and invite Dorothy?" Mabel asked the girls, "As she will only be sitting on her own after everyone has gone to bed until we come home."

"Yes I'll go now." laughed Linda, "as I'm the one that is ready." As Linda walked back into the kitchen Dorothy looked up with sad eyes. "Would you like to come along to the pub with us later Dorothy, and then I will introduce you to everyone I think you will find all us land girls are innocuous, and we do fill the pubs, don't we Gran?" Linda said smiling at Gran. "Oh I don't know," Dorothy said nervously, "you wouldn't leave me sitting on my own would you Linda?" "Courses not, now go and put some make-up on then we will all go along the pub."

After the girls had walked out of Ethel's and closed the door Gran said, "It will do Dorothy good to make some decent friends, as I don't like the look of that Winnie, Aye Prudence has got her hands full, and I will be telling our Eva tomorrow when she comes, to send Prudence over to see Dennis Coates, he has that cottage to rent Cob web cottage it's called, I don't see why our Eva has to carry Prudence's trouble and mark my word that lass is trouble." Ethel looked round and picked her cup off the table it was the last drink of the day Gran was in bed, so was Frank and Colin, the twins had been fed and were in the big wicker basket tucked in together. Ethel sat down on the couch beside Wilf to drink her cocoa, and stared into the deep glow of the fire which she had recently banked down for the night with wet tea leaves. "Are you alright lass Wilf asked concerned? As you look miles away and I don't think you've heard a word I've said to you." "Oh yes I'm fine Wilf," Ethel smiled, I was just thinking about Dorothy and Winnie." Well don't lass you have enough to think about come on let us go to bed it will soon be morning and we have a busy day a head?" Ethel climbed into bed beside Wilf after checking on the twins, she was still thinking about Dorothy and Winnie and thought Winnie would have to suffer the consequences with Prudence. Then Ethel's eyes closed, the accustomed comfort of the sideboard bed and satisfying warmth of Wilf's body tipping her over the brink of drowsiness into sleep.

Ethel woke next morning to the whimper and then the cries of the twins. "I will go and put the poker in to the fire Ethel, and stir it into life and make us both a cup of tea before everyone else wakes up". "Oh yes I could do with a cup Wilf, Ethel liked the early morning and last thing at night best as it was the only time her and Wilf shared on their own she wouldn't like to be without the rest of them but she liked a bit of time with Wilf. It wasn't long until the floorboards creaked upstairs a sure sign everyone was up, and Ethel was frying bacon, for breakfast as Linda helped Gran downstairs. Wilf and the two boys Frank and Colin soon ate theirs then went outside to collect the cows and get them milked, and then the milk was to deliver, so sally the horse ate her breakfast of hay which Colin had cut her a flap with the hay knife while the milking was getting done then she was put between the shafts to pull the milk cart. The milk was taken round the village in churns with half, and pint measures, customers brought own jugs out to collect it Wilf also sold eggs, and any spare butter that Ethel had made. Along at Ethel's the four land girls were setting off on their khaki coloured bikes to the farms where they worked.

"I wonder how Margaret is feeling this morning," Linda spoke her thoughts out loud after Jennie and her had turned off down the lane, leaving Mabel and Susan to carry on to the farm where they worked. "Well I thought Margaret looked a lot thinner," said Jennie, "and she soon seemed to tire, but she has been in bed a while now, but she is recuperating, Gran said she's lucky to have got over that pneumonia." As the girls leaned their bikes up against the wall David came hurrying out to meet them, "you haven't forgotten Linda have you? That our Paul has to go back and see that Doctor again today up at the hall." "No I haven't David." she laughed. What kind of a mood is he in today?" David rubbed his whiskery chin with yesterday's growth on saying; "He hasn't said a word to me, but we have got Margaret downstairs again which is good." David shook his head sorrowfully as he said, "there were times when I thought I was going to lose her, but she's on the mend now I don't know what I would of done without you lasses, but I need to talk to you both about the farm when you come in for breakfast, but I'll let you get on now and bring the cows in for milking, both girls looked puzzled but David didn't stop to enlighten them. The girls talked nonstop as they made their way across the two fields to collect the cows, apart from stooping down to pick the mushrooms, while Meg walked by their sides ready to round the cows up. "Do you think David is going to get rid of the farm with Margaret being so ill?" Jennie asked worriedly, "may be he thinks she will never be fit enough to work the farm again."

"Well we will soon find out Jennie, after we get these cows milked and turned back out, it will be time to go in for breakfast, and then I have to go with Paul up to the hall to see the Doctor." Linda saw Jennie was worried and said to her, "cheer up Jennie, it will be the same for me if you are out of a job I will be as well, but I will never go back home." "Well I will always stay here as Robert and I are getting married when he is no longer a prisoner of war, said an adamant Jennie who wrote to Robert and received censored letters regularly.

Although the girls were worried they still sang the songs to the cows, Jennie said "it stopped them being nervous," Linda didn't know if Jennie meant herself or the cows but she still sang along.

The cows milked and taken back to the fields, the girls made their way indoors after leaving their wellies in the porch; Margaret was sitting on the settee propped up with cushions and a blanket tucked round her, she smiled as the girls walked over to her and kissed her cheek saying, "it is nice to see you up again Margaret." Gladys was busy putting plates of egg bacon and mushroom on to the table for breakfast. Come on then she beckoned the girls, Paul and David, as she carried a small plate over to Margaret. The girls pulled the chairs out from under the table and sat down, neither of them felt like eating until they knew what David had to say. David sat down and started to eat his with gusto, and then he looked over at the girls and saw them pushing the food round the plates.

"What is wrong with you girls this morning David Enquired? You are usually tucking in and enjoying your breakfast." Linda put her knife and fork down by the side of her plate and looked at David. "We cannot eat, David, for worrying about what you told us outside, do we still have a job? And if not when do you want us to leave?" David looked at them as if he couldn't believe these good working girls were talking about leaving. "Surely you don't want to leave me, do you?" David couldn't believe it. "I need more workers not less." Jennie said, "This morning when you said you wanted to tell us something about the farm we thought you wanted rid of us." "No nothing of the kind lass, we have such a lot of work to do and we are going to start with the harvest so," and before he carried on what he was about to say he looked quickly at Paul then said, "We have some P o w s starting tomorrow."

Paul's face turned bright red, as he threw his Knife and fork down on to the table, "Well I've heard everything now, don't you know they are the bloody enemy, look what they did to me made me a cripple and you're going to have them on this farm." Margaret was starting to get upset as Gladys made her way over to her and offered words of comfort as she didn't want her sister very ill again. The girls carried on eating their breakfast relieved their jobs were safe, while David and Paul carried on arguing with raised voices.

Gladys looked up at the window when she heard a car approaching and shouted, "Here comes the Doctor, and so will you shut up Paul?" David turned round to look out of the window as he said "By but he's early this morning," and then he got off the chair and made his way to the window as the back door opened and John. Paul's, brother was standing there with his arm around a smart girl in A T S uniform.

Margaret was the first to speak. "Oh John I didn't expect to see you today and so early, come on in and one of the girls will make you and your friend a cup of tea. Are you going to introduce us to your friend?" John had been dreading this since Millie and he had left very early so they could get back the same day.

"Come on in lad, and what is your name lass? David asked them. John gave a nervous cough and cleared his throat as he said "This is going to be a shock to you Mam and Dad but Millie here is my wife we got married two days ago."

David looked astonished and Margaret had tears running down her face as she said. "Surely you could have told us better than this, surely we deserve better." Well I was going to Mam but you know what it's like in war time and Millie thought we might as well get married while her two sisters were on leave." "Oh I see," said Margaret who was very hurt. "So Millie's family were all at the wedding, and your own family didn't even know, so why have you bothered to come and tell us today?" John and Millie had eventually sat down while Linda had made a fresh pot of tea before going back outside. As Linda past Millie a cup of tea she looked up and said with a scathing smile. "So you must be a land girl, if I hadn't joined the forces, I would have done anything rather than work on the land," she shivered as she said. "I don't like animals and I wouldn't like to live in back of beyond."

David put his mug down and looked at both John and Millie. "So what are you saying? After this war is over you will not be coming back here John to help run this farm." "No I'm sorry I won't be Dad, as Millie lives in Liverpool and it's her home, so that is where we'll be living near her folks." guilt was assuaged as john and Millie exchanged conspiratorial glance. Margaret said, "So that is how the land lies is it? I'm surprised you've even come to tell us." As she took her handkerchief out of her sleeve and dabbed at her eyes which were misted over with unshed tears. Linda and Jennie set off out of the kitchen and then just before they closed the outdoor Linda shouted. "I'll be back in a couple of hours Paul, to go to the hall." Conversation was very stilted Paul was still seething over the P O W s and Margaret couldn't believe what John had done and never even wrote and said, but as she looked over at Millie she could see what she was. "Well John had made his bed now and would have to lie on it, as war made strange bedfellows."

David took a big drink of tea then placed his mug on the table then stood up saying well there's work to be done so I'll away and get started as he reached behind the door for his cap, and then went into the porch for his wellies, As he walked in to the yard he let out a deep sigh what a relief to get out of that house, but by it was a rum do and no mistake. David looked up and smiled as he heard his name being called, it was Linda's voice, "I thought we would make a start with the turnips I hope that's all right we didn't like to intrude this morning did we Jennie?" The girls had dragged the cutter out and were forking turnips into the big drum with a pitchfork each, and then taking turns turning the big handle so the turnips came out like chips, into a scuttle and when it was full they were going to put it into troughs for pig's sheep and beast to eat. David couldn't believe the amount they'd done since leaving the house. "Right lasses you might as well have a rest for five minutes and enjoy a fag. I intended turning the handle on this cutter for you but as you know I got held up in the house, and I think with our John turning up how he did this morning will knock Margaret back. I hope not." he said more to himself than Linda and Jennie. The girls stood and enjoyed their Craven a cigarette and then Linda asked what time is it David?" As David took his pocket watch out of his pocket he said. "It's gone ten Linda; you had better go in and make sure our Paul is ready, and Jennie and I will finish off here, wont we lass?"

Linda hurried towards the door and opened it with a flourish, and found Paul combing his hair with one hand while he held on to the table with the other. Oh I'm pleased you're ready Paul, I thought maybe you'd forgotten, are you sure you can walk right up to the convalescing home?"

"There is no need to walk." John said as he made his way into the kitchen. "I'll run you up, it is Fox hall that they have turned into the convalescing home isn't it?"

"Yes" Linda replied, "The government requisitioned it at the start of the war gran said."

"No you needn't bother." replied Paul. "You've done enough this morning, bringing your stuck up tart here." "Now look here Paul I know it's not easy for you being crippled, but there is no need to speak about my wife like that."

229

"You don't understand at all do you John? Mother has been so ill and then you just come here unconcerned and give her a tremendous shock like that, we had no idea you were intending getting married, I think you could of wrote and warned her anyway time is ticking on, are you ready Linda?" Paul hopped on his crutches towards the door, and Linda quickly opened it as she called ta ra, to anyone who was listening. John made his way back into the kitchen with a heavy heart, his mother didn't look well as she struggled into an upright position, leaning back against the cushions which Gladys quickly plumped up and arranged for her, very rarely did Margaret succumb to ill health, the atmosphere was so thick John thought it could of been cut with a knife, He noticed his wife wasn't trying to be friendly either as she sat there with her nylon clad legs crossed looking bored, while the big pan of stew bubbled on the fire wafting the smell of dinner round the room. John was wondering how to start a conversation hoping to bring his wife and mother together, but as he looked at them he realised they were different as chalk and cheese.

"Would you like a look round the farm," John asked his wife. She looked shocked. "Surely you don't expect me, to trudge round a farm looking at dirty animals, you know I didn't want to come here I'm not a country girl."

Margaret was looking upset as she turned to John and said, "So I presume you will never live in the country again then." "No I won't mother, Millie and I will be living near her relations." John made up his mind as soon as everyone came in at dinner time him and his wife would say their good byes, as he knew he had done wrong, he should of wrote and warned them instead of springing this on them, specially his mother who had been so ill and she was such a kind woman he wished Millie would make friends with her but she was stubborn.

Mean while Paul and Linda had managed to get half the way to the convalescing home when a car pulled alongside of them and the Doctor called to them and offered a lift, "you might as well have a lift," the Doctor told them, "as we are all going to the same place". "It will be easier coming back as it is downhill." Linda told the Doctor. "How are you doing now Paul?" The Doctor Enquired?

Linda chimed in saying, "it is a consultant he is seeing now, and they think they might be able to fit him with an artificial foot, and it will be marvellous if they can." Paul said. "We don't know for sure yet Linda, so don't get your hopes up." The Doctor quickly changed the subject as he could see Paul was getting upset but the Doctor looked at Linda and saw determination in her face and thought if anyone can control Paul she could. "Well we are here now." Laughed the Doctor, "I'm afraid I am here for the day so I can't offer you a lift back." "Oh that's fine we will manage wont we Paul, but thank you for the lift up it was very much appreciated."

Paul looked at Linda's retreating back as she walked in front and opened the door, and then held it open for him. Paul knew he would never of got round to coming here on his own, his eyes filled with tears his expression was anguished, he took his arm off one of the crutches to wipe his eyes before Linda saw and then she would be asking what was wrong with him because she missed nothing, just as he wiped his eyes a woman came hurrying past and bumped him he swayed and nearly lost his balance he struggled to stay upright and avoid the indignity of ending up flat on his face, Linda grabbed hold of him ,and shouted to the fat lass that had nearly knocked him over, the girl had shouted back swearing like a trooper. As Linda helped Paul along the corridor she said, "I know her I've seen her in the pub taking the blokes outside I know what her game is but she won't speak to me like that I'll sort her out next time I see her." Paul was very quiet as Linda led him to a seat; he was lost in thought, he was thinking what kind of a life he had in front of him, no one would want him, never walking or dancing he would never take Linda out, what would she want to go out with him for? A feeling of emptiness engulfed him.

Linda was standing in front of him her hands on her hips saying. "Are you coming to see the Doctor as it is pointless me going in to see him without you." Linda walked in to the little room and sat down leaving Paul to do the Doctors bidding and watching the different exercises' so maybe she could help him at home. Very soon the half hours therapy was finished and Paul was looking very tired, Linda thought it would have been easier if John had given them a lift and then come back for them, as she didn't think Paul could walk back after his therapy, but she knew better then mention it. The Doctor was saying, "Paul was doing very well" "Yes Linda said. "I've told him if he doesn't persevere .he'll be on crutches the rest of his life, but he seems to be doing fine now." As Paul started to leave the room Linda went over to help him. "I'm quite alright." Paul spoke with conviction.

The day had warmed up considerably and Linda could see sweat standing on Pauls forehead. "You have done very well today Paul, but I think we should have a rest," Paul looked at Linda as if she was daft, "where do you propose to rest at?" He asked her. "Just here." She pointed to Tommy's pub just as Tommy looked out of the door, he was surprised to see Paul with Linda as Paul never left the house or so he was led to believe. Linda shouted over. "I know you are not open much through the day due to shortages, but do you think Paul and I could buy a couple of pints?"

Tommy laughed as he replied, "I'll always have a drop of beer for you Linda, and it's good to see you out and about Paul." Tommy put the pints on the bar as Paul put his hand into his trouser pocket and took out a florin; "no this is on the house lad," Tommy told him, as Linda and Paul sat down with Tommy taking a seat beside them Paul picked up his pint and took a long drink and then rubbed the froth off his top lip with the back of his hand, he smacked his lips as he said, "by that does taste good Tommy, I can't remember the last time I had a pint of beer." "You should get yourself out on a night Paul it's no good just sitting in, you can come out tonight with us as this pub is always full isn't it Tommy?" "It is now lass since you and your mates arrived."

just then Lizzie came through the bar saying, "I was wondering who you were talking too Tommy as we don't normally open on a dinner time," and then she saw Paul and Linda, "Well this is a surprise seeing you Paul."

"Hello Lizzie we have been to the convalescent home to see the Doctor and Linda thought we should stop for a rest." Linda finished her pint and Paul and Tommy followed suit, Paul said I didn't intend having two pints but I enjoyed the first one and besides it's my turn to pay so we'll have a pint each as he smiled at Linda, and you and Lizzie get yourselves one as he handed over two florins. The four of them sat and enjoyed their drinks Paul joining in the conversation, and then as they finished their drinks Linda said, "We really must be getting back but I'll see you tonight and Paul is coming as well." "Oh I don't think so; I would feel awful all the able bodied yanks in here and me with my crutches." "Now look lad" Tommy said. "You fought for your country you have nothing to hide away for, so get yourself along here tonight I'll look forward to seeing you." Linda and Paul said ta ra and set off down the road. Linda started laughing,

Paul looked at her and smiled saying, "What is funny now Linda?" "Well us two drinking at Tommy's through the day, and we only went to see the Doctor, did you enjoy it Paul." "Yes I did but there was no one in the pub to see me on crutches."

"Well the pub will be full tonight and no one will take any notice of you when you go with me." Paul was surprised, "Do you mean you would actually go out with a cripple?" "I don't see you as a cripple Paul, and very soon you will be throwing those crutches away."

As Paul and Linda walked through the door David said, "I was wondering where you two had gone, Gladys has kept some dinner hot for you." Linda replied. "We have been to the pub haven't we Paul?" John and Millie were waiting for Paul to return so they could say good bye, although Millie would have preferred to have gone back as soon as they had arrived, she knew she hadn't made a good impression with her new in laws she hadn't wanted to come, as her and John didn't get much time off together and here they were sitting here wasting it, well as far as she was concerned the sooner they left here the better. These land girls seemed too familiar, having meals with the family and now one of them taking Paul to the convalescing home. Millie stood up and rubbed an imaginary crumb off her smart skirt saying, "isn't it time we were going John? We have stayed longer than I expected." And then she looked straight at Linda as she said. "I'm surprised at you, supposed to be working on the land, and escorting people to the hospital, worse still taking them to the pub, now you have relinquished your role of helper to Paul you'll be able to do what you get paid for."

Pauls face was like thunder and colour had flushed his cheeks as he stared at Millie saying, "Mind your own business, it has got nothing to do with you or anyone else, what Linda and I do and there was no need to wait for me, as I'm not bothered one way or another as you are just a stuck up tart and I can't see you bothering to come back here, and you," he pointed to John. "Have just broken mothers' heart, so I hope you are proud of yourself." As Linda and Paul sat down to eat a late dinner everyone said a quick good bye and John and Millie rushed to their car pleased to be out of the house, it was only as they went down the road John said, "I feel awful leaving things at home the way I have, I don't like unpleasantness." Millie replied "I wouldn't bother about them we won't be seeing them again in a hurry if ever." It was that remark that made John realise that he had rushed into marriage, and with a big sigh thought Paul had seen through her, it was a pity he hadn't, as he would miss his family and the farm more than he could have imagined."

The girls made their way down the fields Linda pushing the barrow while she told Jennie all that had happened. Jennie found it hard to believe that Paul had actually gone for a drink with Linda; it had been an arduous day. David was pleased that Paul was taking an interest in things again only he was still as upset as Margaret about the way John had told them he was married, they'd had no idea he was seeing anyone, and she seemed a snooty piece, but he knew they wouldn't see them very often if ever as she didn't seem to want anything to do with them. David turned to ask Paul if he'd enjoyed his time out with Linda and realised he was laid back in the chair snoring, and David thought it wouldn't be easy walking as far as Paul had with the aid of crutches but as least he'd been in the pub so it was a step forward. The girls had unloaded the barrow and smoked a cigarette by the time David arrived. While David and Linda dug out the old fence posts Jennie used a claw hammer to pull out the staples used to keep the wire taut, setting aside those that could be reused, and then rolling up the wire, it took all afternoon as there was the length of the whole field needed mending, after it was all done the girls walked to the bottom of the long field picking up the old posts and laid them in the barrow to take back for kindling sticks.

The girls had just stacked the old posts in the shed when Gladys appeared saying; "I have just poured you lasses a cup of tea, but where is David?" "I have no idea." replied Linda. "Oh I saw him talking to someone up on the cart track." said Jennie as she lifted her arm and pointed but David was nowhere in sight. "Well you lasses might as well come in and drink it while its hot David will likely turn up shortly." Gladys thought. As the girls followed her into the house Linda whispered to Jennie, "isn't it funny how Margaret and Gladys have a lot of the same expressions and mannerisms." Jennie giggled and said, "They even sound the same at times." Paul was awake sitting in the chair enjoying a mug of tea and a slice of Gladys sponge cake with jam and cream in, Linda thought, "Paul is lucky here with food she didn't know how he would have survived on rations a bit like Gran, she liked her food." Paul nodded as they walked in and Margaret smiled and started chatting she was always pleasant, even though she had been so ill. It didn't bother the girls that their friendliness wasn't reciprocated with Paul; mind he didn't seem as nasty today as he had been. As Linda drank her tea she looked over at Paul and asked if he would like to go along to the pub tonight? Just then David walked in and said, "What is it I hear about the Pub tonight?" as he sat down and took a big wedge of cake off the plate. "I was asking Paul if he would like to come with us," answered Linda. "No I don't think so." said a subdued Paul. "Well

I don't see why not you said you had enjoyed a look in the pub today, and now we have double summertime lengthening the daylight until half past eleven or so." Linda was not going to let Paul relinquish his little bit of freedom she was determined. What do you mean by double summertime? Do you think I'm frightened in the bloody dark? "No I don't think you will come out because of the crutches." Paul made up his mind it was imperative he went out tonight just to show Linda that he could. Linda and Jennie ate the last piece of cake they had left in their hands and drank the tea, and then as the girls stood up to go and start creosoting the hen houses.

Paul said to Linda, "I'll see you at the pub tonight," "No you won't Paul Emmerson." she shouted, "as I'm coming to call for you." She said laughing. Jennie looked up at the sun blazing down from a cloudless sky, and said. "I will be coming to the pub tonight, I'll be ready for a drink after we get some of the henhouses creosotated and the cows milked."

The girls wearily mounted their bikes and headed back to Ethel's, they were just coming onto the lane when they met Mabel and Susan the other two land girls who lived at Ethel's. Linda started to tell them about her day with Paul and how she was going to call for him tonight. "Well its unbelievable." laughed Susan. "But do you think you are being a bit optimistic? " Linda shrugged her shoulders "Well it's his loss not mine if he doesn't want to come, I'm still going."

"Oh I think he will come." stated Jennie. "As he won't back down and I think he is smitten with our Linda here." Linda's face coloured as she said. "Don't talk daft Jennie it's a ridiculous idea." she said dismissively, but she had seen a different side to Paul today. Susan said, "I will tell you our news now, Mabel and I were slaving away for old Walter when these P O W s turned up they are Italian." "Yes." said Mabel with conviction; "They were brought on a coach about nine thirty and they have sat around all day while we have worked hard as normal, and then to add insult to injury old Walters wife invited them inside for dinner, while we sat outside with our sandwiches and toasted them over the fire we'd made with a pitchfork" "They blow us kisses," said Susan laughingly, "but I wouldn't want to be alone where they are at." "Well I don't suppose we'll see much of them," said Mabel. "As the coach arrived back for them at four o clock, it's hardly fair as we still have all the work to do."

"Well I don't care about them." shouted Susan, "as I'm going to the pub tonight, and I'm just in the mood to drink a few pints." So are we chorused? The other three, they arrived home at Ethel's and could smell the evening meal cooking inside Ethel's kitchen. The fire was glowing and the smell of fresh bread pervaded the air too as Ethel had been baking all day. While the wooden clock ticked on the mantelpiece a small wicker basket placed at the side of the fire held two tiny babies sleeping soundly. Ethel smiled as everyone came in for tea, the land girls started to set the table and help Ethel dish out, as Colin and Frank took the same stance as Wilf and sat down to wait. It was red hot in the kitchen as they all ate their cooked meal with the fire blazing up the chimney, as Ethel rose to   take the rice pudding out of the oven Dorothy gently pushed her back on to the chair saying. "I'll do that Ethel you've had a hard day." while Linda went to the pantry and brought the big jug of cream off the stone shelf.

"Are you girls going to the pub tonight?" asked Gran "Or is it a daft question?" Jennie started to laugh. "Our Linda had a couple of pints at dinner time Gran with Paul."

Grans head shot up in between spooning pudding into her mouth.

"Well he must be seeing sense, looking at four walls day and night is no good to him, I always said, pride makes a sparse meal, time to eat humble pie, how do you feel about going out with him now Linda? because you've never seen eye to eye, With him"   "Well I thought it was silly to keep up the antagonism and I don't want to give the impression I'm bothered because I'm not, but he seemed pleasant enough today besides I think he should have a look out."

CHAPTER THIRTEEN

Linda was making her way back down to Emmerson's farm at seven thirty; she was dressed in her uniform, and had took particular care over her hair and makeup. As she had leaned over Gran to heat the curling tongs up in the fire Gran had said. "I don't know why you are going to so much bother when he sees's you every day, and I thought you were just been friendly towards him, there's more than meets the eye with you two if you ask me." Linda he was still thinking about it when she saw Paul approaching, she couldn't believe how different he looked, and he'd had his hair cut, Linda remembered now Margaret had said one of the land girls that was staying at the lodge was a hair dresser and was coming tonight to do her hair Paul must have had his cut he looked rather nice. Linda smiled at Paul as he stood in front of her and said. "You have been looking me up and down since you saw me coming, do you think I look alright to escort you to the pub?"

"Yes you do actually and I see you've had your hair cut" "Aye one of your lot did it for me, she is a land girl who lives at the lodge, she was a hairdresser before she joined the land army." Linda's approval was most apparent; as she said "well if you're ready we'll go and surprise Tommy, he'll not expect you in his pub twice in a day". Paul seemed amiable, but Linda kept their conversation colloquialism, she liked Paul when he was being kind but Linda knew he had another side.

They reached the pub door and Paul stood back to allow Linda to go in first, Tommy saw them before they saw him as the pub was packed. "Good to see you again Paul." he shouted over. "Two pints is it?" And when Paul nodded Tommy shouted "grab a seat and I'll bring them over." Paul put his hand in his trouser pocket and handed Tommy half a crown as Tommy turned to get the change out of the till Linda said. "I will buy the next lot of drinks Paul; we girls like to pay our way." Paul laughed at Linda, "yes may be we would take turns if we'd met in a pub but I have brought you out so I'll pay now drink up and enjoy it." Paul became serious as he said. "I wouldn't be here without you Linda, I lost my confidence, I couldn't face coming in here on crutches among the G I s that are here in full force now."

Just then the door opened again and Gary young came in Linda and Paul noticed straight away that he had an empty sleeve; he nodded over to Paul as if he was very pleased to see him, he brought his pint over to where there was a spare seat and sat next to Paul.

"I hope I'm not butting in here Paul? But this is my first time out since I lost my arm, and my confidence, this is the result of fighting a war he said with a sigh of vexation." Linda was pleased that someone had come to join them as the conversation with Paul was inconsequential, as it was only these last few weeks that they spoke decently to each other.

Paul seemed to relax as he chatted to his friend who he hadn't seen for the past two years. Linda saw Dorothy looking lost, as the land girls were singing and Dorothy was not joining in so Linda called her over and invited her to join them. Dorothy had just sat down when the door opened and Lucy walked in with Winnie, Dorothy didn't look very happy. Linda said. "That is your friend isn't it Dorothy?"

Dorothy looked sad as she said. "Well we came here together both being in the same boat but she has that Lucy now and she's a nasty piece." I hope you're not afraid of her Dorothy as I'm going to have a word with her in a minute, I have not forgotten what she said this morning." Paul seemed to have cheered Gary up a bit as Linda noticed they were having a long conversation. Now and again, one of them would laugh about something the other had said, Linda finished her pint and stood up to go for another as Gary saw her and said. "I'm getting these drinks." He got up and made his way to the bar, Linda whispered to Paul. "I would like to go to the bar and help him carry the drinks back, but I don't want him to think it's because he only has one arm." Paul laughed. "I would never think of you as tactful Linda." Just then Gary walked over to the table with Tommy close on his heels carrying a tray of drinks. Linda was surprised at Paul's equanimity he seemed to be enjoying himself. Linda looked over at Lucy and Winnie, and caught Lucy pointing at her and laughing at Winnie. Linda jumped off her seat and grabbed Lucy by the throat and was banging her head against the wall, Lucy was changing colour but Linda carried on until Susan thought Lucy had enough and then she walked over to Linda and pulled her off Lucy, saying. "I don't think she'll bother you again lass." Linda retorted. "She better hadn't." Paul slipped his arm around Linda's shoulders and said. "Don't let the likes of her spoil your night." Linda couldn't help but think Grans words proved to be prophetic. As Linda quickly looked over at Lucy she was scratching between rolls of fat around her waist. Linda thought Paul is right the dirty slut is not worth it. Susan, Mabel and Jennie came over to the table and talked for a while and Dorothy seemed to relax, but Linda had a feeling something was troubling her.

Paul pushed his chair back and stood up "you're not going are you Paul? As you haven't finished your pint."

asked Linda. No I'm not Linda I'm just going to the toilet I'll not be long and don't look like that I can manoeuvre among this mass of body's he laughed.

As Paul made his way to the door Linda found herself worrying in case anyone bumped into him, as this was the first time he'd been in a crowed place since he'd needed crutches. "What is worrying you Dorothy?" Linda asked concerned. "Is it because Winnie has befriended her.? Lucy. "No." Dorothy said emphatically. "Ethel and everyone has been very good to me but I need to earn some money, I know I'm helping Ethel but she doesn't really need me she is just being kind." Dorothy looked down at her stomach and said almost in a whisper. "I know there aren't a lot of jobs I can do, and people will not want to employ me I just don't know what to do." Gary leaned over saying." I'm sorry I didn't mean to be listening, but I couldn't help but hear you mention you would like a job." Just then Paul came back and Linda breathed a sigh of relief, as Paul finished his pint and seeing Tommy collecting glasses he waved him over saying. "Can we have the same again Tommy Please?" "Course you can lad it's nice to see you enjoying yourself, and how about you lass." he said to Dorothy. "Would you like another shandy or something stronger?" "No thank you Tommy, shandy will be fine."I'll have a packet of crisps called Linda would anyone else?" Gary said to Paul. "You know Dennis Flower from Low way farm, his wife died two years ago in child birth, well there is just him and his mother on the farm now and she hasn't been very well I've heard he's looking for help in the house. He then leaned over to Dorothy and said. "If I was you love, I'd pop and see him tomorrow." Linda opened her packet of smiths' crisps; she put her hand in the packet and drew out the tiny blue paper screw of salt. She sprinkled it over the crisps and then shook the bag vigorously, and then sat and ate them between huge drinks out of her pint glass. Nothing seemed to bother Linda, but the way Paul was acting was definitely giving her something to think about. The next thing Tommy was ringing the bell it was closing time. Gary stood up and said I've enjoyed myself tonight it's been nice meeting you and your girlfriend Paul. Linda noticed his Addams apple moved visibly in his throat as he drank the remaining beer in the glass, and then he said.

"Here's our Rodger," as an older version of Gary walked towards them, he acknowledged them all and then said. "I have the car outside, I used it to take Heather home so I thought I would call and take you home our Gary."

"Can you give Paul and his friends a lift?" Gary enquired. "No I will walk with the lasses." Linda quickly told him just take Paul." On the way out of the pub Paul gave Linda a peck on the cheek and asked her. "If she was sure she didn't want a lift." Linda didn't know what to make of Paul it was so uncharacteristic of him. Just then she caught sight of Lucy and couldn't resist going over to her, and then she gave her a push that sent her stumbling on her way. Lucy didn't dare turn or shout at Linda as she had frightened her in the pub and besides her head still hurt where Linda had smacked it against the wall. On the way home Gary told Paul, that his brother's car, an Austin seven had been a recent acquisition purchased two month ago. "Well it seems to run smooth enough, and thank you for the lift as it would have taken me a long time to get home on these crutches."Paul told them truthfully as the car came to a halt in the farm yard. As Paul got out of the car as quickly as he could manage, Gary said. "Do you and your girlfriend fancy meeting me in the pub on Thursday night?" "Yes alright then Gary thanks for the lift Rodger, bye." and as Paul made his way into the house everything was quiet, little did he know that everyone was not asleep, as David was watching for his son Margaret would not settle until she knew her son was in safe and sound.

The land girls made their way out of the pub tripping over one another most of them were still singing. Tommy shook his head and laughed as he followed them to the door to lock up, "good night girls don't do anything I wouldn't do he shouted after them." "Well if we do we'll be careful." Shouted Becky, as, and all the other land girls started to laugh. Tommy turned the key and pushed the bolt along, as Lizzie collected the empty glasses and emptied ashtrays. Lizzie pushed her hand into the small of her back as she straightened up after rubbing the tables down and setting the clean ash trays back where they belonged, then she turned to Tommy and laughingly said, "Did you see what happened tonight with Linda and that common lump from up the cottage?" Tommy stood still as he gathered his thoughts "What are you talking about lass?" he asked his wife. "Well I know the bar was full tonight but I saw what happened, although I pretended otherwise." " I don't know what you are talking about Lizzie, I never saw anything untoward." Oh Tommy I'm sure you stand with your eyes shut I never miss anything." Tommy knew that but kept his thoughts to himself.

"That Lucy came in tonight with Winnie, who is no better then she should be, supposed to be Prudence's sister but there's something that doesn't ring true there, anyway she had seemingly shouted at Linda today when Linda had Paul up at the convalescence home, so when she came in tonight Linda jumped up and got hold of her head and was hitting it against the wall." "Where abouts did she do, that at then Lizzie? As I didn't see anything," "Just over there Tommy near the piano." "Well it's not like you Lizzie, to let things get out of hand like that." "I think she deserves it, she shamelessly parades her illegitimate Babies up and down the village, Martha and me were standing talking outside when she walked past yesterday, we watched aghast." "Oh right Lizzie." replied Tommy. "We have about finished in here I'll go and put the kettle on, while the coals are still hot." Tommy knew to say as least as possible, because once these woman's tongues started wagging they took some stopping, and he couldn't help feeling a bit sorry for Lucy, as she wouldn't have an easy ride with theses country woman, although some of them should have been watching things more closely at home with so many land girls around as they were a bold lot and no mistake.

The land girls were a happy bunch, and as Dorothy walked down the road with them she couldn't believe how much energy they had after a hard day's work and they'd danced all night in the pub, and they were still singing as Dorothy thought about what Gary had told her, she would have to have a job as she needed some money, she didn't know what she would do after she had her baby or where she would live. She was so deep in thought; she jumped as a squirrel ran across the road and straight up the nearest tree, she stopped suddenly to watch the grey squirrel and pulled Linda with her as they were linking arms.

Look at that beautiful squirrel Linda; it is the first time I have seen one so close up." "I don't care anything for squirrels Dorothy, they look like rats with a tail, and they also strip the bark off the trees, and pinch bird's eggs out of the nests and eat them." Dorothy felt sorry for them so she said. "They are probably hungry Linda." "Rubbish." Linda retorted. "There are plenty of acorns and nuts for them."

As the land girls were walking down the road Lucy and Winnie were walking up the bank Lucy heading home and Winnie to Eva's. As they reached Eva's house Winnie saw the paraffin lamp was still burning a sure sign that Prudence was waiting, and Winnie knew why.

Lucy was a good friend she would do anything for a laugh, not like Dorothy who worried about everything, Lucy said life was for living and enjoying yourself, only tonight when they had arranged to go to the pub Lucy had no money and neither had Winnie, but Lucy said prudence was an parsimonious old maid, and Winnie had agreed as Winnie had never seen her spend a penny, although she was paying Eva for Winnies keep. Winnie and Lucy had really wanted to go to the pub so Winnie had taken some money out of Prudence's purse. Next week Winnie would have plenty of money Lucy told her she could go with her to the next village and share her customers, Lucy had laughed at Winnie and said, "You won't need to worry as you already have a bun in the oven." They had reached Eva's gate and Winnie said. "I'd better go in and get it over with." Lucy said. "You can always stay at my house, and don't forget to come along tomorrow as we need milk and eggs, Wilf won't allow Mam anything now until she pays her bill, so we'll get the stuff off him and pretend they are for Eva." "Right I will." Winnie said happily as she wanted to keep in with Lucy. As Winnie reached the door it was swung open and Prudence was standing with her long blue winceyette nightdress down to her feet, and a pink hairnet on her head. She leaned over and grabbed Winnie by the shoulder pulling her in. "Just what do you think you are playing at pinching out of my purse, and going about with that rubbish?" Winnie shook Prudence's hand off her shoulder and said I won't need your money next week."

Prudence was walking ahead of Winnie into the sitting room, and asked. Why won't you need money? Have you found a job?" Winnie looked unrepentant as she smiled at Prudence and said, "I will be working on a night with Lucy, doing the same kind of work." Prudence spun round with a lightness which belied her bulk and slapped Winnie across the face. Prudence was mortified at what she had done as Winnie screamed as she held her red cheek. Eva walked downstairs rubbing sleep from her eyes to see what was going on. Winnie's relief was evident, only it was short lived as Eva said. "I am not putting up with this Winnie, you either live under my rules, or you can find somewhere else to live." Once Winnie had arrived Eva thought, everything and everyone had faded into insignificance as Winnie was Prudence's illegitimate child. A baby born on the wrong side of the blanket, and Prudence lived in fear of Winnie telling everyone, and her a school teacher who should have been above all that.

Next morning Winnie walked up the lane to call of Lucy, who saw her coming and shouted at her to come in. "What is the matter with your face this morning?" Lucy asked Winnie, "As you look very unhappy." "Prudence smacked me across the face last night, and when I shouted at her Eva came downstairs and blamed me she said if I carry on being friends with you I have to find somewhere else to live."   "Well that's not a problem." replied Lucy. "There is plenty of room here, she can stay with us cant she Mam?"

Mildred was sitting picking the food out between her teeth as she said. "She can stay but I need some money off her I cannot afford to feed her on nothing." An idea had come into Lucy's head; she could manage to get money, nylons and make-up she couldn't remember the last time her mother had bought cigarettes, as she had always had a good supply off the G,Is, but if Winnie could get the food Lucy felt sure her mother would allow Winnie to stay. Lucy's mother broke into her thoughts as she said are you listening our Lucy? We need some milk, that miserable bugger that comes round with the horse and cart won't leave me any."

"Why not." asked a shocked Winnie. "I thought he sold milk to anyone that wanted it." "Don't be so naive Winnie, we owe him money but he won't get it we don't like paying for anything do we Mam?" Lucy picked her cardigan up and a can saying. "Come on Winnie we will go and get some milk off Wilf." "I don't understand you."Winnie told her. "I thought he wouldn't allow you to have milk." "He won't." laughed Lucy. "But you can get it for us, as you live with Eva, so we will go and tell Ethel, that Eva has run out of milk, and eggs maybe butter if we can get away with it, as I am sick of margarine or pork fat."

Dorothy had been up early; the same as everyone else who lived at Ethel's and had told Ethel and Gran about the conversation in the pub with Gary Young. Ethel was shocked to learn he had lost his arm. But things looked hopeful for Dorothy as Ethel and gran knew Martha and her son Dennis Flower, who lived at Low way farm. Ethel had told Dorothy how there'd been a big family, and they had all married and left home, apart from Dennis who had married and stayed to run the farm with his mother after his dad died. "She was a lovely lass his wife." Gran said. "Only she died in childbirth three years ago, and I don't think he has ever looked at another woman?" "Oh I don't know." Dorothy was full of doubt, "I can only work there a few month and I don't know what I will do when the baby comes." she cried. "Well I don't think they will expect you to do any work on the farm." Ethel said uncertainly.

"Who won't want help on the farm Mam?" Eva asked as she came in for a cup of tea and a rest, as she had been churning butter all morning for Ethel, and just caught the end of the conversation. "Dorothy is thinking about going to see Martha Flower." Ethel explained. Gary young told her in the pub last night as they need help." Eva looked deep in thought and then said. "I remember now, she hasn't been very well something to do with her legs, I do know they have plenty help on the farm, as three of the land girls who are living at the lodge with Maureen work there." After the tea had been drank and Eva got back on to her feet to resume work, Gran said to Dorothy, "Come on then lass, no time like the present go and talk to Martha she is a decent enough sort then you'll know one way or another." Eva said as she made for the door. "I would go with you Dorothy, but I have some more butter to make yet."

Dorothy set off down the road with mixed feelings; "maybe they wouldn't want to employ her with being pregnant." Gran had said. "It would be grand if she got a start as the farm is tucked away, and Dorothy would be out of sight of prying eyes." It was so well tucked away Dorothy couldn't find it and didn't dare stray too far, at home in the city she thought, she had never got lost, but up here among all these fields it was different as she rubbed away a tear with the back of her hand. She jumped as a voice asked her what she was looking for, Dorothy smiled as she realised it was one of the land girls she'd met in the pub last night. "I'm lost." she admitted sheepishly, after explaining where she was heading too. Shirley said. "It's down yonder." and indicated a lane leading down a farm track away in the distance. She wished a nervous Dorothy good luck then walked away pushing a barrow. Dorothy strolled on down the lane thinking, "what a lovely summer's day the sun resplendent in a blue sky while the birds sang in the trees." The Flowers back door was propped open; it was hot and humid in the kitchen as the fire blazed up the chimney. As Dorothy knocked nervously on the door she could see Mrs Flowers baking a batch of scones.

"Can I help you lass?" Martha Flowers called to Dorothy. "Don't stand on the step come on in. as Dorothy wondered what to say as Martha carried on rolling the pastry, then she looked at Dorothy and said smiling. "Well are you going to tell me lass or do I have to guess?" Dorothy said. "I'm sorry you must think I'm rude but I don't know where to start." Well while you're wondering lass put the kettle on the coals and make us both a pot of tea I'm fair parched. Over a pot of tea Dorothy told her the sorry story. Martha said, as she thought about Dorothy's predicament. "Do you know how to bake lass?"

"Oh yes I can bake Mrs Flowers, Ethel taught me I didn't know how too when I came here but I do now."

"Do you need to hurry back to Ethel's? Dorothy. Because I have a bad back and could do with some help to make the bread. If you would like a job you can start now." Said Martha encouragingly. Dorothy was overwhelmed by the kindness Martha showed to her even though she knew about Dorothy's predicament she knew she had found another friend. An hour after Dorothy had arrived at the Flowers farm she was standing at the table rolling out a huge ball of pastry and lining half a dozen tins in which she would presently place various fillings, as the dough rose in a huge dish in front of the roaring fire. Later as she washed the baking board and rolling pin in the big stone sink, a man walked in and smiled at Dorothy. "Who have we got here then?" he asked his mother. "As I see you've got her working." Mrs Flower introduced them saying. "This is Dorothy my helper she has been baking for me and she is starting here in the morning." The kettle started to boil on the fire and Mrs Flower reached up and took the tea caddy off the mantelpiece and put three good spoonfuls of tea in before pouring the scolding water in. Then she looked towards the open door and asked her son Dennis. "Are those lasses coming for a drink of tea today?" Just then the land girls came in and recognised Dorothy as they had seen her in the pub. Dennis asked Dorothy how she had got to the farm." Oh I walked." she replied. Well you can't walk every day as it is nearly four miles. Dorothy thought in a few months she would be big and didn't think she would still be working here, but for now she shut her mind to her impending worries. Dennis asked. "Can you ride a bike as there is one in the shed?" "Yes I can replied Dorothy." "Right that's settled then after I've drank this I will go and make sure the tyres are pumped up, and you can use it tonight." Dennis wheeled the bike round for Dorothy when she was ready to go home, he held the seat while she slipped her leg through and pulled the pedal up with her toe. Dennis thought she didn't look very confident, and when he watched her wobble away out of the yard, he wondered if she would make it home without falling off.

Winnie and Lucy had arrived at Ethel's; Winnie wished they were on their way back to Lucy's; she had ignored Dorothy last night, and now she had to tell a pack of lies to get a drop of milk. Lucy pushed in beside Winnie and knocked on the door.

"Come in." called Gran. When Gran saw who it was she said. "What do you two want I wouldn't have thought there was anything here to interest you? Lucy gave Winnie a dig in the ribs, so Winnie said. "You know I'm staying at Eva's with Prudence, only Eva has no milk or eggs, so we thought," As she pointed to Lucy, "that we would walk down for them." Gran sat and looked at them as Winnie went from one foot to the other. Gran said what's up with you? You're like somebody with ST vitas dance or is it a guilty conscience?" The girls stood looking uncomfortable as Gran scrutinised them before she picked up her stick and waved it at the window, it was something she did to get attention if she needed help. Colin saw it and went to tell Ethel that the twins needed feeding. "They were only fed two hours since." Ethel told Eva "But I'd better go and see what's wrong with them, you might as well come with me Eva and we'll make a pot of tea."

Eva was shocked to find the girls pretending she needed milk. "I am not putting up with you Winnie, you have got yourself into bad company, and I have had a bad headache all day as I never slept last night after all the rumpus. I know you stole money from Prudence's purse, so I will be having words with Prudence tonight, she can stay as long as she wants but you are not." Winnie dropped her head and turned towards the door, as Lucy cheekily said. "Where is Dorothy has she ran away?" Gran retorted. "Mind your own business and get out." Eva sat down with a cup of tea in her hand saying "honestly I can't believe the cheek of those too." Gran remarked. "Aye those two's lives will never run in calm waters."

"What are we going to do now Lucy?"Winnie asked worriedly. Lucy smiled smugly as they walked past the lodge where the land girls were staying. "We will get all the food we need from there." as she pointed at the lodge door." "We won't be able to Lucy, and I'm not sneaking in there." "You won't have to Winnie." said Lucy with a patronizing attitude." "I think Elsie will be only too pleased to do as I say, after I tell her what will happen if she doesn't comply." Winnie wondered what she had got herself into as they reached Lucy's house, the gloomy interior quickly enveloped her and settled in oppressively the room was sparsely furnished an unpleasant odour permeated the stale air. Mildred, Lucy's mother was sitting in the only armchair that was in the house, with a cigarette dangling from her bottom lip, while Lucy's dirty children were sitting on the floor covered in jam and banging the only pan they possessed with a spoon. There was a huge box in the middle of the floor that acted as a table, and on it was a scraping of margarine and half a loaf of bread, and then Winnie realised there was a jar of bramble jam directly under the sticky fly paper that was dangling from the ceiling, only it must of been there before Lucy and her family had moved in, as a lot of the dead flies had dropped off, and as Winnie looked at the jar minus its lid she thought some of those flies could be in that jar and felt sick as Lucy covered her bread in it unconcerned.

CHAPTER FOURTEEN

Along at Emmerson's farm Paul was contemplating about his next appointment at the convalescence home, and he also wondered about Linda, he had enjoyed his night at the pub and he felt sure Linda had as well. But she wouldn't want to make a habit of it, she probably just felt sorry for him, when there was plenty GIs to choose from who had two good legs, he thought remorsefully. Just then the back door opened and Linda brought a bucket full of eggs in. She left them on the floor in the scullery while she popped into ask Paul if he'd enjoyed last night.

Paul gazed longingly at Linda; she brought a little ray sunshine into an otherwise monotonous existence. "Yes I did Linda it has been so long since I went out anywhere."

Margaret was sitting in the chair smiling at Linda, she was looking a lot better now; David had just been saying she was on the mend. "You look flushed Linda." Margaret commented, and looked concerned. "What have you been doing?" I have been chasing the carrion crows away from those two day old chicks, until David and Jennie knocked the posts in, and fastened the pig netting to them, and then the chicks could strut about safe." Linda was sniffing the air ecstatically as Gladys prodded the roast beef in the oven; she also had a bowl of batter standing on the table waiting to be made into Yorkshire puddings.

"I remember being sent out to scare the carrion crows away." Paul remarked. It's a long time ago now." "Well you were still at school." Said Margaret, "Mind I don't like them I never have." "No me neither." Said Gladys coming into the conversation, "I can watch them from my kitchen window at home, they perch like sentinels on isolated tree tops where they can see what's going on in all directions, they watch other birds building their nests their activities are observed and remembered by the watching crows, and in due course many nests are wrecked and robbed they make a merciless pounce on the tiny chicks, they are notorious as egg thieves, they have a hoarse cry like a "kaaah" they usually utter it three times in succession. Linda was very surprised. "By you know a lot about them Gladys." "Aye I should do lass all the years I've watched and listened to them. I'll tell you something else as well. Huge party's of crows are common in summer, autumn and winter. Once birds are paired they stay together for life, and their bulky nests of twigs and dry grass are usually high in the trees.

Linda hurriedly made for the door saying. "I'd better go or David will wonder where I've got to, as there is plenty of work to be done."

"Yes and I'm going to have a shave," said Paul decidedly. He had been sitting thinking about the night before when he had enjoyed the night at the pub with Linda and the rest of the people he had met up with, he had laughed when the pub regulars had been singing and the land girls had launched into a repertoire all of their own. Paul was now standing in front of the deep pot sink the single brass tap dripped rhythmically the drops of water echoing loudly as they hit the bottom of the sink, he expelled a weary sigh, as he flipped braces off his shoulders and unbuttoned his shirt then proceeded to shave. The cutthroat razor freshly honed against the leather strap, after removing last night's stubble Gladys passed him a freshly ironed shirt saying. "I bet you feel better now."

"No I don't think I will ever feel better Gladys, not when all the GIs are in the pub throwing their money around and chatting all the lasses up and I'm on crutches I don't think I will go any more." Paul said despondently. "They are over sexed over paid and far worse over here."

"Yes but you have a lot more than them our Paul." Margaret told him. Paul looked puzzled at his mother as she said. "You have Linda; it is a long time now since you two put all the previous animosity behind you and she has feelings for you Paul it is time you realised that before she gets sick of asking you out, its time you saw what's under your nose before it's too late as Linda is a lovely lass, and I would love her to be part of this family." Paul flopped down in the chair in deep thought he had no idea that Linda felt that way about him surely his mother had got it wrong, but when he thought about it his mother missed nothing. He rolled a pinch of empire shag licked the edge of the paper and lit up letting out a stream of smoke, and then he shook his head mournfully at his mother saying. "I hope you are right but I can't see her wanting a cripple." He'd been awake most of the night but that wasn't unusual it was damned difficult to sleep day and night as he dozed through the day to put time in from boredom. Gladys had realised that Paul couldn't just sit all day he had become lethargic of late. Linda was just what he needed to shake him out of his doom. Gladys passed him a cup of tea; he accepted it and drank it gratefully.

Along at Eva's house thing were very strained, as both Eva and Prudence waited for Winnie to arrive and collect her things, Eva was worrying over Mark arriving to witness all the unpleasantness with Winnie, and Prudence was wondering how long she could remain in the village as a highly respected school teacher before Winnie told all and sundry that she was her, unmarried mother. Both women jumped as the knock on the door resounded loudly followed by Winnie and Lucy walking in and Lucy banging the door shut noisily behind her.

"I have come for my things." Winnie's wayward tendencies shone through. Prudence was standing ringing her hands; she did not trust Winnie, and the other one Lucy, had a determined look about her. "Go and collect your things then get out." Eva told Winnie. Prudence knew her life had changed dramatically, it was most disconcerting, her assumption had been correct when Winnie arrived with the knowledge, and birth certificate to prove that she was her mother, she'd be more diligent next time, as the time had come for Prudence to move on. Eva was relieved at prudence's acceptance of the situation after all it was her daughter, but Eva was exasperated with Winnie and she knew as long as Winnie was friends with Lucy she would never be any better.

Winnie walked towards the door carrying her possessions' and then turned and scowled nastily as both Eva and Prudence saying. "I won't forget this," Eva knew that Winnie was threatening Prudence, but there was nothing she could do about it, Prudence would just have to hope given time it would blow over but how much damage it would cause in the mean time she didn't know. Eva turned towards prudence as the door closed on Winnie and Lucy. Prudence had an authoritative air about her and it was unequivocal she would not want denunciations.

"Come on Prudence sit down." Eva told her." I'm going to make us a nice cup of tea and don't worry about those two, as your Winnie has enough troubles of her own, as I don't know what she'll do when her baby comes."

Elsie was on her own as Winnie and Lucy walked towards the Grange, she turned from her task of washing the kitchen floor as she heard the latch on the gate banging shut then the door opened and thinking it was Maureen carried on with her chores and then as the footsteps got nearer she looked up at Winnie and Lucy staring down at her.

"What do you want?" Elsie stammered nervously.

"Well everything we need you can supply." laughed Lucy nastily. "And you had better do as I say if you know what is good for you." Lucy's apparent equanimity frightened Elsie. Winnie strode over and lifted the large tea towels off the loaves of bread that Maureen, Elsie and Sarah, had baked earlier. "Do you want one of these loaves?" Winnie asked Lucy. As Lucy was opening the cupboard doors seeing what else she could take. "Yes bring two." Lucy answered. "Mam is partial to fresh bread." And then realising that Maureen, or that nosey woman Sarah, might pop in any minute decided it was time they went with the bread, and on their way out Lucy turned and called to Elsie. "We'll be back tomorrow and you'd better have some ration coupons for me." "What are you going to do with the coupons?" asked a bewildered Winnie. Lucy laughed as she hurried up the road towards home with the bread, "we are going to sell those coupons and get some money." She said gleefully.

Elsie finished washing the kitchen floor with a heavy heart, before Maureen came back. As she went outside to empty the bucket of dirty water she saw Maureen and Sarah coming across the yard from Sarah's home, Badger cottage.

"It hasn't taken you long to wash the floor." Maureen called out. "You're a good girl Elsie." Sarah busied herself getting the huge pans out ready to cook the tea as Elsie went round the rooms adding coal to the fires, and placing an armful of logs on the hearth to help the coal out later, when the land girls would be home as not all of them went out as regular as the rest, more so Rosey, as she wrote to her boyfriend every night and he was coming up in the next fortnight, and Elsie had heard Maureen telling Sarah that it would be alright for him to stay here at the Grange as she, Maureen, would be here at all times so there would be nothing untoward. Elsie thought what Maureen had told her that absence makes the heart grow fonder Rosey's heart at any rate seemed too.

Elsie was brought abruptly out of her reverie as Maureen said. "I must be going daft I was sure we had made sixteen loaves of bread today, and I have just counted them and there is only fourteen. "Can you remember Elsie?" Elsie started to say she wasn't sure when Sarah said. "I could of sworn there was sixteen but." She shrugged her shoulders as she said, "there must have only been fourteen." Elsie loved working here, in fact her life had been good since she had come to stay at the pub with her Uncle Tommy and Aunt Lizzie, but she worried. "What would happen now? Two loaves of bread had gone today, and Winnie and Lucy were coming back tomorrow for the coupons. If she didn't hand them over she dread to think what would happen to her, and if she gave Lucy the coupons it was helping her to pinch, and if Maureen found out she would have no job and no home, if Uncle Tommy and Aunt Lizzie found out. The afternoon went over and the land girls had eaten their teas so after the washing up was done Maureen told Elsie "to get off home." And she added "you have been very quiet are you not feeling well?" "No I'm all right thank you Maureen." and then hurried out of the door with tears running unchecked down her cheeks.

Tommy was just arriving at the door of the pub the same time as Elsie he opened the door and held it open for Elsie to walk through first. "Have you had a good day Elsie?" he asked smilingly as I've been busy." They both walked into the kitchen as Lizzie was pouring them both a cup of tea, after placing the brown teapot under the cosy she took a packet of lucky strike out of her pinny pocket and lit up drawing the smoke deep into her lungs. "Oh I do love a cup of tea and a fag before your uncle Tommy and I start work in the bar." she told Elsie. But Elsie's mind was on other things. What could she do about Lucy and Winnie? If she was to tell Maureen in the morning then she would know she'd been telling lies about the bread, and Maureen trusted her, and she would probably tell Sarah. Elsie knew she had a good job along at the Grange she got on well with the land girls and if they knew about Lucy and Winnie they would soon sort it out. "Would you like to sit in the bar tonight Elsie?" Elsie quickly came out of her reverie as she realised uncle Tommy was speaking to her. She found it hard to concentrate she was no nearer a solution now as she was weeks ago, "Sorry I didn't hear you Uncle Tommy." She said as she looked down at the floor. "Well the others there if you want it, as you are fifteen now and your Aunty Lizzie has agreed with me, you can sit in the bar on a night and have a drink of lemonade, as you know most of the land girls and it will be company for you." "Thank you Uncle Tommy but I won't bother tonight I'll have an early night."

Lizzie was unaware of the situation at the lodge "I don't know what's bothering her." Lizzie told Tommy as she washed the glasses behind the bar. "Bothering who Lizzie?" Tommy asked, as Lizzie always had plenty to say and Tommy didn't always listen. Lizzie stopped what she was doing and stood with her hands on her hips glaring at Tommy." Who the hell do you think I'm talking about? Your niece Elsie. There is something wrong with her." "Oh she's just tired." Tommy replied. "She said she was having an early night." "Well if you believe that you'll believe anything Tommy Gibson, there's something wrong and I intend to get to the bottom of it." Tommy expelled a weary sigh; he just hoped Elsie wasn't in any trouble, because Lizzie was like a dog with a bone she would not rest until she found out what was wrong with Elsie.

Along at Eva's Mark had just arrived, he had four days leave and he was going to spend it with Eva and the four little girls two of whom were his. Eva had taken them in as evacuees. He was single the same as Eva as his wife had died in a fire with her boyfriend. Rationing of petrol had curtailed the use of cars, but Mark was desperate to spend as much time with Eva and the girls as possible, and he was owed a couple of favours, so one of his friends lent him a car while the other one had got hold of some petrol.

"Come to the table and have some tea Mark." Eva invited him; the girls and Prudence were already seated, as Eva dished the dinner out it was his favourite Mince and dumplings with plenty of vegetables, potatoes and gravy. He smiled as he pulled out a hard backed chair from under the kitchen table and sat down saying; "I'm going to enjoy this." There was rice pudding to follow, and a cup of tea that rounded off all the meals, as Mark found out with coming up here. "I'll help you to wash up Eva." He told her as he made his self comfortable on the settee.

"You needn't bother." Prudence thundered. He tried to say something conciliatory to the irate prudence but she just stared back in the aloof way she had adopted. Later in the evening prudence having dispersed and the four children cuddled up warm in comfortable beds sound asleep. Mark decided to speak his mind to Eva, as he sat with his arms around her shoulders. "I have been coming here two years now, and I think it's time we did something about it."

"What are you trying to tell me Mark Parker?" Eva was laughing, after the stress with Prudence and Winnie it felt good to relax with Mark and she did love him. Upstairs prudence had sat down on her bed to open the incongruous looking envelope, which had arrived in the morning post; she had seen the way Eva had looked at her as she had tucked it away, well no doubt Eva wouldn't be interested now she had him to keep her company. There was two letters inside the envelope; one was from her mother apologising, about the lateness of the letter she'd enclosed, Mrs Breaker had gone on to say when the letter had arrived Dad had put it on the bookcase and it must have fallen behind, but never mind it has turned up now. "Better late than never." Her mother had jokingly written. Prudence was in no mood for any jokes, or company, as she tore the letter open as she didn't gleam any information from the postmark. Prudence held her breath as she read the contents; it was from her old friend Victoria Fielding, they had taught at a small school together for a while, and then Victoria and Prudence had gone their separate ways. Victoria had been going through some papers and found Prudence's address and she had some information that might interest her. Prudence held her breath as she read Victoria's letter, seemingly Victoria was teaching in the Isle of Man, and the head teacher was intending to retire, she lived in the village school house, and Victoria wondered if Prudence would fancy applying for the job and they could share the house. Prudence was smiling as she finished reading the letter it was an answer to her prayers, she read through the letter again and Victoria had said Miss Bagley was going to give her six month notice the following week. It was then that Prudence, realised as she looked at the date on the letter that it had been sent four month ago. Prudence was vexed, it was too late she was sure they would have been interviewing people for the post now. She got off the bed, she would go downstairs and make herself a cup of cocoa and take it back upstairs with her, she did not fancy sitting downstairs with those two Eva would be sitting smiling at him, no doubt he would be moving in, more fool her, all men were trouble, she had found that out herself.

Eva looked round as Prudence open the stair door into the living room. "Have you come to join us?" Prudence asked Eva.

"No I've just come to make a hot drink and then I'm going to bed." Prudence said sulkily. Half an hour later Eva and Mark heard the bed springs as Prudence got into bed. Twenty minutes later the loud snores could be heard clearly downstairs.

"Come on Eva" Mark said as he grabbed her hand, "let's go to bed you know you want too," he laughed, "She won't hear," as he nodded his head to the ceiling as Prudence snored on up above.

"Oh alright you've persuaded me," said an embarrassed Eva. Together they hurried up the stairs and were soon in bed it hadn't taken long to get out of their clothes. The desire had been urgent and unstoppable; he had been gentle and persuasive she had no inhibitions so she'd succumbed to his advances. Eva had always thought she would wait for her wedding night for intimacy the second time around but she was revelling in this new found love.

Mark sat up in bed and lit two cigarettes handing one to Eva, "you don't have any regrets do you Eva." he asked, "As my intentions are honourable. "Will you marry me Eva?"

"Yes I will Mark." Eva didn't need to think about it she had fallen in love from the first time they'd met. They both stubbed the finished cigarettes in the ashtray, and then Mark took her back in his arms.

Eva woke and looked at the alarm clock with its luminous numbers, and was shocked to see it was seven o clock Prudence was usually up by now, she must have slept in which Eva was thankful, as she kissed Mark and told him it was time he went back on the settee.

Later as they were all sitting round the table eating breakfast, Mark said to Eva. "I think we'll go and buy you an engagement ring. Prudence nearly choked as she drank her tea.

"Are you getting married Eva?" Prudence was flabbergasted. "I thought you would have stayed single, after your disastrous marriage last time, and don't tell me its wartime and you have to grab happiness while you can, as I personally don't believe it." Prudence pushed her chair back from the table and stood up. "I will be upstairs if you need me Eva as I have things to see too." Prudence picked up the letter from Victoria and thought, "if I don't do it I will never know." Within half an hour Prudence hurried through the kitchen on her way to the post box, looking a little happier than she had at breakfast. Mark watched Prudence's retreating back and asked "Where is she off too in such a hurry."

Two hours had passed since breakfast, but Eva had four little girls to wash and dress, while Mark had offered to wash up thinking. "If he didn't they wouldn't get the ring on this leave."

The little girls were excited as they climbed into the Austin seven, more so when Mark produced a big bag of sweets, when they arrived at the next village Eva told him she needed to buy some material if they were getting married on his next leave, as she would have a lot of dresses to make. The shopping done and material bought they made their way to the jewellers. Eva felt embarrassed choosing the ring not that there was many to choose from. But Eva thought it wasn't everyday you went to choose an engagement ring and took your children along. The jeweller said. "I'm afraid the rings are half gold and half silver due to the war, can't get the gold, but this is a nice little ring." as he picked one out of the tray for Eva to look at. Eva looked in the tray herself and across over ring with two tiny diamonds in caught her eye, she picked it up and with raised eyebrows looked at Mark. "Try it on Eva." Mark told her. "If that is the one you like we'll have it." Eva nodded as Mark took the ring and placed it on her finger. "It's beautiful." Eva whispered. As Mark paid for the ring, the jeweller offered his congratulations.

As they all made their way to the car Eva said. "I want to call and see Mam, I just hope Prudence hasn't called and said we were getting engaged."

Wilf was sitting with one baby in his arms while Ethel had the other, and they had a feeding bottle each as Ethel explained it was easier for her now they were both on the bottle and Wilf even helped to feed them through the night.

"So he should." stated Gran. "He's had his pleasure, and he got that well before you were both married." She told Ethel. "Now he's got his sons, he should give a hand with them as you are not getting any younger our Ethel. Aye you had those twins late in life if you ask me."

"Come on sit down," Ethel told Eva and Mark, "can you girls manage to go in the pantry and get a drink of milk and a cake?"Mark rummaged in his pocket and extracted FRYS five boys chocolate, shining in silver paper, and then shared it out between the four girls.

"Can we go out and play?" The girls chorused, and then hardly waiting for an answer the girls exploded out of the door like corks out of a bottle.

I'll do it in a minute Mam but first I've got something to show you." As she held out her hand to show off her engagement ring, "Mark and I are engaged, that is where we went this morning to buy the ring."Eva was ebullient. Ethel picked her daughters hand up and looked closely at the cross over diamond ring. It seemed a long time since Ethel had seen Eva so happy "It is very nice our Eva, congratulations to you both." as she included Mark.

"Well let me see the ring our Eva." Gran chimed in. Gran squinted as Eva held her hand close to Grans eyes. "Yes it is a nice ring." Gran remarked. "You won't be getting the plain band for a while will you?" she asked. As Wilf rose and passed one of the babies to Eva." I think this calls for a celebration drink, don't you Ethel?" Wilf came back with glasses and a bottle of whisky, "how did you manage to get a bottle like that?" Gran asked. I hope it's not off the black market." "You'll not want a drink then Gran just in case it is." Wilf laughed as he poured everyone a drink.

"Oh I didn't say I didn't want a drink, I like a drop whiskey for medicinal purpose helps me sleep, and I don't suppose anybody will miss a bottle, And as for me drinking it. Well it's for medicinal purposes don't forget as I'm not a drinker." At which Wilf turned and winked at Ethel "Well I did enjoy that." Gran said after she had drank two glassfuls and Wilf had taken the rest back to the cupboard.

"We are getting married very soon." Eva told everyone. That is why I bought some material today for dresses."

"Oh Eva you're not expecting are you?" Gran asked her.

Eva looked shocked. "What a thing to ask me Gran, just because we see no sense in waiting, as If we are starting a family, do you think we would do that?"

"Well don't get all high and mighty with me our Eva, as it wouldn't be the first time you had to get married in a hurry. Just remember you only just made it last time, married three months you were before these twins were born, I don't forget."

"I think I'll put the kettle on Mam." Eva said. "Yes I think we could all do with a cup of tea love." Ethel smiled at her daughter. Eva was forever alienated by gran assuming she was having to get married. "I will show her." thought Eva as she gave an ambiguous reply as she remembered all the nights she had spent with Mark and her face flushed. Oh God I hope I'm not pregnant she thought."

"Well I know I could do with a cup of tea my mouths fair parched." Complained Gran. And if you're bringing those cakes out our Ethel I'll have one. You've made them rather nice this week. I think you must have rushed them last week, Aye, a bit dry I thought. But you know me our Ethel I don't like to complain."

The door opened and Colin and Frank came in looking expectantly at Wilf. "Come and have a cup of tea and a piece of cake first I haven't forgotten." Wilf explained.

"Where are you going Wilf?" Mark asked as he bit into his cake. "These two lads have taken a fancy to these goats so we are going to see them."

"How many do you want?" Mark asked.

"Well I have told them they'll be looking after them; which I know they will." Wilf said. "They are two good lads on the farm and Frank will be leaving school soon."

"Oh and then what will you do Frank? Will you go back to the city?"

"No I'll never go back there, we sorted that out a long time ago didn't we Aunty Ethel?" "We did Frank. These lads will never leave us. I'm pleased to say." After Frank and Colin had drank their tea and eaten three of Ethel's buns each, Wilf got stiffly out of the chair, then took his cap from behind the door and placed it on his head.

"Come on then." he called to Frank and Colin. "And just remember they will have to be tethered on the lane or they'll be away ,and I don't want them in the field as they nibble the grass that far down you can practically see the soil, and you must buy goats in pairs otherwise they will pine."

Another one who was starting to enjoy life in the country was Dorothy. She'd had a hard morning helping Martha to make Braun from the pig heads; it was hot and stuffy in the kitchen, as the big black pans boiled on the fire. It was a relief to Dorothy as she finally sat at the table after helping Martha to dish out; Martha, like Ethel served generous portions and Dorothy was tucking in with relish, she and Martha worked as a team, nothing had been mentioned about her condition, but she was only a couple of month away from having this baby, she sighed as she wondered what was to become of her. Martha looked at her and smiled. Dorothy would cry when she left here Dennis was a lovely man but she was here to help Martha.

"I'm going up the fields after dinner to check on the hay" Dennis told Dorothy. "Would you like some fresh air? You look as if you could do with some."

Dorothy looked alarmed at Martha, saying. "I'm sorry Dennis, your Mam and I have a lot of work to do yet and besides that s why I'm here, or I'd of love too." Dorothy liked Martha very much; she felt an affinity towards her. Martha wasn't daft she'd been watching

Dennis since the lass had come here to work and she knew he was soft on her, after all it had been three years since his wife died in childbirth, and it wasn't natural for a man to be without a woman that long. "After we've washed up Dorothy you might as well go and get a bit fresh air and I'll put me feet up for an hour." Martha told her.

Dorothy s heart was banging like a drum she liked Dennis but to be going up the fields with him was another matter. What would she talk to him about? She quickly washed the pots while lily one of the land girls offered to dry. "There is no need." Martha told her. "Yes there is." Lily replied. "You feed us well so it's the only way to repay you, so put your feet up and I'll help Dorothy." She told her.

Half an hour later Dorothy and Dennis were walking along and it seemed to Dorothy that everywhere in the lanes and fields the scent of wild flowers in profusion was breathtaking and filled the air. Stitchwort, white dead-nettle joined by yellow buttercups, cow parsley and hedge mustard and cowslips. They walked on, alongside gardens and up the lane as Dennis pointed out the different flowers. There were bright flowering whorls of birds-foot, trefoil the yellow and golden orange pea-like flowers, dazzling in the sunshine, and the creamy white blossom of the dogwood. Dorothy felt this life was a far cry from the city, and everyone had been kind to her apart from Winnie who she had been pally, and had arrived with. Suddenly her throat was tight and she felt the prickle of tears behind her eyelids. Dennis glanced at Dorothy as her reticence unnerved him, he had talked nonstop to her from leaving home, as he had made up his mind to ask her today as he could not put off any longer. They came to the stile he climbed over first and then reached for her hand while she clumsily climbed on emphasizing her size. Dennis sat down on the hillside pulling Dorothy down beside him. "We need to talk." he told her. "That is why I suggested we came away from the farm."

Dorothy looked up at him with tears on the ends of her long lashes saying. "If I'd worked on the farm I could have understood you wanting to tell me in private, that you think it is time for me to go to save me any embarrassment, but as I work for your mother I thought it would have been her as she gave me the job." Dennis looked into Dorothy's sad face and smiled. "You have no idea what I have brought you up here to say have you?" Dorothy shook her head. Dennis lit two cigarettes and passed one to Dorothy, he knew he was going to have to tell her now before his confidence left him. "The reason I asked you to come up here today Dorothy was to ask you to marry me." Dennis realised he had blurted it out too quickly as the colour left Dorothy's face. "Look Dorothy I'm sorry maybe I should explain I'm fond of you, and it is going to be impossible for you to work fulltime or ride that bike, Mam suggested you could live in with us if it would help so you could work for a while longer, but as you know I lost my wife in childbirth three years ago, I'm not a drinking man although I don't mind a pint now and again, and I love bairns, so I thought why don't we get married it would give the bairn a name and you would have respectability." Dorothy was so shocked she was speechless. "Surely I'm not repugnant." Dennis laughed to try and break the tension.

When Dorothy collected her thoughts she said. "It's awfully good of you Dennis, and I'm grateful that people are still thinking of me, and trying to help but I couldn't expect you to bring another man's child up, it wouldn't be fair." and then another thought hit her. "What about your mother! What would she say? She has been so good to me I couldn't repay her like that." Tears were running down

Dorothy's cheeks I do like you Dennis and if I'd never been in this condition I would have accepted." Dennis wrapped his arm around her shoulders and kissed her on the lips she returned his kiss, then pulled away saying. "It wouldn't work Dennis through time you would hold it against me. And what if we had children, would my child be pushed aside?" I have thought about this since the day you came for a job." Dennis tried to dissolve her fears. "I have been married, and I know I'm ten years older than you, I want to marry you and take care of you and the baby I'll bring it up as my own."

Two hours had pasted since Dennis had taken Dorothy for a breath of fresh air, Martha mused, and "He must think I'm daft." She had seen the way he looked at Dorothy and she was a nice lass and a good worker. "I have a feeling he's asking her to move in here Martha thought to herself. "Mind he's taking his time they have been away two hours now," she sighed. "I would like to think that Dennis settled down with decent lass as I won't be here forever." She sighed. Just as the kettle started to boil on the fire Martha heard feet coming across the yard. Dennis and Dorothy walked in, Dorothy with a radiant smile on her face.

"Come on then tell me your news and then we'll have a cup of tea." Martha bustled about setting the milk jug and sugar basin on the table. "Well if you stop what you're doing Mam you can congratulate us." Dennis smiled; he had finally got Dorothy to agree to marry him.

Martha wrapped her arms around Dorothy saying. "I'm very pleased lass, and I know you'll settle in here very well, only this wedding going to have to be arranged pretty quickly." As she looked at Dorothy's protruding stomach. "I would say within a month this baby will be putting in an appearance."

The land girls arrived at the door in time for an afternoon cup of tea. Martha was bursting to tell them the news." I'm not only getting a daughter in law she told them excitedly, I'm getting a gran bairn as well to fuss over." As she told them to "help yourselves to the ginger cake, which was sticky topped and smelling of spices, come on Dorothy you have a piece as well as you need to keep your energy up." Martha was going to make sure Dorothy ate something so she passed her a large piece of sponge cake filled with jam and cream. Dorothy appreciatively said. "Thank you Martha for everything." as a tear of relief ran down her face.

"Come on lass think nothing of it we have a wedding to plan." Martha chuckled." I never thought there would be a wedding in the family when I got up this morning; "I wonder what Ethel and Gran will have to say about it?" Jane one of the land girls laughingly said knowing Mrs Brown she will have something to say. I don't think she's ever been stuck for words yet. But I think she'll be pleased for both of you."

Martha rose stiffly off the chair to get back to the task she had been busy with before the arrival of her son Dennis, Dorothy and land girls. She walked back over to the table, where she had left a rabbit already skinned and jointed and surrounded by onions, and was arranged in the big black roasting tin, she picked up the rolling pin and proceeded to roll out the lid of the pastry she'd made earlier. Dorothy having finished her cup of tea and piece of cake followed the land girls outside they were going back to finish the hedging while she went to the shed for potatoes to peel for tea. Dennis got up to go but first came over and gave Dorothy a kiss as the pink suffused her neck.

Dorothy and Martha now had the house to themselves as Martha questioned Dorothy about her intentions of staying with Ethel. "You can move in here tonight Dorothy if you wish? You know that lass don't you, or do you prefer staying with Ethel till after you're married?" Dorothy looked at this kindly woman within the next few weeks she would be her mother in law and she couldn't wish for a better one.

Martha broke into her thoughts as she said. "I've never seen our Dennis look so happy for a long time, and you do care for him don't you Dorothy?" she asked with concern. "As it hasn't been easy for him in the past losing his wife and newborn bairn like that." she sighed. Dorothy put her arms round her future mother in law and said truthfully. "Yes I care for him Martha, I just didn't think anyone could have feelings for me with this." as she pointed to her stomach. Dorothy had thought what a wonderful day she was having as she walked with Dennis and now she smiled, as her day was complete.

Later in the day Dorothy and Dennis arranged that Dorothy would stay on with Ethel until they were married, that was Dorothy's wish and Dennis respected it, knowing that Dorothy loved Ethel, and the family like her own, as Ethel had taken her in when she had nowhere else to go.

"I will walk along to Ethel's with you Dorothy and we'll tell them together, or while you're telling Ethel and gran I'll have a chat with Wilf I don't know." he laughingly told Dorothy. "I never leave the farm for years and then I've hardly done a hands turn all afternoon, those poor land girls have had it all to do I can see your going to be a bad influence he said as he put his arm around her protectively.

They had just past through the gate on to the lane when Harold came by with his horse and cart. "Where are you two young ones off too then?" he shouted. If he wasn't mistaken that was Dennis flower the lad who's wife had died about three years ago having their first child. Aye Martha had been distressed he lifted his greasy cap and scratched his head and if he wasn't mistaken that lass was living with Ethel. She had arrived at Ethel's pregnant and no sign of a husband, so what was on here? He would offer them a lift and presumably they would tell him. He pulled on the reigns talking to his horse and telling the animal to slow down even though they were only going at walking pace Harold never went nowhere in a hurry, folk said he was frightened he missed something.

"Come on jump on the cart I presume you're on your way to Ethel's." He told Dorothy. And what about you young man, are you going to Ethel's as well? You don't usually leave the farm. Mind you've got those land girls now, and as I drive past the farms they are always hard at work".

"Yes I'm going to Ethel's as well Harold." answered Dennis. "Well you won't be going to see Ethel and Mrs Brown are you lad? Never thought you had anything in common with them, unless you're calling with a message for your mother. I will drop you both at Ethel's lad and it will take me about an hour to drop this stuff off. so I can pick you up on the way back down, and call in and have a chat with your mother, Dennis, and she'll make me a bite to eat a lot of woman take pity on me because I live on me own." he told Dorothy.

"Have you always lived on your own?" Dorothy asked him as she was inquisitive. Oh yes been on my own for the past forty odd years since my mother past away never had a wife and never wanted one more trouble than what they're worth." He said lifting his cap and giving his head another good scratch. I'd rather have me horse." Dorothy wondered if he slept with the horse because a good bath wouldn't go a miss.

275

They arrived at Ethel's and as Dennis and Dorothy rose to climb down Harold said. "What was it you said you were going to Ethel s for?" We didn't laughed Dennis. "But all will be revealed when you call back to pick me up." "Oh and by the way Harold called. "Tell Ethel I'll have a cup of tea on me way back and a piece of her beautiful cake."

Dennis felt embarrassed as Dot as he now called her lifted the sneck and walked indoors to a room full of faces, looking expectantly up at him the table already laid and food steaming on all the plates. Ethel turned as they went in as she was just going to join the rest of them at the long wooden table; she smiled at Dot and then said. "Come on sit down Dennis, and I'll fetch another plate." "Oh it's alright Ethel thank you." he muttered.

Linda seeing he was embarrassed started to laugh saying. "come and eat this tea Ethel's made its delicious, and don't mind us as she pushed the bottle of flag sauce nearer him ,the food is served scrupulously so everyone gets plenty as she shoved another loaded forkful into her mouth. Ethel thought there was something she couldn't just put her finger on. It was strange Dennis coming home with Dot unless she'd felt ill so he was seeing she got home alright.

Gran wasn't going to wait patiently, and Dot was blooming. Gran scraped her plate and while she was waiting for the pudding been dished out she asked. "Were you alright today Dot? As I thought you mightn't be feeling well with Dennis bringing you home. Or is there another reason?" "Gran!" Ethel admonished her. "Surely Dennis can walk Dot home without question."

"Well you are wrong there our Ethel, he didn't walk her home they got a lift on Harold's cart. I saw them arrive.

And there is something they are not telling us I can feel it in me bones." Dot looked at Dennis with her fork halfway to her mouth and said quietly. "We are getting married Gran. Dennis came along as we wanted to tell you together." Linda was the first off her chair congratulating the pair and cuddling Dot and everyone followed suit. Gran shouted I wish I'd kept me thoughts to me self till after tea as you lot will be talking now instead of eating and I'm waiting of me pudding." Jennie grabbed the tea towel and lifted the rice pudding out of the oven saying you won't have to wait Gran I'll dish yours out now. The excitement was tangible as everyone wanted to know when the wedding would be. Where they would live? The biggest question on everyone's lips was, would she wear?

Gran looked up and said. "Well by the size of you Dot you'll not have to be too picky it's a pity you won't be able to wear something nice and bright unless our Eva can run something up for you,"

"Oh I'm sure she'll be wearing something bright on her wedding day Gran." said Mabel, "brides like to stand out."

"Oh Dorothy will stand out alright if she wears bright colours. She'll be like a wilting bluebell in a turnip field. And our Eva has clothes to make for her own rushed wedding."

"Gran!" Ethel exclaimed will you please stop associating our Eva's wedding as being rushed. There is nothing underhand about it."

"Well we'll see Ethel time will tell as they say truth will out and you can only hide that kind of thing for so long. Can't you Dot? But it's no good crying over spilt milk."

Rosey was excited up at the Grange. Harry was arriving tonight on embarkation leave; he was the love of her life. She slept with his letters under her pillow. "Do you think I should take him down to the pub or stay in and have a quiet night?"

Maureen laughingly said. "Where are you going to have a quiet night in here? As its never quiet in fact you lot might frighten the poor lad away, He must be brave to spend a couple of days with thirty odd women, or just desperate to see our Rosey.

The next day with the land girls at work Sarah was sitting talking to Maureen with her mending on her knee, as Maureen went to brew a pot of tea; Sarah took her wooden mushroom out of her mending basket then proceeded to push the green wool through the eye of the darning needle in readiness to darn the heel of Charlie's stocking. As Maureen came back carrying the teapot then setting out the cups, Sarah asked.

"What do you make of Elsie?"

Maureen carried on pouring out the tea as she asked. What do you Mean Sarah? She is a good little worker always pleasant, and will do any job that's asked of her." Sarah looked lost in thought. You know when we have been going for a walk, so I could introduce you to people, and you could familiarise yourself with the surrounding area." Maureen was standing staring at Sarah with hand on her hip. "What are you trying to tell me Sarah as I'm starting to worry?"

"Well it could be all and nothing lass, it's just I've been putting two and two together and like Charlie said, I've probably come up with six so forget I said anything."

"Oh no Sarah Foster, I'm intrigued tell me what it is

you know or surmise there must be something for you to notice."

"Well it's my Charlie; he set me off wondering like, when me and you go out for anything, and leave Elsie on her own she has visitors and I wouldn't have thought she would have associated with the likes of them."

"With the likes, of who do you mean Sarah? You've lost me now completely."

"I think Elsie is in some kind of trouble." Sarah told Maureen remorsefully. You will have to tell me all you know Sarah or think you know because if Elsie is in trouble then she'll need help."

"Charlie has seen that Lucy and Winnie calling here."

"Oh is that all Sarah." as a sigh of relief escaped Maureen's lips." I was starting to wonder what on earth you were going to tell me."

"Well that's not all." said Sarah now she had Maureen's complete attention. My Charlie saw those two lasses carrying some bread from here. Or he thought it was bread his eyesight is not as good as it used to be." Maureen sometimes felt as if Sarah rambled on but she did like the old woman who had treated her like a daughter.

"Sometimes we get it wrong Sarah." Maureen said consolingly. "Do you remember when Elsie first arrived here, same time as me actually. She laughed. "How could I forget? Her apparent adroitness and frailty were deceptive in fact, she's as strong as a horse." Although Maureen had tried to reassure Sarah that all was well she had her own doubts now as the lass didn't look well. But Maureen had been so busy and now she felt guilty, but she would get to the bottom of this. Sarah and Charlie were no spring chickens but they knew what they'd seen and there was never smoke without fire." The girls had always talked to Maureen about their problems an arrangement she'd actively encouraged, as Maureen had soon adapted to her new life with ease.

Down at the pub Lizzie was wondering the same. What was wrong with Elsie? the lass seemed happy and friendly the pinched look had left her after she had got some good food into her stomach, after she'd been here a while but now her face was drawn she hardly ever spoke and Tommy had offered her to sit in the bar on a night with the land girls. Nobody could be miserable with that lot about. But Elsie had refused the offer. Lizzies mind was wandering as she cracked fresh eggs into a basin and whipped them with a fork Elsie entered the kitchen and lizzie pointed to the toasting fork hanging on the fireplace and asked her to toast the bread while she added milk to the scrambled egg as she carefully poured her mixture into a saucepan before sitting the blackened pan on the red hot coals. Lizzie turned to Elsie saying. "There's summat the matter isn't there lass? I can see it as clear as daylight." Just then the moment was lost, as there was a noise in the bar and Lizzie hurried through to see to it. As Elsie wondered worriedly when the next encounter with Lucy and Winnie would be?

Rosey was eating her breakfast with red rimmed eyes, Harry hadn't arrived "something must have happened." she'd cried to all the girls. And worse was to come today as the girls who lived at the lodge were sent to different farms where ever they were needed. And today Rosey and Shirley were being sent to old Alec's something to do with sheep they'd been told. Neither girl had ever had anything to do with sheep so they were both mindful that this could be an experience by what they'd heard.

"Come on then." Shirley reminded Rosey. "We are going on our bikes today, so we'd better be going, we don't want to be late on our first day at a new place. It was hot and clammy perspiration was running down their faces as both girls pedalled towards Alec's farm. As they arrived he came hurrying over before they'd dismounted.

I've got a good job for you lasses today." He laughed loudly as he rocked backwards and forwards with his thumb behind his braces. "A nice walk out, so you might as well get started there is forty sheep to bring from that field just up the road a mile or two you'll a past it on your way here there is a few trees in that field. "Do you mean the one up near the wood Mr Parkinson?" Shirley asked him. "Aye that's the one lass, so you might as well get going it should only take an hour or two if you know anything about sheep." Rosey was just about to tell him that they didn't when he walked away.

"How are we supposed to bring those sheep back down here?" Shirley despaired.

"Well I don't know we'll just have to open the field gate and hope they will walk down the road with us." Suggested Rosey "I don't really know I have a feeling nothing is going to go right today it's going to be as bad as yesterday." she sniffed. Oh don't start about Harry he will turn up some time, and if he doesn't there is plenty more fella's to be had. The countries full of GIs."

"Yes but I don't want a GI." whined Rosey." I want Harry." The conversation was sparse for a while as each girl was engrossed in their own thoughts.

Just up the road sitting on the bench was Ronnie his hair was as white as the driven snow, and he didn't have a tooth in his head, his sharp beady eyes constantly darted about taking in all the comings and goings. He was stroking his old dog Mack, with his old knarled hands. He saw the girls before they saw him he thought to himself it's a funny do this, women wearing trousers, land girls come to do a man's job he'd been told, well the sun was shining and he lived on his own so he had no one to answer too, so he decided he'd watch what theses lasses were going to do.

"Hello." they called to him as they passed by.

"Oh hello." he smiled and what do they call you two lasses then?" Are you just out for a walk?"

"No we've come for the sheep they are in that field over there." Shirley pointed. Ronnie laughingly told them. "You lasses will never manage those sheep, have you ever had anything to do with them?" And where is the dog?"

"What dog?" The girls chorused. Ronnie started to laugh. "Well you'll have fun and games with those sheep with no dog."

"No we haven' brought a dog but we'll manage." Shirley sounded more confident than what she felt but she wasn't going to let an old man make fun of them. Ronnie sat back with a smile on his face this would be worth watching as the dog stretched out on the grass and was soon snoring.

It was a sultry day Shirley rubbed the sweat off her forehead with the back of her hand, "come on Rosey not much further now." Rosey stood and looked behind the way they'd come. "We have walked all this way Shirley and then we have to walk all the way back."

The girls finally reached the field; the sheep seemed to be spread all over. "How are we supposed to collect them all together?" Wailed Rosey. "Oh I don't know observed Shirley, just remember the old saying follow like sheep, so hopefully if we get one through this gate they'll all come."

And then she pushed the five barred gate open and the woolly bodies on stick like legs came hurrying through all going in different directions. Shirley ran up the road after eight of them while some in Rosey's care jumped over a garden wall and promptly set to work devouring Mrs. Wilson's flowers. As she was watching her blooms disappearing down the sheep's throat, she came running out flapping her pinny about but the sheep carried on eating their tasty dinner unconcerned.

Rosey didn't like to waste time walking round the corner to get in to Mrs. Wilsons garden, so climbed the wall like the sheep and loosened some stones as part of the wall rushed in onto the grass verge. Mrs Wilson ran into the house and came out waving a stick menacingly at Rosey and the sheep, yelling as she chased Rosey and the sheep back over the rushed wall.

"Take your damned sheep and don't come back or you and your sheep will get some of this." She yelled as she waved the stick in the air. Shirley came round the corner just as Rosey was wondering what to do, the sheep had scattered far and wide with their new found freedom.

"Oh it's alright for you standing there doing nothing." Shirley shouted. "I've been rushed off my feet."

"Well I haven't been standing here sunning myself for your information. I've knocked a wall down trying to stop the sheep eating that woman's entire flowers." as she pointed to Mrs Wilson's house, and she was going to hit me with her stick for all me trouble. What are we going to do Shirley? The sheep are spread all over."

"Well I don't know I bet old Ronnie will still be sitting on that seat having a good laugh at us, but before I do anything else I'm going to have a fag as she took a packet of lucky strike out of her overall pocket lit two and passed one to Rosey, and then sat down on the grass verge with her back to the wall.

"We have never had anything to do with sheep." Declared Rosey, "And he sets us off on our own God knows where they'll end up."

"I know where they would have ended up in the city." And then before Rosey had time to answer Shirley said. "In the stew pot, that's all I've ever had to do with sheep. When Mam made mutton stew she used to send me or one of the younger kids to the butchers for scrag neck, mind you the stew just had a passing acquaintance with the meat She licked her lips as she said. "It was tasty as well with a few onions and a couple of carrots if we could get some."

Rosey threw her lipstick stained stub end down and ground it out with her foot. . "Come on Shirley." she said. "Let's try and catch those bloody sheep." Some of the sheep were just down the road tasting the delights of the grass verge while the others had gone further hoping to find something tastier. "Baa! Baa! Baa! They heard as they turned the corner just in time to see them clamouring Miss Ponds low hedge and starting to eat her cultivated garden. Miss Pond had been up most of the night she hadn't been well, and consequently had over slept. But on hearing the noise had hurried downstairs. With her long white winceyette nightdress on that reached down to her feet, with its high neck and long sleeves, and her lily white hair blowing all over. Rosey screamed, frightening the sheep and Miss Pond. "What the hell did you have to do that for?" asked Shirley. "I thought she was a ghost." Said a shaken Rosey," and we have been entrusted with a flock of sheep without any experience. And I don't know if we will manage to get them back to old Alec." She cried.

"Look I'll run ahead." offered Shirley. I'll walk in front of them, well the ones I can find, and you follow up the rear that way we might keep the few we have left together." Rosey agreed but wasn't sure it would work. Baa! Baa! Baa! There it was again as the girls turned there was another dozen sheep just leaving another garden, flowers hanging out the corners of their mouths, and an old man with a pipe gripped tightly between his teeth waving a stick. Rosey had an uncontrollable desire to leave them as their fat bodies swayed down the road on their stick like legs. Ronnie was still sitting where the girls had left him earlier he was gleefully waiting of the lasses coming back with the sheep, he knew it would be no easy task gathering them in he would eventually help them but first he would sit back and enjoy his morning that flighty piece seemed to think she knew it all oh here they were now but where was all the sheep? When Shirley got nearer he asked where the rest of the sheep had got too,

She had waved her hand airily saying. "Oh they are following."

"Well I've got news for you young lady." he laughed your friend is following with just a handful and shedding tears by the look of her."

Rosey ran to them crying and pointing over to a field full of sheep, "our sheep have gone in with them now we'll never find them. They were progressing inexorably across the field like a plague of locusts."

"Well I've had enough shouted Shirley we are here fighting on with those damned sheep and those Italians are sitting whittling sticks in the barn and not satisfied with that, they get invited in to the farm house for dinner."

Old Ronnie was starting to feel sorry for them. "I will walk back up the road with you and get your sheep out of that field."

"But we can't." Rosey cried, "We don't know the difference they all look alike."

"Yes I suppose they do to us." Ronnie replied. "But to him they don't." as he pointed to his dog Mack, and just remember they will always be idiosyncratically, whether they are sheep or beast it's behaviour of a group."

They had arrived at the gate nearly as far as they'd been to collect the sheep. Alec leaned over to open the gate and let an excited sheep dog through, it didn't take long for Mack to round the ones up that the girls had been sent for, and he herded them through the gate as Ronnie fastened the gate behind him. It didn't take Mack long to gather the rest up and have them all walking together sedately down the road with stomachs full of everyone's flowers. The girls thanked him profusely as he saw them and the sheep inside Alec's farm gate, as he turned to go Shirley shouted if I see you in the pub tonight I'll stand you a couple of drinks." Ronnie waved his stick in acknowledgement.

The girls had just got into the farmyard when Alec came out looking at his pocket watch saying. "I hope you don't intend having your dinners as you have had a good morning doing nothing. I want some work out of you so you can start and sharpen those scythes."

CHAPTER FIFTEEN

The postman had just delivered a letter at the Grange and been invited in by Sarah for a drink of tea. "Here is a cup of tea for you Amos sit yourself down and I'll make you a sandwich." Maureen came through just then. I thought I heard you talking to someone Sarah." "Aye it's the postman lass I hope you didn't think I was talking to myself."

"Oh is there any mail for me?" Maureen asked hopefully. Sarah looked cunningly at Maureen saying, no nothing for you today from my son, but there is one for Rosey and I don't like the look of it." Maureen took the newly arrived envelope from the mantelpiece and turned it over in her hand saying "How on earth do you not like the look of an envelope Sarah?"

Because I have a bad feeling Rosey is going to get some news that will break her heart, once she opens that envelope something she doesn't want to hear."

"Did you think maybe Harry was writing to finish with her, because he hasn't turned up when he should? Because I think that's rubbish he might even turn up after, you know what transport is like Sarah, there is a war on, and the letter might not be from him."

"The letter wouldn't be from him if he cannot write. Now would it Maureen?"

What are you saying Sarah you're making me feel cold I wish you would think sometimes before you open your mouth?"

"Well I'm going to scold another teapot full of tea Maureen but just make sure you are there or I will be when

Rosey comes home to that letter." warned Sarah. "As she will need someone's arms to run into poor lass,"

Maureen shivered. As she thought of all the other times Sarah had predicted things and she was right she seemed to have a knack she just hoped this time she was wrong."

The girls toiled all day in the hot sun and as Shirley and Rosey mounted their bikes Shirley invited Rosey to go to the pub with her tonight. "I could do with a pint now I'm as dry as a bone." moaned Shirley.

Rosey's Eyes lit up and her face was wreathed in smiles as she said. "I will be otherwise engaged tonight Shirley my Harry will probably be at the lodge when we get there."

Sarah was waiting at the window and as she saw the girls coming down the bank she called to Maureen. "They are here."

"I thought you were helping me and Elsie dish this dinner out Sarah, instead of watching folk."

The girls pedalled into the yard and propped their bikes against the wall, Rosey ran eagerly in asking, "Has Harry arrived?"

Sarah passed her the buff coloured envelope and propelled her to a chair saying, "Sit down Rosey before you open that letter, I think it could be bad news."

Rosey tore open the letter and after scanning it cried out like a wounded animal but Sarah was there with her arms wrapped around her, while Shirley picked the letter off the floor where it had dropped." Later on with Rosey tucked up in bed after crying herself to sleep Maureen told the rest of the girls. "How uncanny Sarah's predictions were, and yes she'd been right the letter that Rosey had received was from Harry's Mam saying he'd been killed in action." The house seemed to be shrouded in doom for a few weeks after, so no one noticed Elsie suffering more and more, apart from Sarah, who had become more vigilant and despite this vigilance it was a few days before it came to a head, as Sarah was roseys shoulder to cry on. And no one could have conjectured just how unhappy Elsie was.

The following day after Sarah returned home to her cottage across the yard, Maureen said. "I'm just going out Elsie. Is that all right with you? You would tell me if there was anything wouldn't you?" As Elsie's face and neck suffused with nervous red blotches, Sarah watched Maureen's retreating back going down the road and smiled knowingly.

"There's Maureen away Charlie." she called to her husband. "She has gone to post another letter to our John."

"How do you know where she's going." asked Charlie shaking his head. "Maureen has gone to post a letter to our John she, received one from him yesterday."

"By lass you've missed your calling; you should have been in the secret service." Charlie remarked, "Because you miss nothing."

Across the yard at the lodge Elsie turned her attention to her task's and headed for the kitchen and two sacks of potatoes one of carrots and a sack of turnips that needed peeling for today's tea, as land girls were always hungry. Sarah was still standing at the window looking out, as Lucy and Winnie appeared a lighted roll up, hung from the corners of their mouth's Sarah watched disbelieving as they walked in, their ostentatious way. Sarah opened the door picking the walking stick with the crook on the end and on the way out and calling to Charlie. "I'll not be long." As she quietly crossed the yard, Sarah opened the door quietly and listened to the raised voices, and then the cries of Elsie. Sarah's temper was up as she hurried along the passage towards the kitchen, waving the stick menacingly. Lucy and Winnie had their backs turned towards the kitchen door as they had Elsie's head pulled back and hanging on to her hair, as they demanded the ration books from the lodge. "I warned you what would happen to you." shouted Lucy. "if you didn't find those ration books." As Winnie sneered enjoying Elsie's helplessness.

Sarah threw the kitchen door open with a flourish. Tension bubbled like hot fat threatening to burst to the surface at any moment.

Maureen had forgotten her well worn purse, and decided to return for it as Charlie caught her and told as much as he knew, as a red hot sun blazed down out of a bright blue sky Maureen pushed the sleeves of her dress up to her elbows on this sultry sticky afternoon and broke into a run as Charlie followed. They heard the screams as they opened the door and ran along the passage as Sarah was still beating Winnie and Lucy with the stick, as tears cursed down Elsie's cheeks.

"I think they've had enough lass." Said Charlie to his wife as he took the stick away from her, these two lasses will be black and blue in the morning."

"Well it is only what they deserve." Said Maureen. "Thank God you realised what was going on Sarah."

"Well I think we should call the police and have these two locked up." stated Sarah. "Well it's no good going to tell your mother is it Lucy?" As she is as bad as you probably worse, said Charlie. "But I will go for Prudence, your sister Winnie; she brought you up here so you are her responsibility."

As the school closed for the day Prudence couldn't work out why Mr Foster was waiting, so she made her way across to ask. " It's you I've come to see, he told her, Never heard nothing like it in my life and Elsie such a canny lass and a good worker but those two cheeky buggers won't be sitting very comfortable for the next few days not after the hiding my Sarah gave them. Prudence was alarmed after Charlie had imparted his news, he saw the closed expression on her face but the silent disapproval emanating from her was almost palpable, as her authority had been opposed she had tried to subjugate Winnie but she wouldn't curtail. Lead on then Mr. foster prudence told him with authority. Mable and Susan were busy in the field going round the edges with a scythe they had their trouser legs rolled up to above the knee as the sun shone down relentlessly. I am just going behind the hedge again Susan, Mable told her. Susan put down her scythe and took a packet of cigarettes from her overall pocket; she watched Mable's retreating back until she was out of sight. Susan took a long drag from her cigarette and thought there is either something very wrong with Mable's bladder, or she is interested in one of the Italians. Susan had finished her cigarette and one side of the field by the time Mable came back. "What's your game Mable?" Susan asked her.

Mable looked innocent as she said. "I don't know what you mean, Susan." "You are on with something Mable this has been going on now for a week or two. Are you going with one of those Italians?"

Mable's colour rose from her neck into her face leaving bright red patches. ", Mable begged Please don't tell anyone Susan it would only cause trouble for Salvo and me."

We are not supposed to have anything to do with them Susan, I don't know if my conscience will let it rest."

As the day wore on there was no conversation between Susan and Mable, so when they stopped for a drink of tea and a smoke

Mable went and sought Salvo. "You should not have come here where everyone can see you." Salvo told Mable. "So we shouldn't be sitting on this seat talking." Mable told him. "But what's the harm? But Salvo's didn't reply but his hand sought hers at first hesitantly, then with greater deliberation, their fingers interlacing in the comfort and warmth of a silent unspoken understanding.

Charlie had got all prudence's attention as he explained what had taken place, as she waddled up the road behind him her tongue clicking impatiently against her front teeth. Prudence was sick of Winnie and all the trouble she was causing with those, ne'er-do-wells. Charlie and prudence had reached the grange with prudence breathing heavy. "Are you all right Lass?" Charlie asked concerned. Prudence nodded she wanted to get this over with as quick as possible. They walked in and Prudence dropped her corpulence into a chair. "I don't really know what to say to You, Winnie; I'm so disgusted with your behaviour. But it's plain you cannot be trusted while you are going around with her." Both Winnie and Lucy had stripes across their legs and backs off the walking stick and felt very sore as Sarah hadn't been bothered where the stick had landed. Prudence didn't want a confrontation she'd tried to warn her about Lucy, but Winnie had misinterpreted prues intentions.

Lucy hobbled over a look of pure Vernon on her face. Pointing at everyone in the room and shouting. "You haven't heard the last of this, and you," as she pointed to Winnie, can no longer stay at my place."

"I wouldn't want too." Winnie replied and then wondered where she could stay. "I would have stayed with Mam if she hadn't kicked me out." she cried fuelled by temper, as Lucy banged the door shut on her way out and the hinges nearly dropped off.

"She did not kick you out Winnie." Prudence told her. "And the story you've led everyone to believe is contradiction in the extreme". Sarah who had been sitting having a rest after squaring the girls up said. "Aye Winnies never let the truth get in the way of a good tale". As she wrapped her arms around Elsie, "Come with me love." She bade softly she could feel the hysteria shuddering through her body." "I cannot leave yet," Elsie hiccupped. "Once I go you will not want me back and I don't know what Aunty Lizzie is going to say, she will probably kick me out."

"Oh she won't do that lass." Sarah soothed. Why would she want to do that?" "I have been pinching things from here." Elsie cried. "And I didn't want too but Winnie and Lucy used to come in when Maureen went out, and demand bread and allsorts, they were hitting me today as I would not give them the ration books." Prudence's face had paled to think Winnie had turned out so evil.

Maureen said. "You'll always have a job here Elsie, go home with Sarah she'll look after you and then after you've had a cup of tea we'll start the girl's teas. Maureen thought she would relax better with Sarah's no nonsense attitude. "Come on then Charlie." Sarah called. "We'll all have a cup of tea at home and a bit piece I'm getting too old for this."

Charlie laughed. "Well I don't think you did so bad lass those lasses will not forget you in a hurry."

Maureen reached for the kettle there was only Prue, Winnie and her left and she badly needed a cup of tea, and Prudence looked as if she'd aged before her eyes. Maureen could hear prudence telling Winnie off but Winnie just shrugged a careless shoulder, the response Prudence received was predictable of Winnie as she gave Winnie a meaningful look. Conversation was very sparse while the tea was drank everyone had their own thoughts. Prudence was hopeful a letter would arrive any day now, she was desperate to go, she couldn't stay round here now, all the village would know about Winnies carry on tonight once Lizzie found out what had been happening. She liked a good gossip did Lizzie. Winnie was wondering now after her cleverness and show had come to an end, where would she go for a bed for the night? A tear escaped and ran unchecked down her cheek.

Maureen drank the last drop of tea and stood up saying. "I must get on those land girls will be in shortly for their evening meal and I can't see them taking kindly to what you and that up there did to poor Elsie." Maureen couldn't bring herself to say Lucy's name. Prues authority had been opposed and she knew Winnie would never kow tow to her or anyone else. Yes she knew Winnie would always be trouble but her Prudence would not be around to see it. Prudence knew she couldn't leave Winnie with nowhere to go she would have to beg Eva to take her in until she could work something out, Charlie was sent to the pub to tell Lizzie and Tommy all about the happenings at the Grange, and it was arranged her uncle Tommy would collect her after work on his motorbike just in case Lucy had any ideas. And as Maureen Sarah and Elsie worked in the kitchen among the big steaming pans, the door was standing ajar; an invigorating breeze was wafting into the kitchen. Sarah stood for a moment perspiration standing on her forehead, and wondering if Rosey would eat a bite tonight, as the poor lass was imbued with sadness, but she wasn't the only woman coping with bereavement but while all the land girls were permanently hungry roseys appetite had been all but annihilated by grief.

Rosey was not the only one feeling glum. Mark had gone back to his unit he'd only had a forty eight hour embarkation leave. But Eva with marks engagement ring on her finger seemed to make his imminent departure more bearable, she had made herself a cup of tea and lit a Du Maurier cigarette a packet she'd been given off Linda she would have a quiet sit on her own but her hope crumbled to dust as the door opened and Prudence walked in followed by the dreaded Winnie.

"What are you playing at Prudence?" Eva shouted. "Bringing her here to my house; well you'd better go Winnie I have heard all about your antics today with poor Elsie." Prues face was as hard as granite, while Winnie's equilibrium had reasserted itself. Eva felt like getting up and smacking her, as she stood as if she hadn't a care in the world. Eva raised enquiring eyebrows at Prudence as she asked. "Have you not been to Cobweb cottage yet to see if you can rent it? I don't mind you staying here Prudence you helped me when my late husband turned up and was nasty but I can't do with her." The stew simmering on the fire smelt appetising and Winnie's stomach rumbled in anticipation of a tasty meal. Eva seemed unshakeable in her resolve not to help Winnie. Prudence took a lucky stripe out of a packet and lit it sucking in the nicotine and blowing it out slowly as she tried to calm the tension growing inside her what the hell was she going to do with Winnie. Pru despaired of her irresponsible daughter with a loud sniff and an angry toss of her head she was no nearer a solution.

Eva took pity on prudence after all it wasn't her fault. "Alright." Eva conceded reluctantly. "I am letting her stay for you Prudence. I couldn't care less if she slept in a field. You will do as you're told." she warned Winnie. "And don't even think about bringing Lucy here or she will go out quicker than she came in and you with her." Prudence picked up her hand bag and took out her purse here is my contribution for our winnie I will ask for her ration book as soon as she comes in from the lav and thank you for your hospitality Eva."

I'm the only one daft enough to take her in I dread to think what Gran would say." Winnie came back in doors after being down the garden path to the lav and quietly handed over her ration book. Eva thought that Sarah had knocked the wind out Winnies sails for the time being but she couldn't be trusted, as she was as hostile as a malevolent eye.

Up at the lodge a new girl had arrived just as they were all sitting down to tea. Every one pushed and shoved until they had their backsides comfortable on the wooden bench ready to eat whatever Elsie put in front of them as Maureen and Sarah cooked and dished it out Elsie got the job of running backwards and forwards carrying the loaded plates. As Sarah told her, "Your legs are younger than mine." The new girl just stood quietly by the long table looking hungrily at the food.

"Come on Gwen, Sit down Elsie is bringing you some dinner." Maureen told her. "Sit here next to Shirley, and she'll introduce you to everyone after you have all finished eating." The girls all shoved up as they loaded their forks up they had all had a hard day and were hungry Sarah noticed, apart from Rosey. "She'll be starting to look like a clothes horse if she isn't careful. She is starting to look gaunt now" thought Sarah. "She needs something to occupy her mind."

Gwen was finding it hard to swallow the food although it was very tasty she had just left home for the first time away from her mother's dominance. She was an only child of elderly parents who had not made friends easily as she was lacking in self -confidence so had spent all her time with her mother and had worked in the corner shop, next to her home she was starting to wish she'd listened to her parents as another tear escaped and ran down her face.

Maureen was sitting enjoying a cup of tea but she had a lot of questions for Gwen after she had finished her meal, the first question would have to be what was she doing here as Maureen as warden had not been informed. The girls were starting to leave the table the meal finished Maureen beckoned Gwen over, patting the settee beside her, Gwen walked over to her nervously. "Sit down here Gwen I have to know what you are doing here as I've not been informed that you were coming."

"Well I was supposed to go to Mr Tweddles farm but I was late in arriving and he said he didn't have room for me and sent me here."

"I thought I recognised you walking up the road as we cycled past". Said Shirley. "We work for Alec and we had a merry dance today with his bloody sheep."

"I wish I'd never come." Gwen cried with her hands covering her face as tears ran down through her fingers. Maureen was beginning to wonder what else could happen today as she heard Tommy's motorbike coming into the yard to collect Elsie. Sarah opened the door to Tommy's knock.

"Hello Sarah by it a rum do and no mistake, our poor Elsie and never told anyone but we know now. Winnie and that other trollop need never show their faces at my pub anymore because our Lizzie is fuming."

Elsie heard her uncle's voice she had just finished washing up. Sarah walked back through to the kitchen. "Come on Elsie, Uncle Tommy is here get yourself away home with him. You will feel better after a good night's sleep." Elsie walked through hesitantly and Tommy opened his arms and Elsie went into them he stroked her hair as she cried. "Come on lass we are going home to see your Auntie Lizzie and the way he felt if he saw those two trollops he wouldn't be responsible for his actions. Maureen thought she would sort out Gwen's problem and then she would go up to Pat Greens for her three children they were playing with Beryl she was alright now that she had Pat all to herself.

Maureen turned towards Gwen and said. "Right tell me how you come to be here, because I've had no correspondents to tell me you were on your way, so start at the beginning." I am an only child and my parents are old and protective compared with other girls my age, I have only had one friend as I wasn't allowed out a lot without my parents they were frightened something would happen to me, so all through school I never made any friends, then when I left school Mam got me a job just around the corner from where we live. Cathy also worked there she was a year older than me she had brothers and sisters and was really out going. The first time I had ever been to the pictures was with Cathy". She smiled. Mam and Dad didn't like me going out with her Mam thought she was fast and didn't want me to get into trouble, but I enjoyed going around with Cathy, it was lively at her house where as our house was quiet as Dad read the paper while Mam used to sit knitting and listening to the wireless. I was happy, but with the war starting Cathy said she was joining up and I knew I had to get way or I would be back to having a lonely life, I didn't fancy working at the shop after Cathy left so Cathy helped me to apply for the land army she thought that would suit me better than the forces. I was dreading having to tell Mam so I waited till I'd received the train ticket and my uniform then I broke it to them. Dad forbade me to come. Mam cried and I knew if I was to have any life at all I had to get away. Mam bought me some underwear which was kind of her, but instead of handing me them, she tipped my case out to check I had everything and repacked it for me." Gwen's face was red as she quietly told Maureen that on the station as they were saying good bye as her parents had been determined to see her off, her mother had said. "I have put you an extra packet of STs in your case as you might end up miles away from a chemist." while her father looked down at his shoes embarrassed. Gwen rubbed the tears from her eyes as she told Maureen how she had travelled most of the day, with the train being delayed, and then when I had walked the three mile from the station and arrived at Alecs they had told her she would work for them but she had to find somewhere to live and as she was setting off to find help he had called after her go to the grange you'll be able to stop there as that is where most of the land girls stay. Gwen looked at Maureen with tears in her eyes and asked. Can I stay tonight? Because If I can't I don't know what to do." Maureen put a protective arm round her as she felt sorry for Gwen and she knew how hard it had been for her when she'd come here if Pat and Michael hadn't taken her in she dreaded to think what would of happened to her. "Yes you can stay here but I will have to let the woman from the war agency know we have an extra one here, and if Michael cannot bring an extra bed down from the convalescent home tonight you can share mine." Maureen had already made her mind up where the extra bed would go, it would do Rosey good to have someone to look after, take her away from her own broken heart.

Shirley asked Gwen "When she was starting work for Alec?"

"Well I'm starting tomorrow." She stammered.

"Oh so you will be cycling down to the farm with Rosey and me in the morning." Tears came into Gwen's eyes as she said, "do we have to cycle?"

"Can you ride a bike?" Maureen asked her kindly.

"No I can't." cried Gwen. "My parents wouldn't allow me to have one they said I might fall off and hurt myself, what am I going to do now? How am I going to get to work?" she said as she was wringing her hands in frustration.

Valerie and some of the other girls that were there jumped up off the chairs saying come on Gwen it's the first thing you have to learn if you are a land girl, we will learn you to ride a bike tonight. They all hurried out of the door taking a frightened Gwen with them and as Maureen looked out of her window she could see the land girls were taking turns running alongside the bike holding the seat for Gwen to get balanced and then leaving go so she could manage it on her own. Two hours later a jubilant Gwen and eight tired land girls walked into the kitchen smiling Gwen was going to work in the morning on a bike she had mastered it.

Maureen walked over to the table that held the wireless and switched it on to give it time to warm up, ready for one of her favourite programme, happidrome, followed by the nine o clock news read by Alvar Liddell, but first the last song was just being played called, now is the hour at which Rosey and Gwen burst into tears. Shirley Edith and the rest of the girls made their way upstairs. Kathy was already upstairs removing her dinky curlers which she put in every night before getting into bed and wearing all day under her turban, the girls started to rub gravy browning into their legs as each of them had no silk stockings, then they kept as still as possible whilst the other one drew a "seam" down the back of legs with an eyebrow pencil. The night sky was clear and filled with stars a crescent moon shone as they all made their way to the pub, laughing and giggling at each other's jokes. The pub was packed to bursting, roll out the barrel and we'll hang out the washing on the Siegfried line had just been sung when the pub door burst open and Lucy fell through hanging precariously on the arm of a GI, they were drunk, several elderly men were engrossed in a game of dominoes. Lucy was muttering a profanity that would have shocked some men.

Elsie was sitting in the bar with the land girls and was wide eyed with shock as she saw them coming in, Lizzie saw them at the same time and hurried towards them shouting. "You are not allowed in here ever again you are bard." as she pressed a warning finger into Lucy's chest. "I don't know how you dare show your face now get out." Lucy looked patronizingly at Lizzie and asked, "Are you going to make me?" The land girls had all made their way over and as one opened the door some of the others picked Lucy up and threw her out of the door and when the GI tried to intervene he got the same response, and as Lucy and her GI picked themselves up off the road the girls were singing and dancing as if they hadn't a care.

Along at Eva's she was sitting at her treadle sewing machine, she had a few dresses to make for Dorothy's wedding in a fortnights time, also the date for her own wedding was looming, the air was fraught with tension, Prudence had been inarticulate with rage. Things were not improving between her and Winnie, and as Eva rubbed her tired eyes she felt a headache coming on. Prudence was sitting in the chair her stockings wrinkled like a concertina, and after a trumpeting blow into her handkerchief feigned sleep. Along at the lodge Maureen had tried to enjoy listening to the wireless but as she looked at Gwen and Rosey's face it was very depressing Maureen turned the wireless off and looked at the girls, Rosey had bobbed blonde hair and huge blue eyes she was a pretty girl, while Gwen had a small retrousse nose and enviably slim figure, she was sitting demurely, Would you girls like a cup of cocoa?" Maureen asked as she placed the kettle on the hot coals, it had been a long hard day for her as well but she didn't like to see any of the girls upset, and tried to be a motherly figure to all of them. The girls drank their cocoa with red rimmed eyes and then made their way to bed.

The next morning Gwen mounted the bike nervously and pedalled down to Alec's farm, wondering what lay ahead for her and thinking her parents. They had been right she was missing them, and her home, but then remembered why she had left; they were suffocating her with their protectiveness.

"Come on Dolly daydream." Shirley called to her, "or you'll be left behind, we dare not be late or old Alec will complain."

"I wonder what he has lined up for us today." said Rosey.

"Well it can't be worse than them bloody sheep yesterday." Shirley shouted over to them. As they made their way to the farm yard there was a couple of men talking to Alec and he turned as he heard the girls approaching, and without looking at them he shouted. "Go and see the wife, its pig killing day today". Poor Gwen grabbed hold of Shirley's arm and cried. "I don't want to see any pigs killed; I thought we had joined the land army to look after live animals."

Mrs Tweddle was waiting for the girls standing with her fat arms folded under her monstrous bosom "Now then you girls and you must be the new one are you? She asked as she looked over at Gwen and why are you crying?"

Gwen sniffed. "I don't want to see dead animals." Mrs Tweddle laughed a loud raucous laugh. "Well you're in the wrong job girl unless you stop being so taffy hearted, as you know we are killing a couple of pigs today so I need two girls to stir the blood once the butcher has cut the pigs throat. I usually do it but I'm on me holidays."

"Oh where are you going?" asked a surprised Shirley.

To which Mrs Tweddle laughed. "Oh I'm not going anywhere, I always say I'm on me holidays when I've got me monthlies, as I am on holiday from his advances my Alec he is a randy old goat, it's the only time I get a bit of peace in bed. So are any of you girls having your monthlies, as you are not allowed to make black pudding if you are?"

"Well I am." said an embarrassed Rosey. "And I started mine this morning." Said Shirley her face colouring bright red, "Well I'm afraid it leaves you Gwen, come with me and I'll find you a couple of dishes."

"But I don't know what to do." cried a distressed Gwen.

303

"Well I'll tell you what to do." said the farmer's wife who was losing patience fast with Gwen. "They are going to cut the pig's throat." as she pointed across to the men. You will catch the blood in this dish and stir it well or we won't have any black pudding and you won't have a job." Poor Gwen looked round for Shirley and Rosey but they had already gone to the ten acre field with the scythes to cut the grass out of the dyke backs ready for the next day when the rest of the field would be cut to make hay. Sweat was running down the girls faces as they cut the long grass. "My blade needs sharpening." Shirley called to Rosey, "so I'm going to have a cigarette before I sharpen it."

Rosey walked over to her carrying the scythe and her sharpening stone, "Well I'm going to have a sit down while I smoke mine." as she rubbed the sweat from her forehead.

"Well I reckon it's not far off dinner time." Shirley told her, "So after we have smoked these we'll walk back to the farm and have our bait."

"I wonder how Gwen is getting on." said a worried Rosey. "I felt sorry for her."

"I did as well." said Shirley. "But if we hadn't of had our monthlies, we would have had to do it, I wonder why you can't." Must be old country ways answered Rosey.

A sickly looking Gwen met them as they walked back into the farm yard. I will never stir the blood again in fact I will find out when they are going to kill the pigs and stay away or I will pretend I have my monthlies."

"Well it's over now." Shirley tried to jolly her along. "And we will all have our sandwiches now as I'm famished." Gwen opened her bag and took out her sandwiches which were wrapped in grease proof paper and threw them at Shirley saying. "You two can share them, as the way I feel I will never eat again." After Shirley and Rosey had eaten their sandwiches and poor Gwen had made do with a drink of water from the stand pipe in the yard. Shirley looked over to the field with the high hedge and asked Gwen and Rosey what they should do about the toilet as there were a few men standing round and all the girls needed a wee. "Isn't this embarrassing?" cried Gwen.

"Imagine how we feel then." said Shirley. "They know we have our monthlies and Mrs Tweddle never even offers the use of facilities."

"Well I know I'm not going behind that hedge when those men are there." Rosey declared.

"Come on then you two." Said Gwen with an unprecedented show of courage, "I think we should walk down that track over there." as she tried to see what lay ahead as the sky was high and blue shading her eyes from the sun with her hand we might as well have another cigarette each as I feel as if I deserve another after the morning I've had." As the girls walked through a gate and into a small field well away from prying eyes they noticed a flock of geese well established and grazing as they passed through. The girls had been told a flock of geese were no problem if you ignored them only on seeing the girls the geese started to demonstrate their disapproval in no uncertain terms. Two huge ganders started nipping their heels the girls started to run they were terrified it seemed to be a signal for the rest to join in, hole lots of them appeared necks outstretched and wings beating air squawked in their wake, the girls reached the gate just in time as the gander leaned over for another peck, and as the girls climbed up on to the gate and landed in a heap at the other side. grateful it was between them and the ganders they heard a tear and it was Gwen's overalls that had caught on a nail.

"That's it." cried Gwen. "I can't take anymore of this today, when we get back to the lodge to night I'm going to pack my clothes and I'm going home."

"We still haven't been able to have a pee yet." Shouted Rosey, "and I'm bursting."

"So am I." cried Shirley. "Only my heels are bleeding as well where those damned Ganders have pecked me, and do you girls realise if we don't go back past the ganders I have no idea how to get back to the farm from here."

The girls didn't know but help was at hand, Dorothy was making her way down the road she had been over to see how Margaret Emmerson was getting on with her wedding cake, as her wedding was only a fortnight away and she'd had no word back from her mother to say if she was coming to her wedding she was lost in thought so was shocked to see three land girls coming towards her.

"Could you help us please?" begged Shirley. "I know this must sound daft to you, a country girl, but we have managed to get ourselves lost."

Dorothy smiled. "I'm not a country girl, I haven't lived here long myself but if you tell me where you want to be maybe I can help you." The girls started talking in earnest about their morning and old Alec.

"I know where Alec Tweddle lives." Dorothy told them. "It's the next farm down from ours, I mean my future husbands, and his mothers, we are getting married next Saturday." she added as her face coloured bright red. Why don't you girls walk along with me and have a cup of tea and then you can use the facilities Martha that's my future mother in law won't mind she's a good sort."

Martha was busy giving the broth another good stir as the girls walked into her kitchen she turned around to see who Dorothy was talking too. This is Shirley Rosey and Gwen she told Martha as she introduced the girls then went on to tell her about the morning they'd had at Alecs farm.

"Right sit yourselves down girls." Martha ordered. As she filled them each a dish of broth thick with vegetables bit of ham from the ham shank split peas and barley. "Get that down you." she told the girls. "It will set you up for this afternoon." As the girls ate hungrily they told Martha all about their troubles and poor Gwen having to make the black pudding. Dorothy noticed Gwen was not having any trouble shifting a dish of broth so she must be getting over the black pudding. Martha smiled kindly at the girls after all these land girls had come here to the country and didn't know country ways so it must be strange to them. "I was a farmer's daughter." Martha told the girls. "So when I married my farmer husband my life never changed as that was all I knew, I'm sure you girls will get used to it, and why don't you ask Alice Tweddle if you can use the facilities, as it's not easy when you need to go in the fields more so when it's your monthlies." Shirley stood up and the other two followed. "Thank you so much for the broth and the advice but I don't know if we'll still have a job." Shirley exclaimed.

"Oh I'm sure it will be alright if you just explain to Alice that you needed the lav and you were looking for somewhere and got lost, and you." she told Gwen. "Will have to harden up a bit, call and see me some time and let me know how you're getting on." Martha invited. "Now go down that lane through the gate at the bottom and then carry on through the next field, and then you will be back in Alecs yard.

Dorothy sat down despondently at the table, elbows on the table head in hands. "What's ailing you then?" Martha asked her. "Or can I guess?" she said kindly. "I take it you've had no reply from your mother yet to say if they are coming to your wedding."

"No not yet Martha," Dorothy sniffed. "I should think they have forgotten all about me, and can you blame them?"

"Well I think they will come to your wedding Dorothy, every mother wants to see their daughters married, and I know you're expecting this baby but you are not the first and you definitely won't be the last, so go and bring the treacle out of the cupboard and we'll make a treacle pudding it will go down nice after a good helping of broth. Dorothy smiled as she went to do Martha's bidding; she knew one thing for sure. She was getting a good mother in law not a lot of girls could say that.

Back in London the city of Dorothy's birth. Brenda her mother had received the letter from Dorothy telling her all about meeting Denis Flower and how he still wanted to marry her although she was carrying someone else's baby. Martha his mother is a very nice woman she had told please try and come to the wedding.

Brenda wanted to come but felt like Dorothy's Dad. Dorothy had let them down getting pregnant for all she'd been warned but Brenda still blamed Winnie for her daughters fall from grace, she quickly put the letter back into the envelope and placed it behind the wooden candlestick, and then decided she would write straight away and tell Dorothy they would be there after all she was their daughter and every mother wanted to be at their daughter's wedding, and Brenda had missed her terribly so she pulled open a drawer on the sideboard looking for some paper and envelope and quickly told Dorothy. "You're Dad Michael and I will be at your wedding don't know how we will find our way as you know we have never been to the countryside before." After a few kind words a glint of a tear appeared at the corner of her eye she wiped it away swiftly with the back of her hand, as she realised what was done was done and time for regrets was long past. Brenda quickly licked the envelope and addressed it as Michael walked in Brenda looked in her bag and found a stamp and as she laid the envelope on the table told him to go and post it. She would have to rush now or be late for work.

The blue sky was filled with the iridescence of barrage balloons hanging like fat silver bombs. Brenda had done her early shift and was making her way home when the sirens started she had been in deep thought wondering what food to try and make for tea as everything was on ration and she didn't have time to stand waiting in queues. Michael did that for her she felt guilty when she thought about him, he was only ten he should have been evacuated, but he hadn't wanted to go. just then someone grabbed her arm and hurried her down the street and into the nearest shelter shouting. "Are you trying to get yourself killed woman?" he pushed her down on to the bench then sat down beside her, as everyone moved up to make room for another two bodies.

The man introduced himself. "I'm Arnold I don't suppose you know me but I know your husband Jim, and then he opened his packet and offered her a craven a she accepted and took one with shaking hands.

Just then the door of the shelter burst open and Michael came running in as a tremendous blast shook the shelter, Brenda gave a cry of relief as she held her arms open to her son. "Oh I was worried you would be out doing my messages and get caught in the flying debris." she told her son. "I have spent my day in queues," he told his mother. "But you'll never guess what I got off the butcher?" he beamed. "Hopefully a few sausages for tea but I doubt It." she replied miserably.

"I got a rabbit." He said triumphly. "And I got some potatoes and vegetable, I saw our Marion and she said her and the kids will come along for tea as she hasn't got any food in." Brenda ruffled her son's hair saying, "You have done well. Did you manage to post the letter to our Dorothy? She asked him.

"Oh no I forgot with having to queue nearly all day but I'll do it later." A young woman sitting next to Brenda had been listening and smiled at Michael as she opened her handbag and past him a Fry's five boys in shiny silver paper. Michael couldn't believe it a whole bar of chocolate, "Eat it up she told him I reckon you deserve it if you've managed to get your Mam a rabbit." Brenda smiled at the young woman and offered her and Arnold another cigarette as the bombs dropped and buildings collapsed as children cried, of fright and hunger as mothers dug in their bags for paste sandwiches.

Mrs Milner was a permanent figure in this shelter, as soon as the sirens sounded she hurried down the road in her slippered feet and occupied the same seat every time, "I like to sit facing the door." She told everyone. "So I can watch everyone coming in, I've got to know a lot of the regular ones, and I enjoy knitting my old man's socks while I'm sitting here, there is nothing else to do, is there? She laughed. Brenda watched her as she took her three ply brown wool out of her bag then selected a set of four, size twelve needles and cast on the rib it didn't take her long and she had four inches of rib done and then changed to size ten needles and carried on doing ordinary stocking stitch as the bombs dropped. The incendiary bombs came hurtling down once they hit the ground they burst into flames which would act as targets for the planes overhead to drop more deadly bombs as a continuous stream of bombers passed overhead. Huge columns of smoke darkened the afternoon sky. The planes kept coming and dropping their dangerous cargoes as houses were flattened and then the sudden cut out of an engine suggested that at last our boys in blue were retaliating. An hour later as the all clear sounded Brenda and the rest of the people got stiffly to their feet to climb up the steps from the public shelter they coughed and blinked in the choking air that reeked of cordite although it was only early afternoon the black smoke had created an artificial night. The ferrous fires were burning out of control, and through the smoke burned the angry glow of the setting sun. Voices were screaming and shouting as buildings were still collapsing, ambulances were screaming through the streets with their bells ringing trying to pick up the injured off the streets, the dead would be recovered later. The front had been blown off eight houses in one street wardrobe teetering half on half off the edge they had once been someone's bedroom. Men in tin hats rushing about with burnt blackened faces. Brenda grabbed Michaels hand and hurriedly made her way home hoping her family were alright and her house was still standing. As Brenda got near to her street she slowed down, as her chest was sore and her throat gritty but a cup of tea would go down well she thought, until she got nearer and saw her curtains torn to ribbons flapping through the broken windows in the slight breeze. She started to run to her daughter's house four doors down from her as she had three small children; she hoped they were alright as there was no windows in any of the houses in the street. Marion was just coming to her mother's a baby in her arms and two small children clinging to her skirts, when she saw Brenda she started to cry.

"Oh Mam all my windows have been blown out, the children have all cried nonstop there is no water or gas we can't even have a cup of tea, I can't take anymore." she cried as she passed the baby to Brenda. "Come on then." Brenda said. "Let us go in and see what is left of my house." as she pushed past a crying Marion and three crying children. "What a day this was turning out to be". The messages that Michael had queued all day for were still on the table including the rabbit covered in soot. The letter that Brenda had wrote to her Daughter Dot had blown down on to the floor covered in soot and later after a cup of tea off the w v s van Marion brushing the soot and glass covered floor gathered it all up on the fire shovel and put it in the bin.

Dorothy was beside herself with worry it was only a week before her wedding and she had not had word back from her mother. She thought her family might not come as she had left home under a cloud. But what was done was done and the time for regrets was long pastas her Mam used to say, and she was going to Eva's today to try her wedding dress on, and bring it home to Ethel's.

Eva was getting thoroughly fed up with Winnie, having Winnie back in her house meant all sorts of inconveniences for her and mark, when he was staying with Eva when he was on leave. Eva saw Dorothy walking down the lane towards her house and quickly settled the black kettle back on to the hot coals as Dorothy walked into the room the lid was bouncing on the kettle and steam was pouring from its spout. Eva looked up at Dorothy with a smile on her face saying I'll just scold this tea as she spooned tea leaves in to the brown teapot ready for the hot water from the kettle. As they were both settled on the settee, with a cup in their hand Eva offered Dorothy another cake off the flower patterned plate and she accepted, although she kept looking round warily? Eva noticed and smiled "you needn't be afraid you're going to meet Winnie, as she has gone to see Pat and I told her not to come back here until tea time, so come and try your dress on." The dress was pale blue and dot fingered it admiringly it was intricately smocked with puffed sleeves the dress flowed beautifully over Dots very pregnant stomach. "Oh it's beautiful." Dot cried. "I never thought it would be so lovely, I wish I could sew like you Eva."

"Oh but that is all I have done I started work, making shirts when I was fourteen, Mam said it would stand me in good stead and I would always have a trade at my finger tips, and I suppose she's been right." Eva smiled. "Now there is plenty of tea left in the pot for another cup each, so we might as well use it, waste not want not." laughed Eva.

"Oh alright." said Dot as she sat back down after putting her dress back on. Later as Dot walked back into Ethel's carrying her wedding dress the most beautiful dress she'd ever possessed. Gran looked up and saw Dots eyes shining with happiness, "open the bag up lass, and let us have a look at it then and you can always try it on later when the land girls come in as I'm sure they'll want to see it."

Two hours later with full plates steaming on the table everyone trooped in all ready for their teas, Mabel and Susan had caught up with the land girls from the lodge Rosey, Shirley and Gwen, and cycled home with them and as the girls ate their teas they started telling Gran and Ethel about poor Gwen and the black pudding along with feeling sick she felt sorry for the pig. "Aye it does not do to get sentimental." Gran said. " we have to eat." As she speared a piece of meat and promptly put it in her mouth, later as Wilf went back outside to finish building his dry stone wall that had rushed down yesterday and the boys Frank and Colin had gone to move their goats and stake them a bit further along the lane after milking them. Susan started to laugh and tell Gran and Ethel about Alice Tweddle being on her holidays and Gwen not knowing what she meant had asked her where she was going. "Fancy." said Gran.after being told all about Alice's plight "That is terrible if that is the only bit of piece she gets from that randy old goat is when she has her monthlies." At which everyone started laughing.

CHAPTER SIXTEEN

Dorothy left the table as soon as she had eaten and quickly went upstairs to try on her dress, when she came back in to the kitchen the girls all oohing and ahhing about the dress they thought it was gorgeous, all accept Gran who was staring at it. "Is there something wrong with it Gran?" Dot asked. Gran considered her with a shrewd calculating gaze her lips pressed firmly together.

"The dress is very nice Dot our Eva has made a good job of it but I'm wondering if that baby will hang on till Saturday, as you are carrying it very low and I see you keep putting your fist into the small of your back as if you have an ache, I just hope he gets that ring on your finger before that bairn puts in an appearance."

The hot sun was burning down the week was getting hotter, and Dennis Flower, Dorothy's intended could not put off cutting the hay field any longer. He had greased the entire machine which seized up through winter after he'd been along to Ethel's to see how Dorothy was feeling as she was starting to look tired. Everyone was busy his mother and Ethel were busy baking for the wedding tea while Margaret Emmerson had the wedding cake iced and ready, Eva was finishing off his Mams and Ethel's dress. The mowing machine was a solid machine with two small wheels which was drawn by a pair of horses, Dennis owned two huge horses which he used for the job he would have liked to lend them to Wilf but he needed them himself. Dennis laid the long blade across his knee and started to sharpen it with a stone with a timber handle. The farmers did not commence cutting the hay until the sun was high in the sky and the gentle swaying hay was well dry of the morning dew, they cut the first swaths along the dyke backs it was a hard day walking behind the machine and steering the horses, Dennis saw a pheasant nest further along the field so he halted the horses and picked the nest up carefully and moved it into a corner out of harm's way. As he made his way back to the horses he saw Irene one of the land girls making her way over to him.

"I will take over for you while you go and have a cup of tea." Dennis rubbed the sweat off his brow with his spotted handkerchief as he looked at Irene and said "Do you think you can manage for an hour or so? As I will have to see how Diane is getting on with the pig sty by it's a hot day to be creosoting I hope she has got her arms covered because it burns". Dennis had a lot on his mind as he made his way up the field to the house, his mother would have a pot of tea ready for him and a bite to eat that would replenish his strength. The land girls had already had their morning break; he didn't know how he would have managed without them. As he walked into the kitchen his mother was busy baking, the heat was tremendous as the fire was roaring and the oven was belching out heat. Martha cut a slice off a large fruit cake that was cooling on a wire tray. "I've just brewed the tea." she told Dennis as he walked over to the table and sat down careful to keep out of the way of his mother's rolling pin.

Martha was making apple pies, she had sliced the apples and sugared them and now lifted her pastry and covered the first plate and then began to trim the edges, and then pinching the crust into place with finger and thumb, another one was ready to go in the oven Martha's fingers were so nimble and quick.

"Do you think Ethel and you will be able to make all the food for the wedding?" Dennis asked his mother. "It is in two days time and then there are all the helpers to feed who are coming to help us turn the hay, which will be ready to turn again on Saturday the wedding day"

Just then Dorothy walked in smiling. "I know I can't do a lot and it seemed to take me ages to walk down here, but I thought I might be able to help with the baking."

Martha turned round and looked at her future daughter in law and said. "I will pour you a cup of tea, and you can sit down and take the weight off your feet as I can see your ankles are all swollen lass, and I don't think that bairn far off being born the sooner we get this wedding over the better."

"Has Wilf found anyone to cut his field yet?" Dennis asked Dorothy. "As I'm sorry I couldn't help him as I have all my own ready."

"Oh he's gone with Harold." Dorothy laughed. "You know what Harold is like, if you need anything he always knows where he can get hold of something, Gran said it's because he spends his time with other folks business. "He told Wilf a farmer he knows is selling up, as both his sons had been called up and he wasn't going to have land girls on his land so Wilf has gone to have a look at his two horses, so he needn't borrow horses again." Dennis sat in deep thought trying to think who it would be. "Do you know what this farmer called Dorothy?"

"I think his last name is Bolton." As she picked another pie off the table that Martha had just made and opened the oven door and pushed it in.

"I know who it will be." as it dawned on Dennis. "Do they call him Brian?"

"Yes that was the name I remember now." Dorothy told him as she sat down again as her back was aching. Dennis was looking excited now but not knowing what to do first.

"What 'is the matter with you son you look all flustered, is that the bloke you were going to buy those pigs off?"

"Yes is it Mother, only he wouldn't sell them at the time and we could do with some more but as he's selling up I should go straight away as he'll want to sell them now." He ran his fingers through his hair as he said to Dorothy. "Will you go and get Diane for me, and tell her to carry some buckets of water down the field for the horses, and some oats as they will be ready for a drink and some food and just leave the pig sties for now and help Irene to cut the field."

"Are you going now to see him?" Martha asked surprised.

"Yes I'm going to cycle down and if I'm quick I might catch Wilf coming back with the horses, and I'm sure I'll be able to borrow a cart to bring the pigs back." Martha laughed. "Brian Bolton will probably sell you the lot; he'll think it's his lucky day folk queuing up to buy stuff off him." Dennis never heard her he was peddling down the road as fast as he could go before his mother had finished speaking.

Up at Eva's Prudence was feeling very happy with herself. The scarcity of new clothes to buy particularly since the introduction of clothing coupons was a nuisance, Prudence had been very indignant when going to be measured for a new corset had been told.

"You will have to go to the doctors dear, and if he thinks you need a corset he will give you a certificate and then you can bring it along and purchase a corset, don't you know dear there is a war on and there is steel stays in corsets."

Prudence had hurried across the road to see the Doctor and found she wasn't the only one needing to see someone as three people did look very ill but Prudence would have gone to the front of the queue when the Doctor called "Next." If a young woman hadn't elbowed her out of the way as she manhandled an old man through the door. Prudence sat back down as a woman came in with two young children with snotty noses and coughed constantly, Prudence's patience finally snapped after an hour and a baby crying nonstop as soon as the surgery door opened she stepped inside before her turn and banged the door shut on the others. The doctor jumped as the door banged shut and Prudence shouted. "I have had to sit through there all this time with children coughing all over me babies crying and all I need is a certificate for a pair of corsets." The Doctor had kind brown eyes behind his horn rimmed glasses but they seemed hard now as he stared at Prudence.

"People will cough who come here, babies will cry as they are ill, and you complain and you only want a certificate. Well I would have thought with all the rationing you would not need corsets, but by the size of you I will write one out." and as he scribbled on a piece of paper he said. "That will be two and six, and I think you must be having someone else's rations besides your own." Prudence walked out slamming the door behind her what a cheek that Doctor had but she had got what she had gone for it was no good starting a new life on the Isle of Mann with old corsets

Winnie lying on the bed with hands behind her head was watching Prudence viewing herself in the mirror that was attached to the wardrobe door, standing in her voluminous pink knickers with elastic in the legs, and then she unwrapped the roll of brown paper to reveal her precious pink corsets which she pulled around her body and then pulling herself in, face as red as beetroot and eyes bulging proceeded to fasten the hook and eyes. Winnie thought the garment looked very uncomfortable with the bones digging in to her flesh and the suspenders dangling, but soon her thoughts returned back to her old friend Dorothy, who had been a close friend and had even moved up into the country with her. Winnie felt sorry for herself when she thought what a fool she had been she had lost a good friend, who was getting married on Saturday at least Dot's baby would have a father figure where as Winnie would be on her own with hers.

Back in London life was hectic for Dot's Mam Brenda, who was trying to get everyone prepared for the long journey. Brenda sat at the table drinking the last drop of tea in her cup and stubbing out her cigarette into the saucer before she went to work, then with a deep sigh put the flat of her hands on the table and eased herself to her feet the thoughts of the wedding had been keeping her awake at night when the bombs hadn't. Had she done right in letting Marion accompany them to Dot's wedding with three small children, she had asked herself this a few times after it had been arranged, Marion had wanted to come after all it was her sister who was getting married, and it would do the children good to get a day away Jim thought it was a bad idea as he and Brenda had to find the money and clothing coupons for them all. The black market was thriving more and more as the war progressed, but a friend of Brenda's had told her not to worry over the coupons as she could get hold of plenty, but deception didn't sit well on Brenda's conscience. Brenda walked along the busy street so wrapped up in thought that she never saw her friend Sandra until she caught hold of her arm making her jump.

"Hold on Brenda you seem in a rush this morning you must be going death as well as I've been shouting at you to wait for me."

"Oh I'm sorry Sandra." Brenda replied. "But I seem to have such a lot on my mind at the moment."

I know you do." said Sandra as she linked arms with Brenda. "But I've got those coupons for you in my bag so stop worrying it will be fine," As they walked along Sandra said. "You will never guess what my mother did yesterday when the sirens sounded." And then without waiting for an answer went on to tell Brenda. "My mother has a large shelter and living on the corner of the street she has the bigger garden so when the siren sounds some of the neighbours join her in the shelter. Well yesterday a man that no one knew came in and sat quietly, after the all clear had gone he left the shelter as quickly as he'd arrived, after the shelter had emptied my Mam went to tidy up and found the brown parcel that the man had left and it was ticking, my Mam was so afraid she ran down the garden and had just thrown it at the wall where it shattered into smithereens as the man came back for his parcel, it was his alarm clock that he'd just had mended when the siren sounded." Brenda couldn't help laughing, although as Saturday approached every morning when she woke up she became increasingly worried, about what sort of mood everyone would be in. It was a quintessential summer morning as the two friends made their way into work they would have loved to be able to stay outside in the hot sun but they needed the money, Brenda especially. It was uncomfortably hot with their clothes sticking to them in the factory so hot in fact as the whistle blew for break time.

Brenda said. "I couldn't eat a thing Sandra; I'm going outside for a drink of water and a cigarette."

"I'm coming with you answered Sandra it's too hot to eat." The girls worked hard the rest of the day and were pleased when the final whistle sounded, everyone rushed to grab their bags and get out of the door in to the fresh air, where they all lit their cigarettes and inhaled deeply determined to enjoy their walk home before starting work again preparing tea and seeing to their families. Brenda and Sandra where only three streets away from home when they saw the planes coming over and then the melancholy wail of the air-raid sirens reverberate through the rapidly clearing streets, as everyone ran into the nearest shelter. Brenda and Sandra still had their turbans on their heads with the knot at the front. Although the raid only lasted three hours it made Brenda more and more worried about her children and grandchildren. Sandra's husband was in the army and her two daughters were in the forces so she only had herself to look after, so after watching Brenda rub her eyes and looking so unhappy she decided to offer to go with the family to the wedding on Saturday to help Brenda as she knew she wouldn't get much from Marion.

"Come on Brenda." Sandra spoke kindly as she put her arms around her shoulders. "I will walk home with you when the all clear sounds and help you prepare the tea, and then we will sort Saturday out as I am coming with you to the wedding." she laughed cheekily. The all clear sounded and everyone got stiffly to their feet and shuffled outside to a scene of devastation.

People laying on the red sprayed pavement some sat on the road side covered in blood, Brenda couldn't make out which people lying on the pavement were living or dying there was frantic activity the smell of roasting and burning flesh permeated the air, bodies were strew everywhere, the blazing buildings illuminated the surroundings, people were trying to help but were driven back by the immense heat of the flames, temporary mortuaries had been set up and stacked high with piles of cardboard coffins. Poor souls lay unidentified but they could wait it was the living that needed help.

The two women made their way to Brenda's house as quickly as they could as masonry fell around them, and the thick black smoke stung their eyes and throats. There were large craters in the road, water pipes had burst and people were crying and distraught looking for relatives. But the two women hurried up the road as they turned into Brenda's street she saw her husband dragging bodies from the rubble it was only then that she realised Marion's house had been bombed to the ground she cried out in horror. "Not my daughter and my grandchildren." Just then Jim saw his wife and hurried over shouting they are alright they were in the shelter and they are now at our house waiting for their tea, he laughed trying to ease the tension. He held out his arms and she went into them like a homing pigeon. She paused for an infinitesimal moment before taking a breath and saying shakily. "You'd better go and help those poor folks over there, while I go and see to our family."

It was an eerie quiet that met Brenda has she opened the door into the unlit hall the silence was palpable until she opened the sitting room door to find the kids snivelling with tears which seemed to blend into their colds and runny noses. "Oh no." came the emphatic reply from Marion. "I know you are hungry, but nanna is here now she will cook the tea. What am I going to do Mam? Cried Marion I have lost my home and everything I have nowhere to live." And then she started crying noisily. Sandra made everyone a cup of tea and gave the children a few biscuits that she had in her bag just to get a bit of peace until Brenda started preparing the dumplings she was going to add to the mutton stew she had made with some scrag ends, how many more problems would she have she wondered before they finally made it to the wedding, it was a worry Dot her beloved daughter marrying a man neither her or Jim had met, just to give her unborn baby a name and living so far away in the country. Brenda had never left the city and shuddered when she thought about what lay ahead on Saturday her mind was brought back to the present as the potatoes started to boil and the hot water from the pan splashed on to the hot coals.

Back in the country village Dennis had caught up with Wilf and bought the pigs he was lucky Wilf had purchased both horses, so was able to bring them home for him in a trailer pulled by the two huge horses.

The woman were baking as if their lives depended on it as there was always a good spread put on for a special occasion. Even the elderly brown sisters were baking bilberry tarts and ginger bread, they had offered to come to the farm on the morning of the wedding and boil the kettles ready for the guest returning. Mildred the older of the sisters by two years was rolling out pastry, on her feet were her old cracked shoes with the small cuts on the side to accommodate her bunions. Matilda was stoking the fire up to make sure there was a good blaze to cook the cakes, she had been up early as usual, and cleaned the oven flue out with the long handled flue brush, so when the dog which was a piece of metal that fit the hole was lifted the heat could be sucked under the oven. She was a pleasant woman with a huge goitre it surprised a lot of folks how she managed to swallow, sometimes it bobbed up and down at an alarming rate. Both woman had thinning hair which was drawn back in to a tight bun, neither having married they didn't see the need, they reared hens, and the geese were fattened up for sale at Christmas, which the sisters sold ready for the table as they spent many a day and night plucking them, as they told anyone that didn't know "A warm goose is easier to pluck then a cold one, and do not tear the skin as it blemished the table presentation.

Mabel pressed down the rusty latch and pushed the protesting door which scraped along the stone floor, and after looking cautiously round to make sure she hadn't been seen her and Demetrio slipped quietly inside and shot the bolt across. "I live in Milano and when this war is over I will take you home with me and then we will be together." He had told Mabel as he rubbed his hand up her bare leg, Mabel made no move to stop him as he removed her bloomers and slipped his hands between her legs as his lips fastened on to her nipples she wanted it never to end she had rapturous feelings as they moved together as one. Eventually their movements slowed and then stopped, Mabel thought how romantic he was and foolishly believed him when he spoke of his love for her. It hadn't been very comfortable lying on the prickly straw with his weight on her, but Mabel had made him hers and thought he was worth it. After their abrupt coupling in the little barn Mable opened the creaking door just enough to peer out to make sure there was no one around and after straightening her clothes and patting her hair down kissed Demetrio and hurried down the lane happy in the knowledge they hadn't been seen.

Linda walking down the field had seen them as she carried a huge basket full of sandwiches, cakes and meat pies freshly baked that morning, and a huge can of tea for the girls in the field, turning hay that had been cut the day before and now drying nicely in the hot sun. The land girls were all shapes and sizes, wearing shorts and thin shirts some in bras which made the randy old farmers temperatures' rise, but the wives kept a close eye on their wayward husbands. The girls worked hard all day their sunburnt skin shinning with sweat.

The food delivered Linda set off back up the fields for another basket of food for the P-O-Ws who were working in the far field raking the hay into pikes their bodies glistening with sweat. Linda had renewed her efforts to persuade Paul who had been equally determined to dig his heels in and not acknowledge the prisoners. When the prisoners had arrived at David and Margaret Emmerson's farm they were treated as welcome guests instead of the enemy Paul made no secret of his animosity towards them, while everyone else treated them with kindness and consideration. Grans view. Poor lads were somebody's sons even if they were on opposite sides in conflict and as such deserved to be treated with civility. Well I will not go near them stated Jenny. Paul's experience of losing the bottom half of his leg left him with abiding hatred of Germans the only good German is a dead one was Paul's opinion. Mabel tried to hide behind the hedge as she saw Linda approaching but Linda had seen both her and Demetrio.

"Please don't tell anyone." Mabel begged Linda. "We are in love." "You are a fool Mabel and don't expect me to help you." Linda replied and walked on.

Mabel called after her. A deviant note had crept into her voice "I won't be pregnant we have only done it once."

Well it only takes one match to light a fire replied Linda.

Linda was tired as the cows were still to milk and the normal farm work still went on although it was hay time. David and Wilf had been out all morning although cutting of the hay did not commence until the sun was high in the sky and the gentle swaying hay was well dry of the morning dew, they cut the firth swath along the dyke backs moving the scythes easily but as the day drew to a close everyone slowed down.

The large meadow which Dennis was making his way towards had a high hedge of wild honeysuckle the perfume mingled with the smell of new mown grass. The hay belonging to Dennis was dry on top; it now had to be turned over its damp underside exposed to the sun. Some of the old men from the village were already there, so were the local women helping the land girls who were singing as they worked. The local women toiled in the fields as their children played in the fields or slept soundly in prams. It was a slow monotonous process and a lot of the land girls had some nasty blisters as they had been unaccustomed to gripping pike handles for long. The big enamel bucket of tea was gratefully received along with the basket of food that Dot followed with; it provided a welcome diversion and replenished their strength for a hard afternoon ahead.

Dorothy had been sitting quietly while the workers had eaten their dinners and then she would take the empty basket home to Martha. As Dot made her way back across the lanes the breeze stirred the roses, and Dot sniffed the intoxicating scent, she focussed her attention on the golden brown wheat which was planted in the spring and grew through the summer months the oats' were butter yellow, and across the lane was the barley with its bearded head its pointed stiff hair was sharp. I am very lucky to be living in the country and marrying Dennis on Saturday she thought, everything is under control as long as this baby waits till then, as she rubbed her aching back.

In London at Dots parents thing were far from going well. Marion was living with her parents permanently after being bombed out. Sandra had made things a little easier with providing Brenda with the black market coupons, but sadly Brenda bore the worries of the lot of them she let out a deep sign as she reached for the brown teapot and poured the dregs into her cup. The door was knocked and opened at the same time; Sandra popped her head round the door, as Jim standing at the sink having a shave stripped to the waist, braces hanging down turns around smiling as he says.

"Come in if you can get in as this house gets worse every day." Jim is a serious minded person; he did not always wear a smile with ease. Marion looks up from the magazine she was reading as her three grubby children sit on the floor eating jam and bread, although it is all over their faces she doesn't bother. Marion's head shot up as she cried.

"I hope you are not blaming me for the mess as you know I have nowhere to go because if I had I wouldn't bother you." Brenda anxious to stop another row said "I am sure he didn't mean it. Did you Jim?" As a way of explanation to Sandra she said. "He didn't sleep very well last night, the two hours we had in our own bed, as it was so hot, and it is impossible to lie on the edge of the bed as the springs and mattress sag so we tend to roll together."

"I thought you wouldn't have minded rolling together." laughed Sandra as she nudged Brenda in the ribs."

"Oh that will be my fault." said a disgruntled Marion. They won't be able to get any privacy with me being here, no one seems to want you when you are bombed out." she sniffed. Sandra looked at Brenda's tired face through the haze of cigarette smoke, thinking Marion seemed to enjoy having something to grouse about.

The week had gone by quickly, and with Sandra help everything was arranged, everyone was suitably dressed and just waiting to finish the final preparation Jim was in the kitchen with the shoes that needed cleaning the sound of brushing punctuated by the occasional cling-ting as the cherry blossom tin of black polish falls on the floor. The two friends had spent a frantic few nights rifling through wardrobes choosing and altering clothes, Brenda felt it was all coming together the coupons Sandra had managed to get had made sure they were all turned out decently. Brenda felt happy for Dot if that was what she really wanted, but she had a slight apprehension for her, what wedding didn't have doubts and anxiety attached.

"Come on Michael hurry up and eat your breakfast or we will miss the early train." Brenda was rushing around with her dinky curlers hanging loose in her hair. having brought out her large bag and put the parcels into its cavernous depths "Marion are you going to see to those bairns? I don't know what job to do first and you are sitting on your backside smoking a fag as if you have all the time in the world. Jim having finished his breakfast scraped his chair back and picking up last night's paper, went out into the yard and into the lav he would do two jobs at once and have ten minutes peace. Sandra who had stayed all night took the baby off Marion and plonked him into the waiting dish of water, then proceeded to give him the best wash he'd ever had amid his screams, while Brenda followed suit with the other little boy. Marion decided to strip the little girl and give her a wash, the first one in a week. Brenda turned and shouted at Michael to put his comic down and get ready as she pushed her hair out of her eyes that had now dropped clean out of the curler. Finally after seeing to everyone else Brenda and Sandra went upstairs to put on their best clothes. Brenda looked and smiled as she took her power blue two piece off the hanger, once on she added the white hat with a veil. "It could only be glimpsed by its pattern of fine black dots."

"I haven't had any thing as nice as this for years Sandra, and if it hadn't been for you getting those coupons I don't know how I would have managed."

"I can get most things I need." Sandra said airily, as she changed into her blue crepe-de-chine frock "but keep it to yourself."

An hour later everyone was dressed in their best and ready to walk the short distance to the station all except

Jim, who was standing in front of the mirror in the kitchen, with the tips of the collar pointing up as he knots his tie satisfied with it he turns the collar down gives the tie a few pulls until the knot is centred. Brenda felt she had covered every contingency as far as family appearances were concerned. Marion seemed to have pulled herself together; Brenda thought all her signs of sullenness were melting like dew in the afternoon sun, she just hoped Marion wouldn't air the family grievances with her unruly tongue as she often gave vent to whatever she was thinking, as she opened the brass clasp of her well worn black purse. Sandra had never left the city before so she viewed the trip as an adventure, so with trepidation on Brenda's part, and enthusiasm on Sandra's. They all step out of the door and Jim turns the key then gives it its mandatory three pushes to ensure its locked.

Brenda focussed her attention on the children as they made their way to the station, as Marion had sent them outside to play as soon as they were dressed ready, and Brenda was hoping they wouldn't wander off, and would stay clean.

The children had not wandered off, they had sat at the edge of the pavement, lethargic in the hot sun, taking turns in and out of the house at ten minute intervals and continually asking. "What time is it now? And is it time to go yet."

The little party made their way up the street, Brenda turned to them saying "This oppressively hot day needs a good downpour," as she fanned her face with her hand.

The children started complaining they were hungry, as they walked past a bakery and the smell of cooking reached their nostrils, Jim went inside and bought them all a pork pie at tuppence-ha'penny each he slipped the change into his pocket on the way out, as he handed the pies round he thought he had better be careful with his money or he would have none left for when he arrived in the dales, but everyone was hungry with all the stringent rations.

Finally they arrived at the station Brenda's eyes were going round in her head trying to make sure no one wandered off, although it was early the station was very busy, and Marion was very insouciance at times with her children. Men and woman in all different kinds of uniform, wives and sweethearts saying goodbye to husbands and lovers, wondering if they would ever see each other again. People were used to waiting and queuing but after an hour and a half had passed and the children's whinging cries turned into deep sobs, they were unintentionally piling on the agony, as Brenda started to worry they would not be there in time for the wedding. Jim was just going to find out what time their train would arrive, when he saw a heavily moustached porter coming towards them. They all looked at him as he made his way towards them; Brenda had never seen someone as cadaverously thin.

"I do not know when there would be an available train." He told them. These people take priority." he said as he pointed to the people in uniform. "I am very sorry." He told them as he looked at the tear stained faces of the children. Sandra was staring at him as he stood indecisively in front of them he was so tall and thin that he folded over at the top.

It was another three hours before a loaded train arrived it slowed as if running out of steam and shuddered to a halt in the station, the doors opened then a soldier turned to inform the rest of the service men squatting in the corridors, amid disembarkation the animated voices consisted mainly of servicemen, once they were all off the train they were able to squash into it, Jim had just been to the toilet and came out buttoning his flies by then tempers were much frayed. Jim was sailing in uncharted waters, he was a city man, and although he didn't like to admit it he had never seen a cow and wasn't looking forward to it.

The train door slammed behind them the whistle blew and the train pulled away from the platform with a great puff of steam, and then rolled slowly out of the station then gathered speed, as they past smoking factories and dingy backs of houses. The train speeded up, more and soon fields began to roll past the train windows. The train stopped and started, they all felt they were never going to get there.

Everyone was packed in tight, it was very hot and peoples bodily smells were making Brenda feel sick, Sandra looked across at Brenda and smiled. We will be there in time."She mouthed. "Don't worry." But sadness was running through Brenda like a crack in a cup. It was her daughter's wedding day, and she should have been organising it, not arriving as a guest.

Back at Ethel's Dorothy had spilled a lot of tears. "I wish my Mam was here." she cried. "I thought she would have answered my letter, I don't know how I will get through today without her. Do you think she will come?" Her voice conspiratorial to Ethel, "or do you think she is ashamed of me? I think this is the repercussions of my fall from grace."

Ethel turned and smiled at Dot. "It's irrelevant what I think Dot, but we can always hope besides no mother would want to miss her daughter's wedding whatever her circumstances."

Gran shuffled forward and chimed in. "Well you only have to look at me and our Ethel to see how true that is. Our Ethel has been married twice and both times she was expecting but I went to both of them."

"Yes I know you did Gran." Said Ethel hurriedly, before gran could find some more words of wisdom.

"Come on." said Susan one of the land girls, "we are waiting upstairs for you and we have made a garland of flowers for your hair." Ethel pushed strays of damp hair off her face as she slid another tin of tarts out of the oven; she had also made great slabs of bread pudding full of fruit and brown sugar sticky and extremely satisfying and tasty for hungry workers.

As gran told them, "It will stick to your ribs with a generous helping of custard on." Upstairs Susan was furiously licking the eyebrow pencil to make some imitation seams up the back of Jennie's legs as Jennie had kindly given her best nylons to Dot seeing as it was her wedding day. Dot had washed her tear stained face and was now sitting on the bed while the girls did her makeup and laid her clothes ready. Dot was upset about her Mam but she didn't feel very well neither, She began to wonder what Gran had said about this baby was ready for being born.

Susan seeing Dot staring onto space smiling said. "I know you must be a bit frightened this being your wedding day, but we will all be with you."

Eva helped gran upstairs to get ready while Ethel saw to the twins,

"You needn't make me look too fancy." she scolded Eva. "It's not me getting married; oh I wouldn't fancy that again." she said with a shake of her head.

The sun beats down from a cloudless sky, windows are thrown wide open but in the hot stillness not a curtain moves. Gran has opened her top button on the cream blouse that Eva has put on her, but this is her only concession to this hot day. "Not a breath of air to be had." she tells Eva who already knows, as she has not had time for a sit down this morning. But she knows in a few weeks everyone will be rallying round for her, as she will be the next bride to leave this house, with her secret, as mark had gone back to his unit and the weeks had passed as before and it was as though he had never been. But he had. There was proof she knew she would have five children next year instead of four but for now it was her secret.

Wilf finishes fastening his tie then shoves his arms into the sleeves of his jacket, turning round to ask Ethel as he does.

"Do you think Dot and Gran will be able to walk to the church in this heat?"

"Well I can answer for myself Wilf I might be crippled but my mouth still works, I reckon if someone lends me an arm to lean on I'll manage. I'm not too sure about Dot though."

Down on Emmerson's farm Linda was busy and so were the rest of them hoping to get all the work done so they could all go to the wedding reception. Margaret had cooked the midday meal and the first of the p o w s walked in with David, perspiration running down his whiskery face.

Paul quickly grabbed his crutches and hurried out of the kitchen saying over his shoulder. "I will have my meal later as I'm particular who I eat with."

The p o w s knew all about Pauls leg and felt sorry for his predicament. But they were in this war as well with wives and children thousands of miles away, and no idea what was happening to them.

Linda followed Paul through from the kitchen. "Why do you have to be so bloody nasty to them all the time?" she shouted at him. "Everyone is trying to get along all accept you."

Paul flopped down on to the nearest chair and turned his implacable gaze on Linda saying." I've spent three years of my life fighting and struggling against theses buggers, and now I'm being asked to get into their boat and start rowing with them. Yes they are miles away from home. He gave a harsh laugh. Well I bloody was as well and look how my life has turned out, as he pointed to his leg. "So if you want to eat with them? Do as you want, but I definitely don't." Linda considered him with a shrewd calculating gaze, her lips pressed firmly together. His temper had grown more irascible his moods blacker and more morose of late, she wished the p-o-w-s hadn't arrived but there was a war on and as Gran said. "They were all somebody's sons." Linda walked out of the kitchen swinging her hips there was a dance on tonight and the yanks were coming. Paul didn't see the big smile on her face, or his depression would have been worse. He did care for Linda if only he could tell her but who would want him now?"

The wedding party were just about to leave as Dot came downstairs, everyone was crowing round her saying she looked lovely. Everyone apart from Gran, Ethel turned and looked at gran saying. "You are quiet for a change don't you think Dot looks a picture?"

"Well seeing as you have asked me what I think." Replied gran. "I think the sooner she gets this wedding over with the better, as that baby is not going to wait much longer. Have you invited Grace?" she asked Dot. "Because if you hadn't I think you should have done as I can tell by your face you are not feeling well are you Dot?"

Dots eyes filled with tears. "I haven't felt very well all morning, but I didn't like to say as everyone has been so busy trying to make my day special."

"Come on then said gran let us get to the church before we have the baby before the wedding."

CHAPTER SEVENTEEN

The train shuddered to a stop on a gasp of steam at the Dale Station. Doors were being flung open, weary passengers stretched aching limbs. Sandra's neck was aching as she had been pushed into a corner for most of the journey. The younger children had been lulled to sleep by the movements of the train and were now being wakened. The two small ones were being carried off the train they were blinking in the red hot sun and rubbing their eyes. Michael was still very quiet he had not wanted to come, he did not like weddings, and he certainly did not miss his sister. He could have been evacuated to the country when some of his friends from school had come, but he hadn't wanted to come then and he certainly didn't want to come now.

He looked up as his father was trying to get his attention. "Get hold of these bags Michael. We have come loaded down with stuff, you would think we'd come for a week instead of a day, or a half day by the time we've got here, and by the time we finally reach there the day will be over." The two small children were sobbing now as they were hungry. "Well there is nowhere here to buy them a pie is there?" Jim asked his wife as if it was her fault. Brenda was near to tears but she had survived this far with the sound advice from her dear friend Sandra, who was still helping her so the next step was to find the church.

They walked out of the station and all they could see was fields and hedges. "If we get lost here Dad, at this strange place, will we ever be found?" Michael asked his Dad.

"I don't know son, you wanted to stay at home I wish I'd stayed with you." Brenda's lower lip was trembling.

The mood of euphoria that pervaded for her daughter's wedding once everything had been sorted had now left her.

Sandra who was leading the party suddenly stood still causing everyone else to bump into her. Just as Jim was going to open his mouth and shout at her she said "listen I can hear horses hooves." They all stood still listening they hadn't long to wait as Harold came in to sight with his horse and cart. Harold knew it was Dennis and Dorothy's wedding day today and had wondered if any of her folks would turn up, he decided to say nothing to nobody and wait at the station, and then by giving them a lift and by God they looked as if they needed one, he would get another free meal as she was a good cook was Martha.

Harold came along side with the huge horse Jim backed away he was a bit frightened of them he kept clear of the horses at home that delivered the milk.

"Where are you lot heading off to then?" Asked Harold. "I've never known so many folk on this lane at once."

Brenda felt hope rising. "Please could you help us? It is our daughter's wedding day and we have been travelling all morning, but I'm afraid we are going to be late, and we don't know how to get there." This was just what Harold was hoping to hear. He looked down on them saying. "I could take you but I've got a busy schedule." As he rubbed his hand over is whiskery face, after a moment's hesitation he said

"Come on get on the cart I will take you." They all climbed on wishing they hadn't bothered getting dressed up. But at least they were with someone that knew where they were going. Brenda noticed his old jumper was a patchwork of darns, and was still carrying the remains of last night's supper, but he had turned his muffler cleanest side out but as long as he got them there. Harold gave them another penetrating look as he used his pipe to emphasise what he was saying they all thought they had better show interest or he would slow to a stop. Brenda was suppressing her irritation at Harold's slowness this oppressively hot day needed a good downpour. Harold was talking about Dot now, saying she was marrying into a good family, pity the child was so near. Brenda looked over at jims mutinous set to his mouth, so she made obvious attempt to steer conversation into safer waters, as he did not like being reminded of his daughters condition.

, As Dots wedding party arrived at the church Dennis and his family were already there waiting.

"You must be in a hurry to get married are you Dennis? I didn't think you would have been here this early." Ethel asked him.

Dennis face flashed with colour as he said. "No I mean yes."

"I know what you mean lad." gran interrupted. "you are thinking the sooner you get this over with the sooner you can see to your hay, and I don't blame you as animals have to be fed in winter, and Dot here is getting a good provider." Miss Walker had said she would play a hymn for them on the organ and Dennis was looking for her thinking she wasn't coming as it was a surprise for Dot. Just then her chesty cough heralded her approach, and she slipped in unnoticed by Dot and began to play the wedding march, as Dennis and his best man popped in after her. Wilf held out his arm for Dot to get hold of as he led her down the aisle, she was shaking. Wilf looked at her and whispered. "Don't be frightened we are all here for you, and it will soon be over, just like a wedding."

Harold could see the church from his vantage point but still did not hurry the guests had just gone in and him and his horse always went at a slow pace there was no need to rush. The vicar walked up the church to close the door; he thought it was more personal, when he saw Harold and his cart he could not believe it at first and then he thought may be this was Dots family. Old Harold must have been waiting at the station to make himself a few bob or an invitation for a bite to eat. So just in case he slipped past Miss Walker and whispered. "Please play that again." Then as the family reached the church door the vicar was waiting for them in his white surplice with a gold fringed ribbon around his neck, he held a black prayer book and smiled a welcome as Harold drew up outside the church and the family got down off the cart.

"How much do I owe you?" asked Dots Dad, as he put his hand in his trouser pocket to pay him. "We will see to it later." remarked Harold. "As you will likely all need a lift back for the reception?"

Brenda almost ran into the church, and everyone hearing the door bang shut turned round. Dot saw her mother and started to hurry towards her as best she could. Brenda met her half way with open arms and dot went into them. They cuddled and hugged each other tears were mixed with kisses. "Why didn't you tell me you were coming?" asked Dot. Brenda didn't want to elaborate so she said. "Shh for now go, and get married now we are here." During the wedding ceremony Dot tried to smile and look happy but the pain in her back was getting worse, she had walked to the church against Grans advice, and now she knew it would be impossible to walk back to Martha's. "I pronounce you man and wife." The vicar broke into her thoughts, and then it wasn't long till they were outside and Harold quickly came over and offered a lift, to which Dot was grateful.

Back at her new home, Dot realised how lucky she was with Martha, as her and Ethel had baked all week. The table was full of food everybody was catered for. They had covered every contingency as far as family appearances were concerned. It didn't matter that the bairn was due, or Dennis wasn't the father. No one was going home hungry and Harold certainly wasn't. He was shoving it in as if he hadn't had a bite for a month; he saw Brenda watching him. He laughed and his moustache tilted up to reveal large tobacco stained teeth

Brenda recovered her equilibrium after Sandra whispered to her. "I think all this food is normal for country people." Brenda had been so shocked so had all Dots family when they had seen the spread that had been laid out. Trifles' made with fresh cream, chicken and pork sandwiches, Pasties and pies, cakes galore glasses of fresh milk for the children. There was huge fruit cakes fresh bread that the land girls had baked this morning for Martha with plenty of fresh butter. Jim had never seen such big pieces of cheese. His stomach rumbled in anticipation but he didn't know where to start, after Martha had told him to "eat up lad." he had needed no second bidding. The children were shoving it in to their mouths and when Brenda told them to slow down Martha smilingly said. "It's alright let them fill their bellies, they are hungry." Dot wasn't hungry gran noticed she hadn't eaten a bite, as Dennis took her in his arms holding her as close as her protruding stomach would allow.

Linda was walking very slowly towards the wedding reception; she had finally got Paul to agree to accompany her.

"I don't know why you keep inviting me out with you Linda, as you can have any man you want." it hurt him to say it but he wanted to hear her response.

"I do like you Paul. But you are going to have to be friendlier there is a war on and there is nothing we can do about it. And besides if there hadn't been you wouldn't have known me and look what you would have been missing." she laughed. Jim wasn't a man of many words and everyone was introduced all they got off him was OW'd YA do, until Paul hobbled in, and they seemed to hit it off as they would of both rather have been elsewhere, as both where private people.

Easing her shoes surreptitiously off her feet, Dot rubbed her swollen ankles one after the other. Walking and then standing so long at the church hadn't suited them. Dot was endeavouring to keep quiet about her pains but suddenly the dull ache in the small of her back was making itself felt with renewed vigour. Close to tears she waddled rather then walked now, her backache became more persistent. The woman saw what was happening and to avoid a hasty and unpremeditated exit as some of the men were still eating heartily took Dot upstairs to the clean sheeted bed.

Just then Frank and Colin arrived saying they had brought the horse and cart to take gran home. Gran was already upstairs seeing to Dot, She shouted down "get yourselves something to eat and then take Michael with you, and he can help you to milk the cows and goats, as I'm staying here." Jim had relaxed in Pauls Company, as they sat together at Martha's table nursing their cups of strong sweet tea, while Paul explained who some of the people where that had come along for the wedding.

Just then Lydia appeared wearing a white blouse and blue skirt the waistline of which disappeared deeply into the folds of fat, round her enormous body she waddled into the room to the sound of her own rasping breath and commandeered the best chair, then she sat down with a whoosh of exhaled breath, and carried on wheezing ostentatiously. Her husband owed a small holding just near the woods and had lived there with their grown up family, until their sons were called up, and then they had been forced to apply to the land army for help. The help had arrived yesterday in the form of Mary a city girl who had never seen an animal before. Martha had walked over to Lydia with a full plate of food and when she had enquired about Mary the land girl Lydia's raised voice had risen an octave, as she sat in the chair shaking her head as her heavy jowls wobbled like a plate of jelly, with indignation.

"My land girl turned up all though she was later than expected, she is quiet enough but she is going to take some training. After she had eaten her meal with us I asked her to go and milk the goat, she set off with the stool and pail, the goats were only around the corner, I was just going to tell my Joe to go and look for her after she'd been gone an hour when she walked in with the empty bucket."

"I can't get any milk out of her." she cried. "I've squeezed and pulled gently for half an hour."

"So I had to leave my jobs and go and see why she couldn't milk daisy, I got a shock." she said. "When she pointed out which goat she'd been trying to milk it was the Billy." Everyone laughed but Jim wondered if he would show himself up with the animals while he was here.

The door opened and a young woman walked in slim as a reed, what a contrast to Lydia. Jim thought, as the young woman carried a sleeping child in her fragile stick like arms, and two children clung to her skirt. She smiled showing her huge buck teeth making her look almost rabbity, her dark shadowed eyes contrasted with her pale face. Paul saw Jim looking and said.

"She has only been here a fortnight she was evacuated with her children, her husband is in the services and I think that is the one that is reported missing. We have had a few lately but a lot go back home as they don't like country life."

The man asleep in the corner with his gold watch chain shining across his narrow chest was an old man who lived by himself along the lane. "He always managed to get himself invited to weddings and funerals alike, as soon as his belly is full he nods off", Paul explained when he saw Jim wondering; "he's not much company is he?" Paul laughed as the old man's rheumy eyes were closed, he had eaten a dish of jelly for his tea as a lot of stuff was too hard for toothless gums to chew, and now he was fast asleep with his toothless mouth agape. "They all lived within spitting distance from each other, those that lived down the lane." Paul was saying. While the young women's children sat in the corner with Jims grandchildren, all holding a bag of sherbet dip, they were all quiet, concentrating on dipping the liquorice stick into the paper bag of sugary yellow sherbet. Jim couldn't help wondering how these country people obtained all this food, and his youngest grandson hadn't known how to eat his sherbet, until Brenda had shown him as there was none of that around where they came from.

Dorothy had made her way upstairs quietly trying to retain some dignity.

"Get into bed lass." Gran told her with weary patience, "Because you'll not be back down there tonight." As Dorothy first perched uneasily on the side of the bed then after Grans gentle persuasion turned round and lay on her back the bed springs squeaking loudly.

Dorothy was crying quietly as Gran held her hand saying. "It's no good crying, put it down to experience you'll know for next time what to expect, I learnt quickly I only had the one, but I suppose you'll have to have another at least, as this one isn't your husbands is it?" Brenda walked wearily back upstairs with a cup of tea for gran, she was in a quandary she knew Jim would be wanting to set off home but there was no way she was leaving her daughter in labour, and besides God only knew when she would see her again and this new baby. She made up her mind if the rest of them wanted to go home they could but she was staying. Martha was downstairs with some of the womenfolk tidying up after the wedding. Dot laid on the bed streaks of sweat dripped down her face and her dark hair clung in tendrils to her scalp and let out a scream of pain as she clung to the towel that was knotted to the bed post to pull on. Ethel had gone home with Wilf and the boys and had taken Michael with them. Ethel would return later after she had got all of her jobs done. Sandra had told Marion to get off her backside and help clear the table as Martha filled the huge wicker basket full of food for Emma one of the land girls to take to the hayfield. Dennis had gone on ahead he hadn't wanted to leave Dot but judging by the sky the weather wasn't going to hold much longer and they had the rest of a field to gather in and make into stacks, so they took full advantage of the good weather, as the sun beat down making the heat unbearable. Marion opened her worn hand bag and took out a small case of black mascara and spat on the strip of black, then began to lather it on to her lashes, she had heard one of the land girls mention a pub along the road and she was determined to have a night out, why should she sit here among this lot while they worried about Dot giving birth upstairs, Martha had put the wireless on low, no doubt to drown out the noise Dot was making upstairs,

345

it was playing music interspersed with news, and getting on Marion's nerves, she was also very conscious of the difference in her and dots circumstances now, she knew Dot would never have to queue for food like she had to do, or go without. How she wished she had never come.

"Where has our Michael gone?" She asked no one in particular. "He could have helped me to look after these bairns." Mrs Willis a motherly woman, who had come to see Dennis get married, smiled over at Marion showing a full set of discoloured teeth, saying.

"Pass the two little ones over to me I have a big enough lap to fit them both on, as I've stayed on to offer my help should it be needed."Marion handed them over she couldn't believe her good fortune and then quickly eyebrow-pencilled lines on the backs of her legs in readiness for going out

Paul gave Jim a dig in the ribs and said. "I'd better be on my way or Linda will be coming to look for me besides we are the only men here as Harold is waiting at the door to give Marion a lift along the pub."

"Oh dear I don't know what to do." Jim told Paul as they headed towards the back kitchen door and as he pulled it open it moaned creakily on its hinges. Jim undid his tie and opened his top button he had been sitting near the continually burning grate but he had been told domestic life resolved around it in the country.

Paul took pity on him. "I tell you what Jim I will sit outside with you and then when Linda arrives we will go along the pub. Jim didn't care for this uncivilised remoteness as he sat down beside Paul on the doorstep; he heard the twittering of birds. The skylarks were swooping in the blue sky catching insects for their fledglings they were singing and calling as they hunted in the evening air.

Jim jumped nearly spilling his sweet tea that Martha had brought out for him and Paul, as the screeching cry of the barn owl gave him a fright, as he saw the big yellow eyes, its screeching cry to warn trespassers that this was his territory, as the sky larks headed back to the meadows. A swarm of midges rose from a stagnant ditch in the dyke back and flew around Jims head, as he lifted his hand to flap them away he saw the owl returning with a dead mouse hanging from its talons he settled on a branch and proceeded to rip his meal apart his huge yellow eyes keeping watch over the countryside.

Dennis toiled in the field alongside the land girls and some of the men from the village who were too old or infirm to be called up. What a state of affairs he thought this was his wedding day and here he was working in the field trying to get the hay in before the rain started and looking at the sky it wouldn't be long, and his wife of just a few hours lying upstairs on the bed giving birth to another man's child.

"You haven't heard a word I've said to you." Dennis turned and saw Emma standing beside him.

"Sorry I was just thinking." he replied.

"Well that is another field finished." she told him. "So I'm going to hurry back home and after a quick wash I'm going to the pub."

Back at Martha's the women were keeping watch on Dorothy. "It will take a few hours." said Martha knowingly. "With it being her first, they usually do take longer." Her and Brenda were having a cup of tea as Brenda nodded she knew only too well. In unison they both stopped talking and had a sip of tea, as their cups chinked back into the saucers as one. Then they get off their chairs and hurry stiffly to the door in answer to graces voice, as she hurried

347

in, rolling up her sleeves and excluded an air of capable confidence. Grace stopped suddenly in the bedroom doorway as she saw Gran sitting beside the bed, with her white blouse and black skirt, her usual mode of dress, whether it was a wedding or a funeral. Mrs Brown was alright in small doses, and if only she would keep her advice to herself but Grace knew that Mrs Brown wouldn't budge until Dorothy's baby was safely here. Brenda came into the room puffing from exertion from climbing the stairs again; she walked over to the window and closed the curtains then after lighting the lamp the brass knobs of the iron bed glinted in the corner.

Paul's leg was starting to ache, as he was sitting scrunched up on the well scrubbed step; he started to get up holding onto the door frame very slowly as he was nervous he would fall over. Last week him and Linda had gone back to see the Doctor who was visiting the hall which was given over to the military for wounded soldiers to be used as a convalescent home, and Paul had finally been fitted with his artificial foot, this was the first time he had been out alone without Linda, and although he would never tell her he was missing her, she had given him the confidence and goaded him at times to have this artificial leg fitted he looked around to see if she was coming yet. Jim saw Paul looking worried and asked.

"What is bothering you Paul? If you want to go I don't mind, we could maybe go along to the pub together if you can manage, as this might take all night," as he raised his eyebrows and nodded towards the bedroom window. Paul's slow exhalation of momentarily held breath was less audible then felt. He had an aversion to go out without Linda as she had confidence for both of them. He made his way slowly over to the five barred gate that separated the yard from the hay meadows Jim noticed he was hobbling more so he grabbed hold of Pauls arm. With relief Paul leaned against the gate his arms resting on the top.

"Just look at that." Paul told Jim as he pointed to the hay meadow, with its deep tresses of grass full of lilting colours, tall mixed grasses with the shapely seed heads that sway graciously in the breeze. There is barley grass, timothy, Yorkshire fog and cocksfoot. Bye they look bonny among the wild flowers, the red poppies and blue scabrous along with the corn marigold and marguerites. I always loved the job of going round the outside of the field with the scythe to open it up." When he saw Jim was looking puzzled Paul explained about cutting the fields and making the hay. "Aye this field will be cut tomorrow unless this thunder arrives, I do love the countryside Jim, I would have liked a wife to help me run the farm after mother and father finish with it but it will never happen now." he sighed.

Jim was shocked. "What makes you think that lad? She seems a canny lass the one who came here with you."

"Oh you mean Linda; she is our land girl Jim she has been with us so long now she is like part of the family."

Jim laughed. "Well don't tell me you don't fancy her lad, as she is a bonny lass and she seems keen on you."

Paul shook his head and looked sad. "She wouldn't want me Jim I'm a cripple we didn't get on well when we first met, but now I do care for her but I wouldn't embarrass her by telling her how I feel as she works for my parents no lass will want a cripple."

"Well you have made a start Lad," Jim told him as he pointed to Paul's artificial foot. "Next year you will be opening the fields again ready to get the hay in, and if I was you I would tell Linda how you feel as she'll not wait forever.

Mrs Willis was left to see to Marion's younger children, as Sandra boiled extra water thinking from the noise upstairs that the birth must be imminent. She turned to Mrs. Willis saying.

"If we are all staying here tonight the sleeping arrangements will be haphazard with so many extra bodies, and I don't know when we will be going home as Brenda will want to stay a few days now. The baby will be here before the night is out, and I will stay with her as long as it is alright with Martha, I'm so pleased I paid my rent providently as we will be going to the pub tomorrow night to wet the baby's head."

Brenda turned towards the bed as dot screamed out, and then the terrifying swiftness with which events unfolded, combined with the excruciating pain and then suddenly an overwhelming urge to push and a terrible burning sensation between her legs as a enormous pressure made itself felt, almost as soon as it stopped she could hear gran saying "That's right Dot push". Her body was dictating she couldn't do anything else. Dot thought Grace must have gone home as it was gran who had taken things in hand, a tiny blood soaked baby slipped out and laid between dots exhausted legs gran turned to grace saying.

"Come on then grace, what are you standing there for? You should be seeing to this lass, I've done your job for you tonight," just as the baby emitted a lusty cry. "Well you have got a healthy baby girl." gran smiled. "I'm just pleased I came to the wedding and I was here to see to things as your mind seems to be far away to night Grace."

Wilf and Ethel were making their way back to Martha's with Michael, beside them on the cart. The twins were in bed so Frank and Colin had been left in charge. Ethel had told them. They wouldn't be long. Michael jumped down off the cart as Wilf pulled on the reigns, whoa lad he talked to the horse as the gate swung open, Ethel was looking at Martha's fruit trees they were enormous, they jostled for space with each other their branches tangled together and weighed down with fruit. Ethel knocked and opened the door Mrs. Willis smiled as she walked towards her.

"I have heard the muffled cries of a new born babe." she told Ethel, "but I haven't been upstairs yet as I have just put Marion's two little boys to bed, she went to the pub and has not come back." She said indignantly. Wilf walked in with Dennis who had just finished work in the hay field.

"How is Dot?" Dennis asked worriedly.

"Go upstairs and see her lad." Mrs Willis told him. "The bairn has arrived." Wilf decided to stay downstairs with Michael.

"There will be enough folk upstairs and all babies look alike so I'll stay down here out of the way." he said as Ethel glared at him. As Dennis walked into the bedroom smiling with relief that it was all over and mother and baby were well, a mewing sound came from the small bundle in the drawer. He felt ill at ease in this women's orientated world, more so when gran said. "Congratulations lad, you have a daughter to look after now, next time she has a baby make sure you are the father." The sound of intake of breath filled the room; Ethel was horrified "There was no need to say that gran."

"Why not our Ethel is it not true?" Ethel turned bright red,

"I'm so sorry." she said to the gathering in the room. "Come on gran we are going home."

Gran stood her ground saying." I didn't mean any harm, I have been with the lass all through her labour, and

Dennis must have been worried, as he lost his first wife in child birth, but never mind it has all turned out for the best." Ethel took hold of Grans arm and helped her downstairs. Wilf was on his feet as soon as he saw Ethel he had lost a lot of time to day with the wedding and then her having the bairn and right in the middle of hay time. Wilf looked up at the sky and said. "There is thunder in the air, and I don't think it's far away." Wilf had just put the horse into the stable for the night and was heading towards the back door when the sky became ominously black, suddenly a loud crack of thunder sounded overhead followed by large rain drops. The rain became torrent lightning lit up the black clouds, by morning the storm had cleared and the air was much fresher, but for quite a few got caught and as Gran said as she saw them hurrying past the window from the pub. "They will be wet inside and out." Jim was enjoying himself he was getting on fine with Paul and when Paul suggested he stay until closing time. Jim acquiesced agreed, as he was joining in the sing song and the land girls were dancing. Another bloke sitting along from Jim seemed to be having a hard time with his wife, as Jim had never seen the women's mouth close all night, it was a wonder she didn't have jaw ache. Just then as Jim picked up his pint the women left her seat and went over to the piano to sing the bloke picked his pint up and came and sat beside Paul.

"How are you keeping?" The bloke asked Paul. "I see you are getting out and about a bit lately, that will be down to Linda I expect. Are you going to introduce me to your friend?"

"Oh sorry Norman this is Jim he is staying at Martha's, his daughter got married to Dennis today."

"Oh I see so you've left the wedding party to come and have a quiet pint, well I can't say I blame you, I might

get a bit of peace now seeing as she is singing at the piano."
The women sitting on the other side of Jim turned and gave him a lopsided grin, enabling her to keep the everlasting fag going in the corner of her mouth. The bar door suddenly swung open just as Jim thought he had heard an engine stop outside, land girls came laughing through the door followed by the GIs all smoking and enjoying themselves. Paul saw Jim watching the girls and said. "Aye those land girls surprised me as well. When I first came home after I lost my leg, they will dance and drink half the night, but they will be up at five o clock in the morning ready to milk the cows." Jim watched wide eyed as a woman called Hilary made her way over her pendulous breasts like melons, her smile turned to a scowl as she caught her leg on the rough wood of a chair back , she had just snagged her last remaining pair of stockings. Swearing as she watched the ladder run inexorably from calf to ankle. Jim thought she would likely have more from where they came from as she took an expensive passing cloud cigarette from a bright pink packet. They ended the night at the pub with a rousing rendering of "Kiss me goodnight sergeant major."

Gran was in her bedroom getting ready for bed; Ethel turned the blankets back ready to help gran in.

"I want to have a look out of that window before I get in there." said gran. "As I can hear voices and it is kicking out time for the pub."

"Who are you looking for gran?" asked a puzzled Ethel.

"Well I tell you what our Ethel. Jim went along to the pub with Paul and Linda, and that Marion, Dots sister got herself ready, cheeky madam, and left Mrs Willis to look after her children, she said she was going to the pub. I bet she isn't with that lot who are walking along now I don't think she would go near the pub while her dad was there I reckon she has got herself a GI. Like a moth to a flame that lass she'll be drawn to the men". As the voices grew nearer gran hobbled to the window as her flannelette nightgown flapped around her ankles. "Look our Ethel." She shrieked. "She is not with them; I wonder what she is up too?" Grans sharp eyes and ears missed nothing,

"I think you are being a bit hard on the girl gran, she is only young and with her husband away fighting for his country she is maybe looking for a bit company."

"Aye well you believe what you want our Ethel, but I looked at her with experienced eyes, I just hope her husband doesn't get the blame for something he didn't put there." And as a parting shot as Ethel wrapped the blankets over gran, she said. "Mark my words our Ethel. Marion will likely go home with more than she came with." Ethel blew out the lamp and as she closed the bedroom door she smiled as she called. "Goodnight gran see you in the morning."

Wilf was sitting by the fire with Frank and Colin enjoying his nightly mug of cocoa,

"Come on sit down lass I scolded us both another mug of cocoa I thought we could both do with it after the day we've had."

"Oh thank you Wilf, Gran is getting worse she does say some daft things you should of heard her putting Marion through as I was helping her to bed, she doesn't even know Dorothy's sister."

"Well I wouldn't underestimate gran she misses nothing and you said Marion was in a hurry to go out and her sister was upstairs giving birth but it's nothing to do with us Ethel so drink you cocoa and then we'll go to bed."

Marion appeared at Martha's door in the early hours of the morning, her face flushed, deep red with beads of perspiration visible on her upper lip it had been hot inside that truck even with no clothe on , with the GI she had picked up. He drove off into the night shouting "see you around honey" as she crept into the house, and then out again as she needed to visit the outside lavatory. Marion sat there shivering with the guilt of what she had done while the moonlight crept in through the gap at the top of the door.

Cock-a doodle do rang out bright and clear from Wilf's midden, as Martha's cockerels joined in the chorus. The short summer night was almost over and dawn began to lighten the room as Jim woke and rubbed the sleep from his eyes as his son in law threw the blankets aside and got out of bed. Jim stretched in the comfortable bed and could easily have dozed off again, but hunger and the smell of bacon nudged him into activity he then gave Michael a push as he had his bony knees wedged in his back. Dennis reached for his clothes off the chair at the side of the bed. He would go next door and see how new wife and baby were getting on. He shook his head in disappointment; he had just spent his wedding night sharing a bed with his father in law, and brother in law. Dorothy was sitting up in bed, her mother Brenda snoring gently beside her, on hearing Dennis's voice she shot up wondering where she was at, and then she smiled sleepily as she saw the baby sucking lustily in Dots arms. Dennis walked round the bed and softly stroked the baby's cheek; its head turned causing it to lose its grip on the nipple, and it snuffled noisily trying to latch back on. After a quick kiss on Dots cheek Dennis hurried downstairs to where Martha stood frying bacon, black pudding and eggs for his breakfast. She smiled at him and then nodded to the far end of the table where Marion sat nursing a cup of hot sweet tea.

"I found this young lady in the lav this morning when I paid a visit, she has been there since a GI she met last night dropped her off." Marion was feeling sorry for herself, she was hoping she could eventually forget what happened last night or she would have some explaining to do, as it was a while now since her husband had been home, and it could be years before she saw him again.

"Come on drink that tea lass, or it will be stone cold." Martha kindly told her. It's no good crying over spilt milk what's done is done I just hope for your sake there is no come backs." The smell of bacon floated tantalisingly up the stairs to Dots family, Jim's mouth was watering at the thought of all the food and as he entered the room looking indecisive with Brenda. Martha sensing their indecision told them to. "Sit down and have some breakfast." Brenda and Jim were filled with gratitude for the kindness of Martha and her family for their hospitality. They understood they could not have a bedroom of their own as demand exceeded availability, and besides Brenda had enjoyed the closeness of her daughter and grandchild. The door to the downstairs bedroom creaked open and Sandra walked in holding the hands of Marion's children, Jim looked up thinking it was strange Sandra looking after them and Marion looking unhappy. When he turned and asked Sandra why she was looking after them she was so angry she could hardly speak.

"I have looked after these children all night." She stated "and then she came in early this morning after a GI dropped her off." All the time she was pointing her finger at Marion. "She woke the children up and I had to get them back to sleep to save waking the whole house up, we should have left her at home." Jim stared at his daughter and then blew all the air out of his lungs in an explosive expression of disgust and disbelief, as he realised she had spent most of the night with the GI as she had not been to the pub. Morning was the longest and enervating Marion had ever dawdled through. Martha was busy as hustle and bustle breakfast preparation for the rest of them went on around them.

"I will carry Dorothy's breakfast up to her while you see to Marion's bairns Brenda, as it doesn't seem as though Marion is going to do much today." muttered Sandra.

"Our Dorothy has always been a good worker compared with a few." Brenda replied, as she eyed Marion, who felt this comparison was unfair, and retorted.

"I don't care; I will be leaving here as soon as possible, we will be leaving shortly wont we Mam?" She said enunciating the words so savagely.

"Well we'll see." Brenda temporised as she had no intension of leaving Dorothy just yet as it could be years before she saw her again.

Jim sat back his belly fuller than he could ever remember and gave a huge belch which earned him a hard glare from Brenda, and a knowing smile from Martha who said.

"It didn't take you long to eat that breakfast lad and by the look on your face you've enjoyed it. Would you like another pot of tea?" Then she bent to pick up the huge brown teapot from the hearth. Jim sat back in the chair he made up his mind Marion wasn't going to blight his stay here with these generous people, and as he enjoyed his second pot of tea he looked around the room which was so different from his own home. The kettle here swung over hot coals permanently boiling or just off the boil, it hung on a strong S shaped hook made hotter or colder by hanging the hook higher or lower, on a long heavy chain, suspended from somewhere up in the vast chimney. Martha had told him. He watched her unhook the kettle while she stirred another large pan of porridge its aroma wafting through the cracks in the kitchen door as the prisoners of war made their way in for breakfast, as Martha had a kind heart and fed everyone. Come on in she said as she waved her hand to indicate to them that although she had company they were still welcome to their breakfast's. They walked in with their heads bent feeling embarrassed but Martha wasted no time in introducing them to Dorothy's family. "This is Ubaldino, Pico, Mese and Benetto, my Italian helpers, come and sit down boys and eat your breakfast." she told them. They all said. "Hello." Those of them who went out in groups to help on the farms wore dark blue overalls with distinctive large green patches sewn on to them. Sandra was surprised how different butter was eaten in the country as Martha spread it ever so thick as there was plenty of it, while back home it was so scarce her mother melted hers then spread it with a brush. And Jim was surprised later, as he went out into the fields with the Italians, just how good their English was, and how much they knew about the animals, until Mese and Benetto said. They were brought up on a farm, and it was the only job they had ever done before they were called up." Ubaldino said little and when he did he spoke very fast as though anxious to get the ordeal of talking over as soon as possible. Jim thought he'd had a nomadic existence, according to the short conversation, and wondered what he would go back too, after this terrible war was over.

CHAPTER EIGHTEEN

Prudence knew where she was headed, ever since the appearance of her legitimate daughter she knew she was losing the omnipotence of the village. She had to get away it was bad enough her daughter Winnie turning up, but being pregnant was too much to bare. No one in the village knew she had a daughter; she had done her upmost to keep her a secret, every week she had sent money home to her parents for Winnie's keep, and no one was any wiser, except Gran knew something wasn't right. Oh you couldn't pull the wool over Grans eyes. Pru thought as she watched her huge bloomers blowing on the line blotting out the sunlight. Pru didn't want her indiscretions spread like butter all over the village, she was a proud woman not accustomed to people knowing her business. It was the tail end of the summer, the glorious August heat had mellowed but the frosts had not yet begun. She saw Charlie in his garden and waved. His braces were dangling down by his sides and his beard was yellow in patches from the smoke of his briar pipe. The apples and pears had swelled and weighed down the branches on the trees which they hung it wouldn't be long until the fruit was harvested and Sarah would be busy making jam. Prudence's mind returned to her own problems. The autumn term would soon be underway at the village school, and she had a lot of preparation to do. Prudence set off back into the house and noticed for the first time, the front step worn into smooth hollows by the passage of many feet, and wondered how many more feet would tread it before she would be back again.

Eva cut a slice off a large cake that was cooling on a wire tray, "I've just brewed the tea." she told Eva, as she walked into the kitchen. Eva was making an apple pie. She had sliced the apples, and now lifted her pastry and covered the dish and began to trim the edges, and pinching the crust into place with finger and thumb, all the while watching Prues movements, and knowing something was unsettling her. "We have known each other for a few years now Prue, so why don't you tell me what you are planning?" Eva told her while deliberately staring at her for an answer.

"I am going up to see Pat shortly." Prue answered. When she had first arrived she couldn't have described the wonderful feeling of omnipotence. Having all the evacuees in her care, and being highly respected and now she was intending sneaking away like a thief in the night. After months of procrastinate now, she made her decision to tell Eva the truth, and keep her secret safe, as she was going to under Eva's roof for another week and once Eva got on to something she wouldn't let go a bit like gran Prue thought, so she compressed her lips into a disapproving scowl and sat down so hard on the chair its legs squeaked in protest.

Up at Pat and Michael's home whom they shared with Michaels mother Doris, near the convalescent home. Pat uncurled her legs and slipped them over the end of the couch, she had taken this opportunity of putting her feet up for awhile, she slipped her feet into her shoes and pulled a face when she caught a corn on her little toe and cried out at the discomfort. Doris her mother in law looked over at pat as she withdrew her knitting from her bag, she put the ends of the silver pins under her armpits and settled back to finish the garment her knitting needles clicked rhythmically, as she hummed along to the song on the wireless, Pat knew the song well, but felt too unwell to join in, to "We'll hang out the washing on the Siegfried line" instead she got up off the couch and sat the kettle on the hot coals, then reached up to the mantelpiece for the tea caddy, just as there was a loud knock on the door and it being flung open as prudence appeared in the doorway they had no alternative but to invite her in. Both Pat and Doris were shocked to see Prudence as she hadn't been a regular visitor and wondered fleetingly why she had called, but Prudence wasted no time explaining what she had in mind.

Doris looked up and spoke first. I think you had better sit down Prudence and enjoy a cup of tea with us, as you can see my daughter in law is tired without anymore extra work. Pat had been through to the pantry and brought a chocolate cake with her after slicing it and handing Prudence a piece with her cup of tea she sat at the table with Prue and told her to explain to her what she wanted her to do, as she moved the big brown teapot over the table and pulled the cosy over it. Prudence didn't feel as confident now to ask such a favour of pat as Doris was looking keenly at her, it wasn't only the closed expression on her face but the silent disapproval emanating from her was almost palpable.

Pat expelled a weary sigh, and then said. "You would like us to take care of Winnie until she has the baby. But what happens after the baby is born? Where will she and the baby live? Why can't she stay at Eva's I am sure between you and Eva you could see to her.

Prudence could feel the beads of sweat braking out on her brow, she didn't want to tell these kind people a lie but she needed someone to help Winnie, as she would be starting her new teaching post, miles away from here on the Isle of Man, aye she thought gran had said "war made strange bedfellows."

Doris was watching Prudence as her knitting needles clicked to their own accord and saw she was getting agitated as Prudence kept looking down at her hands twisting them together and flexing her fingers. Prue was mentally assessing the consequences if she told pat the whole truth that she wouldn't be around to see Winnies baby. They might not agree to taking her in as far as Prudence was concerned she would get Winnie into Pats care and her work was done the sooner she was on her way from here the better. Prudence got a shock as Pat nudged her that she clattered the cup in the saucer.

"You were day dreaming there." Pat smilingly told her. "And I cannot make a decision without Michael my husband, being here also, we will have to give it some thought, Wont we Mam?" as she looked quizzically at Doris. But if you leave it with us Prudence I will let you know in a few days and with that said. Pat rose from the table pushing the chair back; indicating to Prudence that it was time to leave, and not outstay her welcome.

Prudence left the Greens household and made her way down the stony lane towards Eva's cottage, she remembered with fond memories the last time she'd walked down this road the blackbirds were hopping about and greenfinches gregariously flitting from hedge to hedge, gorse bushes were richly spangled with gold. The breeze had been sweet with the smell of wild flowers. But she had made a start to get her affairs in order, and was doing all she could to help Winnie, who she could see coming towards her, with an angry look on her face. Winnie saw Prudence at the same time and stood with hands on hips waiting impatiently while one foot tapped the ground. Prudence could sense trouble as Winnie shouted.

"I have been to visit my friend Lucy, and they have gone, just moved out through the night nobody knows where they have gone; now I have no one."

Prudence said. "Well I pity the next lot of people they have for neighbours' as they have caused trouble all the time they've been here." Winnie was getting annoyed so Prudence told her where she had been she couldn't really be bothered with a confrontation but knew it was no good putting it off as time was running out. Winnie swished her hair back off her face and shouting a profanity that would have shocked some men, and then waddled off down the lane as fast as her legs could carry her, with a protruding stomach.

Eva's little girls were playing with their knitted dolls as the door crashed open then banged shut again. Eva dropped the knife she was using to peel the potatoes for tea and rushed from the back kitchen to see what all the noise was about, and then she saw Winnie hurrying upstairs.

"Come back down here Winnie." Eva called.

Winnie reluctantly turned her head and muttered. "If you want to know what has gone on, ask her." As Prudence breathlessly walked in then snecked the door. Eva was thoroughly sick of Winnie but had put up with her for Prue's sake but now she made up her mind Winnie could find somewhere else to live and be someone else's problem, as she had enough of her own. The short time Mark had spent with her on his last leave had left its mark as she was two months pregnant now. Prudence huffed and puffed her way over to a chair and flopped down as the springs twanged under all her weight.

Eva sat down opposite saying. "I am sorry Prue, but she has to go, I will give you a couple of days to find her somewhere but that is all I will allow. She is lazy, selfish and she uses language I had never heard before she came and I'm not putting up with it in front of my children." Eve felt sorry for Prudence so she slid the kettle over the coals to make a cup of tea for her, while Prudence explained where she'd been nearly all afternoon. Eva looked thoughtful and said. "It would be a good thing if Michael agrees to it, also I saw Pat the other day and she didn't look well to me, but we will have to wait and see."

A Long at the Greens Michael was hearing all about their afternoon visitor while he ate his tea. He couldn't help thinking, it was ironic how wayward lass with no morals like Winnie could be having a baby and their longed for baby had never materialised after all the years of marriage. He had been so deep in thought now he looked up into Pats hopeful eyes.

"What do you think about Winnie coming here to give birth? I will be the one looking after her." Michael didn't want Pat breaking her heart after Winnie left with the baby but he couldn't say much as Beryl was eating her dinner and listening to every word. Beryl was their evacuee who had been unloved and unwanted by a mother who was going to enjoy the company of the GIs while the war raged. Beryl had been with them two years and they had never heard a word from her mother. Michael doubted if they ever would, it didn't matter to them, if they kept her after the war as she was one of the family now.

"We will talk about it later." Michael answered as he nodded towards Beryl and then speared a piece of meat with his fork and carried on eating his tea. Doris his mother sitting opposite him kept her thoughts to herself, and loaded her fork up again ready for the next mouthful.

Prudence lay in bed going over the afternoon in her mind, she was tired but her mind was too active for sleep. And the worry about what to do with Winnie if the greens wouldn't take her in wouldn't go away. She threw the blankets aside and stepped out of bed parting the blackout curtains she peeped through the window. It was as black as pitch the antithesis of the warm sunny afternoon long gone. While the fire was burning low downstairs, an oil flame, burning in a tall, highly polished brass lamp, was the only light, except when a log shifted in the grate and sent sparks flying. Eva sat on the mat before it hands clasped round her knees, lost in thought until she heard the floorboards creaking up above, and realising Prudence couldn't sleep neither, decided to make them both a cup of tea.

The land girls were still at the dance hall, the jitterbug from America had been the most popular dance the land girls had been swung up and down the room by the GIs. Dale had swung Jennie over his head; the rest had all joined in energetically.

At last the band stopped for a break, everyone red in the face, from the entire dancing; one of the lads got up to sing after being egged on by his mates, he started singing. "A poor little lamb that has lost its way." And then absolutely everyone was heartily bawling. "Baa-aa, baa-aa, baa-baa." After that he quietly stood facing his audience with his inebriated dignity, and then belched his way back to his seat letting his beer fumes out. Before anyone had time to comment the band was back on stage. "Come on lets have you all up dancing." The lead singer shouted, as the band struck up with Billy Cotton's signature tune. "Somebody stole my girl." Linda tapped her foot to the tune while Paul made his way over to her with the drinks. Linda smiled to herself as she saw him approaching it was a start he was starting to take her out "who knows what might become of them yet?"

Next Morning Jim awoke early as the morning light crept through the parted curtains, and the dog fox barked, as his wife fed the day old cubs in the lair, near the wood. He would go out hunting shortly, for their breakfast. Jim hoped he had rounded all the hens up last night, he thought it would have been better if he'd known how many were supposed to be there, then he would have counted them in before dropping the door down. He stretched then realised he had all the bed to himself. Dennis had said last night they would all be having an early start this morning, as the fields of wheat were all to cut, and stook, before leading them into the stack, for the arrival of the thresher. Throwing the blankets aside he stepped out of bed, the smell of bacon hitting his nostrils, but he would have to go down the garden path first, as he needed a pee. They had only been here a couple of nights, and when Martha had heard Marion complain, how far away the lav was, she'd said.

"If you're stuck lad, there's pittle pots beneath the beds." Jim noticed no one else seemed to use them. The men anyway, and he wasn't going to be the first.

Prudence poured herself another cup of tea and made her mind up to go and see Pat; she had waited over a week now and had not heard anything from her, just as Eva answered the door to the light tap.

"Come on in Pat." Eva held the door open and stood aside for Pat to walk through to the kitchen. Prudence looked up and smiled enquiringly at Pat hoping to get the answer she'd been waiting for.

Sit down Pat and have a cup of tea Eva invited her as she came over with an extra cup and began to fill it. Prudence was desperate to know Pat's answer but Eva had her engaged in conversation now, asking her how Doris was keeping. And then enquiring about Michael, and Beryl. Prudence coughed to draw attention to herself and then smiled ingratiatingly, when she had their attention.

"I have a feeling you have called to see me this morning pat, is that correct? " Prudence asked with her eloquent tone.

"Yes I have." Pat answered guardedly. "We have agreed she can come to us until she has the baby, as we have plenty of room, and my sister is the local midwife so she will be well looked after." Prudence was relieved; she didn't want to look too enthusiastic. But time was running out.

"She can come whenever she wants." Pat was saying.

"I will walk up to your house with her as soon as she gets out of bed this morning, then she can settle in with you." Prudence replied eagerly. Then went over to the chair and took her purse out of the well worn hand bag and handed an envelope of money to Pat, saying. "I don't expect you to look after her for nothing; take this there is enough to see her through her time of need." Then she went upstairs to wake Winnie. Prudence intended having her settled into Pats within the hour.

Winnie stood by the cracked door that hung askew on a broken hinge halfway down the lane to Pats house. "The handle on this case is wearing a ridge in my hand." She tearfully told Prudence. The weight of her suitcase had now fully taken its toll. Prudence nastily grabbed it off the grass then set off with Winnie following behind, and not a word was spoken between them again.

"Come on in." said a surprised Pat she hadn't expected them turning up within the hour. "I'll make a cup of tea."

"Not for me thank you." Prudence said hurriedly. "I must be going." Then she disappeared out of the door, down the lane and out of Winnie's life. Eva was dishing out the tea as she lifted the mince and dumplings out of the oven she called to Prudence upstairs. "Prudence tea is ready." She had been upstairs most of the day. As they all sat down to tea, Eva picked her knife and fork up then looked at Prudence and said. "I have a feeling you will be leaving this week, you have been busy sorting things upstairs all day and you've taken Winnie up to Pats. When are you going Prudence?"

"Tomorrow night Eva, I was going to say goodbye, as we have shared a lot." Things haven't worked out how I anticipated, but hopefully I will find happiness on the Isle of Mann. I would prefer it, if Winnie wasn't told where I'd gone." She told Eva laying a confidential hand on her arm.

Winnie couldn't get to sleep in this comfortable bed, she'd had a nagging pain in her lower back since she'd carried the case halfway down the lane. Pat had reiterated to her that if she felt ill even through the night she should wake her. But Pat had been on her feet all day. And she had seen Doris wincing as she pulled off her shoes before easing her bunioned toes into her slippers after tea .Doris had been baking all day, and Winnie could hear her snoring in the room next door. Winnie got out of bed and squatted down over the chamber pot as Pat had called it, she knew it as a pittle pot. Her back was aching really bad as she climbed back into bed, and cried quietly into her pillow. As dawn turned into day light Pat crept quietly into Winnies room with a cup of tea. She had heard her moving about in the night but had decided if she had needed her she would have called her. Pat pulled back the curtains with a flourish then turned and smiled at Winnie. The day was overcast the clouds black enough to make the threat of rain very real.

Down the road at Eva's, Prue ate her breakfast hurriedly, then without stopping for a chat went back upstairs where she assiduously attacked the rest of her jobs before coming back into the kitchen ready for her journey with coat and hat on and case at her feet.

Eva was shocked. "I didn't realize you were going so early today Prue? How are you getting to the station?"

"Oh I saw the Doctors car at the old ladies cottage, so I asked if I could have a lift when he went back past the station." Just then they heard the car approaching, after a hastily goodbye Prudence walked out of the door, dropping her case near the car, as the driver got out to put it in the boot for her. Prudence climbed in banged the door shut and after a quick wave all that was left was the smoke off the Doctors car.

Gran was sitting in her chair by the fire enjoying a cup of tea, as she saw the car pass by. "Ethel. I've just seen the Doctors car go down past and Prudence was sitting on the back seat." Ethel had just been giving the fire a good poke and after adding more coal looked up at Gran her face bright red from the fire.

"I think you must be mistaken gran, it wouldn't be Prue, what would she be doing riding in the doctors car?"

"Well I don't know that our Ethel but I'm telling you it was prudence, anyway we might find out now I have just heard Grace's bike." She had stopped it with a squeak of breaks.

"Hello it's only me." Grace called as she opened the door and stepped in. Before Grace had time to utter another word, Gran said.

"I'm pleased to see you Grace; do you know anything about Prudence going off in the doctor's car?"

"You don't know that it was Prudence gran, you only saw someone on the back seat it could have been anyone." Ethel explained.

"You were right Mrs Brown." Grace told her as she took the cup of tea that Ethel offered her.

"I have been busy this morning our Pat came and asked me to have a look at Winnie as she is about due to have her baby and staying at Pat and Michaels for the time being."

"Well where has Prudence gone?" Gran wanted to know. "I saw your Eva on the way here and she was telling me everything had been decided quickly, and Prudence left this morning to start a new life, I am not supposed to say where she has gone."

"Well you can tell us Grace." continued gran more or less unabated. Grace leaned forward and whispered confidentially. "She has gone to the Isle of Mann."

"Well I never." Exclaimed gran. "I always said she was a dark horse."

"Well I feel sorry for Winnie." Grace carried on with the conversation. "I have to examine her closely today, you know, down below." She spoke quietly to Ethel.

Grans ears pricked up. "Oh I wouldn't worry too much about that one, it's hardly an untrodden path with her, and she'll very likely have spent more time with her knickers off then on."

"Gran!" Ethel rebuked her. "That is a horrible thing to say."

"Aye but I bet it is true our Ethel." Replied gran, then slurped her tea before holding out the empty cup for a refill.

Pat was getting worried about Winnie, she didn't look well and she was complaining about pains in her stomach. She didn't feel well herself lately, she hadn't seen her own monthly bleed for three months, now she came to think about it, and she had noticed this morning that her nipples were brown now, when they should have been pink, and nausea had plagued her.

"Come on Winnie I will help you up to bed, Grace won't be long." As Pat helped Winnie upstairs they had to stop as another pain took over her body, it went on incessantly or that is how it felt to Winnie, until night fall and Pat lit the lamp. The huge hissing paraffin lamp lit the place up like daylight, making it easier for Grace to see what she was doing. She had popped home to cook her husband's meal, and then with her own meal undigested she had rushed back to Winnie, who had screamed and shouted all the way through it, until now when a tiny blood soaked baby slipped out and lay between her legs, emitting a lusty cry, while Winnie turned her head and looked the other way. Grace picked the baby up and wrapped her in a towel then handed her into Pats open arms.

"Do you not want to see your baby?" Grace asked Winnie. To which Winnie laughed mirthlessly, and said

"You can have her I don't want her." Winnie lay without movement the child suckled with no loving arms around her as she fed greedily. Grace advised Pat to be present all the time. For the babies survival Pat had to be vigilant. Doris saw how tired Pat was getting and after a week decided to swap places, so Pat could spend a night in her own bed. Pat was incensed at Winnie's unfeeling attitude; she had tried to help her but her body was to the point of exhaustion.

Doris was dozing in the chair beside Winnie's bed, when she was woken by Winnie voice, she sounded tearfully as she asked her to bring Pat, she said she was in pain and started to get out of bed holding her stomach.

Doris got stiffly off the chair saying. "Stay where you are I will bring Pat." As soon as Doris walked through the door Winnie quickly put her skirt and jumper on, she had put her under clothes on earlier and had packed her case which was hidden under the bed. Then without a backward glance, she grabbed her coat and flew down the stairs, as the two women made their way back into the bedroom where the tiny baby was snuffling in the drawer beside the empty bed. While Pat lifted the baby into loving arms Doris sucked her tongue against her teeth, to make a tutting sound of exasperation. She rolled her eyes heaven-wards as she said

"Well she has had this planned as she picked up the sheet of paper from the chair, that Winnie had left. Pat said. "Read it out to me Mam, Well it just says. "You can have her and name her, whatever you want." as she doesn't want anything to do with this tiny scrap.

Winnie hurried down the road, but kept turning to look around, hoping that Pat wouldn't send Michael after her, and make her go back to her baby. As she walked on past Martha's gate she could visualize Dorothy playing happy family's she took a deep breath and carried on down the road as she didn't have a family and never would have now. Winnie had only been in the country five months, and it had intensified her longing to go back to the city, only now she was going to a different city, where no one knew her she would put the past behind her and have a fresh start.

The Italians were sitting at Martha's table waiting, for their breakfasts as Marion moodily walked through the door, followed by Sandra and Brenda. The Italians many from farming stock themselves did their work with a mixture of enthusiasm and happy go lucky carelessness, but they had lots of charm, smiling a welcome at the women, while Marion wallowed in self-pity.

Brenda stirred the porridge while Sandra saw to the children. Martha turned and asked Marion. "Could you manage to collect the eggs today?"

"Yes I can do that job." said Marion sourly holding Martha's assessing look and refusing to drop her eyes,

Marion knew what Martha thought about her, but she didn't care, she didn't like her neither.

"You have a good living here, you should be thankful." stated Marion enviously. Dots sister was very conscious of the difference in their circumstances, and was jealous of Dot, as Martha had told them that she had adapted swiftly to her new life.

"Yes but a good living doesn't arrive by idleness, life on a farm may appear idyllic but it is hard work with long hours. We are going into a busy time again next week with the thresher coming."

The passion of fury suffused Marion's face as she said, "I don't have it easy, with the kids to bring up on my own, and you don't have to stand in a queue all day for a small amount of food. There is rationing where we come from." Jim was just walking through the doorway he was totally oblivious to Marion's behaviour.

"Good morning everyone he called cheerily, by that bacon smells good Martha."

"Sit down lad; I'll just fry you a couple of eggs with this bacon and black pudding." After years of toil Martha's hands were knotted and reddened, Jim noticed as she spread butter thickly on the freshly baked bread, after handing him his huge breakfast, which he ate with a vengeance, the country air had heightened his appetite.

"I have never eaten butter this yellow." He told Martha.

"Well we don't have it this colour all year round." She explained to Jim. "The colour of butter reflects the changing seasons, in winter it is almost white as the cows are eating hay, and a bit of cake. But in summer with fresh grass it changes to a rich yellow."

"Can I do anything to day to help out?" Jim enquired. He was filled with gratitude for the kindness of Martha, and Dennis and the hospitality they had shown towards Dot during her vulnerability.

"Well if you don't mind Jim, you could deliver 2lb of butter and a dozen eggs, to the two old ladies who live down the second field from the road. as we have plenty of work to keep us busy in here today haven't we girls?" as she smiled at Brenda, and Sandra.

Jim set off with Ubaldino and Mese; they were only going so far with Jim, but they would point him in the right direction. As they walked past the pig sty, Jim noticed the huge pink pig was lying on her side, while the small piglets squealed and suckled at her, climbing over one another in their haste to feed.

Ubaldino watching Jim said. "This will be an unusual sight for you I suppose, we take it for granted; I know nothing else as I was born in to it." Jim turned to see which one he was speaking too, as they both sounded very much alike, on turning round he realized it was Ubaldino, his retrousse nose facing the sky, a canny fella, although he was a Italian. The men walked on up the road Ubaldino and Mese going the long way round to where they wanted to be; just to help Jim, as they walked they talked to Jim about their home life, on the farm. It seemed to Jim that their work on the farm had dominated their existence. Jim smiled as they asked him about his work in a factory; he was on ground now, which was familiar to him. They had reached the five barred gate, Mese said. "Be careful, and we will see you later." As Jim watched the men's retreating figures, he panicked in all this open space he was completely alone. But he had promised Martha he would deliver the butter and eggs, so the sooner he got started the sooner he would be back into the safety of the farm yard. He whistled as he opened the gate, and then closed it behind him, with trepidation. Jim stuck to the path until he saw the Dutch barn, a roof on high supporting poles. The smell reached his nostrils of hay nicely sweated; full of herbs, natural grasses and flowers he thought to himself. This is a fragrance that nothing can match as he stood admiring the stacked hay, ready to feed the hungry animals in winter.

The gander saw Jim before Jim saw him; the geese had been stepping out in their disdainful fashion, the gander swung its neck protectively over his wives and hissed aggressively as he hustled them through an open gate. it then came flapping its wings advancing on Jim as if it meant business, with its beady eyes, and long beak pecking, its neck outstretched. This wasn't feasible to try and dodge past him even to Jim's uninitiated eyes. Jim's instinctive reaction was to run, as a swarm of midges rose from a stagnant ditch, which spurred the gander into full gallop. Sweat was standing on Jim's brow as he tried to outrun the gander holding on to the eggs and butter at the same time. Events were buffeting him like a leaf in the wind. The gander carried on coming hissing ferociously and wings at full stretch his hefty neck was fully stretched and with pounding feet he charged at Jim like a tornado biting his backside with his sharp beak as he did so Jim ran. The gander buffeting him along that he managed to miss the inconspicuous gap in the hedge and continued on out of breath and terrified, but still going hell for leather.

Mattie Layman was walking on the other side of the hedge and saw Jim running, with the gander still hanging on to his tattered trousers, Mattie ran to the stile and jumped over and started hitting the gander with his shepherds' crook while Jim stumbled over the fence, and

Mattie following quickly before the bat on the head wore off the gander. Mattie took Jims eggs and butter off him. "Come with me lad you need a mug of strong tea with plenty of sugar in it. You are not from round here are you? I can tell. You never run from a gander."

Mattie tapped on the open cottage door and called a greeting to the two grey haired old ladies sitting by the fire; one of them got stiffly out of the rocking chair and came towards them, holding out her hands for the butter and eggs, miraculously only two eggs were broken, the yellow yoke running through the precious brown bag, that could have been used again umpteen times. The other sister pulled the kettle back over the coals, and then reached up to the mantelshelf for the tea caddy that stood on its tasselled red baize cover. Jim turned round as he heard weeping, and realised there was another old woman in the room. She was clad in her widow's weeds and perched stiffly on a wooden chair, her cheeks wrinkled and grey and down these furrows tears ran their uneven course. Mattie saw Jim looking concerned and whispered. "She was just told this morning, her Grandson who was a soldier had been killed." Jim quickly drank his tea, he didn't want to sit any longer than necessary, the seat in his trousers was torn to shreds, and the pain in his backside was unbelievable. He knew he would be black and blue in the morning, and he had a long train ride in front of him, as they were going home.

Mattie noticed Jim shuffling uncomfortably on the chair, so quickly drinking the scalding tea he stood up saying. "Come on Jim, I might as well walk back to Martha's with you, as I have nothing spoiling and it is a grand day."

Jim felt a fool explaining his predicament at Martha's; he told Martha he would pay her for the trousers she had lent him the use of while they had been staying there.

"No you won't pay lad, they were my late husbands, and I was only going to cut the material into strips for my clippie mat."

The stair door opened and Dot made her way in with baby Teresa in her arms; "I know I should still be in bed." she told her family as they all looked surprised. "But it is your last night, and I am going to sit down here with you all, as I don't know when I will see you again." She ended on a sob.

Brenda tried to make light of it saying. "Dennis said, you might be starting the threshing this week, so there will be no more rest for you until you have another baby."

Marion was looking uninterested she was taking out a cigarette machine from her pocket, she fed the paper into the machine, licked the sticky edge, tamped down the tobacco, then closed the lid and turned the rollers to produce a well filled cigarette, after lighting up she sat back and enjoyed it while the women dished out the evening meal.

The night wore on and the women packed ready for the early morning train, all except Marion who had gone along to the pub, and next morning her only concern was seeing to her makeup and getting the seams of her stockings straight. She had already adjusted the neckline on her pink blouse so that it revealed just enough cleavage to be tempting, but not vulgar, as her dad would have something to say. Martha looked at her and muttered "Huh!" The snort was derisive.

After all the tearful goodbyes, and Dorothy's family along with their friend Sandra, loaded on to the cart, Dennis and Martha were off to take the Watson family to the station. They were loaded down with fresh eggs, butter and meat. They didn't have long to wait of the train so sat at the bench on the station platform, next to a pale young girl who coughed persistently. Brenda made her mind up to get in to a different carriage to her.

The train arrived and they all climbed aboard, the carriage doors were slammed. The shrill of the whistle and the hiss of steam almost drowned out their final goodbyes as the train slowly headed down the track.

Martha her thick salt and pepper hair held in place by a hairnet turned to her son and said. "You can start your married life now lad."

Mother and son made their way home on the cart, the horse swishing its tail and enjoying its walk, as they turned into their gate, they saw the binder had arrived to cut the corn. The land girls wholeheartedly pitched in to work as hard as the men, as the binder cut the fields, the girls' stook up, eight or ten sheaves of corn in a stook. The barley oiks penetrating tender parts could still be felt days later.

Dennis helped his mother down from the cart then took the horse from between the shafts, just as dot came to the door smiling, that she'd just scalded a teapot full of tea.

"That's grand lass, just what I need before a good baking day as we'll have some hungry folk to feed this next week or two, while we are threshing."

After the evening meal and all the washing up was done, Dorothy picked up her cigarettes' and matches then went and leaned against the door jamb, watching the land girls still toiling in the fields, as she put the cigarette into her mouth.

Martha was beside her. "I'll have one with you lass, you don't mind? We make a good team me and you." The match flickered and went out. Dorothy struck another one and both women inhaled the smoke.

"Look lass." Martha shouted excitedly. "There's the thresher coming down the lane. Look at the smoke its belching out and all the steam; it's the start of another season."